Death at an Irish Village

AN IRISH CASTLE MYSTERY

Death at an Irish Village

Ellie Brannigan

THORNDIKE PRESS
A part of Gale, a Cengage Company

GALE
A Cengage Company

GALE
A Cengage Company

Thorndike Press, a part of Gale, a Cengage Company.

Thorndike Press® Large Print Clean Reads.
The text of this Large Print edition is unabridged.
Other aspects of the book may vary from the original edition.
Set in 16 pt. Plantin.

**LIBRARY OF CONGRESS CIP DATA ON FILE.
CATALOGUING IN PUBLICATION FOR THIS BOOK
IS AVAILABLE FROM THE LIBRARY OF CONGRESS.**

ISBN-13: 978-1-4205-3165-7 (hardcover alk. paper)

Published in 2026 by arrangement with Crooked Lane Books, an imprint of The Quick Brown Fox & Company LLC.

Print Number: 1 Print Year: 2026
Printed in Mexico

I'd like to dedicate this book to my family, in the memory of my grandmother, Sunny Brannigan, who passed away January 2025 at the age of 96.
She gave me permission to use her name to write the Irish Castle mysteries. She had read the first one, but didn't get a chance to read the others.
She was very proud and kept my books on a special shelf in her home. Her strength and independence left a lasting legacy in her children, grandchildren, and great-grandchildren.
Love you, Gigi!

Chapter One

"Hey, can you lend me a hand, Ciara?" Rayne McGrath squinted against the dappled shadows in the attic to bring her cousin's short bleached-blond curls into focus. They remained a blur. The slate roof was solid without a hint of autumn daylight peeking through.

"On my way."

Rayne adored the cousin she'd inherited along with the family castle when Uncle Nevin had died six months ago, though the pair had started off as adversaries. Ciara and Rayne now had the same goal: save Grathton Village from extinction, population 465, whether the villagers wanted their help or not.

Her uncle must have suspected that he'd be a target of foul play as he'd left very specific instructions for the fate of McGrath Castle in his odd will. Rayne inherited the manor, but Ciara Smith, Nevin's illegitimate daughter, conceived when he and Aunt Amalie were on a break, was to manage the property and receive a stipend at the end of twelve months.

However, if the castle and surrounding grounds was not brought into the black, it was to be sold. Rayne and Ciara could split what was left, if anything.

Rayne, a successful bridal wear designer who'd had a shop on Rodeo Drive in LA, had been robbed by her business partner/boyfriend on her thirtieth birthday. She was practically broke, as was Ciara, who'd had no idea about the state of the household finances her dad had managed.

They had to revive the dying Grathton Village, but not all were on board with a brash American and Nevin's inexperienced daughter taking the reins. Yesterday at church, sitting with Sinead and Liam Walsh, Rayne overheard derisive comments. Father Patrick had just announced that they'd welcome volunteers on Monday to assist with cleanup around the cemetery grounds.

Why waste time and effort into something doomed to fail?

The Walshes preferred Saturday afternoon services because they were up so early on Sunday to bake at the Coco Bean Café. Sinead had glared at the older woman who'd said it but could hardly call the old biddy out.

Ciara and the others from McGrath Castle went to church on Sunday mornings. To those who doubted the cousins' combination of Celtic grit and determination? Step back, and out of the way. Six months was the halfway point and the pressure was immense.

"What did you find?" Ciara shuffled around boxes toward Rayne and lowered her battery-operated lantern. One of the quirks of a historic home meant no electricity in the attic.

"Not sure." Rayne brushed dust from the flat top of a rectangular object. They were searching for authentic pieces to furnish the third bungalow before the next round of guests, due to arrive on Saturday, in six days. After the prior wedding venue fiascos, they didn't want a thing to go wrong.

Correction. They couldn't afford for anything else to fail. Rayne had sold all but two of her collector handbags. If the sheep didn't thrive in March, or she didn't attract new clients to the castle, goodbye pink Hermes bag worth thirty thousand dollars.

Ciara slowly bent down so she was also on her knees and positioned the lantern so they could see the item better.

"Sweet! It's a trunk. Leather, brass hinges." Rayne ran her hand over the curved corner. "Depending on the condition, this might be perfect."

"If it doesn't fit for the cottage, I could use it in my room." Ciara swiped the top. "I don't mind things with dents or dings."

"You should have it." Rayne nudged it toward her cousin.

"Let's see. We're up here in the dust to scavenge furniture." Ciara tilted her head. "What's left to fill in over there?"

The updated bungalow had two bedrooms, a kitchen, a bathroom, and a living area. It was the smallest of the three units for rent.

"The bedrooms are complete. The bathroom just needs towels. The warming rack is genius, by the way." Rayne hadn't required such a thing in LA. "Aine is hemming the curtains for the windows. Amos and Richard are cobbling together furniture for the living room as well as dining area. I don't know how far Richard is with the exterior."

Ciara patted the trunk. "This can be a conversation piece in the living room. Multipurpose storage as well as a table."

"Love it!" Rayne sat back on her heels. Well, flat boots, given the climbing around they were doing. "We could use some lamps. If we don't find any, I might borrow the matching wood pillars from the library."

Ciara stood and lifted the lantern. It wasn't very bright so the illumination it offered barely reached three feet. She groaned. "There's so much in here we haven't touched yet. Let's save ourselves a headache and utilize the lamps we have already."

"Deal." Rayne agreed it was a smart plan. "They're rarely used but will be great in the cottage." Junk, or treasure, depending on who was sifting through it, from centuries past had been jammed in the attic without a system. Tackling it now wouldn't be a priority except they needed a few finishing elements.

Shopping in their attic was budget-friendly while staying authentic to the house.

Ciara turned, bringing her lantern closer to Rayne, and accidentally bumped her boot to the trunk. Dust motes danced in the air, and she coughed, waving her hand before her face. "Sorry!"

"Are you okay?"

"Steel-toed boots," Ciara said. "I hope the trunk is all right."

"It *is* sturdy." Rayne admired the brass edges of the leather. As a designer, she appreciated the numerous details that made something extra special, from dresses to accessories. "Let's get it downstairs."

Ciara placed her lantern on the floor and lifted one end of the heavy trunk. It barely budged.

"Dang it!" Rayne braced her legs, picking it up by the bottom corners on the right, while Ciara took the left.

"On three!" Ciara counted and they lifted in unison.

Despite their efforts, the trunk still didn't move.

"We need some help." Of course, her mind went to Amos Lowell, the McGrath grounds manager. His broad shoulders and muscled arms were the real deal.

"Let's slide it toward the ladder so we know which trunk to grab." Ciara gripped the leather handle on her end, and Rayne did the same.

Rayne had dressed for rummaging through the attic in leather boots, jeans, and a baggy sweater made of soft, durable cotton she'd found at the thrift shop in the village. Plain gray with a scoop neck, it had become her favorite for workdays that required grunge.

On a piece of property like this, with the manor house, turreted tower, barn, gardens, lake, and the new gazebo, it was more often than Rayne ever imagined.

Ciara sent off a text message, then frowned. “It didn’t go through.”

Wi-Fi was also an issue within the stone walls. “I’ll try.” Rayne scrambled to the open hatch door and used her cell phone to text Amos that they needed assistance in the attic. The sooner the better.

Her phone buzzed with a reply. “Amos is on the way!”

“Nice. Oh — what are those?” Ciara took the lantern away from the open hatch to inspect the shadows. The light from the third floor kept it from being totally dark.

When Rayne wasn’t in her sewing studio, or the office to crunch accounting numbers with Ciara and Cormac, she was traipsing outside. There were times when she envied her cousin’s short, bleached locks but her waist-length black hair was something her father had taken pride in, so she kept it long. It was either up in a clip out of the way, or in a braid.

She and Ciara shared the McGrath gray eyes and dark hair. Both young women were around five eight, and slender. Nevin’s murder hadn’t stopped the legality of his will. There was more at stake than just the possibility of earning a hundred grand each, if there was that much to be had from the sale of the land.

The Lloyd family, consisting of Maeve and Cormac, and their nineteen-year-old daughter Aine, would be forced to leave the only home Aine had ever known.

Ciara's lantern created spooky shadows on the slanted attic ceiling as she returned cradling a porcelain vase with a fluted rim.

"That's cute!" Rayne accepted it and examined it closely. "No cracks either. Score."

Ciara's phone dinged and she read a message. "Dafydd is in the field with the sheep. We'll need to help Amos with the trunk." Dafydd Norman was Ciara's fiancé, and the shepherd on the property.

The wooden ladder leading from the third floor to the attic was down and Blarney barked, as if her dog wanted to join them. The stairs were sturdy enough that he probably could climb them, but then he'd need a bath afterward and she didn't have the time for that. The Irish setter was a gorgeous russet with silky fur.

Uncle Nevin had bought Blarney to be a bird hunting dog, but her pup just wasn't a killer. A thief, sometimes, as he liked feathers and jewels, but he was very loyal and intelligent. According to the pet psychic her mother had hired in LA, he'd bonded with

Rayne after her uncle's death.

Blarney entered and exited the castle in mysterious ways. The manor was huge — three floors, plus the attic, the basement, and the tower with the turret, which meant there were places that Rayne hadn't visited yet despite inheriting the castle in June. She'd turned thirty June first. What high hopes she'd had!

In LA, she'd had a very successful bridal-wear design shop that she was sure would go to the next level of boutique department stores. She'd thought her boyfriend and business partner, Landon Short, would propose. Instead, he'd stolen the designer gowns, *women's dreams,* and the money in, she cringed, their joint bank account.

Now she lived in Ireland, in her father's family home. She hadn't seen her mother, Lauren, or her best friend, Jenn, since her unexpected move.

Rayne and Ciara had a ticking time clock of six months left and with the failures of the wedding venue here, Rayne constantly looking over her shoulder for Landon who had escaped jail after carving her name all over the jail cell, and the villagers not being united behind saving Grathton Village, they often wondered if they were running in place.

"The vase will be a pretty accent." Rayne swung her legs over the opening of the hatch, carefully moving the trunk next to her to not get her fingers any grimier than they were already. "This could be the day we find treasure inside."

"That would solve the immediate money woes. I'll go first." Ciara went down the ladder stairs, carefully holding the vase. Her phone poked from the bib of her coverall pocket.

Though not into designer fashion like Rayne, Ciara had natural style.

Rayne descended the stairs and patted Blarney's russet head, as the dog wagged his tail.

"When do the guests arrive?" Ciara asked.

"Saturday morning. They were originally going to be here on Friday, but they're having a hard time breaking away from their jobs. They'll get hitched at the gazebo Saturday at four for the sunset over the lake, and Frances is making a fancy prime rib dinner in the formal dining room that evening. Sunday morning breakfast will be on their own. We can recommend the Coco Bean. Since they all live in Ireland, they'll leave that afternoon."

"How many?"

"Five. Lenni McGee, the bride, Pete

O'Shea, the groom. Her best friend Sharon, and his best friend Brandon with his son, Drake. They're all career people, with the exception of Drake, and simply want to steal away. We've got to make this special for them."

"I hear you. Things can't go any worse."

Rayne knocked on the extended wooden ladder. "Let's not take any chances with statements like that."

Her cousin chuckled. "Fair." Ciara tucked the vase next to the wall. "We should hire a professional to do an inventory of assets."

"Add it to the list!" Rayne sighed. It was already a mile long. Blarney's ears perked and he stared toward the stairs.

Did he hear Amos?

Amos had invited her over for a drink *some time* but that hadn't happened yet. With all she'd had to juggle, sharing a whiskey didn't rise to the top, though she wasn't immune to his wavy dark blond hair, blue eyes, or muscled physique.

Amos and Dafydd had cottages near the sheep pen to the far right of the property, across the field, and adjacent to the gazebo. Richard Forrest resided in a one-bedroom bungalow by the windmill to the back left of the property, behind the barn and horse paddock. Like the house itself, the grounds were ginormous.

Rayne and Richard would probably never be friends, but he treated her with respect now which was an improvement over his earlier behavior toward her. They'd all changed since Rayne's arrival and her uncle's death.

Family dinners were shared with the staff every evening, and on Sundays, there was a late lunch; afterward people fended for themselves. Father Patrick joined them once a month after church for a meal.

It had been Father Patrick's idea for Rayne and Ciara to tackle projects together to show they had skin in the game. So far, they'd repainted the elementary school and the combination middle school/high school. Tomorrow, at eight-thirty Monday morning, they'd begin cleanup in the overgrown cemetery as it was encroaching on the row of vacant offices that were in reasonable condition, according to Bobby Fitzroy, who owned Fitzroy Construction.

They'd hired Bobby to oversee their various enterprises. He'd suggested nobody wanted to rent the buildings because of the trees and tangled bushes. There used to be a caretaker but when the last one died the position didn't get filled. Managing the vacancies was another thing on Rayne and

Ciara's to-do list.

Six. Months.

"Your face is red," Ciara said.

"Thinking about that blasted list," Rayne admitted.

The clomping of men's boots sounded on the central staircase and Rayne smoothed her hair from her forehead wishing she'd had a chance to refresh her makeup.

Ciara noticed her action and rolled her eyes. "You are silly. When will you give Amos a chance?"

"I don't know what you're talking about."

"Good that he's a patient man," Ciara said.

Patient, and smart, and kind, and as Amos reached the top step to walk toward them, Rayne's heart sped. Oh, so handsome. He was dressed in denims and a snug plaid Henley.

"Hi, Amos." She smiled, greeting Richard behind Amos. "Hey." Richard, at fifty, had copper red hair, a slim build, and a distrustful nature. He suffered a gambling addiction, and distrusted Rayne from the beginning. To be fair, Nevin had died under suspicious circumstances, and he'd been a suspect.

Richard had fought with Nevin over the windmill that they no longer used as it wasn't cost effective to make their own bread. Since then, he'd become their handyman. He'd been a big help with the construction of the gazebo, and remodeling the bungalows. Everyone who lived on the property was invested in the castle's success or they could lose their home.

"What are we getting down?" Amos asked.

"The trunk closest to the hatch. It's pretty heavy," Rayne said.

Ciara pocketed her phone. "We can help if you need us."

"All righty." Richard climbed the ladder.

Amos scrambled up the steps after him. With minimal effort, the guys brought the trunk down though they both had red cheeks.

"Where to?" Amos asked as they set it down.

"The blue parlor. That's the most comfortable place to spread out in," Rayne said. "Is that okay, Ciara?"

"Sure." Ciara read her watch. "We have two hours before dinner with Father Patrick."

Frances Coplan, their cook, did an incredible job with the meals served. Sometimes Maeve and Aine helped. If they needed assistance inside for basic cleaning, they hired Dr. Rueben's granddaughter, Sorcha

Ketchum.

"He was so funny at church this morning." Richard wiped his forehead. "Rayne, you missed a good sermon."

"I went yesterday." Rayne didn't like to get up at the crack of dawn for any reason and that included church. She preferred to sleep in until nine on Sunday morning with a cup of coffee at the gazebo, watching the ducks on the lake.

She used to get her Zen fix on the ocean, but the lake was also very rejuvenating. The fact that this was McGrath family land, and had been for centuries, hadn't worn off.

It was a thrill and a responsibility she felt in equal parts. Ciara did as well. Her cousin liked to ride horses after church to nourish her body and soul. Rayne was getting used to the big beasts, but they still scared her.

Amos tilted his head as he smiled at Rayne. "Where will this end up? Should we stick around a bit?"

"Depending on the shape it's in, I'd like for it to go to the third bungalow. A coffee table? This too." Rayne pointed to the vase Ciara had found.

"That's nice," Amos said.

"Looks expensive," Richard said.

Ciara took the vase and turned it beneath

the light. “You’re right. The colors are very bright.”

Rayne admired the hand-painted purple iris with green leaves on an ivory background. “Should we get it appraised sooner than later?”

“There’s no way to know the value until we do,” Ciara said.

“Until then, we should enjoy it.” Rayne tapped her phone to add a note into the notes app. “Let’s have Maeve locate an appraiser willing to come here.”

“All right,” Ciara said.

“Shall we?” Richard lightly nudged the trunk with his boot. “I’m about done replacing the shingles on the roof of the bungalow.”

“Oh, sorry,” Rayne said. “I appreciate you coming in to help.”

“It’s my job.” Richard hefted one end and Amos got the other.

Amos winked at Rayne. “Happy to assist. Anytime. I’m curious what’s in here. Feels like bricks.”

“You’re welcome to join us for the grand reveal,” Rayne said. “Probably junk though. So far, no treasure despite our hopes.”

Amos nodded. “I don’t mind a break from pitching hay.”

The men carefully brought the heavy

trunk down three floors to the blue parlor, next to the office. It was named for the blue furnishings inside it and had a secret whiskey compartment in the bookcase.

Ciara, Rayne, and Blarney followed the guys to the first floor, heading left. To the right were the Lloyds' rooms and more offices, a library, and at the far end, the entrance to the tower that had been refurbished for guests, complete with a turret. Behind the central staircase was the laundry, and to the right, the dining rooms and kitchen. At the far end was the sunroom, and across from that, the game room. A narrow staircase went from the first floor all the way up to the third for when servants weren't meant to be seen.

The parlor door was open as Maeve dusted the shelves with a feather duster. She was slim with red hair, green eyes, a bright smile, and a gap in her white teeth. Aine was her mini.

"Hi!" Rayne said. "Will we bother you if we set up in here?"

Amos and Richard brought the trunk to the carpeted area before the fireplace.

"Not at all." Maeve said, her red brow arched. "And what have we?"

"A mystery," Amos said.

"See you at dinner." Richard tipped his

head before hurrying out the door to finish the bungalow.

"Guess he doesn't care about mysteries." Rayne's curiosity often got the better of her, especially if it was a subject she liked. Fabrics, fashion, and McGrath family history.

"Richard has been struggling with his demons," Maeve said sagely. "Being outside and doing manual labor is very helpful for him."

"A roof shingle isn't likely to offer a wager," Amos said. "I agree with you about Richard. He's been more taciturn than normal, but I'd not given the why of it any thought. I'll be kinder."

Rayne smiled at Amos. He was very patient and nice and handsome and . . . she pulled her gaze from his shoulders and focused on the trunk instead.

She guessed it to be five feet across and three feet wide, with a flat top. If the inside matched the quality of the outside, it would make a great addition.

Rayne tugged the silver lock that latched the container closed. "It's got a padlock. Cool!"

Ciara kneeled before the trunk and fiddled with the lock. "Maeve? Do you have a hairpin?"

"I do." The housekeeper, in her black uniform with the white shirt and apron, joined them, removing a classic bobby pin from her red bun. "Here you are."

"Thanks." Ciara bent the angle of the pin just the slightest bit and jimmied the lock. It popped open.

"Brilliant!" Amos sounded impressed. "Do I want to know where you came by that skill?"

Ciara unbent the pin and returned it to Maeve. "Not necessarily."

"Come on, Ciara," Rayne teased. "Now I'm imagining you as a troubled youth in London living a life of crime."

"It wasn't that." Ciara gave a sad shrug. "Sometimes I borrowed my mom's gold earrings, which she had locked in a jewelry box. I always put them back. I still have those earrings."

"That's really sweet." Rayne patted Ciara's back with empathy. Her single mother had died from cancer ten years ago, which was when Ciara had found out that Nevin was her dad.

"That is nice." Maeve touched her emerald posts, a birthday gift from Aine.

"My mom and I have decidedly different tastes, but I used to borrow her bangles all the time." Rayne's mom, Lauren McGrath, had been on the same sitcom, *Family Forever,* for over twenty years and played a Christian woman in the show that had just filmed its last episode. Lauren was facing her fear of flying to visit in December, with Rayne's best friend Jenn.

Lauren would embrace Ciara as family though they'd never met. When Rayne thought about what might happen at the end of this six months period, she put a fast halt to the outcome. Her life was in LA. Wasn't it?

But being here proved that Rodeo Drive had gone on without her, and Landon, just fine.

"Want to do the honors?" Ciara asked Rayne, removing the padlock and setting it on the slate of the fireplace hearth.

"That's okay. You."

Amos, Rayne, and Maeve crowded behind Ciara, still on her knees. Her cousin lifted the top, the hinges creaking.

The inside of the trunk was lined in thick ivory silk that had yellowed with age. Some of the edges were frayed, so she'd need to fix it before they brought it to the cottage.

"Oh, what is that?" Rayne picked up a framed photo.

"It's got to be a McGrath." Maeve peered over their shoulders. "Those stormy eyes."

"Even in black and white, that's a family trait." Amos playfully tugged Rayne's hair.

"No wonder it was heavy if these are photo albums," Rayne said. "Sorry, Amos. Bricks might've been lighter."

"Not a bother," Amos replied amiably. "I love old pictures. I don't have any of my own."

Rayne patted his denim-clad calf, as it was closest to her. His mother had died while he was at university and his stepdad had gotten rid of everything. McGrath Castle was his home.

Ciara pulled out three more albums that had been filled with pictures. Some photos were loose. "We've hit the motherlode of family history."

Rayne picked up a five-by-seven silver frame of two men in their twenties. Their faces were youthful but their eyes, old. The photo fit crookedly. She took the picture out and read on the back, "Dougal McGrath and Billy McGillicuddy. 1923. Missing Duncan."

"Oh, 1923 — that would have been after the War of Independence. The Irish Civil War ended that year." Maeve tapped her chin. "I wonder if poor Duncan didn't make it?"

"That's a harsh price to pay," Rayne said.

"There were two wars back-to-back?"

"The War of Independence went from 1919 to 1921," Ciara said.

Amos studied the picture. "Some of these men had been fighting *together* to win freedom from Britain, to turn around and battle for the Irish Free State in 1922, against the Irish Republic Army. It lasted less than a year before they came to terms in 1923. North Ireland split to return to Great Britain, as allowed by the Anglo-Irish Treaty."

"It started with the Easter Rebellion in 1916," Maeve declared. She put the feather duster aside to examine another loose photo of men in uniform. "Maybe even before then. Poor dears."

"Ireland won freedom from Great Britain but then spent many years fighting within the country," Amos said.

"Because of their sacrifice we have an independent Ireland — the Republic of Ireland. I wish there were names listed on these pictures." Maeve nodded toward the one Amos held, with Billy, Dougal, missing Duncan. "The McGillicuddys have been in Grathton for as long as the McGraths. Billy is Darcy's dad and Darcy just turned ninety."

"The McGraths didn't live long, did

they?" Ciara said.

"Fighters for the truth seem to live short lives," Amos observed. "It's only been these past thirty years we've had peace."

"Do you remember Grandpa Lorcan, or Grandma Sonia?" Rayne asked Maeve. "Conor talked about them with reverence."

"I do." Maeve nodded. "Sonia O'Sullivan was a beauty and Lorcan was darkly handsome. They made a striking pair. They had Nevin, Claire, and Conor."

"We should do a family tree," Rayne suggested. She ran her finger over the soft old silk. The fabric was high quality.

"I'd like that." Ciara, who usually nixed creative ideas, turned to Maeve, "Is there one already?"

"We can check the family Bible," Maeve said. "I'll ask Cormac."

"Here," Amos said. "Let's pull the trunk out a bit so we can all see better."

"Good idea." Blarney curled up next to Rayne on the floor. Rayne went through the loose photos to put into a pile for a new book. A Polaroid of four men in all black captured her attention. There were no names here. The date, 1921. CC. There was a sketch of a shamrock on a cloud.

"Maeve, do you recognize anybody in this picture?" Rayne asked.

"No. Sorry, love."

"Dark and broody, aren't they?" Ciara asked. "I bet they were soldiers in the war."

Rayne was drawn to it and kept it out on the top of the stack of pictures she'd file later. The next hour flew by and when Aine joined them she burst out laughing. "What on earth is this?" She gestured to the piles of photos and stacks of papers. "I know Mam came into the parlor to dust and now there is more of it."

"We got carried away." Maeve squeaked when she saw the time. "Oh, dinner in fifteen minutes. Why didn't you find me earlier?"

"I didn't realize you were lost in the past." Aine offered Maeve a hand and pulled her mother up to a standing position.

Rayne stood and brushed dust from her sweater. "I don't think that trunk was opened since it was shoved in the attic. These are all from a hundred years ago. As an American, we are less than two hundred and fifty years old, and now, part of the Republic of Ireland, just over a hundred."

"Scrappers." Amos chuckled. "With a wide streak of Independence on both sides."

"I miss my dad." Rayne was filled with sentiment as she regarded the books. "And Uncle Nevin. They should be here with us, to go over this family history."

"I'm a bit mad at my mother for not telling me about Da until she was dying," Ciara said. "I grew up without a father, or family. I might not have been so lonely if I had known."

"It would have been great to know about you, cuz," Rayne said.

"Regrets won't change the facts, my dears," Maeve said briskly. "It's a shame, we can all agree, but it's time to let go what doesn't serve you."

Ciara and Rayne gave identical exhales.

"If we aren't ready for dinner, Frances will serve us instead of roast lamb to Father Patrick," Amos said.

"What should we do with this stuff?" Ciara asked Rayne.

"I'd like to leave it so we can go through it later," Rayne said. "I'll clean up the mess."

"I'm not worried about that," Maeve said. "It's valuable family history but not exactly gold or jewels. Cormac assisted Nevin with many things so he might know of a family tree."

"All right," Rayne said. "We'll reconvene later, but I need to freshen up before I meet you all in the dining room." Once in the hall, everyone dispersed.

Blarney trotted at her side as she raced up the stairs to her room on the second floor. She'd kept it unlocked as they didn't have guests at this time, though she always locked her sewing studio out of habit.

"What to wear, what to wear?" Rayne had a limited selection of clothes in the wardrobe here and the rest stashed in her Aunt Amalie's impressive closet in her sewing studio.

She washed up and chucked off the comfy sweater and jeans, choosing a simple navy-blue sheath with a pattered blue-and-white jacket. Blue heels, lipstick, and — voila!

Down the stairs they went, and Rayne let Blarney outside before rushing to the non-formal dining room. Father Patrick stood talking with Amos and Cormac. Richard and Dafydd were getting drinks. Ciara came in behind Rayne, smelling like lemon and lavender soap.

Maeve and Aine carried dishes through the door that led from the kitchen to the dining rooms, followed by Frances with a platter. On these occasions, everyone ate together.

Though Rayne had known of her McGrath family in Ireland, at home in Hollywood, it had been her, and her parents, who she called, Lauren and Conor. She'd never had a pet. Her dad had died from an illness when she was only twelve.

It had been her and her mom, something she and Ciara had in common. She was lucky to have Lauren, her dearest friend. Jenn was her next bestie. Landon had fooled them all.

If Landon was smart, he was hiding from the law in Mexico somewhere, though he'd been on a flight into Dublin back in September. She hadn't seen him and while a part of her was on guard, the other had to live her life.

"Drinks, ladies?" Amos asked.

"Whiskey." Ciara glanced at Dafydd, talking with Richard. "I can get it."

"Let me," Amos said smoothly. "Rayne?"

"Whiskey for me too." Though it had been an acquired taste, she loved the peaty notes of the amber spirit. She'd even grown to appreciate the lack of ice. Yes, she drank her whiskey neat.

"Here you are." Amos handed Ciara a tumbler and then Rayne. He went back to where he'd set down his glass and joined them to observe everyone as they chatted.

"Thank you," Rayne said, as Ciara echoed the sentiment.

"What can Dafydd and Richard be discussing so intently?" Ciara asked. "He didn't even notice me walk in."

"Sheep, no doubt." Amos laughed. "The ram was returned to the owner last month so now we need to wait to find out how many lambs are pregnant."

"Trials of dating a shepherd," Rayne said.

"It's a fact." Ciara didn't appear happy.

Maeve clapped her hands. "Let's eat before this delicious meal gets cold." Everything but the lamb was covered so there was little chance of that. It was the principle of the matter. Dinner was served at three, and it was now three ten.

Rayne sat begrudgingly at the head of the table. Just as she didn't like using the Lady title, she also didn't want the courtesy of being in charge. She and Ciara were equal partners in her mind no matter Uncle Nevin's will.

It was an argument Rayne had lost as Maeve, Ciara, and Cormac all sided with Ciara, and the law, that Rayne was the head of the family. Since Ciara hadn't filed the adoption papers showing that Uncle Nevin had wanted to adopt her, there wasn't much she could do.

Not only did they share a wild Celtic temper, stubborn also ran in their veins.

Father Patrick O'Murphy sat on the opposite end, as Ciara had given him her chair. He had compassionate blue eyes beneath thin black brows, and his hair was dark with silver at the temples. His white collar gleamed from his black button-up shirt. The chair had better back support and Ciara was considerate of their guest.

Rayne liked Father Patrick very much. He cared for his flock and clearly supported their venture. After several minutes where everyone feasted with roasted potatoes, carrots, and lamb, the conversation started up again.

This time sheep weren't the subject. Rayne was glad not to discuss the breeding habits of the wooly beasts at the dinner table. She had a grudging respect for what the animals brought to the manor, but it was a lot of work.

They were trying so many things from different angles. *Tick, tock.*

"Maeve mentioned you'll have wedding guests this weekend," Father Patrick said after he'd swallowed a bite of roasted potato.

"Yes." Rayne dabbed her lips with the cloth napkin. "A small wedding party Saturday and Sunday. Keep your fingers crossed."

"I will double my prayers for you," the priest said.

"Even better." Ciara ignored Dafydd, sitting next to her.

Dafydd realized that the snub was on purpose and scowled. Yet, didn't seem surprised. Trouble in paradise?

Rayne looked at Ciara's finger and noticed the Claddagh engagement ring was absent. Her cousin didn't always wear it, as she didn't want to lose it, so it might be nothing.

"I asked for more volunteers today during the service." Father Patrick smiled with satisfaction. "We should have thirty to clear the old headstones and debris. Eight thirty sharp."

November in Ireland was chilly, and it was common for the temps to drop to the forties with a high of fifty-two. Not only early, but cold too. Rayne didn't share the *doomed to fail* comment she'd heard yesterday during the service.

"We should wear layers," Ciara said. "Once we begin working, it won't be as cold."

"I'll join you ladies after I do my rounds here," Amos said. "It's grand you're putting in the hard labor too. Beetle said he's heard support from the villagers that he hasn't in some time."

"Oh?" Beetle Randall was the bartender at the Sheep's Head pub and had his thumb on the pulse of the village.

"He's got that vacant house next to him," Cormac said. "It needs to be rebuilt or destroyed."

Rayne sipped her whiskey. Where did that fall in the list of priorities? "We'll have Bobby Fitzroy look at it."

"Houses get old, and others might just need paint," Father Patrick said. "Some of my parishioners are of an age . . . Darcy McGillicuddy, 90, passed away this morning in his sleep. We have an entire generation that will be meeting the Lord soon."

"I'm sorry to hear that." Rayne nodded toward Maeve, who'd mentioned Darcy's birthday earlier. "We saw a picture of his ancestor, Billy, with one of ours. Dougal." Missing Duncan. 1923.

"It's a shame," Father Patrick said. "His family lives in Dublin. They'll want a service and have Darcy buried here in Grathton."

"Good you're cleaning the old cemetery," Dafydd said. "To find the McGillicuddy plot."

"It is full," Father Patrick said. "So, he'll go on the new side."

"There's a new side?" Rayne asked.

"Yes. Seventy-five years ago, give or take," Father Patrick said, "it was before my time, the tiny cemetery was full. The McGraths had a plot for family already on the other side, as they were the landowners. They provided more space."

"Now, that's a slogan we should find a way to use," Ciara said. "Welcome to Grathton Village — we have room to grow."

Rayne burst out laughing. "Love it!"

"You should both join the council," Father Patrick said. "I know you're busy, but again, this will show that you're serious in your commitment."

"I'm getting up at dawn to help clean a cemetery," Rayne protested.

"I don't want to be on the council," Ciara said.

"One of you has to be." Father Patrick swallowed his honeyed carrot.

"She's the lady," Ciara jerked her thumb toward Rayne.

"Can we share the duties?" Rayne shook her head, overwhelmed. "I can't do it alone."

Father Patrick hummed, pleased. "I'm sure it's been done before. Tinsley? Tinley?"

Rayne wondered at how well he knew them all. The priest's job was to guide his people, but she felt like she'd been herded in the direction he wanted her to go like one of the sheep.

Frances served a warm apple tart for dessert. As Rayne was finally relaxing, Father Patrick said, "One of the volunteers will be Owen Hughes."

"What?" Ciara spluttered.

Rayne had a lump in her throat, or she might have said more than, "Sugar cookies."

"Calm down, now. He's square with the law which means we need to welcome him back into the fold." Father Patrick stood. "Thank you for a lovely dinner, and I will see you all tomorrow morning, bright and early."

Chapter Two

Rayne hadn't slept well the night before and blamed Father Patrick's bombshell that Owen Hughes was in Grathton Village. The solicitor had drawn up Uncle Nevin's wonky will. If he was back, then she and Ciara could fire him. It would be first on the list. She was up before her 7 AM alarm and hopped into the shower rather than toss and turn.

Rayne arrived at the kitchen for breakfast. "Morning!" She sidled to the side door to let Blarney outside.

"Hey," Ciara said in a perky tone, the opposite of surly Frances. It wasn't early for Frances — that was simply her nature.

Maeve and Aine were there, as was Cormac. All had their beverage of choice. The ladies would be doing household chores while Ciara and Rayne were at the cemetery. Amos, Dafydd, and Richard all had breakfast in their own houses.

Rayne didn't have a strict schedule during the day. Her wedding gown business was steady, thanks to Aine's tweets and social media photos. Her December dresses were complete and ready to be mailed. There were two on the schedule for January. The fitting for Saturday's gown would be the first in person for Lenni. The CEO said her measurements hadn't changed.

"Will you be home for lunch?" Frances asked.

"I'm not sure." Rayne fixed her coffee and helped herself to a scoop of scrambled eggs with ham, adding two slices of whole wheat toast — with butter. Life at the castle was so active that she had no problem burning calories.

"I can make sandwiches," Frances offered, "but don't expect me to feed the whole village unless you give me time to run to the market in Kilkenny."

Ciara dipped her head to hide a smile.

"It wouldn't be the whole village," Maeve said in an even tone, "but there might be thirty or forty volunteers. You're right, Frances. It would be a supportive thing to do."

"That is very thoughtful. Thanks for thinking of it!" Rayne said. "Maybe Cormac or Aine could deliver the sandwiches around noon?"

"It won't be fancy given the short notice," Frances warned. "Good simple food. I've got ham and pickle for a ham salad. I'll do some egg salad for any vegetarians."

"Thank you, Frances," Ciara said.

"There's money in the jar if you need to buy anything," Maeve said, nodding to the tin by the window.

"We should tempt people with lunch so they work a full day," Ciara suggested.

"Good plan," Aine agreed.

"We have to knock off by four, I imagine, due to the lack of daylight." Rayne sipped her coffee, enjoying this part of the day before things went crazy. "I wonder how long it will take to clear the area?"

"I have no idea." Ciara shrugged. "But the more hands the faster the job."

"Father Patrick said he had thirty volunteers, plus us, so forty would be just right." Rayne finished her coffee and stood, ready to get to work.

"Have fun today," Maeve said.

Rayne and Ciara left the manor and walked toward the church. The cousins each wore jeans, boots, and T-shirts covered by layers of sweaters and topped by a wind/rain jacket. Work gloves were in their back pockets.

Blarney joined them.

The air was brisk, no doubt, Rayne thought to herself, but she enjoyed the fresh outdoors a lot more than she'd thought she would, considering she was raised with blue skies and warmth.

Ciara, as if reading her mind, said, "You must miss California right now."

"I miss being warm," Rayne agreed with a smile, "but it's not as bad as I feared. Now, I'm not sure what I'll think when winter comes. I've never had a white Christmas."

"Maeve goes all out for the holiday," Ciara warned. "It's her favorite. She hangs evergreen branches from the chandelier."

"I can't wait. It's going to be an extra special holiday once Lauren arrives. I miss my mom a lot more than the blue skies."

"That's saying something," Ciara said.

Rayne smiled. "You know, we should fire Owen Hughes as soon as we see him this morning."

"That's perfect. He's got a lot of nerve showing up."

They walked across the street, carefully looking both ways with Blarney, who wasn't on a leash. He didn't like streets and usually stayed by her side.

The church was a few blocks down. Across the road from the church was the *newer* cemetery where the McGraths were buried or interred depending on the choice made. When it was her time, she wanted to be ashes, as her father had been. Uncle Nevin had been buried.

In Ireland, Rayne had learned that the people accepted death as a topic of conversation, not to be shied away from, as one did in LA. It was a fact of life and unavoidable.

When they arrived at the church to the left of the road, the parking lot was full of trucks and cars. Bobby Fitzroy's construction truck — bigger than a van, but covered, had the tail open. Garden tools of all kinds were showcased. Of Bobby himself, there was no sign.

"Are we late?" Rayne asked, worried. Her watch read 8:15.

Ciara shook her head. "Eight thirty is when Father Patrick said to be here."

A man possibly in his seventies called out a hello, followed by an announcement. "Our ladies have arrived."

About forty people in the parking lot turned toward Rayne and Ciara, shouting morning greetings. None of them were Owen.

"Can I get you a cup of coffee?" asked a thin-voiced older woman next to a silver truck with the tailgate down and an array of coffees, hot water for teas, and disposable paper mugs. She wore silver framed glasses.

"Yes!" Rayne said. "You are my new best friend."

"I'm Shauna Dennehy, milady. How do you take it?"

"Call me Rayne, please — and sweet."

Rayne strode through the volunteers and realized that most of whom were over seventy, and possibly into their eighties. A few younger folks in their sixties, and three men in their forties.

Monday mornings would be regular working hours. Were these men in need of jobs? Or perhaps they had flexible schedules.

"Here you are." Shauna blasted her bright smile to Ciara. "Tea, dear? That's what you drink at church."

"Thank you," Ciara said. "You are very kind." She turned to face the volunteers. "We will provide sandwiches from the manor at noon in appreciation of your labor."

Rayne nodded at her cousin. It seemed Frances had saved them. Blarney ambled through the folks toward Father Patrick, who patted the dog on the head. His black uniform was covered by a black wool coat.

"And a splendid morning, everyone,"

Father Patrick said. "It's good of you to volunteer your services." He tilted his head at a couple so old Rayne feared they would break by lifting shovels. "Murray and Olivia O'Brien were married here."

"And plan to be buried here," Olivia quipped. "But not anytime soon. Nothing wrong with the new cemetery. Not sure why we need to clear this one out, but if Father Patrick thinks we need to do it, then I'm happy to help."

"I explained, Olivia dear, about the weeds taking over the offices for rent," Shauna shouted into Olivia's ear.

"Mrs. O'Brien is deaf as a doornail," one of the younger men said. He had thick brown hair and a hooked nose. "My grandma says she won't get hearing aids — too vain." He stuck his hand out to Rayne. "I'm Don McElroy. I know Aiden from work. He was mentioning vacant offices that might be suitable if we branched out? We're in mobile phones."

Rayne shook his hand. Getting in younger people would revitalize the village, which was in line with what Uncle Nevin had wanted. "Let's talk later. I'd be interested in hearing your idea."

"Me too," Ciara said. "Which one is Aiden?"

"The boyo with the red hair and freckles." Don gestured toward a man about his age with a lovely young blonde in her late thirties. "That's his girlfriend, Treasa. She's not staying to help, but they share a car. Lucky guy."

"That would explain why she's dressed so cute," Rayne said. Treasa had on a calf-length plaid trench coat, boots with three-inch heels, and wavy brown hair to her shoulders.

"She works as a receptionist for a solicitor," Don said. "Not sure how Red gets the ladies he does. His ex Sheila was a looker too."

Was that jealousy in Don's voice? He didn't wear rings of any kind on either hand. Looking toward Father Patrick, she saw panic in his demeanor. He'd been sidetracked from his instructions by a woman in her eighties who had a death grip on his elbow.

"Ciara and I need to find out what our jobs are. Be sure to talk with us later." Rayne hooked her arm through her cousin's and dragged her toward Father Patrick.

If Father Patrick jerked away too fast, the woman might topple over. Next time they had a volunteer event that required manual labor, they would need to set an age restriction of eighty and younger.

Could Rayne and Grathton Village be sued if someone had a stroke or heart attack? Her pulse sped. In the states, this would be a legal suit waiting to happen.

"Rayne, Ciara." Relief appeared on the priest's expression. "I'd like you to meet Elizabeth McGillicuddy. She's arrived early from Dublin. Her brother passed away yesterday."

"Darcy," she warbled. "He was in perfect health. I don't understand what happened."

"He was ninety, wasn't he?" Rayne asked, wanting to make sure that she had the right person. The one who had died in his sleep.

"And he was on track to be a hundred, like our parents," Elizabeth said with an unhappy sniff. "I'll be eighty-eight this year. Healthy as a horse."

Rayne was glad that the woman wasn't here for the weed clearing and she did appear to be in good health. Of medium height, thin, yes but not like she'd get blown over by a sturdy wind. It was her grief that had her bowed.

She wore slip-on leather boots without a heel and leggings with a long cardigan sweater and a turtleneck underneath. Her white hair was pinned back from her face. Lovely blue eyes shone from a fishnet of wrinkles.

"How did you get here?" Ciara asked.

"I drove." Elizabeth's brow furrowed. "How else did you think? I'm well-off but not flighty with my money." Rayne looked toward the car Elizabeth pointed to, which was a brand-new Mercedes. "Our father taught us better than that."

She recalled the name Billy McGillicuddy on the photo with Dougal McGrath. Missing Duncan.

Rayne liked this spunky woman. "I am so sorry for your loss."

"Thank you." Elizabeth shifted from Ciara to Rayne. "You both have the McGrath look about you. I didn't keep in touch with the family as I've been in Dublin for over fifty years now. The stories I've heard," she waggled her bejeweled finger, "that's enough to keep you up at night."

"What stories?" Rayne asked. Being Ireland it could be anything from leprechauns to the latest in politics.

"About the War of Independence," Elizabeth said. "Our kin were heroes."

"I think so too." Ciara smiled. "We found a trunk of photos from that time."

"Ancient history," Don remarked. He'd evidently followed them. "My family goes on about it."

"And they are?" Rayne asked.

"Dorothy and Sheff McElroy." Don pointed to a stooped man with silver hair, and a round woman with dyed brown hair. "I told them not to worry about cleaning this place, but I couldn't stop them from showing up today. I'm happy to help them."

Elizabeth narrowed her eyes on Don. "You young people have no respect for your elders. I've taught my children better manners than that. They'll be here tomorrow to discuss Darcy's estate." She dabbed at her lower lashes. "I just am stunned that he's gone. Life is short. Father, please excuse me. I'll see you tomorrow at noon." She nodded to everyone and climbed into her Mercedes. The windows were tinted.

"Well, pardon me," Don said. "Was that polite enough?"

Aiden joined them and Rayne turned as a newer red sedan peeled out and sped toward the road. Elizabeth remained in her car. Maybe she was listening to music or talking on the phone. Absorbing the loss of her brother. Even though it seemed like a *good way to go,* it was obvious that Elizabeth was stricken by her brother's death.

"Hi. I'm Aiden Dennehy." The man had hair even more startling a red than Richard's, and freckles across the bridge of his wide nose. He shook Rayne's hand and then Ciara's. "I'm thrilled to help. I've been wanting to meet you both and this is a great opportunity. Where do you want me to start?"

"We were going to ask Father Patrick the same thing," Rayne said.

"I wasn't expecting Elizabeth McGillicuddy until tomorrow and she was quite upset that I couldn't talk with her right now." Father Patrick bowed his head. "I feel bad, but we have plans and appointments for a reason."

"She rich?" Don asked, probably still offended by Elizabeth's rudeness. "Rich people think they have different rules."

Father Patrick gathered his composure. "Let's get started." He looked for Murray O'Brien, who was hand-in-hand with Olivia. To be married for such a length of time and still take such good care of one another gave Rayne hope for the future.

Weddings and partnerships to last a lifetime. Unlike her and Landon. But when she thought of Amos, her stomach tightened for a different reason.

She glanced at her watch. Only quarter to nine. Blarney joined her and Ciara.

"Mr. Fitzroy!" the priest called to Bobby. He was in his sixties and wore a ballcap over gray hair. His shirt was a waffle-print of thermal and clung to muscles he no doubt earned doing his construction work. "You've got a system for us?"

"Yes." The man whistled for everyone's attention. "Hey all — I'm Bobby Fitzroy. I'd like us to be in teams. Everyone should have work gloves. If you don't, come see me and I will loan you a pair." He gestured to a stack of gloves in a cardboard box that read Fitzroy's Construction.

"Thank you." Shauna waggled her arthritic fingers. "I knew I forgot something."

"Grandma," Aiden said. "I think you should leave the hard work for me."

"I may not be able to saw down branches, but I can certainly gather trash," Shauna replied pertly. "Right, Luke?"

"So true, a chumann." Luke wore a worker's cap and a flannel shirt over heavy jeans. "Just turned eighty-nine last week and Dr. Ruebens said we need to get more regular exercise than our work on the farm."

"It must be something in the Irish air," Rayne murmured, impressed. Six couples in their eighties, and Olivia and Morris were ninety. Darcy had died at ninety, and Elizabeth, still in her car, was eighty-eight.

"Our villagers are hearty," Ciara said.

"Could this be a Blue Zone?"

"What?"

"An area where the majority of people live to be a hundred."

Ciara appeared faintly terrified.

"Healthy hundred, too," Rayne continued. "In Greece, they even have happy hour."

"I don't know if I want to be that old," her cousin said.

"If my mind and body were in decent condition then I wouldn't be opposed." Rayne smiled at the plump woman next to her and the woman smiled back.

"We haven't met yet. I'm Dorothy McElroy and this is my husband Sheff. You were talking with our grandson Don. We know Ciara, dear, from church."

"Hi!" Rayne said.

"Nice to meet you." Sheff shook Rayne's hand with a firm grip, despite his slight stoop. He and his grandson shared a larger hooked nose.

"Do you also have a farm?"

"Small homestead a few miles over that hill," Sheff confirmed. "The McElroys have been friends of the McGraths for centuries. You ever need a thing, you can call on us."

"Thank you!"

"We are fortunate that our three kids — one son and two daughters, have given us four grandchildren. No greats so far." Dorothy shrugged. "They have homes on our property. Being able to work remotely allows them to have the best of both worlds. Don's mother is an accountant, and his dad manages the siblings' jam business."

"It is nice that they are all so close!" Rayne said. Jam business?

"Did you have siblings?" Sheff asked.

"No."

"It's a shame." Sheff shook his head. "Our Don is single. Are you seeing anyone?"

"Oh! Uh . . . I am very involved in the business right now."

Ciara covered her mouth with her hand to hide a grin as she stepped toward Bobby. "Rayne?"

"Coming!" Rayne nodded at the happy couple. "Nice to meet you both."

She raced to her cousin.

"You owe me." Ciara pulled her work gloves from her back pocket.

"Like ten times over."

"Not a fan of Don McElroy?"

"I don't know him!" Rayne slid her gloves free. "He's definitely not my type. When are we getting directions for this shindig anyway?"

"People keep interrupting poor Bobby." Ciara gestured toward the man who was handing out gloves because the people hadn't been able to get beyond that first step.

At last, the box of gloves was empty.

"People. Please let me finish giving instructions. I will answer questions afterward." Bobby lifted a sheet of paper. "For today only, we are going to clear the weeds and debris. Tomorrow, if necessary, we will trim tree branches or hedges."

"That's good," Rayne said. "Nobody over seventy should be messing with any chainsaws. Do you think they'll need naps?"

"Rayne!"

"Sorry. It's a legit question. In Greece, that's one of the Blue Zone superpowers."

"Pay attention," Ciara said.

Bobby next showed a map. "This is the graveyard. We have a list of graves from as far back as 1760. Father Patrick has shared the manifest of known burials from the church records. I am a bit of an ancestry buff so I'm very excited about the headstones. Be gentle with the old stone, alright?"

A chorus of yesses came from the crowd.

"All right. If you see a tombstone knocked over, come and find me or Father Patrick. Do not attempt to lift it or raise it yourself. Depending on the age, and condition, we might prefer to leave it as is or contact a professional restorer." Bobby shook the papers in his hand. "I only have ten maps so please break up into ten groups of five or less. When you're done, appoint one person as your leader and pick up a map."

Rayne and Ciara were joined by Amos and Richard. "Nice of you both to come!" Rayne said. She bumped her arm to Amos, next to her.

"Amos helped with the roof, so it's done," Richard said.

Olivia and Murray O'Brien joined Shauna and Luke Dennehy, with Aiden as their muscle. Don stayed with Dorothy and Sheff McElroy. Rayne overheard Dorothy ask Don about Paddy O'Brien, Olivia and Murray's grandson. It seemed the kids had all been close as children.

Paddy would join them after he got off work at the dairy in Cotter, if he could. He was staying with them on the property.

Rayne met Bronagh Wilson, Bran's mother. She seemed like a nice woman, who also checked out Rayne's bare ring finger.

"And how is Bran doing?" Rayne asked politely. He had been very vocal against the rejuvenation of Grathton Village.

They had some folks who believed that Grathton would be better off if combined with Cotter Village and the McGraths absorbed into a bigger whole.

Cotter had two thousand residents, while they had less than five hundred.

It was up to Rayne and Ciara to change their minds and show that the McGraths cared about the villagers *and* could provide security such as jobs and housing.

"He's busy," Bronagh said. "Still looking for his soul mate. Are you dating?"

"I'm much too busy to date."

"I overheard Sheff suggesting Don." Bronagh smiled. "He isn't as wealthy as you are so it wouldn't work. My grandmother used to be the village matchmaker."

"That's a real thing?"

"Not anymore, but it was a vital position." Bronagh sighed. "What this village needs is babies. Don't you want children?"

"No. Well, I didn't. I had my career."

"Designing dresses?"

"Modern Lace. I wanted to make sure that my gowns were in every high-end department boutique." Now that had changed. Maybe someday she'd be open to the possibility.

If the right Viking, er, man came along. Rayne looked for Amos, who was conversing with Father Patrick and hadn't heard Bronagh's questions.

Richard was the captain for their team, so

he went to get a map. Bronagh had a cheery attitude and struck up a conversation with the church members next to them.

Oscar Wharton, seventy-five, a widower. Colleen Randall, Beetle's sister. Moira and Keith Morton, grandparents in their sixties with twin blond girls, five, who would start school the following year. Shannon and Shayna Morton were Hollywood cute, right down to the upturned little noses and precocious personalities.

"Are we ready?" Moira asked the two groups.

"Yes!" Rayne said.

"Cemeteries are spooky," Shannon declared as they walked into the gate that surrounded the lawn and tombstones.

"So scary!" Shayna seconded, her blue eyes round.

Blarney trotted next to Rayne.

"I wish my Corrine wasn't at preschool," Colleen said. "Maybe I can bring her tomorrow to meet you two sweethearts."

Shannon nodded. "We'd like that," she said, speaking for her and her sister.

Rayne bet that happened a lot.

"Will your dog protect us?" Shannon asked.

"Of course," Rayne said. "But there is nothing to be afraid of."

"Ghosts," Shayna said. "Leprechauns."

"Skeletons. And fairies," Shannon said. "They are the worst."

"All right, darlings," Moira Morton said. "That's enough." To Rayne's surprise, the kindly grandmother leaned down and clasped her granddaughters' shoulders. "Do you see that red door over there in the tree? It's a fairy house — it will trap the bad fairies, so never fear."

"Bad fairies?" Rayne asked.

Amos moved close and peered into her eyes. "The fairies enter those doors which go nowhere, confusing them. It keeps the mischievous ones from harming humans."

Blarney barked, his tail wagging. Were they serious right now?

Richard handed Rayne the map of the cemetery. "Let's start in the back corner and work forward, all right?"

"Sure."

Bobby Fitzroy was on the opposite corner with his group, doing the oldest tombstones first. Don and Aiden were on the outer edges of the land to clear it and see what was there. Inside the cemetery were a variety of trees — pine, to oak that had shed its leaves.

"Will we find any of your ancestors?" Moira asked.

"No. Father Patrick said the McGraths always had a private plot of land for their dead. When this was getting too full, they opened it to make it available for the villagers."

"That's pretty amazing to have your ancestors all in one place since 1760," Oscar said. "We came around the nineteen hundreds. Is Wharton on the map?"

Rayne scanned the page. "The names aren't in alphabetical order." She squinted "Wilmington. Wharton!" She gave it to Oscar. "It should be in the newer section, on the outskirts, where Aiden and the Dennehys are."

"Do you mind if I go look?" Oscar asked.

"Not at all."

"I'll go with you, Oscar," Colleen said.

Rayne looked at Moira and Keith. "Should we check for Morton?"

"No," Keith said sadly. "We've only been in Grathton for twenty years. We were driving from Dublin to Kilkenny where our daughter and son-in-law lived and fell in love with the fields. I used to be a teacher but retired last year. Moira has her own dried lavender business. We grow it, dry it, and ship it all over the world."

Lavender!

"We love it here," Moira said. "You have

our support in the village debate. We need young blood."

"We're trying to convince our daughter to move here." Keith pointed to their granddaughters. "Free babysitting is a pretty good lure."

Somehow, hours passed in companionable conversation. They were moving in ten-by-ten squares that Bobby had suggested after realizing folks had scrambled to the headstones without any organization. Bronagh, Bobby's sister, was a very diligent worker.

Rayne pulled vines from a four-foot-tall headstone, smiling at Amos as she put the debris in the trash bag. He'd already gathered and exchanged one with Father Patrick who remained at the church to manage stragglers. Blarney had nosed around the base of this grave, so she'd started here. The dirt was softer and not as hard packed as elsewhere in the cemetery.

"Here's another M name," Rayne said. "Lots of Monroes. The McGillicuddys had an impressive mausoleum." She paused and wiped more dirt free. Bobby, Murray, and Richard gathered around. Ciara and Bronagh joined them.

Ciara peered over her shoulder, catching some of the excitement. "Does that say McGrath?"

"Yes!" Rayne brushed the dirt from the letters of the first name too. "Thomas."

Bobby scanned the map and the list of names. "It's not on the roster."

"Is there a date?" Bronagh asked.

"1923." Rayne's heart filled with sorrow. Recalling the history lesson from yesterday, she said, "He must have died in the Irish Civil War."

"Not Duncan, from the photo?" Amos asked.

"Nope." Rayne traced the engraved letters. "Definitely Thomas."

"I wonder why he was buried here?" Ciara asked.

"We might never know." Rayne's imagination went to the photos of handsome soldiers they'd discovered yesterday. "Maybe he was the product of an affair?"

"You and your Hollywood ideas," Ciara laughed. "Maybe though. We'll ask Maeve and Cormac. They might know."

Her phone rang. Speaking of, it was their butler. "Hello?"

"Brown bag lunch is ready if you want to let everyone know to come back to the church parking lot," Cormac said.

"We will — thank you!"

Rayne brushed her hands free of dirt. "It's lunch time, folks. Amos, let's leave the bag here so we know where we left off. I can't believe we found a McGrath."

The group tromped out of the cemetery, Bobby murmuring to Bronagh that the grave shouldn't be there.

Rayne had learned that in this life, things that weren't supposed to happen, happened all the time. They reached the church parking lot, where Cormac had set out a spread on the table that Bobby had been using earlier for the gloves and maps.

Frances had outdone herself even with a simple lunch. Ham salad, or egg salad, crisps, an apple, and sweet cookies.

It was just what the volunteers needed to push through the next two hours of the afternoon. At three, Rayne, Ciara, Amos, Bronagh, and Richard had gathered five huge bags of leaves and debris. Everyone met back in the parking lot.

Bobby collected tools he'd loaned, and they tossed the bags of trash into the back of his pickup truck. "I'll take it to the dump," he said.

"What's the plan for tomorrow?" Rayne asked.

"For those that can help, it will be the heavier activities like branch removal and tree trimming," Bobby said. "Meet here at eight thirty again, like this morning. Great job, folks."

More than half of the volunteers were in the parking lot, and they applauded.

"We'd love to thank everyone for helping out by buying a pint at the Sheep's Head," Rayne said.

"Or your beverage of choice," Ciara said.

It was like a game of telephone as Richard spread the word and the volunteers in the cemetery, not quite finished but well in line to be done by the next day or two, emptied to the church parking lot.

Father Patrick bowed his head. "Thank you all for coming today, and Lord's blessing upon you." He raised his gaze. "I'll go clean up and meet you there in a few minutes."

Rayne, Amos, Ciara, and Richard headed to the pub that was several blocks away. Pub life meant community.

"Hey, Beetle." Rayne greeted the tattooed bartender when they entered. Blarney would wait outside on the bench beneath the awning. His eyes were almost black, and every visible piece of skin had ink on it, even his shaved head.

"Richard, Amos, ladies," Beetle said.

"We'd like to buy a round for the volunteers helping at the cemetery today," Rayne said. Some expenses, while not tangible, such as good will, were still important.

Cheers erupted behind her as at least twenty of the forty piled into the small space. The place smelled like fish and chips and hops — smells Rayne was growing to appreciate. She'd learned to like an amber ale but would choose a whiskey after the day's hard work.

"It's just me here to serve," Beetle said. "Colleen is with Corrine."

"I'll help." Richard adeptly delivered the drinks.

"Pour one for yourself, Beetle," Rayne said. "I'd like to toast to the Grathton villagers. It's because of your kindness that we will grow again to what my Uncle Nevin wanted this place to be — a hub of community that looked out for one another."

"Slainte!" Ciara called, raising her whiskey glass.

Claps sounded around the room.

"That was lovely, Rayne," Amos said.

"Ah, thanks. I mean it." She reached for Amos's hand and squeezed. "You especially have been so supportive."

"I care for you," Amos said.

"Oh!" Rayne hadn't expected that declaration.

"I've been waiting for you to be ready to hear about my feelings," Amos said. "And I think you might be." He searched her face.

"I am." Rayne leaned to him and kissed him softly.

"Another round, Beetle," Amos called. "This one's on me."

Later that evening, three rounds in, Rayne was feeling no pain and floating on air. Anywhere Amos was in the room, she knew it just by his energy.

This was special and brand-new. She'd never felt like this before.

"It's about time." Ciara grinned at her. "He's a happy man. And you?"

"I'm happy. Is it stupid of me to be happy? Landon really broke my trust." Rayne sipped her whiskey.

"Landon is an imbecile," Ciara said firmly.

"I second that," Richard said.

Rayne blinked. She hadn't realized Richard was around.

She looked for Amos, and located him near the Jakes, chatting with Beetle. Murray and Sheff were both talking loudly, which happened in a crowded room of drinking people, but this caught her attention. There were angry raised voices.

Aiden and Don were playing darts with a third man. Don called him Paddy — must be the McElroy's grandson. He had bleached hair in spikes. Treasa, Aiden's girlfriend, had stopped by for a quick drink and left after Paddy promised to give Aiden a ride home.

Bran walked in and went to join his mother, Bronagh, who was sitting with Olivia and Shauna. This was the community that she and Ciara were part of — would it be enough to prove to the villagers that they wanted the best?

"I'll be right back," Rayne said. "I want to ask Don and Aiden about their new business."

Ciara propped her elbow on the high-top table. "Everybody uses a mobile. Wonder how soon they could move in? We could offer a discount on rent."

"Do we own the building?" Rayne asked.

"I don't know." Ciara's cheeks were flushed pink. "Maybe we should find out who does before making any deals."

"Good plan." Rayne decided to stay put. Richard left to talk with Bran. "Where's Dafydd?"

"He's busy with the sheep." Ciara drank her whiskey. "He knows where I am if he wants to join me."

"Things okay?"

"I don't want to talk about it."

"All right." Rayne understood that.

Just then, Beetle gave a growl of rage and

hauled back to punch Aiden in the nose. Blood spurted everywhere.

"What on earth was that about?"

Amos was at Rayne's side in an instant, literally protecting her with his body. "We should probably get going."

"What happened?"

Amos sighed. "If I tell you, will you leave with me now?"

"Yes."

"Beetle has a little sister."

"Colleen. I know her. So?" Ciara said.

"Well. Aiden has a girlfriend, Treasa. The blonde that just left."

"Yeah?" Rayne had a bad feeling.

"Aiden messed around with Beetle's sister and then had the nerve to not only show up here tonight, but invite Treasa. Colleen sometimes helps Beetle out here at the pub."

Another punch sounded.

"It's time to go." Amos curled his fingers around her hand. "You promised."

Chapter Three

Rayne woke up in the middle of the night to Blarney howling at the door. The last time that had happened, it had been Ciara's fiancé Dafydd trying to scare her.

Not cool.

Still, he'd apologized. Blarney had never barked or howled like this as if knowing Dafydd was not a danger to her.

It was possible the castle was haunted. Enough dead McGrath ancestors rested here to make it likely even that one or two resided in these walls. Uncle Nevin, Cousin Padraig, and her Aunt Amalie.

Her mom said that none of those people would want to scare Rayne.

She was right. "Blarney," Rayne called softly. "Come here, boy."

Blarney glared at the door before giving a final growling bark. His hackles were raised — not in fear, but warning.

Rayne thought for about two seconds of

getting out of bed to open the door and see who it might be . . . but decided she would not be that heroine in the movie that was too stupid to live. Instead, she pushed her night table in front of the door, turned on the TV, and returned to her safe bed, cuddling her dog.

She dozed until dawn.

"Another early morning for us, Blarney. You're a good boy." She petted his fur and looked into his eyes. "You're the best protector."

She climbed from bed, showered, and as she dressed, thought of Amos — another fierce protector.

Though she'd promised Amos she would leave last night, things had grown complicated because Paddy had called the police on Aiden's behalf after Beetle had punched him. Aiden hadn't pressed charges. Rayne and Ciara couldn't desert their friend once the chaos had calmed.

Beetle kicked Aiden out of the Sheep's Head permanently. Shauna and Luke apologized for their grandson's wild behavior, though Murray and Sheff put it down to boys being boys.

"No harm done," Sheff had said.

"My sister is brokenhearted." Beetle had been resolute. "Colleen thought he'd broken up with Treasa because he told her he was single. That's not an act of integrity. Don't tell me you'll stand by Aiden's behavior." He'd pointed toward the door and the couples left.

Rayne, Ciara, Richard, and Amos stayed to help Beetle clean up. The music was loud and cathartic. Beetle had a great rock voice.

They'd arrived home in time for dinner at six, the roast chicken and potatoes sobering them up. Oh, maybe the whiskey had kept her from a sound sleep last night? It made more sense than ghosts wandering the halls.

Now, fresh from the shower and ready for breakfast, Rayne and Blarney left her bedroom, making sure to lock the door once she and Blarney were in the hall.

"You heard the noises too, Blarney. And you were sober as a judge." The dog wagged his tail, and they went downstairs to the kitchen.

Ciara wasn't there yet, but Maeve, Aine, and Cormac were seated at the table. The Lloyds were dressed in their uniforms for the day. Amos and Richard had other duties today so couldn't join them.

"Sandwiches again?" Frances queried.

"That would be wonderful. I don't know how many volunteers we'll have but I don't think as many signed up. It's tree trimming day." Bobby had asked that they leave the Thomas McGrath section alone until he talked to Father Patrick.

"Let me know when you get there," Frances said. "I've got poached eggs this morning and bacon for breakfast. Soda bread, and jam."

Rayne's stomach rumbled. "That sounds delicious. I met the McElroys yesterday and they have a jam business."

"What kind of jam?" Maeve asked.

"I didn't ask. To be honest, I was trying to dodge them setting me up with their grandson Don."

Ciara entered the kitchen with a low laugh. "They wanted to nab the Lady McGrath to add to their family tree."

"I am not available." Rayne ducked her head but couldn't stop her wide smile.

"Not anymore," Ciara sang as she grabbed a mug from the counter. "She and Amos kissed."

"Yes!" Aine pumped her fist.

"Ah, did you now?" Maeve asked with a grin.

Cormac buttered a piece of soda bread. "The lad has had a soft spot for you since you arrived, intrigued by all of your . . . suitcases."

Rayne's cheeks burned at the memory of

Blarney running off with her Jimmy Choo and her lingerie packed around a small sewing machine.

"We have agreed to see one another on a social basis." Rayne watched for their reaction to be sure she wasn't doing anything wrong. Amos was an employee. Sort of.

Ciara fixed her tea with honey the way she liked it best. "Maybe someday one of these weddings will be for you."

"Let's not go so fast! We haven't even had a single date yet," Rayne protested. Not even a coffee at his cottage. Yet, she knew Amos was a decent man, with a compassionate heart. And damn sexy. She doubted the connection to him would ever fade.

And though it was the perfect opportunity to bring up Dafydd, Rayne did not. Neither did the others around the table, as if they all sensed a riff.

Last night at dinner, Dafydd had noticed that something was off and was extra attentive, but Ciara remained polite.

Polite wasn't good.

It wasn't passionate or loving.

Well, Rayne was here if Ciara wanted to talk. Had her cousin ever had a female bestie to chat with about guys? Dreams? Expectations?

"No more teasing!" Rayne said. "We have

a lot to do today. I'd like to hire a new solicitor, actually. Maybe Treasa, Aiden's girlfriend, can recommend one? I don't want to use Owen Hughes. He never showed up yesterday or we would have fired him already."

"Fair," Ciara said. "Cormac, do we own the land in the village?"

"Aye, I believe so," Cormac said.

"I'd like some help finding the deeds to all of that."

"If we don't have copies here," Cormac said, "it should be filed with the Registry of Deeds. They probably have a main office in Dublin."

"I love Dublin," Aine said.

"That's where the office for the McGavin Property Management company is headquartered," Cormac continued. "It's a family-owned business. Five generations. Nevin went to visit them in April of this year."

"Around the time he started taking heart medication," Ciara said, lowering her eyes.

"The McGavins manage this property?"

"Yes," Cormac said. "Would you like me to make an appointment with them for you?"

Rayne and Ciara exchanged a bemused glance. "Yes," Ciara said.

"As soon as possible," Rayne said. Six months wasn't very long. "Thanks, Cormac. You're sure Nevin went to Dublin in April?"

"Yes. He didn't want me to go with him," Cormac paused for a beat, "when normally that was something we would do together."

Maeve patted her husband's hand. "You couldn't have known anything, dear."

Cormac lowered his head, concentrating on his bowl of porridge.

"While we are there, I can pick up ivory silk thread for Lenni's dress. I have an alternate, but I'd prefer silk."

"For the wedding this Saturday?" Ciara asked.

"Yes. I have a back-up, but it isn't silk. I would know the difference, but the bride wouldn't. Also, I can pick up some ivory fabric to mend the lining in the trunk."

"I can meet Nolan," Ciara said.

Aine's face fell. "I adore him. He's a fabric wizard."

"Next time, you can come," Rayne promised. "Once we catch a breath around here, we should go for a day of fun. The Zoo, museums, everything."

Ciara shook her head. "Fun. There is *always* work to do."

Rayne saw the time. "We should go and make sure we beat them this morning." She told the others around the small table that though they'd been early, the elders had already set up and had coffee and tea.

It was half past seven and thanks to her lack of sleep she was already wired for the day. She stood and tucked an apple in her pocket.

"Wait for me!" Ciara wrapped her soda bread in a paper napkin.

They called goodbyes, with Frances reminding her to message about lunch, and went outside. It was cold and woke up any remaining sleepy parts of Rayne's body.

Blarney raced from the barn, dirt on his muzzle. What on earth?

Rayne brushed it free. "Should I ask, boy?"

The pup woofed. Blarney seemed to know where they were going and trotted at her side. She had on the same lightweight all-weather jacket as yesterday, and work gloves in her pocket. Jeans, boots, and a knit cap that she'd tucked her long hair under.

Ciara walked beside her with a confident stride. Her canvas coat was olive green, and she wore coveralls. Her short bleached-blond curls were uncovered.

Her cousin slapped her gloves against her opposite palm. "I hope Cormac finds the deeds to the property, but either way, we will meet with the management company. We'll need to talk with Treasa this morning — she'd be a good place to start. I imagine in her position as receptionist she'd have all the intel on the local solicitors."

They crossed the street. Liam and Sinead from the Coco Bean Café waved to them and shouted a greeting.

Ciara and Rayne, with Blarney, kept walking past the forlorn shops before the landscaped section and the small general store, Dr. Ruebens' office and Owen Hughes's office. It was dark and seemed vacant. Rayne hoped that Father Patrick's information was incorrect.

They rounded the quiet corner. Bobby Fitzroy passed them in his work truck, headed toward Kilkenny. He seemed intent and didn't notice them.

"Wonder where he's going?" Ciara asked. "Maybe he forgot something and had to go back. That's a twenty-five-minute drive each way." She looked at her phone. "Seven forty. He'll be roaring in on his back wheels to reach the church by eight thirty."

"Maybe he's just going for coffee," Rayne suggested.

"You rushed me through my tea so I could use a second cup." Ciara unwrapped her soda bread. "But at least I've got this to keep me going."

The church parking lot was quiet. "We beat them!"

Fog rolled over the hills giving the cemetery to their right an eerie vibe though the church property and older cemetery, including the small house behind the church where Father Patrick lived, hadn't yet been ensconced.

Gray skies promised a drizzle later but for now, it was clear.

"Treasa's car is here," Rayne said, recognizing the red sportscar. "Maybe she's dropping Aiden off?"

"Great! We can talk to her before everyone else arrives," Ciara said. "Did you notice that for a bunch of people who need hearing aids, they are the worst gossips?"

Rayne chuckled. "That, and matchmakers. Bronagh's grandmother was one. I feel bad in a way for Don. Paddy is divorced, and Aiden a ladies' man, but Don hasn't had a steady girlfriend, and everyone knows it. There aren't a lot of single women around — unless you go to Dublin."

"Do you think the McElroys and Dennehys asking you out is why Amos shared his feelings?" Ciara teased.

"He had nothing to fear, believe me." Rayne liked this time of being with Ciara on a joint venture to save the village. Things had been easier between them as they learned to work together and trust that the other had Grathton Village's best interests in mind.

"Hallllooo!" Ciara finished her soda bread and wiped her fingers with the napkin.

Rayne looked in the red car. Nobody was inside. Blarney darted into the cemetery. Someone had left the black metal gate wide open.

"Blarney!" Rayne called, hurrying after him.

"He needs a trainer," Ciara said, staying at her side.

"I know." Definitely not a priority.

In fact, Blarney being trained fell way to the bottom of the freaking list. Cemetery cleanup, the Lenni-Pete wedding this weekend, joining the council, finding the deed to the McGrath land, an appointment with the property manager, and locating a new solicitor, all came before Blarney's sometimes willful behavior.

He'd stolen a Jimmy Choo shoe and lingerie. They'd never recovered all the gemstones on her designer heels, though they'd found a few. Maeve said it was either the leprechauns or fairies returning the crystals, but Rayne knew it was Blarney.

Honestly, Rayne liked that Blarney had a unique personality. He'd adored the feather boa she'd used in one of her latest gowns and liked to curl up with it. So what?

Trees shaded the headstones and Rayne shivered in the sudden cold as the temperature dropped. Her dog maneuvered around the cleaned grassy spaces. Squirrels chittered in the pines.

They'd made a lot of headway yesterday. Part of today's agenda would require chainsaws and axes as Bobby and his crew removed branches.

Blarney stopped suddenly and howled.

Goosebumps rose on Rayne's arms. "Blarney?"

The dog circled a man with red hair slumped against the Thomas McGrath tombstone.

Blarney dug at the base. A clear stone that looked like it came from her Jimmy Choos was visible in the fresh dirt.

"Is this your hiding spot?"

"Oh, damn," Ciara said. "Who do we have here?" She walked closer. "Aiden Dennehy. Drunk? I don't see Treasa. Did they have a fight?"

Rayne reached to tap his shoulder. "Hey, Aiden. Bud."

His nose was bruised from where Beetle

had punched him yesterday. His eyes were open. Rayne's stomach clenched and she was glad that she hadn't had a big breakfast as it rose up her throat. Blood pooled to the grass.

"Snicklefritz. Sugar cookies. Lemon drops."

Ciara clasped Rayne's shoulder. "What's wrong?"

"Aiden is dead." Rayne pointed to the cellphone salesman's back and the partially buried silver blades. The orange safety grip on the handles. Fitzroy Construction written in black marker on the side. "Can't be true."

Blarney sat and howled.

"It fecking looks that way." Ciara pulled her phone from her pocket. "I'll call the Garda station." She zipped up her jacket against the chill and dialed.

Rayne couldn't tear her eyes away from the orange handles. The blood on the grass. It had to be a joke. An awful joke. People didn't just go tripping over bodies all the time.

Father Patrick, shrugging into his big cardigan sweater, sans his white collar, as he was in a rush, arrived. "What's going on? Blarney, hush now."

The dog stopped.

"Aiden is . . . no longer with us." Rayne glanced at the slumped figure with the garden shears protruding from his back. The blood. In order to not fall apart she had to pretend that he, this situation, wasn't real.

"Oh no." Father Patrick crossed himself. He went to Aiden's side and even though it was obvious he wasn't alive, he felt for a pulse, and then made the sign of the cross over Aiden.

"Hello — this is Ciara Smith. I'm at Grathton Church. Aiden Dennehy is dead. He's been stabbed by garden shears."

Rayne was very proud of how steady her cousin sounded on the phone and pinched her wrist to get it together. "Father Patrick, why don't you go back to the gate to keep anyone else from entering the cemetery? We'll stand guard until the police arrive."

"I will. Oh, dear God in Heaven. What an awful start to this day." The priest hurried off. Blarney stayed with Rayne and Ciara.

"Where is Treasa?" Rayne wanted to know as they huddled near one another. "What if she's also hurt somewhere?"

"We just need to wait here and not mess with the crime scene." Ciara's chin trembled. "I hope she's safe."

Rayne pocketed the clear gem to add to the vase in her room with the others. "I wonder if this is where the rest of the Jimmy Choo crystals will be?"

Blarney slunk out of sight.

"Not good, pup," Ciara said. "If it wasn't so awful I'd laugh. Blarney used the McGrath headstone as his hiding spot. How could he know that was a McGrath?"

Rayne gave poor Aiden another peek. His knuckles were bruised. He was in the same clothes he'd worn last night when Beetle had kicked him out of the pub. "We saw Bobby in his truck. What if . . . Bobby had to pass by the church from that road?"

"Not a good job cleaning up after himself if he's the killer," Ciara said. "The garden shears have his company's name written on them." Her mouth pursed. "Could be an act of anger. Maybe Bobby's leaving the country?"

"I can't imagine it." The construction company owner had been diligent and hardworking, like his sister, Bronagh. Bran, his nephew, must take after his father.

Father Patrick returned with mugs of coffee. "From the house. I've asked Sheff and Murray to stand guard."

"Thank you." Rayne cupped the steaming mug. Though she preferred hers with cream and sweet, she didn't complain. Hot kept the shock at bay. Sheff McElroy and Murray O'Brien were here to help with the cleanup, though that seemed strange as they were practically ancient.

To be fair, their ages hadn't kept them from hard work yesterday. It was good to have a purpose.

Within moments they heard sirens. Blarney didn't let Rayne out of his sight.

Garda Williams and Garda Lee arrived, coming through the cemetery lawn. Ciara, Father Patrick, and Rayne had moved several headstones away from Aiden, keeping him at their back.

"You're certain the person is dead?" Garda Williams asked.

"Yes," Ciara replied. "His eyes . . ."

Garda Williams and Ciara used to date a long time ago, which left some unsettled feelings between them. He tended to be more formal with Ciara and Ciara liked to call him Dominic in return. Out of uniform, he looked like the boy next door — fair skinned with blue eyes. Fit.

Garda Kaitlin Lee had brown hair and eyes and a friendlier manner than her counterpart, but she hadn't dated either Ciara or Rayne and had no personal history with the cousins.

"Again?" Garda Lee quipped. "I hope you didn't trample the crime scene."

"And good morning to you both," Rayne said. "We've been standing in the cold to make sure that the . . . scene . . . stayed pristine, after we discovered poor Aiden." She gulped.

"Thanks," Garda Willliams said. "Dr. Rhodes will be here shortly. I didn't call for the ambulance since you said that he was dead. There's a fire in Kilkenny so the paramedics are needed there."

The medical examiner had been very professional, as Rayne recalled.

"Oh no!" Father Patrick said. "It's a shame."

"No injuries so far," Garda Lee said. "A bonfire out of control. Kids being silly."

Rayne preferred silliness to deliberate murder.

Don startled Rayne when he called from the entrance that was just out of sight, about a hundred yards away. "Hey! What's going on? Treasa's car is here. Where is she?"

Garda Lee hurried toward the gate and motioned Don back to the other side of the fence. "We will know more shortly. Why are you all here?"

"We're volunteers to clean the old cemetery to tempt new businesses. Place was overgrown with weeds, but we've got it looking nice," Don said. "It's somewhere me and Aiden can see ourselves branching out for sure."

"Please join the others." Garda Lee adjusted the brim of her cap. "Father Patrick? May they wait inside the church where it is warmer while we continue our investigation?"

"We should send them home." Father Patrick lowered his voice. "I don't think we'll be working today. I can't imagine this — Aiden dead, a young man in his prime. A member of our church. Shauna and Luke are here — his grandparents. They need to be notified."

Garda Lee rocked back on her bootheels. "I don't want anyone to leave the premises. We will need to speak to everyone here — and talk with his family. Do his parents live here too?"

"No," the priest said. "He wasn't really close to them, not like his grandparents."

"How old is he?" Garda Lee asked. "Not a minor."

"No," Rayne said. "He's forty-ish. He has a girlfriend, Treasa. In fact, they share that red car, and she dropped him off yesterday."

"Did you say someone is dead?" Don shouted. The metal fence rattled.

"I'd like everyone in the church," Garda Williams told Father Patrick.

"All right." The priest slowly made his way around the tidy tombstones to the black metal gate. He put his hand on Don's shoulder. "We must wait for the police in the church." He scanned the volunteers, his gaze skipping over Shauna to Dorothy McElroy. "Dorothy, could you please get coffee started? I'll be in shortly."

Don dug his heels in. "Why is Treasa's car here? Where is she?"

Rayne wondered if they should be looking for Treasa — her body, or her, as the killer. She didn't see it, but it made more sense than Bobby Fitzroy.

Treasa might have had a reason to be angry, after finding out that Aiden had been sleeping with Beetle's sister.

Rayne cupped the mug and drained the coffee which had cooled quickly. "How can we help?" Blarney slunk next to her and sat, shivering.

"You were first on the scene," Garda Williams said. "Together. Did you know Aiden?"

"Yes," Ciara confirmed. "Through the church. We're trying to prove to the villagers that we care about their fate. To show that we have a stake in Grathton too." She gulped and tossed the cold coffee to the tree next to her.

"You okay?" Rayne asked.

"Staked was the wrong word, considering."

"It's all right," Garda Williams said in a softer voice than he'd used so far. "I see paw prints in the dirt."

"Yes. Blarney must be using this place to hide his treasures. I found a piece of the Jimmy Choo crystal he'd stolen."

"Oh no," Garda Lee said. "Spendy shoes boyo."

Blarney lowered his ears.

"How long have you known Aiden Dennehy?" Garda Williams asked.

"I just met him yesterday," Rayne said.

"Like I just said, we met at a few church things." Ciara gave a miserable shrug. "I didn't know him otherwise."

"What can you tell us about this Don person?" Garda Lee asked. "Just meet him too?"

"Yes, yesterday. He was the one that explained that he and Aiden's girlfriend shared a car. She's a receptionist at a lawyer's office," Rayne said.

"But she isn't here?" Garda Williams asked.

"Not that we noticed. We stayed here after discovering his body," Ciara said in a serious tone.

"Why is that?" Garda Lee asked.

"Just in case the murderer came back to disturb anything," Rayne said. "Blarney barging in here might have scared them off."

"Not the same answer I was going to give," Ciara said. "I just remembered how upset you were with Da, and the scene being disturbed because of not realizing that it wasn't an accident."

"How many times do I have to apologize for that?" Garda Williams exclaimed.

Rayne and Garda Lee exchanged a surprised look.

"Nobody realized it," Garda Lee said, sharing the blame. "It seemed like an accident. It would have been easier if it had been, eh? But not justice. Williams scoured the tractor for clues to be sure and that's when we realized there was more to it."

"I wasn't blaming you — I was sharing why I was staying close to Aiden's body." Ciara raised her chin.

Dr. Rhodes, the medical examiner, arrived with his assistant and equipment.

"Can we go?" Rayne tried not to focus on Aiden, or the garden shears in his back. The blood.

"Wait for us in the church," Garda Williams said. "We will certainly have more questions. I know this is a hard task, but don't discuss this with anyone."

"We are entering gossip central," Ciara protested. "Can't we go home?"

"No." Garda Williams turned his back on them to speak to the medical examiner.

"Rude," Ciara muttered. She patted Blarney's head. "You should probably go though, pup. You can't be in the church."

Blarney darted before them to pace at the gate. Murray, Paddy, Sheff, and Luke waited there with Don, tensions high. What might Don have overheard? When had Paddy arrived?

Luke moved toward her and Ciara. Rayne held up her hand. "We can't say a word. The gardai will do their jobs and be out to talk with you."

Sheff opened the gate for them and held it. Blarney went first, bypassing the church and parking lot, to a path that led to Father Patrick's small home. He climbed the porch stairs and made himself comfy on the cushioned bench.

"Not his first time here," Rayne remarked. "I'll ask Father Patrick about it. I hope Blarney doesn't bother him."

The priest stood on the steps of the church. "Come on in where it's warm. Dorothy and Olivia have made coffee."

Moira Morton had arrived with her husband and their twin granddaughters. Realizing that something was amiss, she had the kids stay in the car. Keith remained behind the wheel as Moira exited. "What is it, Rayne?"

Rayne took responsibility for her actions and decided to send them home. She'd let the officers know but the twins didn't need to be cooped up in the church.

She met Moira midway across the parking lot. "Don't ask me any questions — just turn around and head home. Please stay there until I call you later."

The woman was smart, noted the police vehicles and the medical examiner van, then retreated. "Thank you."

Rayne nodded. "I appreciate your cooperation."

Moira climbed into the family car. "Who wants to go home and make pancakes with chocolate chips?"

"We do!" Shannon and Shayna cheered.

Keith eyed Rayne with concern but drove off without argument.

"Why do they get to go?" Paddy asked.

"Let's wait inside the church as the gardai instructed," Rayne said without answering his question.

"Why should I?" Paddy's attitude was

blustery. His leather coat was studded in silver. Punk rock energy.

"It's on you to freeze then." Ciara shrugged, as if she could care less if he was acting the maggot.

Rayne stood next to Father Patrick. Ciara took up the spot on his other side. Father Patrick rubbed his hands together, uneasy. It was clear he wasn't doing well. "Should we go get a cup of coffee?" Rayne suggested. "There's bound to be some whiskey somewhere. Seeing a dead person is a shock."

"Let's go in. I keep some in the cabinet in my office for emergencies. Death never gets easier." Father Patrick put his fingers to his temple. "I have the funeral arrangements to make with Elizabeth McGillicuddy and Darcy's family. I tell you, it's a lot easier to accept a man's dying at ninety than one at forty. He was an altar boy, once upon a time."

Rayne opened the door for the grieving priest. Ciara kept her hand on his back in comfort.

"Any news?" Olivia asked.

"Not yet," Rayne said.

"Where are you landing? I can bring coffee or tea," Dorothy said. "Our family knows this church and the priest's house like our own. My mam was the caretaker/

housekeeper when she was alive, and now me and my girls take turns cleaning it."

"With this old man's thanks." Father Patrick's face remained pale.

"You're not old," Olivia chided. "I've got over thirty years on you, Father. God help us."

Shauna had her phone in her hand, tears on her cheeks.

Did she suspect something? Did she know it was her grandson? What exactly had Don overheard? Shauna caught Rayne's gaze. "I texted Treasa. She's livid that Aiden took her car. She had to catch a rideshare to her job."

Well, that answered the Treasa question.

"Oh," Rayne said inadequately.

"I only had her number because we'd planned a surprise party for Aiden last year when he turned forty." Shauna reached for Rayne's hand and squeezed.

Rayne bowed her head rather than answer the question in the woman's gaze.

Shauna swallowed a sob and plonked down. Rayne couldn't leave the poor lady alone in the pew, so she sat next to her.

Olivia brought coffees, Dorothy added whiskey, and Ciara sat on Shauna's other side. Father Patrick kneeled and prayed in silence.

Colleen Randall read quietly to a little one who had to be her daughter. They had matching brown curls with auburn tints. The child had pink glasses with thick lenses and was quick to turn the page.

"Who is that?" Rayne asked Ciara.

"Corrine, Colleen's wean. She's four. Poor thing was born early and lucky to be alive. She's got some learning issues. Beetle is very protective."

"I see why!" Colleen exuded maternal energy. They'd met yesterday during the cleanup at the cemetery. "Is she married?"

"No. Corrine's da died in a car accident but they had planned to marry. Colleen has always been kind to me."

Before Rayne could talk with the young woman who had a full plate and a child besides, the door slammed open.

Sheff entered, Murray, Don, and Paddy holding Luke upright as the man had gone limp.

"It's Aiden," Sheff stated. "The lad is dead."

Chapter Four

"Aiden!" One of the other ladies gasped. "How?"

"They aren't answering our questions," Sheff said. Don and Murray, with Paddy's help, brought Luke to a pew to sit him down.

"Not my grandson." Luke seemed in shock. "Where's Shauna?"

Shauna exhaled and stood, and Rayne was impressed by the older woman's sudden strength. She would be the backbone of the couple during this time.

"Here, dear." Shauna reached for Dorothy's whiskey — she must have found the bottle in the priest's cabinet — and poured some into her empty coffee cup. She walked slowly, solemnly, to her husband. "Drink this."

Luke accepted the mug and shot it back, his wrinkled hand trembling.

Father Patrick finished his prayer and

stood, also visibly calmer now. “Did you speak with the gardai?”

“No.” Murray’s voice was thick, and he cleared it. “No. Paddy snuck into the cemetery and saw the medical examiner. Aiden’s red hair.”

“Do the gardai know you saw them?” Ciara asked.

“Yeah. Sure do.” Murray’s mouth thinned. “Paddy screamed like a fool.”

“I never saw anything like it. Never.” Paddy shook his head. “We were mates from the time we were born.”

“Didn’t I tell you I heard the gardai say Aiden’s name?” Don typed something on his mobile phone. “Just let Sheila know.”

“Why would you do that?” Paddy demanded. “They were over.” The man spread his arms to his sides. “Oh, that’s right. Sheila sometimes takes pity on you and lets you sleep with her. Bleedin’ chancer.”

Rayne and Ciara exchanged glances. So, Don was not a complete loner anyway. The pair were close enough for hooking up. Would Don think he could sweep in and take care of Sheila by taking Aiden out of the picture?

What time had Don shown up this morning? He’d been around the cemetery working with Aiden yesterday and knew the layout. Had he set up a meeting about the new business and then something got out of hand and so he stabbed his friend with Bobby Fitzroy's garden shears?

Rayne could imagine the argument, sure, but not the stabbing. There was no good reason for such a violent act.

"I bet Beetle had something to do with it," Paddy said. "Punched him in the nose, didn't he? So what if Aiden was sleeping around."

Beetle had punched Aiden and kicked him out of the Sheep's Head permanently. What if Aiden had tried to come back?

Beetle had been mad, sure. And now that Rayne had seen Colleen with sweet Corrine, she understood his protective actions.

He'd also closed early to cool off. He'd told them while they'd cleaned up the bar that he planned to hang out at Mary's Pub, eat curry fries, and drown his sorrows.

On Monday nights they offered karaoke. Beetle had an awesome voice — she hoped that he had a lot of alibis. Heaven help him if he didn't, not with this lot wanting a scapegoat. She believed deep down that Beetle, while tattooed and brooding, wasn't a killer.

"Beetle said he was going to Mary's Pub," Rayne said.

"All night, milady?" Sheff challenged. "He was plenty pissed off."

"He'd cooled down after everyone left," Rayne said.

Colleen joined them, little Corrine on her hip, drowsy.

If Aiden wasn't already dead, then Rayne would want a word with the playboy for messing around with a woman who had an innocent child.

"Not certain this matters right now," Ciara said. "We need to wait for the gardai to let us know what they can. We can't go blaming people because we're angry."

Well, her cousin had shown a degree of maturity that proved she had her Celtic temper under control while Rayne's was making its way to the surface more often.

"Wise words." Don opened the door of the church to peer outside. "Where are the gardai?"

Paddy joined him, his shoulders braced. "What is taking so bloody long?"

"Boys," Father Patrick admonished. "I'd appreciate it if you'd come away from there. Let's pray for guidance in this terrible time."

Though they were over forty, the pair did as the priest asked. Father Patrick waited until everyone was kneeling and prayed for the soul of Aiden Dennehy.

It was a savvy way to stop people pacing, worrying, and questioning, Rayne would give the wise priest that.

Twenty minutes passed before the door opened, and the gardai entered with bowed heads. Rayne had sat toward the back with Ciara. Colleen and Corrine were on the right.

Father Patrick finished the impromptu sermon with thanks to God. Everyone stayed seated but turned around in their pews.

"What news?" Father Patrick asked as he walked away from the pulpit.

"We regret to inform you that Aiden Dennehy is deceased, though it seems you already know that," Garda Williams said. "I add my condolences to the family here today."

Luke and Shauna nodded, grief clear to read on their expressions.

"We will be speaking with all," the officer counted those in the church, "thirty of you, individually. We want to know about Aiden's recent activities."

"Beetle Randall punched Aiden last night," Paddy shouted. Murray smacked the younger man on the back of the head with a hiss to be respectful.

Garda Lee stood to the right. "I'll start here, and Garda Williams will take the left."

Ciara and Rayne happened to be to the left, as were Olivia, Murray, and Paddy O'Brien. Luke, Shauna, and Don were on the right side, like Colleen and Corrine. His sister and his niece were the reason Beetle had punched Aiden in the first place.

Garda Williams gestured for Rayne and Ciara to step away from the others. "I'll interview you both together, since you found Aiden. What can you tell me? Rayne, what time were you here today?"

Rayne turned so her back was to the people waiting to be interviewed. "We wanted to be here earlier than the other churchgoers, who were very early yesterday. We were to start at eight thirty, but they'd gotten here at eight. We felt it made us appear late."

"Though they were early," Ciara interjected. "So, we planned to be here close to seven-thirty to be on time."

"Did anybody know that?" The garda kept his gaze neutral.

"No," Rayne answered. "Not even Father Patrick. We saw Liam and Sinead at the Coco Bean, and oh, Bobby Fitzroy was driving the opposite way — but he had to have passed the church . . ."

"From Fitzroy Construction?"

"Yes," Ciara confirmed. "We hired Bobby and his company to help us organize the various projects we've been doing. It was nice to see the cemetery cleaned up. We hope it will make the buildings across from it more appealing as rentals."

"Did you see anybody else?" Garda Williams asked.

"No," Rayne said.

Ciara shook her head.

"We will need to get footprints. We know you both were there, Father Patrick, and Blarney." Garda Williams narrowed his eyes. "He didn't stab himself in the back, so we must find out who is responsible. Tell me what happened after you found Aiden?"

"We called 999," Ciara said. "Father Patrick was alerted by Blarney's howls that something was wrong, and he found us at the gravesite. He checked Aiden's pulse though it was obvious Aiden was gone."

Garda Williams nodded and shifted his attention to Rayne.

"You heard Paddy shout about Beetle earlier," Rayne said. "It's true that Beetle punched Aiden in the nose for sleeping with his sister," she quietly added, "Colleen, who is here right now. Aiden had told her he was single, when in fact, he was living with

Treasa Boone."

"How do you know about the punch?"

"We saw it," Rayne said. "At the pub last night."

"Yeah. Beetle was angry but not out of control — there is a difference," Ciara said. "We were home by six, so before that."

"If buttons are pushed, tempers can erupt," Garda Williams said. "Who else might have a grudge against Aiden?"

"Don McElroy." Rayne glanced at Ciara, who nodded for her to continue that train of thought. "Don was jealous of Aiden's success with women. He's sleeping with Aiden's ex-wife, Sheila."

"Sheila?"

"I don't know her," Rayne said.

"No lack of enemies then," Garda Williams commented.

"Nope." Ciara shrugged. "Don't understand that behavior myself. If you don't want to be with someone, just say so. Don't lie and mess around with people's feelings."

"Exactly," Rayne said. Colleen and Corrine were two innocents.

"Would Bobby have anything against Aiden?" Garda Williams asked.

"Since the Fitzroy Construction garden shears were in his back?" Rayne shuddered. "Yesterday Aiden was kind of full of himself, but Bobby just shrugged it off. Right, Ciara?"

"That's what I saw too." Ciara tapped her chin. "Aiden seemed interested in renting an office here once they were renovated. Hence the reason to clean up the overgrown weeds so it wasn't an eyesore."

"What business?" Garda Williams asked.

"Mobile phones," Rayne said. "He and Don would operate it together. It's what they do now in Kilkenny."

"Who owns the vacant businesses?" Garda Willilams asked.

Ciara turned red. "We think that we do."

Garda Williams chuckled. "That makes sense. Grathton Village would be owned by the McGraths."

"I'm a Smith," Ciara said.

"By choice," Rayne said. "By blood you are equal. Let's take a DNA test right now — that should silence any contenders." She glared at the people on the pews, but nobody was paying them any attention.

"What are you talking about?" Garda Williams asked.

"Doesn't matter, Rayne. My father left you in charge."

"We have joint responsibilities. Without you, I fail. Without me, you would have a harder time but still succeed." Rayne knew this to be the truth.

"Can we stay on topic?" Garda Williams looked at Paddy especially and the others all waiting to be interviewed.

"Hurry with the questions then," Ciara grumbled.

"Do you have any clue who might have killed Aiden on your ancestors' grave?" Garda Williams nodded toward Father Patrick. "He said the other McGraths are buried across the road and have been since the beginning of Grathton Village."

"I just assumed it was a coincidence," Rayne said.

"It's possible." Garda Williams sighed. "All right. Take your worried dog and go home. Call me if you think of anything else." He shook his head and muttered, "*Think* you own the buildings. That's something else."

Rayne and Ciara waved goodbye to Father Patrick and left through the front door of the church. The old stone had stood since the eighteen hundreds. Rayne had an affection for history because of the way her father had spoken of Ireland in a romantic, poetic, way.

Just then, a taxi dropped off Treasa Boone. She paid in cash and the cabbie whizzed away.

"Hi," Rayne said. Did she know that Aiden was dead?

Treasa noticed her standing in the parking lot with Ciara and burst into tears.

Yes. "We are so sorry for your loss," Rayne said.

Ciara stepped toward the woman, in sync with Rayne to offer consolation.

"I need my car," Treasa said. "I can't believe Aiden took it. I can't believe he is dead. Dead! I can't fathom it."

Rayne patted her shoulder. "I'm very sorry. I only met Aiden through his kindness of volunteering."

"Aiden was here because he had community service hours for reckless driving. He wasn't supposed to drive." Treasa sucked in a sob. "We had the worst argument last night. He'd drunkenly confessed to messing around again. Well, he had a broken nose and black eye. Couldn't hide it. I demanded that he press charges for assault against Beetle and that's when he admitted there was more to the story."

Rayne's compassion kept her from shaking sense into Treasa. Community service hours? She'd be better off without Aiden. She was an attractive woman with a car and a job — why settle for someone who treated her poorly?

"Where is everyone?" Treasa put a lock of hair behind her ear. "Don texted me, and Sheila. I like Shauna. She's a sweetheart." She sucked in a calming breath. "This will break her and Luke."

"Inside with the gardai, and Father Patrick," Ciara said.

The front door opened and a garda that Rayne didn't know exited with Paddy and the O'Briens. Murray and Olivia were old, yes, but strong people. It was beneficial for long life to have a farm.

Maybe they could tout that as clean Irish living? There were young people in the village, but they needed more of them.

Don came out of the church next. His gaze was like sonar, landing on Treasa. He walked toward her and gave her a hug.

"I need my keys," Treasa said to the female garda.

"You are?"

"Treasa Boone. Aiden was my boyfriend. He took my car, and I need to get back to work at McArthur's Solicitors before I get my hours docked."

"About that," the garda said. "We will need to impound this vehicle for possible evidence."

"What?" Treasa shook her head.

"I'm sorry for your loss, but this is connected to a crime scene."

Treasa cried some more, and Don patted her shoulder ineffectually.

"I'll need to get your statement," the garda continued. "Here, or at the station?"

"The station in Kilkenny?" Treasa asked. "That's close to the solicitor's office I work at. You should give me a ride since you're taking my car. For how long?"

"I can help you," Don offered.

Paddy shook his head. "Pathetic. Always after Aiden's crumbs."

Treasa glared at Paddy. "What do you mean?"

"Ask your boyo, there," Paddy snickered. "About Sheila Martinet, Aiden's ex-wife. They are friends, if you know what I mean."

Treasa gave Don her shoulder. "I know he's friends with Sheila. Whatever."

Don scowled at Paddy. "You wouldn't know the first thing about being polite, would you? If there's nothing in it for you, then you don't do it."

"Lads," Oliva said sternly. "Now is not the time. We've just lost one of our own and you will be respectful."

Murray seemed to have aged another decade as he nodded morosely. Two gone, if one counted Darcy as well as Aiden.

Blarney came around the side of the

church. He wagged his tail and loped toward her which caused her spirits to lift slightly.

"Should we walk the back road to the manor?" Rayne suggested. "To see the difference of the cleanup from the street." She fluttered her fingers at those coming out of the church to leave for home.

"All right." Ciara zipped her canvas jacket against a gust of wind. It would begin to rain within an hour.

Rayne had gotten good at predicting when she could dart outside without getting thoroughly soaked.

Though her main job was to manage the wedding venue, and make bridal dresses, Rayne liked to be outside and didn't mind getting a little wet. Drenched, not so much, but she'd learned to have a hood or a shawl.

Umbrellas often fought with the wind and so weren't as successful in the effort to stay dry.

The road between the church and the businesses hadn't been paved in some time. Who had to pay for that? Rayne had a bad idea it would be her and Ciara.

It must have been so overwhelming for her uncle. He'd trained Ciara as his right-hand man and wanted to adopt her but hadn't before his death.

"This could use an upgrade," Ciara said.

"I was just thinking the same thing."

"Surprised that nobody has complained before now." Ciara paused to admire the black metal fence that was no longer covered in weeds. It had protected the shiny black color of the inch-thick rods.

"The trees definitely need to be trimmed, but this is nice." Rayne turned so that her back was to the cemetery, and she was facing several blocks of vacant houses or empty businesses. "Does this come up against the Sheep's Head pub?"

"No," Ciara said. "There are two blocks in between."

"Of what?"

Ciara shrugged. "I'm afraid to look."

But, being made of stern stuff, the cousins braced their shoulders and walked the quiet blocks.

"It's like a ghost street across from the cemetery, until the next main road. For some reason these haven't been cared for." Ciara stopped. "Were they just abandoned?"

"Don't know." Rayne didn't discount the idea of ghosts out of hand as she stomped around a single-story house of cement and stone construction. "It might have had a thatch roof at one point." She peered through a window that had no glass. Rats and cats lived inside.

"No doors either. Could have been used for firewood for someone during a hard winter," Ciara suggested as she walked into the structure.

"Think it could be fixed up?"

"Dafydd is the one who knows construction. He's teaching Richard. We don't have enough people to live in them, anyway. It's why they are vacant."

"Maybe if we made them habitable, people would return. I can sell charming Irish cottage like nobody's business."

"In your spare time?" Ciara asked.

"Yes, we have a lot on our plate. Getting these homes filled with young people would be a start." Rayne thought of Colleen and Corrine and hoped they had a better home than this.

"Businesses on that road will be easier — they don't have this dilapidated feel. I wonder if these homes were built after them so that the owners had a place to live?"

"I don't know. We'll have to make a list before we go to Dublin." Rayne brought out the crystal in her pocket and smoothed it like a worry stone.

Blarney stayed at her side, chasing birds or squirrels, or rats, with half-hearted enthusiasm. Was he sad about her finding his treasure, and calling him out for it?

"I'm ready for a shower, and," Rayne snapped her fingers, "lunch. I forgot to let Frances know how many not to make."

Ciara snickered. "You're gonna be in trouble."

"How about I text her, and we can stop at the Coco Bean for a sandwich instead?"

"Rayne McGrath, are you being a coward right now?"

"No. No." It was noon. "I'll call." She dialed the house phone, and Maeve picked up.

"McCormac Castle, this is Maeve."

"Hi, Maeve!"

"How are ye?" The housekeeper had a distraught tone. "We heard sirens."

"We are fine. One of the volunteers was killed though. It's why I forgot to text Frances."

"Oh, don't worry about that. Are you coming home? She's made a hearty mutton stew with biscuits. You can tell us all about it when you get here. Also, Freda Bevan called and left a message for you to give her a bell."

"We are on our way!"

Maeve hung up.

"Nice way to steer the subject," Ciara said.

"We get warm stew and biscuits."

Blarney's ears perked as well.

"Let's go home and eat. They've got to find out who murdered Aiden very, very quickly." Rayne was thinking of the wedding guests due to arrive on Saturday.

"I hope it wasn't Beetle," Ciara said. "That would really break Colleen. And Corrine. She loves her uncle."

"Same. I like him."

"I had no idea he could sing like that," Ciara said. "I don't do karaoke though, so being at Mary's Pub on Mondays wasn't ever on my radar."

"What do you do to relax?"

Ciara shrugged. "I like horseback riding. Hiking. Reading."

"What do you read?"

"Old mysteries. Da and I would share books all the time. And our library is stocked. Do you like to read?"

"Magazines," Rayne admitted with a shrug. "I have a short attention span for anything that isn't dress-related."

"Aine has some that she gets ordered to the house. Maybe she'll share."

"She likes her fashion magazines. I feel really bad about not bringing her to Dublin with us. I hope Cormac remembered to call McGavin Property Management. If not, I'll do it."

"Yes. As you said, next time. I'm looking forward to meeting Nolan, the fabric wizard."

"That's an amazing nickname Aine coined and actually very apt." Nolan Rourke managed Oasis Fabrics in Dublin, and he'd saved her behind more than once.

They stopped and waited for traffic to cross the road. Blarney was patient but once they reached McGrath property he darted into the leaves, his tail wagging as he chased a robin.

"It's like he was being so good and just exploded with energy," Ciara said.

"He's trying. He probably thinks he's in trouble for the Jimmy Choos and burying the crystals who knows where."

"Are the crystals worth money?"

"Not really. It's the design of the whole shoe that makes it so valuable. These are just fancy cubic zirconia pieces." Rayne took it from her pocket to study and then dropped it back. "I'll add this to the others I found. I only have one shoe. The other is long gone."

"Maeve thinks the fairies bring them to you," Ciara said.

"My money is on Blarney. He might've eaten the entire shoe." Or, it could be buried in the cemetery. "It is a little odd about Aiden being found on Thomas McGrath's tombstone. Don't you think?"

"I didn't until Garda Williams brought it up. He doesn't like coincidence," Ciara said. "Probably can't trust it in his line of work."

They arrived at the manor house and climbed the steps. Cormac opened the door for them. "Ladies."

"Cormac!" Rayne said. Ciara smiled.

They entered the foyer. "You have an appointment with McGavin Property Management tomorrow at eleven thirty," Cormac said. "They'd had a cancellation. I put the information on the desk in the office."

"Brilliant," Ciara said.

"Thanks, Cormac. That stew smells heavenly." Rayne's stomach rumbled at the savory scent of rosemary. "I'm starving."

Maeve brought the landline to Rayne, covering the earpiece. "It's Freda. She's all worked up so you might as well get this over with and then you can enjoy your lunch."

"Thank you!" Rayne accepted the handset and took it to the office and sat at Uncle Nevin's desk. Though she and Ciara did use this space, it remained his in both of their minds. Like Cormac had said, the information with the date and time for tomorrow's appointment with the property management company was also on the desk.

"Hello. This is Rayne."

"Freda Bevan here." Freda's voice on the phone was as loud and boisterous as the woman in person, who favored bright colors and patterns.

"What can I do for you?" Rayne aligned the note from Cormac with the edge of the desk.

"Are you coming to the council meeting on Thursday? We need someone from Grathton to fill the board."

"Yes. Ciara and I will both be there."

"Only one of you can officially hold the title."

"I'm not sure that's true," Rayne said. "We're positive the position has had co-chairs before." She wasn't though. Father Patrick was going to check on it, but things had gone haywire.

"Not for Grathton," Freda said. "It was for a teensy village named Tinsley, that was absorbed into Cotter eventually, as you will be. Why not stop wasting time and taxpayer funds?"

Rayne swallowed a sharp retort. "What do you mean?"

"We all know how this will end up." Freda's tone was very smug.

Rayne didn't like it one bit. "No, Freda. I think you're wrong."

"I saw you poking around my village today. Well, the gloves are officially off. I want Grathton and I will do what I can to get it."

"Thanks for the warning." The woman was a bulldozer.

What did she mean about Rayne being in her village?

Before she could ask, Freda had ended the call.

"Well!"

Rayne left the office, the door automatically locking, and went to the informal dining room where the staff had gathered.

"What did Freda want?" Ciara served herself a bowl of stew from a sideboard against the wall. Fresh rolls steamed from a basket and pats of butter glistened.

Maeve, Aine, Frances, and Cormac were already seated as were Amos, Dafydd, and Richard. They all must have heard the sirens and wanted information. Frances had no doubt arranged everything like a master sergeant in the kitchen. They didn't always lunch together as a family, like they did dinner.

"Freda wanted to be sure that we're coming to the meeting this week. She let me know that she'll fight to get Grathton for Cotter Village. We knew it was her goal —

now she's made it official." Rayne filled her dish and brought it to the table. She sat on one end, and Ciara the other.

"How rude!" Aine said.

"She's losing her mind. She accused me of *poking* around the village today. Which I did not, as Ciara can attest." Rayne sipped her water and pointed at her cousin. "We've been together all day."

"Yep." Ciara dipped her roll into the stew. "She's always had a crazy side. Remember when she punched Da in the arm at a meeting?"

Rayne hadn't been there for that, but the others murmured their assent.

"We need to be careful when we go to the meeting on Thursday. Tried to tell me that we couldn't be joint chairs, but when I told her I was sure it could happen, she admitted that it had already been done."

"What?" Ciara blustered.

"Yes." Rayne stirred her stew so it would cool. "Some poor little town called Tinsley or something — like Father Patrick had shared."

"She's a tyrant," Amos decreed.

"Now," Maeve said, with a glint in her eye, "it's time for you to tell us about what happened at the church."

Rayne took another sip of her water. In

the states, she used to drink it with ice but had grown used to beverages at room temperature.

"Aiden Dennehy was killed. He was stabbed in the back with gardening shears, of all things." Rayne patted her lips with the cloth napkin. "We found him first thing this morning."

"Oh no!" Maeve said.

A chorus of commiserating sounds rounded the table.

"Aiden, that had the altercation with Beetle?" Amos asked. His shoulders seemed to triple in size.

"Yes," Rayne confirmed. "I saw Colleen and her sweet daughter Corrine. No wonder Beetle is so protective."

"Surely the gardai don't believe Beetle killed Aiden?" Richard stated. He was probably the closest to Beetle of them all at the manor.

"They are investigating," Rayne said. "It doesn't look good, so I really hope that he's got a pub full of alibis."

"He was singing at Mary's," Richard confirmed. "I was there until about midnight and called it early because I had to feed the horses this morning, and then I painted the inside of the third bungalow. It's done, by the way. Ready for the furniture and trims."

"Thank you," Rayne said. "Aine and I will fit it out this afternoon. Amos, I'll need your help with the trunk, once I get a chance to look through it. I promise by Friday!"

"Happy to help however I can," Amos assured her.

"What time will the guests be here?" Cormac asked.

"Not until Saturday morning. They are busy professionals who are stealing away for a romantic weekend." Rayne's pulse sped. She ate a bite of stew, and then another.

She had a dress to finish but would get the thread tomorrow. The gown was done but she'd learned not to fix the zipper until the last step. A visit with Nolan always energized her.

Maeve smiled at Rayne across the table. "We will get everything done. It's a good thing that Aiden didn't die here on the property, as sad as it is to say."

"You're right. I don't think our wedding venue could handle another mysterious death," Rayne agreed.

Chapter Five

Rayne and Ciara left the castle at eight Wednesday morning — the drive would take ninety minutes and get them to Nolan's place at nine thirty when he opened. The appointment with the McGavin Property Management, MPM, company was at eleven thirty.

She noticed a missed call from her mom. It would be two in the morning there. While in the car they discussed whether or not to bother Treasa Boone. They needed a solicitor, and she had connections at McArthur's, where she worked.

"Whoever we hire can fire Owen Hughes," Ciara said.

"Finding someone who won't rob us shouldn't be that much of a stretch." Rayne set her purse by her feet.

With all the challenges they'd faced in the past six months, it seemed as if they'd been working with one hand each tied behind their backs. The will was legal and held, despite Nevin's murder and Owen's shady part in it. They'd ignored Owen until he'd returned to Grathton Village, content to kick legal representation down the road.

The time had arrived. Even though it was a major pain in the neck, they needed a solution to save the manor and the village and couldn't hide their heads in the sand anymore.

They weren't sure what they owned, to be clear. They received a quarterly check from MPM but given the obstacles they'd faced they hadn't messed with that income as it wasn't large but steady.

"Should I call my mom first, or Treasa?"

"Your mother. She's grand."

Rayne dialed her mom and put her on speaker phone.

"Lauren!" Rayne said, smiling to hear her mother's voice on the other end of the line. "Are you still up?"

"Darling! Yes, yes, seems I'm a night owl now that I don't have to be on the set so early. Are you all right? You were on my mind every second. I feel like you need me. Have the police found Landon yet?"

"No — you're on speaker, so say hi to Ciara."

"Hello, sweetheart. Well?"

"Hi, Lauren. Your mam-radar is on point but not because of Landon," Ciara said.

"Uh oh. Let me top off my herbal tea."

"We don't really know anything," Rayne said. "Aiden Dennehy, one of our volunteers, was stabbed at Grathton Church cemetery yesterday morning. Lots of possible suspects but so far nobody's been arrested. He was working off community service hours at the church and didn't have a car. His girlfriend drove him everywhere. Beetle is under suspicion."

"The bartender with all the tattoos?" Lauren said.

"Yes. Aiden lied to Beetle's sister Colleen, a single mom, saying he'd broken up with his long-term girlfriend, Treasa, when he hadn't."

"I despise men like that," Lauren said. "What happened?"

"Beetle punched Aiden the night before, but he wouldn't have killed him. It was enough that he'd kicked Aiden out of the Sheep's Head for life."

"It's not possible that Beetle did it? Protection is a strong motive."

"We don't think so. Unfortunately, Beetle passed out at home after drinking and has no alibi since he lives alone," Rayne said. "He has an apartment above the pub."

Richard had given them all an update about Beetle last night at dinner. Afterward, Rayne and Aine had made the third bungalow the cutest yet in bright yellow, purple, and charcoal accents. The vase with the hand painted iris tied in the colors. She'd left space in the floor plan for the trunk which would serve as a coffee table with storage. They were delivering on rustic luxury for the discerning, high-end client.

"You should be on guard too, girls. People act out of passion, wanting to protect loved ones." Though her mother's series was winding to a close, Lauren had plot and motivation ingrained into her brain. "What are you up to today?"

"Driving to Dublin. We have an appointment with our property management company to see if we own the land the village is on," Rayne said. "We think we do but the paperwork we have at the castle only goes to the eighteen hundreds. Oh, and Freda Bevan has dropped the gauntlet — she wants our village to combine with hers."

"Maybe considers herself a political figure," Lauren said. "Don't you get more power the bigger the population as a councilman? It works that way in the states."

"She's a political pain in the arse."

"Ciara," her mother said with a laugh.

"You are correct — so, we know what she wants, and you two are working together to stop her from taking it. I guess you've decided that you want to save the village for yourselves and not just because of the will?"

Rayne's eyes welled. "You nailed it, Mom. Some of the people who showed up at the cemetery on Monday to help clean were in their seventies, eighties, and one couple was ninety. They were married at Grathton Church. This is their home."

"Will they physically lose their land if the village is . . . sold, or, absorbed?" Lauren asked.

"I don't know." Rayne watched the cars speed by as they drove to Dublin. "Today's mission is to get answers. From what I'm learning, small villages sometimes become rural wastelands because the young people move to bigger cities for work. There is nobody left to care for the family homesteads."

"People in rural areas live longer, healthier lives for a reason. Natural activity in their daily lives, and community. But if there is no money to support that land, the system falters." Lauren sighed. "A philosophical discussion we can have when I'm there, sipping whiskey by the fire. I've bought my ticket, Rayne, and I will be there on the first of December."

"Yay!"

"On that note, I've got to hit the sack. Paul and I are having lunch tomorrow."

"Forward me your flight information. I'll pick you up with bells on!" Rayne laughed, her mother's imminent visit an immediate mood boost. Lauren ended the call.

"I can't wait to meet her. And," Ciara sent her remorseful side eye, "I'm sorry about what a jerk I was when I picked you up from the airport."

"I'm sorry I was such a brat. I'm glad to have a cousin." It was nice to have family.

"Should we try Treasa next?" Ciara suggested. "She works at McArthur's in Kilkenny."

"I'll find her." Rayne pulled up the information on her phone. "Dang. I don't know that she can help us after all. They specialize in labour law."

"Just try."

"All right." Rayne dialed the office number. It was nine on the dot.

"McArthur's Solicitor's office," a cheery voice sounded.

"Is Treasa Boone there?" Rayne asked.

"Speaking," she said, lowering her tone.

"This is Rayne McGrath. We met yesterday . . . at the church." How to talk around her boyfriend's death and car impound?

Treasa sniffed. "I remember. What do you want? Does this have to do with Aiden? I didn't know he was such a piece of work. I trusted him. Oh, did you get involved with him? I don't want to hear it."

"No, no. That's not why I'm calling."

Ciara's cheeks were red, and her shoulders shook as she tried to contain her laughter.

"Well?" Treasa demanded.

"I wondered if you might suggest a list of lawyers you'd personally recommend? I am from the US and could use your advice."

"McArthur specializes in labour law. What do you need?"

"We need an all-purpose lawyer," Rayne said.

"Well, I can't help you."

"It was worth a try. Thanks anyway." Rayne glanced toward Ciara. Now what?

"Sorry to be so short," Treasa said. "I didn't sleep well last night. The gardai didn't release my car so I had to walk to work. It reflects poorly on me to be involved with someone who had a reckless driving ticket, and then was murdered."

"It's not your fault."

"Right? I told the police I didn't know anything, but Mr. McArthur seems suspicious of me. Like I did something wrong.

Good luck in your search."

Treasa hung up.

"What if she did it?" Ciara suggested. "She said they'd argued. I can't see it, but it seems she was willing to forgive him for messing around."

"I don't get it."

"Well, maybe she's guilty of having bad taste in men. Don't think that they can fire her for that."

"So many of us would be out of work," Rayne said.

Ciara burst out laughing.

"We are back to square one about a solicitor." Rayne drummed her fingers to the dashboard.

"Why not look at reviews on your phone?"

"Good idea." Rayne scanned the list of local solicitors near Grathton. "One in Cotter Village, which is close, but I don't want to support Freda."

"Fair."

"Lots in Dublin. Do you mind driving so far every time we need something?"

"There was convenience to Owen's office being across the street." Ciara kept her hands loosely on the wheel as she glanced at Rayne. "What if we advertise for a solicitor and give them a break on rent?"

"I like how you're thinking." Rayne starred

several possibilities within a ten-mile location. "We can call a few on the way back." She nodded to the highway sign. "Here we are!"

Ciara exited and parked in a multistory garage near Oasis Fabrics. They walked down the street and arrived at nine forty, entering the fabric shop. Vibrant colors stacked on shelves beckoned Rayne, but her gaze was drawn to the manager.

Nolan Rourke was tall, thin, and had gorgeous flowing rockstar hair. He took one look at Ciara and put his hands to his heart.

"Just as beautiful as our Rayne. I adore your hair," Nolan said. Ciara had added gel, so it was shiny and curly.

"I like yours too," Ciara said.

"How have you been, my sweets?" Nolan ushered them past the center aisles toward his back office.

"We could be better," Rayne said with a hitch in her chest.

"Why is that?" His dark brown eyes oozed compassion.

"Aiden Dennehy was killed the other day in Grathton." Rayne still felt like it was surreal to have another dead body in their village.

Nolan gasped.

"Did you know him?" Ciara asked.

"Yeah. I know his ex, Sheila, too." Nolan leaned his hip to his desk. "She went back to her maiden name of Martinet after their split."

"I can see why. Aiden was kind of a player," Rayne said. "Do you know Don McElroy?"

"I do." Nolan opened a dorm fridge and handed out miniature cans of lemon lime fizzy waters. "Did Don do it? I know he and Sheila have an occasional thing. Not serious on either of their parts."

"I don't want to think so," Rayne said. "But we don't know. He was there that morning soon after we had arrived. Paddy O'Brien too."

"They're questioning Beetle Randall." Ciara popped the tab on her can of water, then took a small sip.

"I know Beetle from his band days," Nolan said. "He was a regular in the weekend party circuit."

"I knew it!" Rayne said. "He's so cool he had to be in a band, and his voice is amazing."

"He doesn't really talk about it," Ciara said. "What do you know?"

"Beetle was on track to be a superstar," Nolan shared. "He could play any instrument. And sing, as you said. Don't know what happened, but he suddenly left the music scene and moved back to Grathton."

"I wonder . . ." Had Beetle known Aiden here in Dublin? Did they have a past together that might explain more of their animosity?

"I never realized Beetle was so talented," Ciara said. "He pours a great beer."

"That is true. I hope he doesn't get tossed behind bars just because of an argument with Aiden — protecting his sister, no less. Aiden had an ego the size of Ireland and no reason for it that I could see." Nolan crossed his arms on the table. "How did he earn a living?"

"Mobile phones," Rayne said. "Aiden was a salesman. Don and he were interested in opening a business in Grathton Village."

"Hmm."

The front doorbell chimed, and Nolan shot to his feet. He had caged tiger energy. "I suppose I best get to work but I'll be thinking about Aiden. I bet Sheila would know more of his enemies, besides Beetle."

"If you could ask her, that would be an incredible help." Rayne finished her water and put the can in the trash. The mini cans were the perfect size.

"Good morning," Nolan called as he left the office. "Welcome to Oasis Fabrics."

"I can see why you and Aine adore him," Ciara said.

"Right? He's just so friendly and engaging." Rayne stood.

"Don't forget your thread," Ciara said. "And the silk fabric for the trunk liner."

"Thank you!" Rayne grinned, her blood singing as she walked along the aisle of assorted fabric.

"Why are you smiling like that?" Ciara demanded.

"Cotton, silk, lace . . . I love it all."

"You're nuts."

"Do you mind if I just do a quick spin around the store? I'd like something in emerald velvet for my December bride."

An hour later, Ciara dragged Rayne to the counter.

"Do we have to go?" Rayne complained. It was eleven.

"Yes. Or we will be late for our appointment at the McGavin Property Management company."

"Fine." Rayne passed her selection to Nolan. The ivory silk fabric would hopefully be a perfect match for the lining that she'd fix before they moved it to the bungalow. She also gave him the emerald gossamer fabric. "Oh! A dozen spools of ivory silk thread too."

"Not just one?" Ciara asked.

"No. It's a staple in the wedding gowns. And lingerie. Though for this bride she didn't request anything but the wedding dress."

"And a ten percent discount just because," Nolan said.

"Thank you!"

"That's one way to keep repeat customers," Ciara said.

"I very much appreciate the business of Modern Lace," Nolan said.

"It's mutual!" Rayne assured him. The last wedding had floated them financially, and she'd paid off her credit cards. Though it hurt, she'd be using one of them today. It was part of doing business.

"I'll reach out to Sheila about Aiden." Nolan stuffed the receipt in the bag. "She's a nice lady who got screwed over by him."

"We'll share that with the gardai," Rayne said. "The sooner we get this killer caught, the happier I will be."

"And what about that other loon?" Nolan gave a dramatic toss of his hair.

"Landon?" Rayne suggested. Her life was usually drama-free. She preferred her drama in the dresses.

"That's the one," Nolan said.

"He's at large." Ciara jerked her thumb

toward Rayne. "She's not worried."

"Should we be concerned?" Nolan's pierced brow arched.

"No," Rayne said. "I can take him. Honestly, I think he's probably hiding in Canada or Mexico."

"Well, just be careful, love." Nolan crushed her in a hug.

Ciara squeaked when he hugged her too.

Nolan was just great company.

"See you later," Rayne said. She had one bag and Ciara a second.

"Say hello to that minx Aine for me, all right?"

Rayne nodded. "She sends her regards!"

They left the shop and hit the street at eleven ten.

"Can't believe we just spent so long in a fabric store," Ciara said. "The MPM offices are only five blocks away."

Rayne's phone dinged. Her heart sank a little. "Hey, MPM needs to push our appointment back two hours. They know we made a special trip, so will see us at one thirty instead. Shall we drop the bags at the car?"

Ciara lifted the bag with the spools of thread. "Mine isn't heavy."

Rayne's slim bag of fabric wasn't either. "Same — let's keep moving." She'd have to be blind to miss the legit castle across the street. She stepped toward the sidewalk.

"What are you doing?" Ciara asked in alarm.

"Is that a castle?" Rayne waved toward the tall and imposing structure. "It's bigger than ours."

"Yes. Dublin Castle." Ciara's lips twitched with amusement. "How about we visit after we look for the records on our property? I know that the management company should have that information, but if they don't, it won't hurt to ask."

"Promise we can come back?"

"Promise!" Ciara raised her right hand.

"All right." They walked to the offices on Merrion Street and went inside. After several minutes they were told by a snooty receptionist in a dark-blue suit with a skirt that they needed to make an appointment.

Rayne sighed. It had been a longshot. "We just have a question on how to find the deed to the property we own that's been in our family since 1750."

"Give me your number, and I will have someone call you. Shall we make an appointment for next week?"

"Fine," Ciara said.

"Tuesday at ten, all right?"

"Yes," Rayne agreed. "But if someone can

call us sooner that would be great."

"Of course," the woman said.

Rayne feared the message would be in the trash can beneath her desk as soon as they left — known as the circular file. They reached the bustling street. "Well, that was a waste of time, but I think we should check out the castle since we're here. Have you ever been?"

"No. Da and I worked at the manor and didn't really do things outside it. Well, one time we went to the Dublin Zoo, but that's it."

"Okay. Let's check this place out then!"

They went inside Dublin Castle where a white-haired museum curator welcomed them. "Hi there. Can I help you?"

"Well, we're in Dublin because of our property, McGrath Castle in Grathton Village," Rayne said.

"You have a castle too?" The museum curator winked. "I guess stone and arched windows were quite popular in the architecture scene about eight hundred years ago."

"Ours was built in 1750 give or take," Rayne said with a laugh.

"A baby compared to ours!" she said. "This beauty was built in 1204. Do you have a turret?"

"We do! Nothing this grand," Ciara said,

getting into the spirit.

"That's all right. We're happy to share in the glory. Tell me what you know about Dublin Castle? I hate to waste your time if you've already done the tour. It's popular for kids in school for a field trip. But you are American? And you . . . was that a London accent beneath the Irish?"

"You're good," Ciara said.

"I was easy," Rayne complained. She shook her head. "Yours is as Irish as Maeve's, our housekeeper."

"Born and raised in Dublin," the curator confirmed.

"Neither of us have been to the castle before," Ciara said.

"Well then let me give you the rundown. How much time do you have?"

"All day," Rayne said.

"Two hours," Ciara countered. "We have an appointment with our property manager at one thirty."

"I will take care of you." The energetic curator rubbed her hands together.

Rayne was reminded of a chipper Santa's elf. The elderly woman was short, petite, and engaging. Considering this was Ireland, maybe a leprechaun rather than an elf.

"Dublin Castle has had a castle in this exact spot since King John, the very first

King of Ireland. The name Dublin comes from two words, meaning dark pool."

By the end of the hour-long tour, Rayne was still enthralled. "I hate to go!"

"Well, let me leave you with a bit of scandal that happened right here." The curator's white brows rose.

"Scandal!" Rayne grinned. "I'm from LA — we eat up scandal with a golden spoon."

"This has a mystery too."

"I'm interested," Ciara said.

The curator spoke in a low voice to draw them in. "It involves the Irish Crown Jewels."

"Rayne loves jewels." Ciara ruffled her curls. Her jewelry was silver and black, compared to Rayne's chunky multicolored beads.

"It's true," Rayne said. They each took a half-step toward the curator.

"Well, these were stolen and never recovered."

"When?" Rayne had heard something about this, but where? Her dad? Grandpa Lorcan? Her memory eluded her, so she returned to the curator's mesmerizing story.

"In 1907. Right from Bedford Tower. Sir Arthur Vicars was in charge of the jewels, and they were taken directly from his office."

"And they were never recovered?" Ciara exclaimed. "What were they?"

"Emeralds, diamonds, and five ceremonial collars of various gemstones. Stolen right here in this castle," the curator said. "A star, and a badge for the grand master, and four other collars for the Knights of the Shamrock. There were four. The jewels officially belonged to the Order of Saint Patrick."

"How?" Rayne gestured to the stone walls. "This is a fortress."

"It's a known fact that Sir Arthur liked to drink." The curator tipped an imaginary glass back. "Theory is that he was gotten knackered on purpose so the thieves could take his key and empty the safe. Smuggled them out with no one the wiser."

"Did Sir Arthur steal them?" Ciara asked. "The guard is often the thief."

"Vicars says no . . . so they hired a detective to investigate, which meant digging into people's pasts. Secrets were uncovered about the possible suspects that the royal court didn't want to reach the light of day." The curator waggled her white brows. "Vicars was later killed in a deliberate house fire. In his will he claimed he didn't steal the jewels but was set up."

Rayne sighed. "Was he innocent?"

"Rumors abounded that the detective's

report was stifled to protect the guilty. Drinking. Wild parties. It remained a scandal. And despite many different books on the subject, the jewels have never been found." The curator's eyes shone with excitement.

"How incredible!" Rayne shook her head. "I'd like to see those beautiful jewels."

"There are only photos. They came from Queen Charlotte's personal collection and were of the highest quality," the curator said. "They were stolen right before King Edward VII was due to visit, and appoint Lord Castletown into the Order of Saint Patrick, which was meant to show unity between England and Ireland's gentry. I've always wondered if they were stolen as a protest."

"Stolen for the good of all? Like Robinhood?"

"Too bad," Ciara said, "that the only thief in our family is Blarney, our dog."

Rayne's alarm went off. "One fifteen. We have to go but thank you so much for this very entertaining and informative tour. We might give our butler Cormac some tips."

There was a jar for cash donations, and Rayne put in twenty euro, which was all she had on her.

"Dublin rocks," Rayne said as they quickly

followed their walking map app to the two-story brick building that housed the MPM company.

The initials, MPM, were embossed in gold on the glass panel of the front door.

"Fancy," Ciara said.

Rayne opened the door. Like many older buildings, the ceilings were low, and the space dim. A sitting area with three sage armchairs surrounded a marble table with magazines. A fireplace took up one wall, and the window to the street another. The third was the entrance with the glass door and wooden panels on either side.

An umbrella stand was situated to the right, and a coat tree to the left. Where a fourth wall might have been, was a counter reminiscent of a bank. Behind the counter were a dozen shelves, filled with books. Two desks, a phone, and laptops.

A long hall disappeared into shadows, but Rayne could make out at least two offices with frosted windows in the doors.

"Welcome," a voice echoed toward them. The scent of coffee teased Rayne's senses.

"Hi!" Rayne replied.

A young woman, not even thirty, popped out of the first office door with a harried smile. "Howareyetheday? I'm Haley McGavin. What a mess it's been — not your fault, and I apologize for cramming everything in."

"Hello," Ciara said. "It's fine."

Mock-scowling at the dark foyer, Haley put her hand on her hip. "Come on out of the cave. I've been on Da and the sibs to add some fecking light, oh, sorry. But — well, they want to keep the atmosphere. If you can't see, what's the point?" She waved for them to follow her into the shadows, toward the smell of coffee.

At the end of the hall, they turned into a brightly lit kitchen that had a wooden table and six chairs. Haley had brown hair with blue tips and a bustling energy that made it impossible not to fall in love with her immediately.

"My family would shoot me dead if they realized I'd hosted the McGrath family in the kitchen, but it's spooky. This place could be haunted. There, I've said it." Haley grinned and shrugged. "Coffee, or tea?" She put the electric kettle on and pointed to a Keurig. "I'm on my third hot chocolate. Can you tell?"

Being as Haley didn't actually seem at all afraid of the consequences of serving them in the kitchen, Rayne pegged her as being one of the lucky ones who had an adoring large family.

This room was decorated with paintings, art, and many, many photos of the McGavins, young and old, throughout the centuries.

"Coffee, but I can get it," Rayne said.

Ciara was also by the counter. "Tea. And there is no need to wait on us. We appreciate you fitting us into your schedule."

"My sister creates custom tea blends so you can't go wrong. I like the orange zest the best." Haley's shoulders drooped. "I am soooo very sorry about Nevin's death. I liked him so much and considered him an uncle. He's been part of my life, always. I was in Barcelona, or I would have been to the funeral."

"Your family sent a large arrangement that was very thoughtful," Ciara said.

"Do you travel often?" Rayne asked.

"Yes, it's part of my life studies in art appreciation." Haley pointed to the picture of her and two others. "My brother Sean — he's a writer, my sister Kailyn. We each spend three months a year on call in Dublin. The other nine months, we pursue what makes us happy. Mam and Da each have their own things too, but do a month here, since they are retired." She gave the cutest snort. "As if they could walk away. This company has allowed us to guide others in property and wealth management. It's very soul-satisfying, you know?"

"I would love to know more about that particular balance," Rayne said.

"Grab your drinks and we will brave the hallway to my dungeon, er, office," Haley said. "I hope you don't mind but I've pulled up the history of the accounts so I can answer whatever questions you might have."

Rayne, coffee in hand, followed Haley. "Are you the only one working in the office today?"

Haley stopped to open the frosted glass door she'd come out of earlier. "We have four fulltime people on staff. We have three days of everyone in the office here — I love that wonderful creative energy, and the other two days are remote. Mondays, Wednesdays, and Fridays. It's been a nice mix." She ushered them in.

Her office was in stark contrast to the entrance, and the kitchen. Sculptures in metal or wood decorated the space. The walls were a soft green, with emerald accents. Her adjustable desk was up, as if she'd been standing.

The landline rang — she glanced at it, but didn't answer.

"Have a seat." Haley used a remote to lower the desk. She sat behind it, and Rayne and Ciara took seats opposite hers. She clicked on her laptop, in rainbow colors, and tapped her fingernails. "Our family has been managing the property for your family since eighteen-fifty. Isn't that wild?"

"It is very cool," Rayne said.

"What can I help you with?" Haley asked.

"We stopped by the registry office to find out about the deed and property lines." Ciara balanced her teacup on her knee. "They couldn't tell us what we own, so we have an appointment for next week."

Haley hummed and nodded, pressing a few keystrokes. "You need to know what you own, exactly?"

"Yes," Rayne said. "We learned that Uncle Nevin, Ciara's dad, was here at your company in April. We don't know why, and he never told his butler, Cormac, who was also his best friend. Do you know?"

Haley made a note on a scratch pad. "I'll check. It might be in the notes of whoever he met with. It wasn't me, of course."

"Thanks," Ciara said as Rayne nodded.

"What is it that you do as a property management company?" Rayne asked. "Forgive my ignorance. I had no idea that we would inherit the property in the manner that we did."

"What do you mean?" Haley asked.

"Rayne is the one who inherited," Ciara said. "I was kept on to manage it for her to get the castle and village out of debt. If we don't bring the property into the black then we are supposed to sell the manor, and property, and split what is left, if there is anything."

Haley's jaw dropped. "That's insane."

"Right?" Rayne agreed.

"Is that even legal?" Haley wondered.

They shared what had happened with the crooked solicitor but yes, Uncle Nevin's will was valid.

"You need a new solicitor," Haley said.

"We do! We've been looking around but haven't made any progress. Do you have a recommendation?"

"Hold onto your hats, ladies. I am going to share with you the best solicitor in Ireland — even better and beyond that. Her name is Fionagh Quinn. She works freelance for us sometimes, but she won't commit to a salary. She's expensive but worth it."

Rayne's stomach tightened. "We're living on what we bring in with the weddings, my gowns, and rental income that you send in quarterly. I've been selling purses to keep us going in between."

Haley laughed but stopped when she realized they weren't. "What are you doing for money?"

"I used to own a bridal boutique on Rodeo Drive, and so was familiar with the wedding industry. Because I am not allowed to go back to the states until the terms of the will are over, I had to figure out a way to satisfy my wedding gown orders and bring in money. McGrath Castle is rustic and charming. It makes the perfect romantic getaway for a quiet wedding."

Haley snapped her jaw closed. "How's it going then?"

"Better now. We had a few hiccups."

"Hiccups?" Ciara shook her head. "We had a fire in the turret, a member of the last wedding was killed, not to mention that Landon Short, your ex in LA, stole everything from you, went to jail, and escaped with revenge on you in mind."

"You can't know that," Rayne said, arguing with the last point because everything else was spot on.

"Are you both okay?" Haley reached into the bottom drawer of her desk and handed them each a piece of dark chocolate. "Rayne, are you a citizen of Ireland?"

"I have dual citizenship. My dad took care of that before he died."

"That helps with the legal stuff." Haley read the screen on her laptop.

"It's a lot, is all," Rayne said.

Haley swallowed her chocolate, her gaze speculative. "First off, I have the rental income listed here for the last two years. It has been declining, I'm sorry to say. Nevin was right to be concerned. Second, you own the entire village and most of the property. Rayne, if the will says it belongs to you, then you alone are responsible. Please, make an appointment with Fionagh. I'll give her a heads-up to expect your call. Maybe she can adjust the will. Or you can, as the person in charge." She looked at Ciara. "Are you willing to share the burden? I wouldn't blame you if you didn't want to do it."

Ciara slowly exhaled. After a minute, she nodded. "I would help Rayne. It wasn't right of Da to stick her with it."

Rayne felt relief that she wasn't actually on her own and clasped Ciara's hand. "Thanks."

"I'll print everything out for you. Let's brainstorm some ideas to build up the village." Haley raised her palm. "You do want it to succeed, right? You could let it fall and nobody could fault you."

Success meant saving not only the property but the livelihood of the Lloyds, the Walshes, the church, everyone in the village. If they didn't bring things into the black,

they would all lose their homes. There was no guarantee that being absorbed into Cotter Village would save them. Freda could decide to tear it all down and build a mall. This was not just about Rayne, or Ciara.
"We do!" Rayne said.

"That's right," Ciara said. "We will do whatever it takes."

Rayne blew out a deep, heartfelt breath. "How do we fill all those empty buildings?"

"Freda Bevan wants Grathton, but we can't just let her win. We will fight for our villagers, even if they don't care." Ciara spoke with assurance.

"Who is Freda Bevan?" Haley asked.

"The councilwoman for Cotter Village," Rayne said.

"You are on the council?" Haley asked.

"We agreed to do it together," Rayne said. "Our first meeting is tomorrow night. We need to attend armed with the information you give us."

"You got it," Haley said. "I am all about goalsetting. When is the deadline?"

"June first," Ciara said.

Haley whistled. "I realize this might be a personal question, but do you have an accountant?"

"Not anymore," Rayne said. "We've been doing the accounts — us, and Quicken. The program has been a lifesaver. It's working for now."

"What is your annual income?" Haley grabbed a pen from a ceramic pot on the desk.

"It's hard to say what that will be," Rayne said. "Income depends on the sheep and the rental property, which is declining. According to Uncle Nevin's books, when he was paid for something, it was needed for the next thing. Selling sheep, means buying hay and other supplies. It takes every last penny to keep the castle and village property going. There was a theft, so again, it is difficult to know the true numbers."

Haley studied them with empathy.

"We've been so focused on putting out the next fire, that this is the first we've been able to pop our heads up and look around," Ciara said.

"You've landed in the stew, no doubt," Haley said. "Let's find a way to get you out. What businesses might be a good fit? Do you have decent Wi-Fi?"

"We do," Rayne said. "I needed it for the online wedding dress orders."

"Splendid. Remote work is a possibility. I'll help you with an ad." Haley tapped her pen to the desk. "People are all about the digital nomad lifestyle, and tech is booming right now in Dublin. Grathton Village isn't that far. We can target professionals in their thirties who are tired of the party lifestyle and ready for something quieter in a quaint village. You have," she read the list of businesses turning in rental property, "three pubs. That's good. We haven't raised the rent in ten years, so we can start there — after we bring in some new tenants."

"I love it," Rayne said. "What else can we bring in to grow the place?"

"A bigger market than just the general store. It's so eclectic that you don't know what you'll find. Could get stuck with cream of mushroom soup when you want ramen." Ciara scrunched her nose.

Haley laughed. "What about crafters?"

"Moira Morton dries lavender and has an online business. It's possible we could tempt her with a storefront," Rayne suggested.

"What about yarn?" Ciara said. "Maeve, our housekeeper, is always knitting."

Haley wrapped her hair into a messy knot and stabbed the pen through it. "I adore knitted scarves. My favorite. I sculpt and draw but two needles at once is beyond me."

Rayne chuckled. "I can sew like a dream, but I'm with you." She thought of how Amos and Dafydd managed the animals on the property. "What about an actual veterinarian?"

"Brilliant," Haley said.

"What about an urgent care center?" Ciara suggested. "Or a dry cleaner, or a laundromat."

"We have Dr. Ruebens for medical help, but a walk-in clinic might be nice, considering the age of our villagers, and Dr. Ruebens."

"They are old," Ciara agreed.

Haley narrowed her eyes. "What do people *need*?"

"A bookstore," Ciara said.

Rayne shrugged. "You can get books at the general store sometimes. The An Post carries a limited selection. Our villagers aren't rich."

"A library?" Haley rattled the sheet with the rental income. "It won't make money."

"It could be one of those free libraries run by volunteers," Ciara said. "We could not charge for the rent of the building. Reading is an escape, Rayne. It's for mental health."

"I won't argue."

"What about an estate agent?" Haley said. "The right one could really make a difference in filling those vacant properties." She scanned the list. "There are two apartment buildings with twenty flats each that are empty, begging to be occupied."

"Forty apartments?" Rayne asked. "We can have Bobby Fitzroy check them out to see what they need to get them livable and attract those digital nomads." She and Haley exchanged a smile. "Jams! We can talk to Dorothy and Sheff McElroy about a business."

"We better taste them first," Ciara said, only partially kidding.

"You ladies are on the right track," Haley promised. She stood. "I'll print out this information, with Fionagh's phone number. I suggest you celebrate with lunch, just in case I have any questions. Oh, you need to sign a new agreement with us. Totally forgot in our chit-chat." She took their hands — one each, to make a circle. "You both have a burning entrepreneurial spirit and the McGrath drive. You *can* do this."

Though riddled with doubt, Rayne needed to believe her.

Chapter Six

Talking Ciara into a fancy meal took some arm-twisting, but Rayne knew the credit card bill would get paid. They deserved a chance to splurge. It felt like a light had been shone at the end of a dark tunnel. The paperwork from Haley and the MPM company was in a folder in the bag with the ivory silk, thread, and emerald gossamer fabric.

"My mind is spinning with possibilities," Rayne said as the meal ended. She'd had scampi, and Ciara, fettuccine. They'd been quiet, each lost in their own thoughts.

"Mine too."

"I hope Fionagh Quinn calls us back today. I'd love for her to settle the will thing for us. When Haley asked if you were willing to share the burden, I almost couldn't breathe." Rayne's stomach tightened.

"I saw your face, and realized how unfair Da was to give you this mess. He didn't think he'd die, but a part of him must have known or suspected. If the will can be changed, then yes, we can make it legal. If not, you have my support anyway. You didn't have to stay, Rayne. You could have returned to LA."

Rayne's cell phone rang. She couldn't have returned to her life with a clear conscience, knowing she'd be responsible for Ciara, the Lloyds, Amos, Blarney, the sheep, everything would have been sold, and the manor shut down. She cleared her throat and answered, not recognizing the number and hoping it could be the new solicitor. "Hello?"

"This is Marty from the land registry office."

"I'm Rayne McGrath. Thank you for calling me back." She put the phone on speaker so that Ciara could hear too. The other diners were so loud that they weren't bothering anyone.

"You say the family land has been in your hands since 1750? That's remarkable. I have the deeds all on film here. The line is continuous. What was your concern?"

"Well, my cousin and I inherited the property six months ago. I'm from America and I just wondered what our responsibilities for the village would be."

"You work with someone to handle the rentals?"

"Yes. McGavin Property Management."

"They could tell you better. Let me send you the exact property lines via email. Will that be okay?"

"Yes." Rayne gave him her email address.

"There is a nominal fee for the transfer."

"Not a problem," Rayne said. It was only money and would be paid back eventually. "We appreciate it. This way we don't need to come back on Tuesday."

"I'll cancel that appointment for you. You must be very proud of your family heritage," Marty said. "It's not something to be taken lightly. You have a responsibility to protect this for future generations. So many times, these little villages get swallowed up into larger ones."

"We are trying to avoid just that." Rayne and Ciara exchanged a look. Her cousin lowered her fork.

"Join the council, vote, be active in your community. Do you still have your church?"

"We do," Rayne said. Gossip central.

"Good. And An Post I see," Marty said. "Those things are the heart of the villages."

An Post was a post office, and theirs was small but quaint. "Thank you very much. I appreciate the email."

Rayne ended the call and lifted her tumbler of whiskey to Ciara's hard cider.

"To us, and to Grathton Village."

After their toast, Rayne felt lighter. They had a property to be proud of, and yes it was definitely worth fighting for. They shared a slice of apple cake for dessert.

"Ready?" Ciara stood.

"Yes. I can't wait to share the good news." Rayne grabbed the bag with the fabric and information from Haley, to be added to the deeds from Marty. It had been a very productive day.

They were ten minutes outside of Dublin on the motorway when Rayne's phone rang. "Nolan," she said to Ciara. "Wonder what he wants?"

It was four in the afternoon and starting to get dark. Ciara didn't mind, she said, she loved to drive on the fast highway. She also loved horses, so maybe her cousin was a secret thrill seeker.

"Hello!"

"Rayne? Have you left town yet?"

"We just did."

"Any chance you can turn around?" Nolan asked.

"Oh — let me put you on speaker phone so Ciara can hear. She's driving." Rayne hooked up the Bluetooth. "There."

"Ciara, love, can you turn your metal steed around?"

Her cousin laughed. "Sure, what for?" Ciara flipped on her turn signal and crossed two lanes of traffic to be in the lane for the next exit.

Rayne gulped down a squeal.

"Sheila Martinet wants to talk to you both, actually," Nolan said. "She already knew about Aiden's death when I told her."

"What about?" Rayne asked. "We've never met her."

"She has something to share but doesn't want to tell you over the phone," Nolan said. "Better at the pub."

"Oh!" Rayne glanced at Ciara, who was focused on traffic. Though it was a Wednesday evening, downtown was still packed.

"She sounded like it was very important, or I wouldn't bother you with it — what's the matter with a call, right?" Nolan said. "You mentioned you wanted information."

Ciara looked intrigued. "I don't mind. Not like I have to be home at a certain time."

"No lucky man at home?" Nolan sighed. "Not for me either, lass. It's wrong that we are all three on the market."

"Ciara is engaged," Rayne corrected him. "And, I've been asked to coffee."

"Coffee!" Nolan snickered. "Is that what they call it over in the village?"

"Let's stay on topic," Ciara said. "Can you send Rayne the address of the pub? Will you be there too?"

"Alas, I am not invited even to gossip. It concerns Aiden and I believe Beetle. Sheila seemed unsurprised that Beetle would be a suspect in Aiden's death."

Ciara exited as Rayne's phone dinged. "Got it! Thank you."

"Sheila has mermaid blue hair so is easy to recognize — she's already there and has a booth in the corner."

"Thank you!"

"Talk to me the next time you're in Dublin. Let's do lunch or dinner!" Nolan ended the call.

"I wonder what on earth she's got to say?" Rayne asked.

"It better be good. I hate to waste petrol, even if we have the time."

"It's kinda cool to hang out like this," Rayne said. "I'm not mad about it."

"Don't get so mushy," Ciara said.

It took several tries but they at last found parking within a block of the busy, popular, pub.

They entered the brick building with wood trim and a wooden door. It had been modernized about a hundred years ago, Rayne guessed. Around the time of the War of Independence.

The interior had the familiar fish and chips scent that warred with the smell of hops and other fried foods that seemed to be the staple of the Irish pub.

The low lighting allowed Rayne to make out the back corner, and a woman with the bright blue hair Nolan had described sitting at a booth.

"Hi!" Rayne said. "Are you Sheila?" She spoke in a murmur as this seemed on the clandestine side. No Nolan *and* a secret about Aiden.

"Yes." Sheila half-smiled at Rayne and looked over Rayne's shoulder to Ciara.

"Hey. I'm Ciara."

"Have a seat, both of you," Sheila said. She had an empty wine glass before her and had started on a second. A bowl of pretzels was about halfway eaten. Her manicure was turquoise with black tiger stripes.

"All right." Rayne scooted into the booth first.

Ciara tossed her purse in between her and Rayne and then sat. "Should we get drinks?"

"The waitress will come," Sheila said. Her eyes were heavily made up with blue shadow. While Aiden had been just over forty, Sheila had to be older. Probably closer to fifty.

Her face was pretty, with lines around her mouth and eyes. Sheila smelled of cigarettes though this wasn't a place to smoke. Like in the states, smoking was banned in public venues.

"I recommend the house wine," Sheila said. "It's buy one, get one, during happy hour. Apps are half price. I thought I'd wait for you before I ordered food."

Well, that explained the second glass. Sheila wasn't ready for AA but on the second drink of her special.

"Sounds great!" Rayne said. "We just had a late lunch, so I am not ready to eat."

"Speak for yourself." Ciara perused the small menu. "I've never met a toastie that I didn't like."

"The cheese and onion is my favorite," Sheila said.

"What is it?" Rayne didn't mean to, but her shoulders braced. Everything in this place was loaded with fat.

"A grilled cheese sandwich but better," Ciara said.

"Ten times better," Sheila agreed with a grin.

"I'm full," Rayne repeated.

"You'll be sorry, and I'm not sharing,"

Ciara said.

The waitress arrived. Ciara and Rayne split the buy one, get one house wine special. Sheila and Ciara each ordered a cheese and onion toastie. "Crisps?"

"No, thanks. You have scampi fries?" Ciara asked.

"I'm down to my last bag," the waitress said. "You want it?"

"Yes. I'll share with the table," Ciara offered.

Shrimp in wine sauce was one of Rayne's favorite meals. She was intrigued that it might be on French fries. The curry sauce was out of this world.

Rayne sent a text to Maeve that they were a little late and not to hold dinner for the cousins. They would be full.

Maeve sent a thumbs-up emoji in reply.

"I let the others know not to wait for us to have dinner," Rayne said.

"Good idea," Ciara agreed.

"What's it like to live in a castle?" Sheila asked. "Nolan told me that you both inherited it recently."

"Are you familiar with Grathton Village?" Rayne asked.

"I've heard of McGrath Castle, but Ireland is dotted with historic landmarks." Sheila sipped her wine. "Aiden being from

Grathton Village is the only reason I was ever there, but that was many years ago."

"How long ago?" Ciara asked.

"How old is Corrine?" Sheila asked in a speculative tone.

"Colleen Randall's little girl?" Ciara clarified.

"Yes." Sheila drank her wine.

"Four," Ciara said.

"Five years ago, give or take." Sheila's mouth pursed and lines grooved her face.

Rayne felt like there might be more to this, but the waitress arrived with a basket of a grilled cheese sandwich for Sheila and Ciara and a bag of what looked like potato chips but were in fact a strange item called scampi fries.

Ciara opened the packet and a smell nothing like her beloved dish escaped the package. "Want one?" Ciara pointed it toward Rayne.

"No, thanks," Rayne said quickly.

"Your loss, cuz. Sheila?"

"Yes, please." Sheila drew a handful from the bag and put them next to her cheese and onion toastie.

"I won't ask how you can eat something that looks like Styrofoam," Rayne teased.

"I suppose it's an acquired taste," Ciara said. She smacked her lips.

Rayne waited until Sheila had finished half her sandwich before bringing up Aiden again. Sheila had requested an in-person meeting in a dark bar. The mood was perfect for a secret to be shared. "Nolan said you had something you wanted to tell us?"

Sheila patted her lips with a napkin and wadded it in her palm. "I do." She exhaled. "I just . . . I could never prove it, you know?"

"Prove what?" Rayne sipped her wine.

Sheila exhaled and crumbled a crisp into her basket. "You said that Beetle was a suspect in Aiden's death?"

"The gardai think so but we don't," Ciara said. "He's a friend of sorts."

Sheila's expression turned to one of doubt. "I remember him from the band days, and he had a terrible temper."

"Did he?" Rayne had only seen the controlled version of Beetle.

"Before he punched Aiden in the nose, he had always kept his cool that I'd witnessed." Ciara reached for her wine, sipped, and quickly set it back down, reaching for her water instead.

Rayne snickered, thinking of how scampi fries tasted with pinot grigio. Ugh.

"You both think so? I guess people can

change, unless they are provoked." Sheila arched her brow. "And Aiden was one for provoking someone."

"How long were you married?" Rayne asked.

"We met at one of the music venues. Aiden wanted to be a rockstar but had no rhythm. Couldn't carry a tune in a bucket." Sheila shook her head. "He had dreams of grandeur that didn't match his level of no-talent."

"Did he win you over with a dance, then?" Rayne asked. Aiden was average in looks and even though older, Sheila had more going on. She was a catch. Paddy had remarked on that as well, when he'd accused Don of scooping up Aiden's exes in front of Treasa. Of the men, Don was the least attractive of the three.

"Nah." Sheila shredded a piece of crust off her toastie. "Aiden worked for extra money helping the bands set up their music equipment."

She wasn't answering how they'd met. Interesting.

Rayne glanced at Ciara. Ciara's brow furrowed.

"So, Aiden dreamed of being a musician but had no talent," her cousin summarized. "He worked around music and had no rhythm. Muscle was probably always appreciated when moving equipment."

"Aiden made decent money doing it, but it wasn't a steady gig," Sheila said.

"Did he live in Kilkenny?" Rayne asked. "Or Grathton? The grandchildren of the older families all have ties there it seems." Paddy, Don, Aiden. Did the McElroys have grands in that age group, or the McGillicuddys?

Sheila swallowed a bite of her sandwich. "Aiden was working at the Gray Boar here in Dublin when we met. That's where I met Nolan too. When Aiden wasn't helping the bands, he was a bartender. He poured a much better beer than he could sing."

"And it was love at first sight?" Rayne prodded. She normally wouldn't mind Sheila's meandering style of conversation, but they had things to do, like get ready for the upcoming wedding this weekend. Now that she had the ivory thread for the dress, and the silk lining for the trunk, she was eager to get the projects completed.

"Not exactly." Sheila stared into the depths of her almost empty wine glass. "I was lonely," she admitted. "To have a younger man like Aiden interested in me beyond just serving me drinks was a thrill."

"How old were you?" Rayne asked. "If you

don't mind my asking."

"I'd just turned the dreaded thirty with no prospects," Sheila said. "I wanted a relationship, but I wasn't into kids." She shrugged. "I had my house and a boring but steady job in accounting. One drunken Christmas eve, Aiden suggested we get married, and I stupidly agreed. I thought we'd raise rescue cats and be happy." She drained the glass and looked toward the bar, but their waitress was not paying attention.

"You have cats?" Ciara asked. "We have two barn kittens."

"Three." Sheila's eyes lit up in the dim lighting. "It turned out that Aiden was allergic. I should have known that it was an excuse to not be home very often. As stupid as it sounds, I honestly didn't realize that he didn't love me anymore."

"That sucks," Ciara said.

Rayne's body filled with empathy.

Landon had never loved her either but had used her, to steal from her. Just because he could.

"Or that he never had," Sheila confessed. "He was using me. I think I lied to myself and made excuses for him. A part of me would've rather had him in my life than to be alone."

"What happened?" Rayne felt for this

woman who didn't value herself enough to stand up to a Grade A jerk.

At least Landon had gone to jail for his crimes.

Then again, someone had killed Aiden.

"Aiden was messing around," Sheila said. "He'd moved into my place after we got married. I didn't know that he'd kept his flat. I believed him when he said he was on the road some weekends to travel with the bands."

"A roadie," Rayne said. It would be the perfect job for a cheater.

Ciara crumpled her empty crisps bag.

"Yeah." Sheila swept her hair back, her nails catching the dim candlelight. "I must've suspected something more because I insisted on going along for one of the trips. Suddenly it was cancelled so he was able to spend the weekend with me, and our rescue cats, after all."

"Dang!" Rayne said.

"For my fortieth birthday I thought we'd do something special so when I heard him murmuring on the phone, I thought it was a surprise for me." Sheila shrugged, her eyes filling with tears. "Turned out not to be true."

"I'm afraid to ask!" Rayne could relate on so many levels to Sheila.

"Me too," Ciara said.

"I showed up at the bar that Aiden worked at that night, though he'd told me not to, thinking it was a surprise. I was surprised all right. My husband and Colleen Randall were attached at the face." Sheila puckered her lips to make kissing noises.

"Oh no!" Rayne said.

"That was seven years ago." Sheila looked up from what was left of her sandwich. "I broke up with him right away."

"Of course you did! What a fecking eejit." Ciara bristled with anger on Sheila's behalf.

Though it was dark, shame poured from Sheila and Rayne imagined her body would be red with embarrassment. "Aiden convinced me to take him back . . . not sure why, in the end, except to see if he could get away with it."

"Aiden sounds like a sociopath," Rayne said. "What happened?"

"I discovered that he and Colleen never broke up." Sheila's voice wavered.

"No!" Ciara said. "Colleen Randall, as in Beetle's sister?"

"Yes. The slut."

"Hey!" Rayne said.

"I don't understand," Ciara said. "She's . . . surely, once Colleen knew you were married, she wouldn't take him back?"

"Aiden lied to her, it's true. I didn't know until later. Our marriage license is a matter of public record," Sheila said. Her voice sounded indignant. "She could have done some due diligence on her end rather than believe him."

"That's really awful." Rayne couldn't stand liars. What made people think they could get away with them?

"It is," Sheila said.

Rayne had the feeling that it wasn't over yet and braced herself. Her wine glass was empty, as was Ciara's.

She drank her water just to wet her throat.

"Beetle was furious when he found out and cut Aiden from his friend circle." Sheila made a slicing motion across her throat. "That's when Beetle moved back to Grathton Village full time."

"He's from Grathton?" Rayne asked Ciara.

"The Randalls have been in Grathton Village over a hundred years," Ciara said. "Like the others in the community."

"Beetle had been living in Dublin and had grown a following for his band. Nolan and I were both fans. He and Aiden got into a terrible argument." Sheila shrugged. "Aiden had been drinking, but not Beetle really so . . . to be fair, Beetle pulled his punches."

"I can see that," Rayne said.

"We did see that. Do you like Beetle?" Ciara asked.

"No." Sheila's tone didn't waver there.

"Is it personal, or is it because of Aiden?" Rayne watched the woman closely. What did Sheila hope to gain by putting Beetle down? They would support Beetle no matter what. Unless he really did kill Aiden.

"Aiden was a weasel but like I said, I didn't realize that at the time. Maybe he had it coming . . ."

"What are you talking about?" Rayne demanded.

Sheila was quiet, letting the tension build.

Ciara's knee bounced beneath the table.

Rayne curled her fingers around the bench seat so she didn't reach over and shake Sheila silly.

"You said that Beetle hit Aiden for being in the Sheep's Head bar." Sheila's eyes were narrowed to slits.

"Not just that. Beetle punched Aiden for seeing Colleen while he was also still dating Treasa," Rayne said. "Treasa confirmed that she'd learned the truth from Aiden that night, because she'd wanted Aiden to press charges for assault against Beetle."

"Aiden came clean with what was really going on," Ciara said.

"Another woman, taken in," Sheila shrugged. "Poor fool. Especially if Treasa loves him, but I really doubt that."

It sounded like Sheila knew Treasa too. Was she keeping an eye on Aiden for a reason other than jealousy?

"Beetle pulled his punches that night, despite learning that Aiden had lied to him, and to Colleen," Rayne said. "He is very protective of Colleen, and Corrine."

She didn't understand why Sheila was looking so smug.

"What if there was another truth?" Sheila asked them, making eye contact with Ciara and then Rayne.

"You're not making sense," Ciara said.

Sheila leaned across the table. "What if Beetle discovered that little Corrine was Aiden's daughter?"

Chapter Seven

"Is that true?" Rayne gasped. Corrine, so sweet, with her pink glasses and fun style of clothes. Her cheery attitude. Colleen's air of sadness.

Sheila shrugged. "I don't know, but I suspect it to be the truth. What color hair does the little lass have? Is it red, like Aiden's?"

"Brown," Ciara said. "Maybe there's a red tint, but this is Ireland, so, not a big reveal." She leaned over the table to peer at Sheila. "Why would you even say that? That's how rumors get started. Ugly ones."

"Didn't Colleen have a fiancé that died in a car accident?" Rayne put her guard up against the gossipy Sheila, not liking her style after all. How could Nolan be her friend? Maybe he'd never been on the receiving end of her slander.

Could be why she hadn't wanted Nolan there with them to hear her jealous tale.

"I never met Colleen's fiancé." Sheila turned to Ciara. "Did you?"

"No. But I've only been around for ten years. I knew the Randalls had been in Grathton for so long because Da had mentioned it. The McGillicuddys and McElroys have been part of Grathton for even longer. The O'Briens, and the Dennehys."

"Was Uncle Nevin friends with the families still?" Rayne asked.

"I think so." Ciara's brow furrowed. "The McElroys, definitely. He talked about the Randalls, who still have a small farm," she said. "Beetle and Colleen's mother Connie worked as a nurse for Dr. Ruebens until she retired. Not sure what she does now. Their father is a mechanic in Kilkenny."

A nurse! "Grandma Sonia was a nurse in the war. That could be another position to fill," Rayne said. "And a mechanic seems like it would be needed. Does Mr. Randall live and work there? Kilkenny is not an awful drive but what if we created a shop in Grathton to tempt him to stay local?"

Sheila nudged her basket. "Probably money. What can a mechanic earn in Grathton compared to a bigger city? Not that Kilkenny is big but it's certainly bigger than your village."

Rayne sat back, slightly stunned at the

overwhelming task of bringing people into the village in a way that would make them prosper. "Where do we start?"

"People want to thrive." Ciara correctly read Rayne's panicked expression that had zero to do with Corrine's paternity, or Beetle's motivation to take out Aiden. "Da was right to put you in charge. It's too much."

"We are a team." Ciara couldn't change her mind! Her mom was right — this was more than the money but family pride. Rayne focused on the gossipy Sheila. "What would convince you to move to Grathton Village?"

"Me?" Sheila's brows rose so high they disappeared behind her mermaid-blue bangs, and she burst out laughing. "Not enough money in the world. I thought I'd come eventually with Aiden once he inherited the Dennehy family property, but I have no reason to move to that puddle of sheep piss now."

"Hey!" Ciara said, taking offense.

"Not necessary," Rayne agreed. "Those sheep are vital to our community. That wasn't an invite, by the way. I'm curious what might tempt someone close to fifty to move from a city."

"I am forty-four," Sheila said indignantly.

"Forty-seven, if you turned forty, seven years ago. Sorry," Rayne said, not sorry at all for calling the woman out.

Sheila fluttered the uncomfortable truth away with a wave of her fingers. If this was how she lived her life, it was easy to see how she could have ignored the Aiden problem for so long. She'd been thirty when they'd first met. Seventeen years was a long time.

"Dublin is my home so I wouldn't leave." Sheila blew out a breath. "But if I was looking to relocate, the village would need to have modern amenities along with rural . . . charm."

"Charm is good!" Rayne said. "We have satellite for Wi-Fi that is provided free for the village. We started a wedding venue at the castle with that idea in mind. We've painted the schools and just cleaned the cemetery. Next on the village to-do list is update the office buildings for curb appeal. Don and Aiden wanted to open a mobile phone center."

"That can't happen now," Sheila said, sounding cheery about it. "Your list must be pretty long."

"It is, it is." Ciara peered at Sheila over the rim of her water glass. "You sure you weren't upset about not getting your fingers on the Dennehy property? It's grand. Lots of acreage and a creek. Plenty of outbuildings that are all in decent repair. Once Luke and Shauna pass, I mean."

Sheila drummed her fingers against the table. "Why would I be upset? I just told you that I am happy with my life in Dublin."

"Who will inherit now that Aiden is gone?" Rayne asked. "Did he have other siblings?"

"No. He was an only child and spoilt," Sheila said. "As you say, his grands are still alive, as is his mother. His dad's name is Allan Dennehy. He had a falling out with his parents over something and turned his back on Aiden and the whole family. Aiden hadn't heard from him since he was a teenager."

"His mom is still alive?" Rayne asked.

"Yes. Lives in Spain though and is remarried to an artist. I'd be surprised if she came home for the funeral as they weren't close," Sheila said.

Rayne made a mental note to check into that situation. Could Aiden have been killed over his possible inheritance? Just because his dad had walked away decades ago didn't mean he wouldn't be around now.

Should the gardai be taking a closer peek at Colleen Randall and her daughter, Corrine?

Because while Beetle had punched Aiden for sleeping with Colleen behind his back and lying, it looked very suspicious for Beetle, if he'd found out — if it was even true, that Corrine was also Aiden's daughter — he might have exacted revenge in a fit of passion.

She recalled how things had gone down at the Sheep's Head the other night, and that Beetle had called Aiden's name before his punch.

Aiden had been stabbed *in the back* with gardening shears. It was cowardly.

Not the same as confronting someone in a pub brawl.

Rayne believed that if Beetle had found out about Aiden, Colleen, and Corrine, the worse he would have done is force Aiden to take responsibility.

"Does Treasa know your theory about Colleen and Corrine?" Rayne asked. "It could be very hurtful to spread this story."

Sheila pursed her lips. "Treasa Boone thought she was too good for Aiden. Possibly she had her own money, and yes, she is above average in looks, but she had her faults."

"What were those?" Ciara asked. Her cousin invited Sheila to share with a smirk.

"Well, for one thing, she wanted Aiden to

marry her, but he wouldn't do it." Sheila hooked her pointer finger. "She led him around by the . . . nose . . . in order to get her way."

"Why wouldn't he marry her?" Rayne asked. "As you say, he wasn't in love with you. Could it have been Colleen he loved all along?"

Sheila's eyes widened.

"Oh, yeah," Ciara said. "If Aiden loved Colleen for real, then that would be a brilliant reason to drag his feet regarding Treasa."

"I guess you should ask her," Sheila said, sounding annoyed that the subject was no longer her in the starring role of victim.

"Treasa did tell us that Aiden was serving community service hours and that's why he was volunteering," Rayne said. "Do you think she suspects about Corrine's paternity?"

"I knew there had to be a reason Aiden was there cleaning up an old churchyard," Sheila said.

"Treasa already thinks you're nosy, Rayne, so we can always call her back at the solicitor's office," Ciara said.

Rayne tapped the back of her cell, face down on the table. It was true about her curiosity, but she tried very hard not to hurt people. “Except that if Treasa didn’t know, I would be spreading an unfounded rumor about someone and that adorable girl could get hurt. So, no. We will keep this ugly rumor here.”

Sheila’s phone rang and Don’s grinning face showed on the screen. Rayne remembered what Aiden and Paddy had said about Don being satisfied with Aiden’s leftovers.

When it came to human connection, there were some things best left unimagined. Rayne couldn’t take another minute here with Sheila. “You ready, cuz?”

“Yes.” Ciara slid off the bench, seemingly as eager to leave as Rayne.

Rayne scooted to the edge of the booth.

Sheila’s phone dinged with notifications starring Don like a pinball machine. She smacked her palm over his face.

“Are you guys dating?” Rayne asked. “Don seems nice.”

Sheila shrugged. “He’s all right. Another Grathton Village man.” She scrunched her nose. “You might just see me in your village after all. Even though I wasn’t invited.”

Ciara tugged Rayne up from a sitting position. “Let us know.”

“So you can avoid me?” Sheila asked.

“We appreciate your time, Sheila,” Rayne said. “I don’t know what to think about the insinuation of Aiden as Corrine's dad. I guess a DNA test would prove one way or the other."

"For what purpose?" Sheila asked.

"Well, if it is true about Aiden being Corrine's dad, then she will be quite wealthy," Ciara said. "The Dennehys are loaded."

"They are?" Sheila's mouth rounded. "I didn't realize."

"Yep. Old money from before the War of Independence."

"Oh!"

It was sad but Rayne realized that Sheila was calculating what she'd possibly lost by divorcing Aiden.

Would Sheila have stayed if she'd known about the money despite the cheating?

Rayne shook her head. No cheating man was worth a dime — in her perhaps jaded opinion. "You were smart to put yourself first."

"What can you possibly know about it? An American," Sheila said with disdain.

"You're right!" Rayne stepped away from the table toward the door, stopping on the way out to pay their tab. Even Sheila's.

"Why did you do that?" Ciara asked. "She was rude."

"She's a mean woman. Sees herself as a victim. I don't want that energy around me because you and I, Ciara, are not victims."

Ciara slung her arm around Rayne's shoulders. "No. We are fighters."

They were driving home in the dark though it was only six PM. Ciara chose a radio station that had a mellow vibe that was conducive to sharing.

"What made you see Sheila as a victim?" Ciara asked. "I thought she was self-centered more than anything."

"Her expression when she realized that Aiden was wealthy, and she'd divorced him for cheating. It wasn't her fault, but it was what had happened to her. I suppose that's true, but she took it for years before she finally had enough. When she caught him with Colleen, she couldn't deny it anymore."

"I wonder if she's handy with garden shears?" Ciara quipped.

Rayne chuckled. "Nah. She might break one of those fabulous nails." She sighed and continued, "I never wanted what Landon did to me to define me," she said. "It still is a struggle to separate my expectation of unimaginable joy to the reality of what happened. I am not a girl who gets walked on! Or taken advantage of, and yet, here I am."

Ciara nodded, showing she was listening.

"My mom is an actress. My dad a handsome Irish poet. We lived in Hollywood. My childhood was magical, Ciara. And then Dad died."

Rayne stopped and pressed her hand to her heart.

The pain of that would never go away.

"It changed my world and showed me that the magic could be tainted. What was your childhood like?"

"A lot less dreamy than yours," Ciara said. "Being raised by a single mum in London wasn't abnormal — there were plenty of single parents and all kinds of blended families. I always had enough to eat and was expected to work hard on my grades. If I wanted something special, I had to get it myself."

"That explains your work ethic," Rayne said.

"I didn't mind because it taught me that my life was what I made of it, you know? Until Mum got cancer and told me about Nevin McGrath being my father. I was angry with her for keeping that a secret and wasn't kind to her when I should have been. She didn't have long to live. I regret that," Ciara said softly.

"I'm sorry."

"It's all right."

Headlights from oncoming cars on the other side of the highway flashed into their windshield before passing by at sixty miles per hour.

"Da and I figured it out, but it wasn't easy having a grown woman on your doorstep," Ciara said. "Proof of a fling while separated from your wife, the love of your life."

"It must have been awkward."

"Maeve welcomed me immediately. If it wasn't for her giving me cups of spiked tea in the kitchen while I cried my eyes out, I don't know if I could have made it."

"Maeve is who I remember as well being so compassionate. I learned that biscuits were cookies," Rayne said. "That was the summer I came home and told everyone in LA that my family was royalty and that I should be treated accordingly. I was insufferable."

"I can see it!" Ciara chuckled.

"Lauren sent me to deportment classes and that straightened my *wild, Celtic ways* for the most part anyway. Conor just laughed it off. My dad was a true artist."

"Da spoke so highly of him, and you," Ciara said. "Lauren too."

"I loved him and Aunt Amalie, and Cousin Padraig, so much. It's hard to believe that everyone but us is gone." Rayne sighed thinking of the trunks of family history. "It's awful that we don't have the elders that the others in the village have. Our family members died protecting Ireland and their belief in freedom."

"Makes me both sad and proud," Ciara said.

"You and Dafydd will need to start procreating pretty quickly." Rayne peered over the console to her cousin, who didn't crack a smile.

"I'm not sure about that."

"Oh?" Rayne waited, giving her cousin the time and space to discuss her problems. The car was the best place for confessions.

Ciara tapped her thumb to the steering wheel.

She still wasn't wearing her engagement ring.

Dafydd and Ciara had been a united front when she'd arrived, though Ciara had seemed surprised by Dafydd's jealousy regarding Garda Dominic Williams.

They'd had a relationship before he was on the force and when Ciara had returned from London the second time, after breaking up with her toxic boyfriend.

"Da liked Dafydd."

"He's an incredible shepherd."

"Top-notch mechanic," Ciara added.

"He's been an employee for a long time."

"Practically family." Ciara glanced at Rayne.

Rayne kept her expression neutral.

"You might not be aware that when you get married in the Catholic church, you need to go through marriage classes," Ciara said. "Father Patrick has been a rock in our community."

"That's good. Is it a rule? Like you can't get married if you don't take the classes?"

"No, but it's recommended, to make sure that both people are ready for such a commitment. Marriage is not to be taken lightly."

Ciara's jaw clenched.

"I agree with you." Without being Catholic but Rayne kept that part to herself. If more people took their vows seriously, perhaps divorce wouldn't be so readily used to solve a problem.

"I thought Dafydd and I were on the same page."

"Oh?"

"We've been going to these classes for three months. I was considering a wedding in the spring or maybe next summer. After we know what happens with the village. It's not like life has been running on a straight course."

"True."

"With Da's death, and then Dominic's scrutiny into our lives, and the will! It's been a lot to handle. Getting married took a back seat."

"Fair."

"Dafydd wanted to start back up with the classes."

"He loves you."

"Yes." Ciara's knuckles whitened on the steering wheel.

Oh, but no immediate return of affection from Ciara.

She quickly glanced toward Rayne. "We were talking about commitment and Father Patrick said something about since neither of us had been married before that it didn't apply to a particular lesson he'd been teaching."

Rayne's stomach knotted. Ciara's grip strangled the wheel.

"And Dafydd, who I have been dating for years, and been engaged to for over a year, says, 'about that, Father Patrick . . .' "

"What?"

"I don't know who was more surprised, me or Father Patrick." Ciara shook her head, her tone bemused.

"Oh no. Is Dafydd currently married?"

"Not that bad," Ciara said. "But still — bad." She exhaled a shaky breath that had

Rayne's empathy on high. Relationships were so complicated.

"What happened?" Rayne asked quietly.

"It seems that Dafydd was married for a time before he went to jail. I understand and applaud his reasons for going to jail. He stole food for his siblings, got caught, and did the time. His siblings are now grown and happy with families of their own." Ciara spoke with conviction.

Rayne nodded.

"At no time did Dafydd mention that he'd been married to his secondary school sweetheart. They were together and only divorced after he got out." Ciara's mouth pursed. "Not good, Rayne."

"No."

"Not illegal, not immoral, but not totally honest." Ciara released the wheel with one hand to pat her chest. "It doesn't sit right with me."

The truth was a big deal to them both. "What does Dafydd say about it?"

"Dafydd doesn't think he did anything wrong. He'd wanted to make a good impression on Da." Ciara returned both hands to the wheel. "He had me in his sights as the woman he loved."

"All is fair in love and war?"

Ciara smacked the dashboard with heat.

"It shouldn't have been a battle. Dafydd created this mess by his lies of omission."

"You're right." Rayne shifted on the passenger seat. "What does Father Patrick think?"

"It's up to me to either decide whether I can live with this omission, and forgive Dafydd with my whole heart, or not go through with the marriage." Ciara again glanced at Rayne, raising her brows.

"Good advice." Father Patrick must have counseled a bunch of people over the years because that really was on point.

"It's solid." Ciara focused on the highway.

"And?"

"I just don't know if I can do it. Forgive him, when he was silent about his past, and this love he'd denied for his first wife, saying that I was his first love." Ciara sounded filled with regret as she shared her feelings. "Stupid, I know, but I can't let it go."

"Those are your feelings, and you are entitled to them." Rayne tapped the console between them. "You are one of the smartest women I've ever met. And my bestie Jenn is an accountant."

"I'm so confused." Ciara tilted her head, gaze intent on the road ahead. "I just told Dafydd not to pressure me — he is so certain that things are okay that he doesn't get it."

Rayne had seen his confusion firsthand over the past few nights at dinner. "Should we fire him immediately? Oust him from the property?"

Ciara's lips twitched. "You are a good ally to have."

"The best. Whatever you want, I have your back."

"Thanks." Ciara exhaled. "I think we should keep things status quo at the manor. It's been easy to keep my distance from Dafydd. I guess that's my answer?"

"You don't have to decide right now," Rayne assured her. "It's your choice. You can take a break, and Dafydd should give you room."

"We made a promise to each other." Her words were filled with pain.

"He wasn't honest with you."

"I know," Ciara said. Her tone lifted. "Let's talk about something else."

"Okay." Rayne rested her elbow on the passenger side armrest. "How on earth are we going to fill the homes and businesses in the village in six months?"

Ciara ruffled her curls. "I'd almost rather talk about Dafydd."

"It's a problem we've got to address.

Aiden's dying in the cemetery doesn't help our slogan for smaller villages are a safer choice to plant roots."

"Nope."

"We can try the Blue Zone idea instead. How many villagers do we have in their seventies and eighties? Who's to say how long our ancestors would have lived if they hadn't died in the war?"

"And Da was killed." Ciara glanced at Rayne, kindly not bringing up Conor's death. It had been natural causes but at such a young age. He hadn't even been forty. "You think Sheila and Don will end up in Grathton Village for real?"

"Sheila won't give up her house unless she's getting a better one, so, what are the McElroy finances like?"

"We can ask Cormac and Maeve. They'll know."

"It's a matter of public record, like, what properties and stuff people own. At least some of it."

"We can also ask Sorcha to research for us."

Sorcha Ketchum was Dr. Ruebens' granddaughter. She worked part-time for her grandfather at the doctor's office and part-time at the castle, helping with the cleaning that came from extra guests. She was a whiz on the computer.

"And Haley McGavin could help too. I can't wait to share our findings with Cormac and the crew."

"Without our team, we would be lost." Ciara glanced at Rayne. "We started this conversation about Landon . . ."

"I'm good." Rayne turned up the radio and they sang the rest of the way home. Each shared experience brought the cousins closer.

While there was loss, there'd been gain as well. They'd be home by seven and she could finish the ivory wedding gown and check out the silk lining on the trunk to mend it.

Rayne's plans for the dress and the lining of the trunk went out the window when there was a crisis at home. One of the sheep was ill and Dafydd rightfully worried she'd lose the lamb she might be carrying.

If it was a sickness, then would the other sheep be at risk? That would be a nightmare as it would severely hinder their spring income.

Not that Rayne knew squat about what to do for the sheep, but she could pitch in with moral support. Personal feelings were all set aside as they focused on the wellbeing of the sheep. Dafydd and Amos were in the barn while the others waited in the kitchen for news.

Cormac went back and forth with updates and strong tea.

"When do we call a veterinarian?" Rayne asked.

"Dafydd knows what he's doing," Ciara assured her. "We just need to follow his lead. Keep the tea coming."

At two in the morning, the sheep passed what would have been a lamb, but it was too soon to save it. Ciara, Cormac, and Rayne joined Amos and Dafydd in the barn now that it was over, and they wouldn't interfere.

"Nature's way," Dafydd said sadly. "It wouldn't have been a healthy lamb."

"The good news," Amos said, "is that it wasn't a sickness that will spread to the others."

Cormac passed out whiskey for them all.

"We'll take all the positive we can get. Well done, Dafydd, and Amos," Cormac said.

Dafydd was an integral part of the McGrath team and during the emergency, he and Ciara had worked together for the good of the flock.

"Slainte," Rayne echoed.

Chapter Eight

Rayne, Blarney, and Ciara walked from the manor house to the cemetery. The Thursday morning trek was brisk and overcast. They had to meet Bobby Fitzroy at eight, when they all would have preferred a slower start. Nobody was especially cheery due to the lack of sleep but at least it wasn't worse.

The mama sheep was alive, and what had happened wouldn't spread to the others.

The fog rolled over the green hills and around the new cemetery on the other side of the street. They reached the church, and the parking lot was empty of cars. Not even the Fitzroy Construction trailer was there. Rayne checked the time on her phone. Eight sharp.

"Bobby isn't here yet," Ciara said. "I could've had another cup of tea."

Just then, Rayne's phone dinged with a notification. She read it and sighed. "Bobby's running a little late." With Aiden's murder, the schedule for Grathton Village cleanup had been thrown off kilter.

"How late?" Ciara asked.

"He didn't say." Rayne nodded toward the cemetery. "Should we see how much work has been done?" They hadn't been here since Tuesday morning, and the tragedy.

"Sure."

The cousins walked in sync. Father Patrick's vehicle was parked behind the church, before his cottage with the small porch and bench seat on a gravel drive.

No caution tape blocked the gate which meant the gardai were done with their investigation of the premises and crime scene.

The metal posts of the cemetery fence shone black with rust on some of the pieces. "I wonder if we should paint this?"

Rayne liked things to be pretty. It was why she wanted to fix the lining of the trunk before sending it over to the third bungalow.

Yesterday while the cousins were in Dublin, Richard and Amos had gotten everything ready, with Aine's help. They were waiting for the trunk, lamps, and possibly the vase. Would a frayed edge in the lid of the trunk bother anybody but her? Probably not, but it wasn't the point.

"It will just get rusted again," Ciara said.

Rayne sighed. Her cousin was more about being practical than dressed up. "Let's take a look at the progress and decide what's next on the list for priorities."

"Okay."

They entered the cemetery, the gate hinges squeaking. Trees created shade as well as outlined paths to walk along the lawn. The first part of the tombstones had been cleaned and the engraved names brushed so they were easier to read.

The Dennehy family had their own section, as did the McGillicuddys and the McElroys. The Walshes were there, as were the Randalls. The O'Briens too.

"Darcy McGillicuddy should be buried here, with the rest of his family," Rayne said. There was a two-foot-tall white picket fence around a large mausoleum that read MCGILLICUDDY. Someone had done a wonderful job.

"Only if there's room for a coffin," Ciara said. "Father Patrick was thinking he'd need to be in the other cemetery. According to the manifest of bodies, this one is full."

"The manifest that Thomas McGrath wasn't on, so how accurate can it be?"

The McGraths, across the street, also had a fancy mausoleum in addition to monumental tombstones. The first ever McGrath to own this land was buried there. Andrew McGrath in 1780.

"It's fantastic how our families have been connected all through the centuries," Rayne said. "In good times, and in bad."

"It's a connection that creates community. I didn't have anything like it when I lived in London. Mam moved around a lot."

Blarney went to the Thomas McGrath headstone where Aiden had been killed. With Fitzroy Construction garden shears. The only reason Rayne wasn't freaking out about meeting Bobby here was because it was like Ciara had said — it would be a very sloppy cleanup after murder, and the gardai hadn't arrested him.

They were focusing on Beetle.

"Come here, pup," Rayne said.

The dog ambled back to her, golden eyes shining, tail swinging. She and Ciara walked to the four-foot-tall headstone. They'd left the grave alone as Bobby had requested. He was interested in testing the age of the stone to see if it matched the date. 1923.

Boot prints and footsteps had created mud around it, but the caution tape was gone. Nothing else was left as a reminder of Aiden's death, other than Rayne's memory.

Which was plenty. She would never forget the handles of the garden shears protruding from Aiden's back. She pulled out the crystal that was still in her pocket and smoothed it between her thumb and forefinger.

"Should we move poor neglected Thomas?" Ciara asked.

"So he can be with the others?" Rayne smoothed the crystal again, the action easing her anxiety. "What if he's over here in the old cemetery for a reason?" She studied the gravestone and read aloud, "Thomas McGrath. 1923." They'd cleaned it but not too hard. There were several spaces with hollows or indents. One was in the upper corner. Bobby had said it might take several times to get the dirt free without damaging the limestone.

"Like because he's illegitimate?" Ciara put her hand in her pocket. "I can see that, especially back in the day. We should right that wrong."

"Our ancestors were willing to die for freedom. Guess it didn't pertain to infidelity, being as they remained primarily Catholic. What other reasons might he have been separated from the rest?" Rayne tilted her head. The tall trees shifted in the breeze, moving the barren fall branches.

"What if he'd been somebody's guilty secret?" Ciara placed her hand on the tombstone. "He died during the Irish Civil War. Brother against brother. He could be an unsung hero."

Blarney howled.

"I guess he likes that one," Rayne said. Thomas McGrath wasn't on Father Patrick's master list, so it was definitely a secret. Hero was better than where her mind had gone. If not a hero, then . . . "What if he's a Protestant?"

Ciara blinked, startled. She started to laugh. "That would be something to hide, all right. But maybe not on the grounds of a Catholic church."

"All right, all right," Rayne said, swallowing her own laughter. "Don't hurt yourself. I wonder how old the other headstones are in this section?"

"Bobby might know how to test them, since he's so interested in history. Our Thomas is dated 1923." Ciara scanned the others around them which were in different stages of aging. "Does it matter?"

"I'm just curious. We could try to match the moss to other moss . . . except that we just cleaned all of the stones, so, maybe not a good idea." Rayne pocketed the crystal. "It's the bane of my existence."

Ciara put her hand over her heart. "And mine, if I'm honest. How about we use that curiosity to figure out how to get the buildings filled with businesses and families?"

Rayne led the way to the rear of the property and the back fence. Though the weeds had been cleared, the trees still needed to be trimmed.

"Doesn't look like Bobby got this done." Ciara patted a tree trunk with a fairy door on it, painted in blue and yellow. The branches were overgrown.

"I hope he can finish quickly. The sooner he's done with the trees, the sooner he can start on the buildings across the street."

"Fitzroy Construction. When we hired Bobby, I bet he wasn't thinking he'd be working on the never-ending project." Ciara shrugged. "Has he texted you with an update for his ETA?"

Rayne had her phone in her hand, just in case. "Nope."

"It's getting cold. Maybe we can go back home to wait. Or, we can go to the Coco Bean and get a chai latte with lavender." Ciara rubbed her tummy. Sinead's latest concoction was her cousin's favorite hot beverage.

"We'll give him five minutes and then, yes. That sounds great." Rayne looked out at the street beyond the black fence and trees. The row of concrete and brick businesses was so sad.

"We will fix you up, Grathton Village," Ciara said.

Rayne looped her arm through Ciara's. "We will."

"Ladies!" Father Patrick called from behind them.

Rayne's heart raced in alarm.

Blarney was at the priest's side.

She hadn't realized the dog had slipped away from them.

"It's so good to see you here." The priest's face was etched with concern. "I'm afraid we have a small problem."

"What is it?" Rayne stepped toward him. "Are you okay?"

Father Patrick shook his head, his palms together before him. "Elizabeth McGillicuddy is up in arms."

"Why?" Ciara stayed at Rayne's side as they neared the troubled priest.

"Darcy's death. She's insisting that something is wrong, but, well, Darcy was ninety and died in his sleep." Father Patrick eyed the clouds before focusing his gaze on them. "She's threatening an investigation which will delay the funeral proceedings for Sunday. I made a special exception to hold the mass on the Lord's Day to accommodate her and the family, coming from Dublin.

We've already put it in the bulletin and on the website."

"I'm sorry . . ." Ciara said.

"Me too." Elizabeth was a powerful, and wealthy, woman. "Can she ask for the medical examiner to have a second look?"

The priest's shoulders quaked. "The problem is that Darcy was already *cremated.* There is no body to examine."

"Oops." Rayne scrunched her nose. Good news was that there was sure to be room for his ashes to be added to the family mausoleum.

Father Patrick held his hands out to his sides. "He wasn't supposed to be cremated in the first place, so I don't know where those wires were crossed."

"Sugar snaps," Rayne said. What a tragic mistake.

"Ms. McGillicuddy is threatening to sue, and she has plenty of money to back her up. It's terrible." Father Patrick's brows drew together. "Terrible. She can't sue the church."

"I'm sorry, Father!" Ciara looked at Rayne with panic that had to be mirrored in her own gray eyes. Could the village be found at fault?

"It's a shame. It wasn't anything that I did wrong, so I am not personally beholden, but Darcy is a member of my congregation, and I know he didn't want to be cremated. I don't believe his soul is in limbo, but he was adamant that he wanted his body to become one with the earth. Ashes to ashes, dust to dust . . ." Father Patrick shook his head.

Blarney leaned against the priest's leg. He patted the dog's head.

Rayne also wanted to help. "What can we do?"

"The funeral home in Kilkenny is responsible, and thank Heaven for that." Father Patrick made the sign of the cross with a heartfelt look of thanks upward. "Grathton Village is not at fault."

"We couldn't take another hit," Ciara said.

Rayne also said a quick prayer of thanks and stepped closer to Ciara.

"Here I've been going on — what are you two doing here this early, anyway?" Father Patrick asked.

"We have a meeting with Bobby Fitzroy. We're trying to arrange a time to finish the project. Trees trimmed, and the fence painted." Rayne glanced at her phone, but there was no update from him.

"He's running late," Ciara said.

"Bobby was being interviewed by the gardai yesterday and seemed very upset. His garden shears were the murder weapon," Father Patrick said.

"We were the ones who found Aiden, remember, Father?" Ciara said.

"Oh, that's right. It seems ages ago, and my mind is a jumble with everything going on. Bobby was here earlier that day to assess what tools would be needed," the priest continued.

"We saw him drive by," Rayne said. That didn't look good for the construction company owner. "He'd donated all of the tools and equipment."

"Those were his personal shears and had his prints on them," Father Patrick clarified.

"But we all wore gloves!" Ciara said.

"It is a mystery," the priest said. "Bobby was here to do his assessment and then left. He swears he didn't go into the cemetery but dropped his trailer off in the parking lot. It was unlocked so anybody could have accessed the tools. It was a good deed."

"That's strange," Rayne mused. She thought back to the parking lot. The Fitzroy trailer was there, but not Bobby, as he'd said. Could he have killed Aiden, left sloppy prints, and then what — panicked?

It didn't make sense.

"Does Bobby even really know Aiden?"

Ciara asked.

"Bobby knew him from when Aiden had had a summer job a long time ago, working for him. He hadn't seen him in well over twenty years."

"What does Garda Williams think?" Rayne asked.

The priest shrugged.

"Garda Lee?" Ciara asked.

"They don't talk to me, not even in the confessional, so don't pry. They go to church in Kilkenny," Father Patrick said. "That's where Garda Lee lives. Garda Williams was asking her about flat rental prices as his lease is up and he wants to move from Cotter."

"We could make him a deal," Rayne said. "That would give our little village onsite protection."

Ciara didn't say no.

Interesting.

"Father, do you know of anyone else who might be interested in moving to Grathton? Or a business that could flourish here?" Ciara asked. "Once the buildings are done, that's the next step for us. We need warm bodies!"

"I'll give it some thought."

"Thank you," Rayne said.

"Let's go back to my house while you wait

for Bobby. Can I interest you in a cup of tea? Dorothy sent over fresh biscuits this morning." Father Patrick rubbed his hands together. "She doesn't come until nine, usually, so these are warm from the oven."

"That sounds great to me," Ciara said. "We can brainstorm ideas."

"Sure," Rayne agreed. "Father Patrick, you are the pulse of the village. You see areas that are wanting. What do you know of the Randalls?"

"They are a good family," the priest said. He led the way through the headstones to the gate. It was open. He stared at it with confusion.

"What's wrong?" Rayne asked.

"I know I closed this," Father Patrick said. "I guess I'll have to lock it though I never thought I would need to do so in this parish."

"Why is that?" Ciara asked.

"Don't get upset." The priest stepped through the gate to the church parking lot. "Sometimes we have vandals in the cemetery playing pranks, especially around All Hallow's Eve."

"Okay . . ." Rayne looked from the priest to Ciara, and back to Father Patrick. The man was being squirrelly.

"This time the prank involved scarecrows

with your names on them. Not a big deal — silly stuff is all." Father Patrick headed toward his little house and made it as far as the edge of the gravel driveway.

Ciara stepped in front of the priest and crossed her arms. "Then why haven't you mentioned it before now?"

"I didn't want to upset you!" Father Patrick eyed the front porch, but Rayne had him hemmed in on the other side of his small car.

"When was this exactly?" Rayne demanded.

"On Halloween." The priest cleared his throat. "And . . . last week."

"What are they, exactly?" Ciara asked.

"Straw figures with your names, that's all." He spread his arms to his sides in a way that said everything would be fine. Relax.

Rayne wasn't buying it. Not that the priest would lie exactly. Would he? "Father? What happened?"

Father Patrick frowned. "It's possible that the scarecrows had been lit on fire."

Rayne didn't like that at all. "We should tell the gardai. We need to find out who is behind this — burning scarecrows with our names goes farther than a prank."

Ciara nodded, her mouth agape.

"I don't know." Blarney stayed at Father

Patrick's side, his tail wagging. Her dog was in the everything would be okay camp, clearly.

"Why shouldn't we complain?" Ciara demanded.

"Who are you protecting?" Rayne asked.

"Nobody!" The priest darted between Ciara and Rayne and reached the bottom step of his porch.

"No offense, Father, but that didn't sound convincing." Rayne couldn't believe her ears. Or her dog.

Father Patrick opened the door of his house. "Let's talk about it over a cuppa. Come on in. Blarney, outside, boy."

Blarney leapt up to the cushioned bench and sprawled over it giving Rayne a doggy grin.

"Dorothy doesn't like for the dog to be in the house, so we compromise. She makes the best biscuits — don't tell that to Mrs. Dennehy, or Mrs. O'Brien." Father Patrick hung his coat on a hook in the foyer.

"We won't." Ciara reached the inside of the tiny sitting area with Rayne at her heels. She had no choice but to follow so close. "Now, spill it."

The interior was just big enough for a love seat, round table with four chairs, and a bookshelf. The kitchen was off to the far wall. Two closed doors led to a bedroom, and a bathroom. The open door showed a small office with a desk and computer.

"Try to remember when you were a wean," Father Patrick said. "These kids are just out of primary really. Not one of the altar boys, but his brother. I'll have a talk with him."

"You're sure he's the culprit?" Rayne asked.

"Pretty sure." Father Patrick didn't quite meet Rayne's gaze.

"What family?" Ciara asked.

The priest busied himself with closing the front door and ushering them to the small kitchen table. He wouldn't answer.

"If it happens again, I want you to tell us, all right?" Rayne unbuttoned her coat. "It feels so overwhelming to try and grow the village when they hate us."

"Nobody hates you," Father Patrick said.

"A burning scarecrow makes me have a different opinion," Ciara said. "They won't get past that I was raised in London and Rayne is an American."

"It's the reason we are cleaning the cemetery in the first place and refurbishing the buildings." Rayne shrugged out of her jacket and placed it over a chair. "We care, blast it."

"About that," Father Patrick said.

"What other news?" Ciara demanded. "You are at our house for a monthly Sunday dinner, and you might have brought these issues up sooner."

Rayne sent Bobby a text that they were visiting with Father Patrick while waiting for him to show up.

"It wasn't the time. Take off your coat, dear." The priest put on the electric kettle, his back to them.

"I can't take any more bad news," Rayne said. She placed her phone on the table.

Ciara unzipped her canvas coat and took it off. It was too bulky to stay put over the rounded back of the chairs. She ended up placing it across her lap.

The priest turned to face them. "All right." He raised his palm. "I got the idea from you ladies, creating the wedding venue. Using rustic to your advantage."

"Okay . . ." Ciara said.

"The majority of pushback you get is about modernization," Father Patrick said. "Is that right?"

"It's a tie between that and Rayne being American, and me, raised in London," Ciara said cautiously.

"Close enough. Hear me out."

Rayne folded her hands over her knee to

keep it from jostling. Was the priest about to share the answer they'd all been praying about?

"I think we should create an eighteenth-century village experience." Father Patrick smiled wide. "The entire village would need to be involved."

Ciara scowled. "They won't go for it. They'll go from burning us as scarecrows to attacking us in person."

Rayne, however, could totally see the idea playing out. Probably the advantage of having a movie star mother and visiting the set often. "Come on, cuz. Let's not rule the idea out."

Chapter Nine

"Rayne McGrath, put that idea in the circular file you were telling me about earlier," Ciara advised. "It would be a lot of work."

"So?" Rayne asked. "If the villagers were behind it, we could get them on our side for once."

"The lads who are burning our likenesses — how do their parents feel about us and our mission to save the village?" Ciara asked the priest.

Father Patrick had turned his back again and busied himself with making tea. When he rounded toward them, he carried a tray with a ceramic pot in a knitted cozy, biscuits, and jam. "Dorothy's berry blend. Shall we?"

He brought the tray to the small table and proceeded to hand them each an empty cup, then saucer, with the accoutrements of small knives for butter and jam.

As they waited for the tea to steep, Rayne cleared her throat. “Father Patrick, you didn’t answer Ciara’s question.”

“Help yourselves to the pastries,” the priest said. “I couldn’t say for sure. Isn’t this a lovely tea cozy? Bronagh knitted it for me.”

“Bronagh Wilson?” Rayne asked. The Irish name was one of her favorites as she liked the soft sound. “That’s Bran’s mother. Bran does not support us. Does she?”

“Yes, she does. Lovely woman. She retired early from An Post where she’d worked for years to take care of her ailing husband.”

“And the husband?” Rayne pressed. “How does he feel about it?”

“Not as supportive.” Father Patrick exhaled. “Donald thinks he would get more services if his farm would be combined with Cotter Village. They are on the edge of the property line.”

“Which is just like Bran,” Ciara said. “Probably trying to take up his Da’s position. Is Donald all right now?”

“He had a stroke but maintains his small property.” The timer went off. Father Patrick removed the tea leaves from the metal container shaped like a sheep. “A few goats and cows. A garden for family veg.”

“What services does he think we lack?”

Rayne asked, genuinely curious. Kilkenny was only twenty to forty minutes away depending on traffic and location. It would be the same for Cotter Village, possibly even farther.

"Emergency medical," Father Patrick said. "Donald feels like waiting for an ambulance from Kilkenny, twenty miles away, is too far."

"I understand that," Rayne said. "What would it take to have an urgent care center here? Maybe we could expand Dr. Ruebens's practice."

"Dr. Ruebens would like to retire," Father Patrick said, "but doesn't have anyone to replace him for those families in need."

"I didn't realize," Ciara said.

Of course, the elderly doctor was in his eighties.

"You'll be at the meeting tonight?" Father Patrick asked.

"Yes," Rayne said.

Ciara nodded.

"Good. Maybe you could bring up the idea of the old-fashioned town and see what the feedback might be," the priest suggested. "If you think it has merit."

"I will do that."

"We own the property and the businesses," Ciara told the priest. "The meeting yesterday with McGavin Property Management was very helpful."

"Of course you do!" Father Patrick said, blowing on the hot liquid in his cup.

"Doesn't that mean we can do what we want?" Rayne asked. "And to heck with Freda Bevan?"

"Doubtful," Father Patrick said. "There are rules for our quaint old villages. Deciding to make this go back in time, shouldn't be a problem. But, it's best to be sure."

"So many questions, so few answers," Ciara said.

A knock sounded on the priest's front door.

"Who could that be?" Father Patrick asked as he stood and crossed the small living room to open it.

"I told Bobby we were here," Rayne said.

Ciara tapped Rayne's hand. "I never thought you of all people would want to mire Grathton Village in the past. Aren't you for modernization?"

"True, but I'm also for saving Grathton." Rayne applied berry jam to her biscuit and bit the corner. "This is really good." How to convince the McElroys to open a storefront?

"Bobby!" Father Patrick widened the door. "We were just having tea. Why don't you join us? I'll get an extra cup."

Blarney peeked into the room, spotted Rayne, and melded back to his position on the bench.

"If it's no bother." Bobby entered and removed his gloves. His hands were chapped from work and weather, and his sturdy work boots clomped inside. Jeans and a canvas jacket completed his ensemble.

"Hi," Rayne said.

"Ladies. Sorry I was late. It's been a helluva morning." Bobby's cheeks flushed. "Sorry, Father."

"No big deal. These biscuits and jam are excellent." Ciara lifted hers with a happy smile.

"I'd like to continue with trees today," Bobby said.

"We want that as well," Rayne agreed.

"The gardai were questioning you?" Ciara asked bluntly. "About Aiden's death?"

Bobby shrugged out of his coat and hung it on a coat hook by the door. "Yes, that's so. As if I'd be daft enough to leave my own shears in Aiden's back."

"That's what we thought," Ciara concurred.

"It looks bad, though," Rayne said.

"The problem is that I was on the grounds earlier." Bobby crossed the small room. He took off his cap, stuffed it in his back pocket, and mussed his graying, shaggy hair. His brows were as gray. "They've got me on CCTV and all that. I turned in my dash-cam as well. I have no secrets."

"We saw you," Ciara said.

"Why were you there?" Rayne asked. "Was it really to see what tools were needed?"

"Right. I was excited by the grave of Thomas McGrath, if you must know." Bobby accepted a mug and sat down on the love seat. "Thanks."

Father Patrick gestured to the lazy Susan with the accoutrements. "Cream and sugar, if you like."

"Thank you," Bobby said.

"It's good that we are here together to get to the bottom of what happened to Aiden," the priest said solemnly. "He was an altar boy once upon a time."

"Why excited?" Rayne asked, returning to the subject. Why had Aiden been killed over their ancestor's grave?

"It shouldn't have been there." Bobby slurped his tea, drinking it dark. "And when I asked Father Patrick, he agreed with me."

The priest nodded. "Not anywhere on the manifest."

Rayne recalled how Bobby had repeated that over and over. "We were wondering if maybe Thomas was illegitimate or something, so wasn't allowed in with the rest of the family."

"Or if Thomas had a falling out with the others over something. Possibly religion," Bobby said, picking up Rayne's trail of thought when she'd suggested Protestant. "I wanted to study the headstone itself to see if it was rounded or had details that might give me a clue to its real age."

"According to my records," Father Patrick said, "that section of graves was filled in around one hundred years ago, but it is not a hard fact. People weren't thinking that they'd need more room to plan a cemetery for the future. It started with a few plots outside the church and grew from there."

"I see that, all over Ireland," Rayne said.

"We have a lot of churches and a lot of graves that weren't properly marked." Bobby sounded enthusiastic about it rather than upset. "It's a hobby of mine to research and identify what I can to share with a local website."

"Would you know someone who could help us with it in an official capacity?" Rayne asked.

"Yes." Bobby slurped his tea again. "It's why I was here early Tuesday morning before Aiden arrived. I took pictures of the headstone to share with my group. He wasn't here."

"What time was that?" Rayne asked.

Ciara leaned forward to watch Bobby as she sipped from her cup.

"Six that morning."

"Why so bleedin' early?" Ciara blurted.

Bobby chuckled. "I have many specialty jobs around this area. I have a lantern that allows perfect vision in the dark, so it wasn't a problem. If I didn't find a workaround for weather and daylight, I'd be homebound for half the winter." He gave a horrified expression.

Rayne cupped her tea in her palm, the aroma soothing. "We saw your construction truck around seven thirty, though, not six. I don't get up that early for anyone."

Bobby's gaze hardened. "I drive all over this area doing small jobs from painting to landscape. Dropped off my trailer here at the church at six. Delivered paint to a crew out west, and was back by half past six, when I took pictures of Thomas McGrath's grave. Time-stamped, six thirty. Aiden wasn't there." He showed Rayne his phone. "I went to fill up the truck at the petrol station, got coffee and chatted with the clerk. Had a delivery for trim at seven, and must've been on my way for a second cup when you spotted me. I've shared this with the gardai."

"What were you looking for?" Rayne wasn't sure she believed that Bobby was there just to study a grave. It was good that the police knew about it.

"What do you know of the War of Independence?" Bobby countered. "The Irish Civil War?"

"A little." Rayne took a bite of biscuit. Dorothy was indeed a master for her pastries and jams. "Some of our ancestors died for Ireland's freedom."

"Thank God for them," Bobby said. "There was a rumor of men in Grathton Village who wanted Ireland's freedom at any cost. Possibly from the eighteen hundreds."

"Oh?" Ciara perked up. "Like a secret society?"

"That is very cloak and dagger." Father Patrick's brow arched. "There have been many secret societies in our history. It's been a bloody battle between brothers. North and the Republic. Thank God for peace."

Rayne nodded as Ciara and Bobby did too.

"Peace is something we have thanks to our heroes. They weren't always considered heroes, and some were wanted by the law," Bobby said.

"I guess the winner in a battle would depend on the side that you're on." Rayne's cup was empty. For every winner there had to be a loser.

Father Patrick brought the teapot around again to top off their cups with more steaming brew. "Do you know who these men were?"

"No. They were all sworn to secrecy and to mention names meant instant death. They took an oath to put the Republic of Ireland above personal cost." Bobby sighed, his gaze faraway. "Can you imagine such dedication to a cause?"

"Yes," Rayne said."It's what we are trying to preserve here. Ciara, do you remember the museum curator who gave us the tour of Dublin Castle?"

"Of course. She was a hoot."

"Well, she mentioned the Knights of the Order of Saint Patrick." Rayne sipped her tea. "They weren't a secret society, but they stood for protecting Ireland's interests."

"Under Britain's thumb," Bobby said. His mouth twisted.

"What was the name of the society that you were thinking about?" Ciara asked Bobby.

"I've asked around plenty, believe me, and what I've discovered in common is the symbol of the shamrock on an inverted crown." Bobby set his cup on the floor at his feet. "It's believed that there were four men involved in this group."

"And you wonder if Thomas McGrath was a member?" Rayne asked. She recalled the mountains of photos they had in the trunk. Searching through it became a priority, to see if they could find his name somewhere.

"Possibly. What do you know of him?" Bobby asked.

"Nothing," Ciara said. "Father Patrick?"

"Let me peruse my records for the family," Father Patrick said. "It seems important to find out why Thomas McGrath ended up here."

"The timing is right," Bobby said with excitement. "1923."

"Can you imagine if Thomas McGrath was a hero?" Rayne's father would have been so proud.

"Or worse, not a hero," Ciara shuddered. "Think about it — what if he'd committed a war crime of some kind and that's why he wasn't included in the family mausoleum?"

"Either way." Bobby sounded wistful.

"Uh, I'd prefer hero, please," Rayne said.

"Me too, honestly," Ciara said.

"I'd like to investigate the headstone further, if you don't mind." Bobby tipped his mug toward the priest. "Father thought it would be a courtesy for me to ask you both first. It is on public land."

"Actually, the cemetery is on private land." Father Patrick's forehead furrowed. "What you're looking for might be harmful to the McGrath name when the ladies are doing their pure best to bring the village around. I'm not certain it's a grand idea."

Rayne wondered the same. Was it possible that Bobby had been taking photos of the grave, and had been interrupted by Aiden, so had killed him?

"The McGraths have a stellar reputation for bravery in our community," Ciara said. "And always have. I'd hate to dig deeper and discover that there was a black sheep in the family."

"Every family has them. Why should yours be any different?" Bobby's mouth twisted with censure.

"That isn't what I meant." Ciara's shoulders hiked.

"We have plenty of black sheep," Rayne said. "And a lot that we don't know. It would be great if you could help us learn more. But, let's put the headstone aside until after the New Year and focus on filling the buildings to revive the village. Thomas isn't going anywhere."

Father Patrick asked, "Do you have any suggestions, Bobby?"

Bobby considered this. "We could use another restaurant."

"I think so too," Ciara said.

"It would be nice to have other options besides the pubs, the café, and the diner," Father Patrick agreed.

"I would love a good Asian-fusion option," Rayne said.

Ciara tapped her fingernails to her teacup. "Bobby, we have two apartment buildings with twenty flats each that might be ready to find renters for. If you don't mind checking them out, I can send you the addresses. We would hire you for any of the construction needed."

"Not at all." Bobby ate a bite of biscuit. "Thanks."

"What does Colleen do for work?" Rayne asked.

"Colleen Randall?" Bobby's face clouded.

"Yes — do you know her?"

He shrugged.

"Well?" Ciara asked.

"I was friends with her mam in school. Her and Bronagh were in the same year.

Connie was brilliant, so it was no surprise Colleen went to Dublin for university. And now, well, Corrine is the spitting image of them both."

"Did you know her fiancé?" Rayne asked.

"What fiancé?" Bobby drank his tea.

"Corrine's dad."

"Never did," Bobby said.

"I guess he died in a car accident," Father Patrick said. "Colleen's been home from Dublin for almost five years now."

Bobby's gaze softened with empathy. "Oh."

"What?" Rayne asked.

"Well, I heard that Corrine's dad might be Aiden Dennehy." Bobby's face turned red with rage. "If it was true? I don't blame Beetle one single bit for killing him."

Chapter Ten

Rayne wished that Bobby's fingerprints weren't on the murder weapon of the garden shears in Aiden's back.

He had a quiet affection for Colleen's mother, Connie, and was definitely steering the blame toward Beetle, just as Sheila had done. Was he guilty himself of murder? He seemed too intelligent for that.

Who would set the construction company owner up?

Why was Beetle such an easy scapegoat?

"What are you saying?" Father Patrick asked in a shocked tone.

"We heard that same thing from Sheila Martinet yesterday, so maybe not that big of a secret if we've all heard the rumor," Rayne said.

"I didn't," Father Patrick said. "Colleen's fiancé was killed in an accident in Dublin and so she came home to Grathton Village to raise her babe."

"At the same time as Beetle?" Rayne asked.

"Perhaps around that," Father Patrick said.

Would Beetle have given up his rockstar career to support his pregnant but alone sister?

It would be in keeping with the man she'd come to know across the bar counter. They would need to find out more from Nolan and Sheila if Beetle himself proved to be not forthcoming with information.

Rayne didn't see the man as a killer, but he did love his sister.

Bobby stood, bringing his empty cup to the small sink. He rinsed it and put it aside before walking toward the front door. "What are the instructions for the day?"

"As you had suggested, trim the trees," Rayne said. "Tomorrow, we can discuss refurbishing the buildings by the cemetery."

Bobby nodded and walked across the living room.

"Nice to see you, Bobby," Father Patrick said.

"And you all. If I think of any other business ideas, I'll let you know." Bobby put his hand on the doorknob. "And please let me know when I'm allowed to look at the headstone."

The emphasis Bobby put on allowed let them know he wasn't happy with the decision.

The construction company owner jammed his cap back on, grabbed his jacket, and left.

Silence filled the tiny home as they waited, hearing bootsteps on the porch and then gone.

"We should buy a lock for the cemetery gate," Ciara said.

"I hate to agree," Father Patrick said. "But you're right."

"Do you want me to go with you?" Rayne offered. "Or Amos could go — we should get a sturdy one."

"I'll call Amos and arrange it later," Father Patrick said. "I have a few other things to pick up at the hardware store."

"Do you believe that Bobby is innocent?" Rayne asked.

Father Patrick immediately started to say yes but then slowed his agreement to a maybe. "I didn't know he had feelings for Colleen's mother, Connie. She is a married woman still, even if her husband works in Kilkenny."

"As a mechanic," Rayne said.

"Obviously, Bobby's feelings for Connie don't matter in this situation." Ciara shrugged. "The Randalls are still married, even if they are all three miserable."

"Ciara!" Father Patrick said.

"Sorry." Ciara shrugged.

"You know, you never answered what Colleen did for work," Rayne said.

"She helps at the preschool where Corrine goes," the priest replied. "Also, at the Sheep's Head. Why?"

"We need businesses to fill those buildings," Ciara said. "We are hoping to improve the lot of our own villagers first."

"Dorothy's jam is delish," Rayne said.

"Would she be interested in a storefront?" Ciara asked.

"I can ask," Father Patrick said. "She is here once or twice a day. Well, her or her daughters. I'm a fortunate man. Shauna comes on the weekends to help at the church as does Olivia."

Rayne's phone rang. "It's Don."

"Answer! Ask if he still wants to rent a space."

Nodding at Ciara, Rayne answered, "Rayne McGrath speaking."

"Hi! It's Don McElroy."

"Hey Don."

"Do you have time today to talk about the building rental? I'm still keen to let a space. Me and Paddy will go together on it."

"Instead of Aiden?"

"Well, obviously," Don said.

Ciara cracked up — silently.

"It would be the mobile phone store?"

"Yes."

"I think that can be arranged. When would you like to get together?"

"I'm in the area right now," Don said. "Will you meet me behind the cemetery?"

"Sure. I have Ciara with me." And Blarney, in case Don turned out to be a murderer.

"That's fine. Paddy is staying with his grandparents, Murray and Olivia, so is only a few minutes away. I'll have him join us."

"See you in ten minutes," Rayne said.

Ciara and Rayne cleaned up their mugs and saucers, as well as Bobby's, and set the dishes in the dish rack to dry.

"Thank you, Father. Let us know about the McElroy jam franchise, would you?" Rayne said with a smile.

"I will — take care, ladies. Good luck tonight at the town meeting."

They left and Blarney joined them for the walk around the cemetery.

Ciara peered around the street. "Where's Bobby's truck?"

"Or Bobby?" Rayne had expected to see the business owner trimming trees as he planned to finish this project today in order to start the painting tomorrow. He had a crew to help, and he hoped to knock it out over the weekend.

There were five independent stone buildings. Behind them was the row of houses and adjoined townhouses for possible rentals. Two apartment buildings with forty flats.

How to fill the village?

How did one go about advertising for new businesses to grow what was failing here? Haley McGavin had suggested creating an ad targeting digital nomads. Folks in the tech industry.

Did Father Patrick's idea of making this a living history village make sense? It went against anything modern.

It wasn't a bad idea and would give Grathton something unique to bring people to — a reason to stop on the tourist tour.

Being close to Dublin was a bonus though they weren't on the coast and as Sheila pointed out, ruins were everywhere in Ireland so hardly unique.

"He probably had to go to his shop. What does someone need to cut trees and trim hedges?"

"I wouldn't know." Rayne's ears perked at the sound of a car coming toward them. "That must be Don."

A black newer vehicle with silver trim arrived and Don climbed out behind the wheel while Paddy O'Brien exited from the passenger's side.

Don, conservative in looks, was even more bland next to Paddy, who had bleached hair ala Billy Idol — he even wore leather pants and a jacket. Don's McElroy nose was prominent.

"Thanks for meeting us here." Paddy jammed his hands into his pocket, rather than offer them in greeting.

"Hi," Don said. His jacket was brown wool. His slacks were also brown, but he had on black dress shoes and a tie.

"Did you just come from work?" Rayne asked, nodding at the tie.

"I go in at eleven," Don said. "Paddy is between jobs."

Rayne swallowed her retort. He'd been at the dairy on Monday. Maybe he didn't want anything steady.

Ciara elbowed Rayne discreetly probably just as curious as to when the last time Paddy had held a job was — well, to be fair, he could work at a pub without a problem. Heaven help the O'Briens if he was also a musician.

Paddy scowled at Don. "Thanks?" He smiled at Rayne and Ciara, exuding charm that Don lacked. "I can pour a Guinness with the best of them but I'm hoping for a change of direction in my career. You know, something during the day."

"Why is that?" Ciara asked.

"My girlfriend is a dentist, and I'd like to match my hours with hers if possible."

"A dentist?" Rayne asked.

"How long has she been practicing?" Ciara asked.

Don touched his jaw with a wince. "Got a filling last month and it didn't hurt a bit. I have some dental anxiety, but she was great."

Rayne said, "We should add that career to our list."

"I can ask her if she feels like branching out on her own, but she's got a sweet thing going right now," Paddy said.

"Not good if she moved and then the village went arseways," Don said. He studied the row of businesses that could use sprucing up.

"True." Paddy went to the first one and rocked back on his heels, shading his eyes to look upward. Each standalone was three stories high but narrow. "Solid bones. Stone isn't crumbling but could use a wash and paint."

"That's what we thought too. Bobby will

be around to confirm that. We are thinking white paint with navy blue trim."

"Better than bland stone," Don said. "Businesses on the bottom, or all the way up?"

"We haven't decided. Bobby would like to have the paint complete this weekend. When would you want to begin?"

"December first is fine with me," Don said. "I'll be splitting my time between the store in Kilkenny and here."

"And I'll be full time," Paddy said. "What's the cost?"

"Ciara and I will need to run numbers on our end, but we can give you the first month free of charge if you sign a twelve-month lease."

Ciara nodded. "In exchange, we'd like you to spread the word."

Rayne glanced at Ciara before asking, "What would you think of making this place an old village for tourists to come and experience life two hundred years ago?"

"Not a fit for us, and our mobile phone shop," Paddy said immediately.

"Good point," Ciara said.

"You aren't doing that, are you?" Don asked. "I couldn't sign a lease if that was the plan. Not smart."

So, Don had a business brain.

Rayne had to agree with him. "It was an idea brought up by someone in the village but it would have some drawbacks."

"I can't rent here if that's the case," Don said.

"I thought I'd ask is all." Rayne kept her smile in place.

"I agree that what we have here in Grathton Village is unique," Paddy said. "I've traveled around the world as a bassist for hire. I can see the appeal of all this history."

"What? You have always complained that this is a place to keep in your rearview," Don said.

"I'm older now," Paddy said. "Forty. It would be grand to find a way to combine old and new. Not sure that the old village is the way to go."

"It isn't," Don said firmly.

Ciara laughed. "You two sound like me and Rayne."

"Have you traveled, Don?" Rayne asked.

"I've been to London a few times," Don said. "I never had the wanderlust to go farther than Ireland really. We have such variety in our country. Going to the coast is like being in another land."

"Bogger," Paddy said fondly. "That sounds like GrandDa going on about the lovely green hills of Ireland."

"Mine wax on too. We've been rooted to this earth for centuries. Just as long as you McGraths." Don adjusted his tie.

"We noticed that in the cemetery — the Walshes, McElroys, Randalls, McGillicuddys . . ." Rayne said. She trailed off when the last name caught Paddy off guard, and he started to cough.

"Okay?" Don patted his friend on the back.

"Yeah." Paddy ruffled his spiked hair. "Darcy's funeral is on Sunday. GrandDa is upset about it is all. Spent the morning mooning over being old. Then Grandma was out of sorts about Elizabeth being around."

"Why?" Rayne asked.

"Hard to fathom that they were all so young and good looking once upon a time," Paddy grimaced. "GrandDa and Elizabeth were an item before Gran swooped him up." He shuddered.

Don laughed. "I've seen pictures of them all in their youth. It's true but hard to believe. You think we'll look back at these days? Remember when you and Aiden . . ."

Paddy's eyes welled. "Poor bloke," he said.

"Aiden will forever be handsome. Never get older," Don said. "We've got to find out who killed our friend."

Paddy turned to Rayne and Ciara. "I heard the gardai suspect Beetle? And that they were sniffing around Bobby. What do you know?"

"Not more than that." Rayne patted Blarney's head.

They shared a moment of mutual sorrow for Aiden Dennehy.

"It seems wrong to laugh," Don said. "Or carry on with our days as if he wasn't gone." His phone rang. "Sheila."

"You didn't waste time there," Paddy complained.

"We've been off and on for a year," Don said. "Aiden knew about it."

"Sure, he did." Paddy snorted. "Who will argue with you now?"

"He treated Sheila like crap," Don protested. "You know it."

"Yeah. Aiden never met a woman he didn't like." Paddy scuffed the street with his boot. "Well, we should go. I am not sure about the village tourist idea. It could work but it would be difficult."

"Thanks for keeping an open mind," Ciara said, tongue in cheek.

"Let's touch base on Monday after the buildings are repainted," Rayne said. "We should know by then."

"Deal." Don pocketed his phone.

"See you birds later," Paddy said.

The men got into the car.

"Interesting pair. You think they will make it work?" Ciara asked.

"People probably say the same about us," Rayne said.

"True."

The sound of a work truck slowly made its way down the street toward them.

"Bobby at last."

Chapter Eleven

Rayne, Ciara, and Bobby spent an hour discussing paint colors and what repairs to do to make the buildings presentable and safe.

For all Bobby's confidence that he was cooperating with the gardai, Rayne could tell the man was nervous. She didn't blame him. She just hoped he wasn't guilty.

The cousins next helped Bobby with the trees.

At noon, Bobby laughed. "Ladies. I mean this in the nicest way — but you are slow, and my crew will go much faster if you go home for lunch and stay there."

Rayne was affronted at first but soon joined Ciara in laughing.

"No offense taken," Ciara said.

"You are both hard workers, and I can attest to that. It's skill I need though." Bobby doffed his cap in respect. "Ta."

Rayne, Ciara, and Blarney, walked back to

the castle where lunch would be served at twelve thirty.

Amos was on the steps with Richard and Dafydd. The guys had seen Rayne and Ciara walking down the lane and waited for them.

"Hi!" Rayne said. "Are you out here because something is wrong, or just being friendly? I hope it's friendly."

Ciara nodded. "We were just politely fired from our volunteer construction jobs."

Amos laughed. "The only disaster this morning is one of the horses catching a rock in his hoof — easily fixed."

"Several sheep strayed off, but I was able to find them before they reached the road," Dafydd said. "Good news there. The sheep from last night has made a full recovery. When can we talk fencing?"

"Not until the spring," Ciara said. "We can't afford it. Richard?"

"Everything is done except for the trunk. Not a problem at all."

In fact, Richard had a dab of paint on his cheek that Rayne kept quiet about. "Good job then everyone." Her stomach rumbled, to the amusement of her coworkers.

Dafydd tried to take Ciara's hand, but she kept them in her pockets. "Bobby will be finished with the tree trimming today at the cemetery and start the businesses tomorrow."

Ciara skipped up the stone steps.

Cormac opened the door for them.

They all went inside. The foyer had a round table with a bouquet of fall flowers. Maeve knew how much Rayne and Ciara loved them.

They all veered to the right and took turns washing up in the downstairs bath before filing into the dining room.

Maeve, Aine, Frances, and Cormac joined them to eat a meal of sandwiches and carrot and lamb soup. Rayne and Ciara each took an end of the dining room table. Amos sat next to Rayne, and Dafydd next to Ciara, with the others filling in around the table.

"How's your day been?" Amos asked.

"Busy — you?" Rayne looked at Amos, admiring the lines of his strong jaw and nose. His blue eyes studied her with frank approval.

"Also busy. I love this time of year, though, where we get to harvest what we've sewn. It's a tangible reward for our efforts." His tone was low and rumbling, affecting her on a physical level.

Amos, since he was the grounds manager, was in charge of outdoor activities while

Cormac, and Maeve, managed the indoor ones. It took an entire team to run the day-to-day at the castle. Then, they had the MPM company to deal with the village.

Rayne had learned to appreciate each person for their skills. Aine, also her apprentice in the wedding gown biz, was the seamstress for the castle. At nineteen, almost twenty, she radiated positive vibes and unflagging energy.

Each person here, even Richard their handyman, played a role in their success, or, she gulped, failures. Rayne and Ciara had taken Uncle Nevin's books apart to find out how to cut back on expenses though he really ran a tight ship.

"I like knowing that our vegetables come from our own land. Can't get more organic than that." Rayne finished her soup. Organic was a Hollywood buzz word, but also worked in the Blue Zone areas that had people who lived longer, healthier, lives.

"Healthy living," Amos said.

"It's why we have so many octogenarians in our village," Rayne said. "I'd love to use that as a lure to get new, younger professionals. Haley, from MPM, suggested marketing to the digital nomads. It seems Dublin is having a tech boom. Being under two hours away is a big deal."

"On the other hand, Father Patrick thinks we should consider turning Grathton into a tourist destination as a place to experience the eighteenth century in an all-encompassing way." Ciara looked at everyone before she settled on Cormac and Maeve. "What do you think?"

"Aren't we trying to modernize?" Cormac said.

"Yes," Rayne said. "We would need to be outwardly historic. Would being inwardly techno forward be against the rules of authentic eighteen hundreds?"

"I'm not sure," Maeve said, her brow furrowed.

"I don't like the idea," Frances said. "Not that you asked me. I think the wedding venue with the tower is quaint enough. Can you imagine the cost of trying to go backwards? What would we have? Horse and buggies instead of cars?"

Rayne nodded, not surprised by Frances's cross opinion. The woman could cook though, so she didn't mind her outbursts.

"I agree with Frances," Amos said. "We lost a lot of our youth to bigger cities because they wanted amenities."

Rayne gave another nod. She had felt the same way. She still did.

However, it was up to her and Ciara to

save Grathton from being lost and forgotten. Making it a tourist destination could be its saving grace.

"I hear what you're saying," Rayne said.

"We need to examine all the options," Ciara continued. "Discover what could bring the most income into Grathton."

"We promised Father Patrick to check with the council tonight to see if it was something that was even possible." Rayne sipped her water. "It might be a moot point."

"You are the bosses," Dafydd said. "Just say no."

"But what if it's the golden ticket and we just don't want to acknowledge that it would mean going backward?" Ciara asked in a very serious tone.

Dafydd frowned at Ciara in response.

Rayne knew it was more than just a simple disagreement over the future of the village, but more to do with their future as husband and wife. Dafydd should have been honest with Ciara from the start.

She looked at Amos, who sent her a smile that made her stomach flutter.

"How's your schedule for a cup of coffee at my place?" Amos asked.

"I wish I could say today, but I have a meeting with Sinead about the wedding cake for Lenni and Pete's wedding, then I've got to work on the dress, fix the silk lining in the trunk, and then the council meeting tonight." Rayne was exhausted just sharing her plans.

"What about tomorrow?" Amos brought his knuckle next to her arm. An accidental touching of skin?

Rayne mentally ran through her to-do list for Friday. If she got everything else done today, she could clear time in the afternoon. "Well, I might be able to meet you for happy hour instead. Say four? The wedding party doesn't come in until Saturday morning."

"Deal!"

She grinned and then bowed her head. Happy hour with Amos was a plan she anticipated.

"When should we move the trunk?" Amos asked.

"I'll get in there to work on the lining today and tomorrow so it should be good in the afternoon. I need to be on call for Bobby if he has questions regarding the buildings but he's an expert." Hopefully not a killer. "Hey, how well do you know Colleen Randall?"

"Pretty good," Amos said. "Why?"

"I would love to help her succeed. Father Patrick said she works part-time at the preschool that Corrine attends and sometimes at the Sheep's Head to help Beetle."

"What if she's already happy?" Richard said, overhearing their conversation. "Not everybody wants a career while raising their weans."

Rayne nodded at Richard. "You're right. I'd hate to interfere. Would it be rude to find out if she'd be interested in running her own business?"

"I can ask. We talk after church a lot." Richard tapped the table. "Amos, let me know when you're ready to move that trunk. It will take us both, even with a dolly."

"I will," Amos said.

"Colleen likes to knit," Richard said. "She always has yarn and needles in her bag. She said she learned while she was pregnant, and it soothes her. She offered to teach me, but men don't knit." His cheeks flushed.

"They do so!" Aine said. "Gerard Butler knits. I would rather sew."

Richard ate his sandwich without further comment.

Rayne asked, "How is Beetle doing?"

"Not good. He's worried because the gardai keep coming up with reasons he might have killed Aiden." Richard drained his water glass.

"Could Beetle be responsible?" Rayne

watched Richard closely.

"No, of course not. He's a decent man." Richard shook his head emphatically.

Ciara dipped her roll into her soup. "Do you know who Corrine's dad is?"

Richard shrugged. "A guy she was engaged to who died in a car accident. It's why she came back to Grathton after university in Dublin."

The same information that Father Patrick had.

Rayne and Ciara exchanged a look and mutually decided not to bring up the possibility that Aiden was the lass's father.

It could ruin Colleen's reputation and that wasn't worth it — for now. Unless . . . well, Rayne put that aside to focus on those around the table.

"Is there anything we should know before our first town council meeting tonight?" Rayne asked.

"Yeah," Ciara said. "I am not into politics."

"I would observe," Maeve suggested.

"For the first time," Aine agreed.

"But you must be prepared to fend off questions regarding the direction of the village. I'd bring up the population of Grathton Village as well as the projected income for the year," Cormac advised. "You have the information from MPM as well. Let the others know you want to make this a thriving community once again."

"It's been seventy years," Frances chortled. "Moving the highway took us off the main thoroughfare."

"That would have been the death knell," Ciara said sadly. "I wonder how our ancestors handled it?"

"The McGraths have always been self-sufficient and one to buck the normal trends," Cormac said. "We will stay the course."

"I like that." Ciara nodded at Cormac.

"Me too!" Rayne said.

"I will run the property assessment by after lunch," Amos said. "And then head to the hardware store in Kilkenny with Father Patrick to purchase a lock for the cemetery gate."

"I should bring the maps from the land registry office, but I've got to print them out," Rayne said.

"We have printer paper," Cormac said. "I can help."

"Thanks, Cormac." Rayne's pulse sped and she waved her fingers before her face as if they were a fan.

"I heard that Darcy McGillicuddy was cremated at the funeral home in Kilkenny,"

Maeve said in a curious tone.

"So?" Richard asked.

"He wasn't supposed to be." Maeve shook her head.

"No!" Frances said. "Oh no."

"Elizabeth McGillicuddy is out for blood. She called here looking for Father Patrick. The priest must be avoiding her, poor man." Maeve finished her soup and dropped her napkin over her dish.

"We heard," Ciara said.

"I feel awful for Father Patrick but he is not responsible so I don't see why Elizabeth would want him to do something," Maeve said.

"She's an entitled rich Irish woman," Frances opined. "I knew her when I was younger when she would sometimes return to the McGillicuddy property from Dublin."

"She's a lovely lady," Maeve said. "If prickly."

"Barbed," Frances said.

The pot calling the kettle black. "Is the McGillicuddy property as grand as this?"

"No, love," Maeve said. "Nothing in Grathton is as grand as this. And it always got under Elizabeth's skin. She married and moved to Dublin and never looked back."

"But kept her maiden name?"

"It has more historical power than her

British husband's, so yes," Maeve said. "I respect a woman who knows her mind. I don't respect how she dismisses others who she considers beneath her. We are all equal in God's eyes."

"That's true," Ciara said.

Everyone agreed with Maeve.

On that cheery note, lunch was over, and the staff split to their different directions. Rayne, to visit Sinead about the wedding cake, and Ciara, to help in the kitchen. Rayne noticed that her cousin avoided Dafydd.

That evening at six, after an early dinner with the others, Rayne and Ciara drove to Cotter Village where the town council meeting was being hosted. Each quarter, one of the four villages would hold the gathering.

Luckily, Uncle Nevin had hosted the quarter before so it wouldn't be their turn for another eight months.

Just six months until Rayne and Ciara had to prove that the village was in the black and decide their futures.

Rayne had the idea of returning to America with Ciara running the castle. Or, maybe Rayne would be more hands on. It meant the world that Ciara had agreed to share the responsibility with her.

They were playing phone tag with Fionagh Quinn.

Could it work if she split her time between LA and Grathton? She had dual citizenship, so it wasn't out of the question, legally.

Emotionally? Rayne really didn't know and that was why she kept putting the decision off.

Ciara parked the Fiat before a modern white office building with lovely landscaping and a smooth, paved parking lot.

While the main street through Grathton seemed deserted, Main Street in Cotter Village had been recently redone. There were clear lines on the cement road while the one through Grathton was gone.

Streetlamps illuminated the area. It just seemed a nicer, more exciting place — like the neighborhood was newer somehow though it had been started in 1800.

All the old buildings had either been painted white or torn down for new. The cars were newer too.

Rayne decided to study every detail for anything she might be able to use for Grathton's sake.

"Freda Bevan has two thousand villagers in Cotter," Rayne said as they left the car. "Are we doing our people a disservice by not offering them this?"

"If they want it, they can move," Ciara replied in a curt tone. "Don't tell me you're being swayed by these bright lights?"

2,000 to 465.

"No, ma'am." They entered the front door to a lobby. It was as white as a hospital interior and about as welcoming.

Freda opened a door to a generic meeting room that could be any corporate gathering space in the world.

Rayne would rather have her decrepit brick than this bland façade. Freda's bright yellow cardigan sweater over orange pants missed the fashion mark for simply atrocious.

Her bright pink lipstick and gaudy blue eye shadow added insult to injury.

"Rayne and Ciara!" Freda called. "Welcome!"

Rayne hadn't forgotten Freda's remarks about absorbing Grathton into Cotter — she'd made no bones about her desire to take them over.

Well, it would happen over Rayne's dead body. The McGraths were fighters. Her kin had died for Ireland's freedom.

"Come on in, and meet everyone," Freda said. "That way you can stop sneaking around. Silly cailin."

"I haven't been," Rayne insisted.

They entered the meeting room.

A long table that seated six people on either side took center stage. What was Freda talking about? A man who had bright red hair and brilliant blue eyes stood and held out his hand.

"Hello! I'm Berny Fincher, councilman of Westford. Nice to finally meet you both. The rumor mill, depending on who was talking, had you as demons or goddesses." The red-haired man winked. "Just so you know."

A woman about sixty-five, with grayish white hair and aqua blue glasses, scooted her office chair back with a smile. "Damned rumors. You look lovely and capable to me." She fluttered her fingers and cast a wry glance toward Freda. "I'm Dania Louis-Smith, councilwoman for Hinsdale. Our tiny village is holding strong at a thousand."

"That's twice of us," Ciara lamented.

"Nice to meet you." Rayne waved.

"I'm LuLu Sneed," a British accented voice at the other end said.

Rayne turned to see a woman with dark skin and hair — tall, and glamorous, with a turban over her head.

"Hi!"

"I'm the councilwoman for Kendalport. Our village has eight hundred people."

"Which leaves me," a garbled male voice said.

Rayne shifted her attention to the other side of the table, halfway expecting a gnome from the tone alone.

"Hi." Rayne leaned her shoulder to Ciara's.

"I'm Mickael Warbington. Been on the council for Pickstone in some way or another for forty years."

It looked like it. Again, Rayne attributed the length of life for the villagers to being on farms and healthy living. She pegged him to be in his nineties.

"We have seven hundred and seventy-eight folks in our village."

"We are here to learn," Rayne said. "Four hundred and sixty-five."

Applause rounded the table.

"Ha!" Freda remarked loud enough over the clapping.

"Please come in, come in," LuLu said.

Rayne and Ciara took seats. There was no way Rayne would remember everyone's names so she created a cheat sheet with people's initials on her phone.

Surprisingly, the others were informative and helpful, though Rayne never let her guard down around Freda.

The meeting was almost over when Ciara

brought up the idea from Father Patrick about making the entire village of Grathton a historic tourist stop.

"What do you think?" Rayne asked, looking at them all one by one.

Freda snickered.

Mickael turned and arched a brow. "What is it, Freda?"

"Go for it," Freda enthused, her hand to her stomach.

"Why?" LuLu demanded.

"Yes, Freda dear," Dania said, looking over the rims of her glasses at the councilwoman from Cotter Village. "Be clear as to what you mean?"

"Well," Freda said.

"Yes?" Berny echoed the impatient sentiment around the table as they all wanted to go home and think about the fate of their villages. Maintenance was paramount for all of them in some way.

Rayne and Ciara looked at one another.

"I think they should do it." Freda brushed her fingernails to her collar, acknowledging the others and snubbing the cousins.

"We are right here." Rayne said.

Freda turned in her chair to face them. "I want you to fail in a big way. I want Cotter to take up Grathton, and Westford, Hinsdale, Pickstone, and even Kendalport."

Freda's expression bordered maniacal. "I want you all."

The council folks pounded their fists on the table.

And if that wasn't the worst ending of the evening, Rayne received a text that the wedding guests would be arriving Friday afternoon after all.

Chapter Twelve

"Freda is nuts," Ciara said as they sped home to the manor house. Her grip on the wheel of the Fiat was steady.

"She is!" Rayne's nerves were all chaotic. She couldn't settle down.

"What should we do about it?" Ciara asked.

"Well, nothing at the moment. I think we need to decide whether or not we would move forward on our own. With making the village historic or not."

"Da wanted modern so I think it is a backward step." Ciara glanced across the console at Rayne.

"I hear you," Rayne said. "And Don and Paddy wouldn't be behind it. So far, they are the first clients once the paint dries."

"So, we would start off in the negative."

"What did you think of Cotter Village?"

"It was too modern for my taste," Ciara said. "It had no personality."

"I agree. I'd prefer crumbling brick to shiny white and metal."

"Should we take a poll?"

"From who?"

"Our current tenants." Ciara eyed Rayne. "We have a meeting room between the general store and the doctor's office that seats three hundred."

"Oh! So we could legit call a town meeting?" Rayne chuckled. "We should get bedazzled gavels."

"Trust you to turn it into a fashion show." Ciara peeped at Rayne as they turned down the tree-lined drive toward the manor house. "But we should do it and get to the bottom of the issues. We want to help. We don't deserve to have our likenesses burned. Scarecrows, Rayne."

"I agree!"

Ciara parked by the barn. "Next step?"

"We have to let the others know about the wedding guests arriving tomorrow afternoon instead of Saturday morning. That's priority one."

The ladies exited the car. Blarney bounded toward her, his fur flowing behind him with his speed.

She knew he wouldn't jump on her, so she waited calmly as he skidded to a stop next to her. "Hey, boy."

She looked down the path for a sign of Amos, but he wasn't there. Dafydd, Amos, and Richard were no doubt snug in their cottages ready for bed.

Manor life started earlier than dawn during the fall and winter.

Her lips tingled as she recalled Amos's promising kiss.

"I guess the direction of the village isn't the most immediate issue. We can mull it over while we fix the buildings and try to get in businesses." Ciara shrugged. "Though, if we are going for old, we would need a candlemaker instead of a solar light specialist."

"You make a legit point. Let's handle the wedding first. I want to check out that silk on the trunk lining. If it's quick, I'll get it done before two in the afternoon." Happy hour, with Amos, might have to wait until next week.

Ciara read her watch. "It's after nine and I'm beat. Can we talk about it in the morning?"

"Of course."

The ladies walked down the gravel path toward the castle. Tires sounded to their right and a police vehicle, driven by Garda Williams, rolled to a stop before the manor.

"Maybe he's found who killed Aiden!"

Ciara said.

"That would be great and take a weight off so that I could focus on the wedding for Lenni and Pete."

The garda exited his white car. "Sorry to bother you so late," Garda Williams said, looking at Ciara first, then Rayne. "But I saw you drive in."

"Stalking us?" Ciara queried.

"I was at the Sheep's Head, talking to Beetle, actually." His cheeks remained pink.

"He didn't kill Aiden," Rayne blurted, hoping it was true more than having any proof. He was a man with integrity. He could have beat the crap out of Aiden multiple times but pulled his punches from what they'd seen, and heard, from Sheila.

"He has motive," Garda Williams said. He didn't seem affected by the cold weather, in his navy-blue jacket and cap. "And I think you know it."

Ciara shrugged. "Should we go inside and discuss this over tea?"

"We just got back from the town meeting in Cotter Village, and I can't take another sip of tea. How about whiskey?"

"I'm on duty," the garda said. "Another time, maybe."

Ciara sniffed. "I can't stand out here all night."

"I'll hurry, then," Garda Williams said.

Rayne slung her arm around Ciara's shoulders for warmth.

"Beetle doesn't have an alibi for the time Aiden was killed, between three and eight in the morning."

"He was at Mary's Pub," Ciara said.

"Singing," Rayne added. Three and eight? Snicklefritz. Richard had told them that Beetle had passed out in his apartment above the bar. No witnesses or alibis.

"He left Mary's Pub at one thirty in the morning. He was drinking heavily after he'd punched Aiden in the nose for messing around with Colleen Randall, his sister. You said you both were at the Sheep's Head when it happened."

"It's true. But, Beetle was controlled and then kicked him out permanently," Rayne said.

"What if Aiden came back?" Garda Williams asked.

"Aiden was found in the cemetery," Ciara said. "Beetle would have no reason to be there too."

"You can get around this village by foot quite easily. Beetle lives in a flat above the bar." Garda Williams sounded terse.

"I'm following you, but why the gardening shears from Bobby Fitzroy?" Rayne asked.

"Beetle wasn't part of the group that was cleaning the cemetery grounds that day," Ciara said.

"Was Colleen Randall a member of the cleaning crew?"

"Yes," Rayne said. "At least part of the morning."

"She helped out while Corrine was at preschool," Ciara explained.

Garda Williams nodded.

"Whoa, are you suggesting Colleen killed Aiden?" Ciara asked in surprise.

"I am not suggesting anything. We know that Colleen and Aiden were lovers," Garda Williams said, his voice hitching on the word. He kept his gaze on Rayne.

"Aiden had lied to her about being single, according to Sheila and Beetle," Rayne said.

"We've talked to Sheila Martinet who mentioned that she'd had a conversation with you both about Corrine's possible father."

Rayne and Ciara nodded.

"It's a rumor," Ciara said. "You don't do rumors, Dominic."

At that, Garda Williams turned to Ciara. "I prefer facts."

"Have you asked Colleen about who Corrine's dad is?" Rayne asked.

"Not yet. It's a delicate subject," Garda Williams said. "She maintains that the lass's da is a man she was engaged to who died in a car accident and was the reason she came home from Dublin to raise her child with family around."

"That's what she told me too," Ciara said. "It's none of my business."

"Unless it's *not* true," Garda Williams said. "And Beetle found out, and acted in a fit of rage, stabbing Aiden in the back."

"And just so happened to have the garden shears?" Rayne shook her head.

"It's possible the garden shears were left behind from the cleaning crew the night before," Garda Williams said. "Bobby didn't have them numbered or counted as to what was loaned. He said himself that his trailer was in the church parking lot, unlocked!"

It was true, and matched what Bobby had told them. The trailer had been left on the property for the cleaning crew while he'd been away for a job.

"So, what?" Ciara said, thinking aloud. "Beetle followed Aiden into the cemetery and grabbed the closest weapon at hand to stab the man in the back?" She scrunched her nose. "It doesn't fit with Beetle's personality."

"But, this is his sister we are talking about," the garda said. "We all know how protective Beetle is of her and always has been. Colleen is a gentle soul."

Rayne shivered in the cold and stuck her hands in her coat pockets. "Bobby Fitzroy's prints are on the shears. We had tea with him and Father Patrick this morning."

"I don't think you can focus solely on Beetle," Ciara said.

"I know how to do my job. I simply wanted your statements regarding what Sheila had told you concerning Corrine's parentage." Dominic Williams stepped back.

"Sorry," Ciara said.

This was progress. Months ago, her cousin would have let him have it with both barrels for not believing her about Nevin's death being more than an accident.

The garda gave a nod and went on, "Can you tell me exactly how the conversation went?"

Rayne did so, ending with, "Sheila seemed a little shocked that the Dennehys were well off financially, as if she regretted getting divorced from Aiden even though he was a cheater. Did she call you with this information, or did you call her?"

"Funny about that," Garda Williams said, "she was on my list of contacts to talk to, but she called me first."

"Sheila is jealous of Colleen," Ciara said.

"Jealousy is a strong motive." Rayne's mom always said so.

"But wouldn't the target of Sheila's rage have been Colleen?" Ciara said.

"What if Aiden and Colleen were meeting that early morning in the cemetery?" Rayne mused. "And she followed them?"

Garda Williams bit back a smile. "Let me know when you're ready to enroll in gardai school. I can sponsor you."

Ciara and Rayne both laughed.

"We are curious, yes, but feel responsible too. This happened in our village," Rayne said.

"About that," Garda Williams said. "I was wondering if you had any flats for rent? I'd prefer a house but I'm not sure what's available."

"Moving out of Cotter?" Ciara said.

"The prices keep going up and it's hard to afford what I want on my salary," the garda said.

"How soon do you need it?" Rayne asked.

"The first of the year would be great." He shrugged.

"That works for us too," Ciara said. "We can find you something at a decent price."

"Thanks. I should get back to the station

with Beetle's statement. It's funny that you had mentioned someone following Aiden to meet with Colleen. I didn't quite piece that together, but it would make sense if that's what happened. Not Sheila, but Beetle might have been the one tracking them."

The garda drove away and Rayne's stomach twisted. "I hope we didn't just hand the garda a reason to arrest Beetle."

The cousins, with Blarney, walked into the house. It was quiet as everyone was in their rooms. Frances had a small space of her own off the kitchen, Maeve and Cormac had their personal suite, and Aine her own room too all on the first floor. She and Ciara had the second floor to themselves and whatever ghosts remained in the castle.

"That would be awful," Ciara conceded. "But we found out several new things — like, time of death for Aiden."

"And that Sheila had called the garda first. She is a suspect in my mind, more so than poor Beetle."

Ciara crossed the foyer to the steps. "I agree." She flexed her hands. "I've got to hit the hay."

"I'll be up in a minute. I want to check the silk lining and hope it won't be a big mend so that we can move the trunk tomorrow."

Ciara waved and trudged up the stairs with a straight back, though her shoulders bowed with exhaustion.

Rayne and Blarney went to the blue parlor.

The trunk from the attic had been pushed to the side wall nearest the fireplace, the lid closed. It was a lovely piece with thick wood panels and brass slats as well as brass screws. The lock was open, thank heaven, because Rayne didn't have the heart to go get Ciara.

Blarney sniffed the trunk with canine interest and wagged his tail.

Rayne, not quite as tired as everyone else, was wired from the confrontation with Freda and the news from Garda Williams.

How much strength was required to kill a man in the back with gardening shears? Could a woman, say a tall, strong, angry, woman with blue hair be the culprit?

Sheila came to mind, but then, unfortunately, so did Colleen.

Rayne went to the hidden panel in the shelf and pulled out a tumbler and a bottle of whiskey, pouring herself two inches.

She'd learned to take it neat and now appreciated the smooth peaty scent just before the flavors trickled over her tongue. It was no wonder her father, Conor McGrath, had kept a bottle from Ireland in their Hollywood home.

"Slainte," she said to Blarney, who watched her with love, love she reciprocated, in his golden-brown eyes.

She carried the tumbler to the trunk and sat on her haunches, putting the whiskey to the side.

"I hope the silk fabric matches," Rayne said as she carefully opened the lid. The silk lining was ivory with age though still in good condition other than the small tear to the side.

"If we take the books and photos out, then that will make it easier for the guys to carry it over." Rayne did that, piling things to the side.

When finished, she rewarded herself with a deep sip of whiskey.

She ran her fingers along the edge of silk at the top, which was flat rather than curved.

But not smooth as she expected.

Was there a reason this side of the silk was loose? Carefully, Rayne tugged a little more. If it ripped, she would need to do more than sew it tighter but would have to replace the entire silk piece. Well, she'd bought it from Nolan just in case.

She got up and went to the desk in the parlor, locating a slim metal letter opener.

Returning to the trunk, Rayne sliced the fragile threads. Inside was a very thin sheet of paper the size of a business card with writing in Gaelic. It was in pencil, and accompanied by a sketch of a three-leaf shamrock on top of an inverted crown. Two Cs interlocked.

"Sugar cookies." She couldn't read Gaelic, but this felt important.

This matched what Bobby had been talking about — unsung heroes, doing unheroic things.

Her phone dinged with a message.

Amos.

Night, Rayne.

You still up? She felt stupid as soon as she sent it.

Yes. Couldn't sleep. Thinking of a certain gray-eyed lass.

Wondering how the meeting went?

No.

Rayne's stomach warmed and she finished her whiskey. Temptation in Viking form called to her.

She gave the text a heart, not sure what to say that wouldn't sound silly in the light of day. At night things were different.

What are you doing?

She considered telling him that she was getting ready for bed but didn't want to sound like she was a tease.

Do you know how to speak Gaelic? she asked instead.

A series of dots before his message. Yes.

Of course he did. He was a wonderful surprise.

She put the words she'd found on the paper in a text, keeping the rest to herself until she had a chance to show it to Ciara and sent it to him.

Amos sent an emoji of him laughing.

I was hoping for a second to receive a photo of you in some of that sexy lingerie, but I should have known better.

Her cheeks flamed. What does it say?

Can I have context? Where did you find it?

With the pictures in the trunk. I was clearing it for you to put in the cottage tomorrow. The wedding couple are going to be here in the afternoon rather than on Saturday as planned.

Still working this late.

What does it say?

I believe it says, Long Live the Republic.

That makes sense and matches the time period of the books too.

Anything else?

She smacked her palm to her forehead. I still need to replace the lining. Good thing I bought some in Dublin.

You should go to bed, my sweet, and we

can do it in the morning.

Good idea. The whiskey made her bold. And Amos, when you see me in my lingerie, it will be in person.

Chapter Thirteen

Friday morning, Rayne was up and dressed for the day in her comfy work jeans at seven, filled with energy as if she'd gotten a good night's sleep.

Dreams of Amos had kept her up all night, but she didn't mind the least.

It was better than her old nightmares of Landon.

Last night, Rayne had examined the lining and realized it would at least need to be repaired if not replaced. She'd locked the small secret message with Long Live the Republic in Gaelic, and the shamrock on an upside-down crown, in the office file cabinet, after putting it in a plain letter envelope marked 1923.

How to bring income to the castle and the village? The one idea they'd had suggested went against what Uncle Nevin had wanted for Grathton. Modern Father Patrick had put out authentic historic.

What Grathton offered was unique to the rest of the world. Cotter Village was very modern, and bustling, compared to them.

She would call her mom to get Lauren's advice. Sending a text to call when her mom was awake, not an emergency, Rayne went to kiss the picture with her Da and realized it was missing. She often moved it between the sewing studio and her room. It was probably there.

"Go on down, Blarney. I'll be a few minutes," she told the pup when they'd reached the central staircase.

The Irish setter went down the stairs to the kitchen where she knew that Frances or Aine would let him out.

She walked to the end of the hall where her sewing studio was, passing Ciara's room as her cousin was exiting. The secret message would be very cool to share. "Hey!"

Ciara held up her hand. "You are literally vibrating with energy. I need tea before I can talk to you in this good mood."

Ciara went toward the staircase, but Rayne didn't take offense.

It was something she could feel in herself, and she knew it was because of Amos. It had been simmering, this attraction, and their flirty vibes last night had brought it to flame.

She wouldn't act. Didn't dare do more than flirt, as she had terrible judgement and couldn't put the manor staff at odds. What would happen when she left for America?

She didn't plan on staying here and giving up her old life.

Amos made her feel desired. He knew her past. He had to understand that her future was out of her control for now, so she would need to live in the moment.

If he could agree to that, then, well, they could have . . . coffee.

Singing beneath her breath, Rayne unlocked and entered her sewing room, going for the ivory thread in her thread cabinet which had a glass door. She dropped it in the pocket of her cardigan sweater, then brought the silk fabric too.

She selected her finest scissors, determined to do her best to salvage the lining, but if it wasn't salvageable she had a replacement.

It wasn't authentic to the time period so if she couldn't repair the tear, it would be ruined so far as a collector went.

Given the dates of the picture and items in the trunk, she figured it was well over a hundred years old if not more.

Rayne and Ciara were caretakers for the next generation. Babies. Oh, Ciara would have the cutest babies. Dafydd's brown eyes? Ciara's gray?

Of course, the wedding was rightfully on hold due to Ciara and Dafydd's disagreement.

Well, his withholding of information, like that he'd been married before. Rayne would support her cousin either way.

It would be interesting to watch what might happen between Ciara and Garda Williams (Dominic) once he moved here. He was fair to Ciara's dark. Her cousin hadn't opposed the idea.

Rayne scanned the sewing studio for the photo of her dad but didn't see it. She'd toned the pink walls down with shelves, utilizing every inch of space.

It wasn't here. She collected her supplies, then hurried down the hall to the main staircase, where she practically floated down the stairs to the blue parlor, Amos in her thoughts. She deposited the thread and scissors on the desk, noting that the trunk was closed though she'd left it open last night.

Probably closed on its own. Shivering, she went to the kitchen where her senses were met with sizzling ham and fresh soda bread from the oven.

"Morning!"

"And to you," Cormac said.

Aine passed Rayne a cup of coffee while Ciara looked up from her tea with bleary eyes.

"I couldn't sleep a wink," her cousin complained. "I heard noises outside my door all night."

"Maybe you should get a dog?" Rayne suggested. "Blarney keeps the ghosts away." She scanned the empty kitchen. "Thanks for letting him outside."

"Not a bother," Maeve said.

"Ghosts?" Cormac shrugged. "They must be keeping to the second floor or the tower. I didn't hear a thing."

"I don't need a pet," Ciara said. "Not a dog anyway. Maybe a kitten would be the thing."

"I thought Dafydd was allergic to them?" Aine said.

Ciara shrugged and helped herself to a piece of bread, applying a golden ribbon of butter. "It's a thought is all."

"Pass the jam, will you?" Rayne asked, taking the attention from Ciara. "Oh, we tasted the McElroy jam yesterday at Father Patrick's and it is delicious. He said he would ask Dorothy and Sheff about opening a storefront."

"But we might lose Paddy and Don if we decide to make the village a tourist spot stuck in the eighteen hundreds." Ciara bit into her bread.

"How did the meeting go last night?" Cormac asked. He sliced his ham and stabbed it with his fork.

"Freda wants us to do it so that we will fail," Rayne said. "She lost her mind and told the other village councilmen that she wants to absorb us all to make one big town. Is that the next level of incorporation? Village is the smallest, then town, then city . . ."

Aine shrugged. "I don't know about that, but her plan can't work. She's ridiculous."

"Can you imagine Freda Bevan holding power like that?" Maeve shook her head. "The woman has always been just a little bit too grabby for my liking."

"I think she showed her true colors last night, so she might have overplayed her hand when it comes to the other villages." Rayne sipped her coffee — light and sweet, the way she liked it best.

"I hope that stops her." Cormac ate another bite of his porridge. "Frances, well done, again. Thank you."

"My pleasure," their cook said as she stirred something savory on the stove.

"What's the plan, now that I've had tea and breakfast?" Ciara asked Rayne.

"I found a hidden sheet of paper with

Gaelic writing in the trunk lining last night, beneath the silk, which was why it had sagged and torn," Rayne said. "I'll need to fix it right after we finish here."

Aine, Maeve, Cormac, and Ciara gasped. Frances whirled around, spoon in hand.

"I sent just the Gaelic text to Amos. He said it meant Long Live the Republic, which makes sense if the trunk is a hundred years old." Rayne sipped her coffee. "That matches the photos and the albums for that time period."

"That's very interesting," Cormac said. "A secret letter."

"It is! It's locked in the office file cabinet as we need to switch gears before I can do more investigating. Last night, Lenni texted me that she and Pete will be here today around three or four, and they are ready to relax before their wedding weekend."

"But they are early," Aine said. "The bungalow needs furnishings."

"I was panicked too until I remembered that they are staying in the biggest cottage, which is already done. Their best friends will each need a cottage, but they won't be here until tomorrow. We have to focus on furnishing just the one. Amos will be here this morning to help."

"Have you met them?" Maeve asked. "Are

they easy going?"

"Just on video call so not in person. Lenni is a CEO of a tech company and Pete is a history professor who is interested in studying our manor."

"All right," Cormac said. "The house is always ready for company."

"I think this is a special break for them as they both have big jobs with lots of responsibility. They've been dating for years and decided to make it legal. This was the only time this year they could both get away."

"We will make it very special," Maeve said.

"I know it!"

"No disasters," Ciara said.

"If we don't count dead Aiden, that is," Rayne said. "We are offering a full dinner tomorrow in the dining room. Should we offer breakfast? Lunch can be in the heated gazebo, or we can suggest going out. The view of the lake never gets old. They'll get married at sunset."

"Romantic." Aine sighed.

Rayne finished her breakfast, a million things racing through her mind. "Sinead will bring over the wedding cake tomorrow at noon and help set it up in the gazebo. Aine, and Maeve, will you let Sorcha know to wear her white uniform with the Irish green trim? I'd like you all to match."

"I'm not coming," Ciara said.

"You don't have to be at the wedding. I'll feel them out to see about the formal dinner. They are being married by a notary, she didn't call it that, but someone from Kilkenny."

"Not the priest?" Maeve asked.

"It's not what they want." Rayne shrugged. "Our job is to make our guests happy so they spread the word about our venue."

The last wedding hadn't gone according to plan, but it had been a good dress rehearsal, and they'd all learned how to fine-tune for this time around.

"They seem to be low-key about everything. Thank you for all you do to make this happen!" Rayne lifted her cup.

Though they hadn't gotten the reviews Rayne had hoped for, the castle had gotten paid very well, enough to ease the brutal summer months and prior wedding fiascoes.

They were hoping on the sheep in the spring but until then, they had this wedding. Rayne had two November gowns and three for December that were ready for mailing. She had two orders for January, and the buildings for rent as well as the apartments.

The phone rang, startling her.

"Only eight," Maeve said in a dreaded tone.

Aine's eyes widened.

Ciara, Cormac, and Rayne all watched the housekeeper — Frances continued stirring though not as vigorously.

She got up to answer the landline. "McGrath Castle."

A knock sounded from the kitchen threshold and Amos's broad shoulders filled the doorway. His expression was concerned.

Maeve covered the handset. "Elizabeth McGillicuddy is demanding to speak with you, but I wouldn't. Shall I take a message?"

"All right," Rayne said, going with Maeve's decision.

"She's not available. Nor is Ciara Smith." Maeve nodded. "I'll let them know." She hung up the phone.

Amos waited, watching. "What is it?"

"Elizabeth has cornered Father Patrick. She's demanding that you find out what happened to Darcy, or she will sue." Maeve's lips pursed. "And the village will be done for. Well, she said more than that, but I won't repeat it."

"Sue us?" Ciara blinked.

"We own Grathton Village," Rayne said, stunned. "Can she? What does she want?"

"For you to meet them at Father Patrick's house." Maeve clearly disapproved.

"All right, of course. I don't know what we can do, but I'll see if I can calm her down."

They all looked at Amos, who cleared his throat. "I'll go with you, Rayne. Be your bodyguard."

"All right." Rayne stood as her stomach fluttered with awareness of her Viking. She'd never wanted a protector but how could she say no?

Chapter Fourteen

"I think it's grand that you speak Gaelic." Ciara rose to her feet. She gave her last sip of tea a longing glance before returning her focus to Amos.

"Thanks," Amos said. "Long Live the Republic was a common phrase around the time of the War of Independence as well as during the Irish Civil War."

"It was," Cormac agreed.

"We can talk about this when you get back." Maeve shooed them toward the door. "We don't want poor Father Patrick harangued by that harridan."

"I have so much to do," Rayne said. She glanced toward her staff.

"What is the priority?" Maeve asked. "We can help."

"I need to sew the zipper in which isn't something that can be passed on, the interior of the third bungalow needs the finishing touches, which Aine can manage until I return — leave the trunk — and if Frances, you can adjust the menu to include food for tonight, and possibly breakfast — Maeve, will you make sure the fridges are stocked through Sunday?"

The staff all nodded.

"Thank you!" Rayne exhaled and blew out a breath, shaking her hands to release stress. "We've got this!"

Her phone dinged with a series of notifications, and she winced, bracing herself before she read the messages on her phone.

Her mom, promising to call later, Don, sounding on the fence about signing any sort of lease if they were going to be a tourist town, and Lenni, in a panic because the solemnizer cancelled.

"What on earth is a solemnizer?" Rayne asked.

"The person who performs the ceremony, since they aren't having it at the church," Maeve said. "Ask Father Patrick if he can step in."

"Is it the same as a Notary Public?" The previous wedding had been at the church in the village and the Montgomery family had handled the requirements behind the scenes. Rayne and her crew had provided the venue.

"I'm not sure," Cormac said. "Talk to the

priest while you are there."

"Two birds, one stone," Frances said.

Amos put his hand on Rayne's elbow. "Should we drive? It's lashing rain."

"That would be best," Rayne said. "Thank you."

A rainy day probably meant that progress on the buildings would be slow.

"I hope it stops by tomorrow," Aine said. "But even if it doesn't, the gazebo is covered and will provide shelter."

"And warmth," Rayne said. "It's one of my favorite places. I bring my sketchbook and watch the lake. I've come up with some nice dress designs." Though she was a business owner, her creativity was an important outlet.

Rayne waved at everyone who remained in the kitchen, her mind rushing with what to do for Lenni and Pete. Lenni had dropped that bombshell, but no more news had come from the bride-to-be.

Amos drove with Rayne in the passenger seat and Ciara in the back for the five-minute trip that would have had them drenched no matter how many layers of latex on the raincoat or wellies. An umbrella, thanks to the wind, was out of the question.

Blarney had been kept at home, though he hadn't liked it. Aine had given him a piece of ham to appease him.

Amos parked the Fiat close to the church steps. "No help for it, you'll have to dash inside." He turned the engine off. "One, two, three — go!"

The trio exited the car. Rayne ducked her head and sped inside the church with Ciara leading the way and Amos at her back.

The cold made Rayne shiver. "Brisk," she said. In LA, the rain was warmer and softer than this wild downpour.

It spoke to her Celtic soul. As her mother liked to say; she didn't melt. Rayne stopped abruptly as she noticed Father Patrick and Elizabeth McGillicuddy exchanging heated words.

The pair were outside of the kitchen in the hallway, and each held a mug.

"I will find the responsible party, and if it leads to negligence in this backward village, those upstarts will pay through the nose," Elizabeth said. She was without her coat, her solid black clothes striking against the silver of her hair.

Darcy McGillicuddy, her brother, had been a vital ninety, according to her. Elizabeth was eighty-eight, and still had lovely features, even in her anger and grief, with brilliant blue eyes.

"I'm so sorry for your loss," Rayne said.

She stepped forward with her hand out, forcing Elizabeth to choose — either transfer the mug to one hand, and shake Rayne's, which would require a truce of sorts, or snub the greeting. "I'm Rayne McGrath. We met a few days ago at the church."

Elizabeth, with gracious manners, held her mug in her left hand and accepted the greeting with her right. Bands with gemstones graced her slender fingers. No arthritis bumps dared show on those hands though there were age spots.

"Elizabeth McGillicuddy. I remember you. Did you know my brother? He didn't speak highly of either of you McGraths."

Ciara's cheeks burned.

Rayne gave a small shrug. "We've been so busy trying to stop the village from disappearing that I never did meet Darcy. I'm sorry he was so quick to judge. As a respected elder here, his support would have been invaluable."

"You're right there," Elizabeth said. "You're no fool, I can see that. Pretty enough. You have the McGrath gray eyes. Your grandfather Lorcan had them."

"My dad and Uncle Nevin too." Rayne hooked her arm through Ciara's. "As does my cousin. We deserve to be here, on this land, to protect it for the next generation.

Your opposition could hurt our plans to save the village. What would it take to gain your cooperation?"

Elizabeth blinked. "Brash American." Her lips lifted upward. "I respect your directness." She sipped from her mug.

"I am a product of both my parents. I believe that the blending of my Celtic ways with my American ones gives me a new perspective."

"Modernization," Elizabeth said.

"Wi-Fi makes life easier." Rayne smiled.

"Amen to that." Elizabeth glanced at Father Patrick. "You have an ally in your priest."

"We are grateful to him," Rayne said.

"Not everybody agrees though." Ciara's eyes narrowed. "We've had scarecrows with our names on them burned in the fields. What would your brother think of that?"

"Darcy would never stoop so low as that. If my brother wanted to move against you, you wouldn't see it coming." Elizabeth sipped her tea.

Amos stepped out of the shadows, supporting Rayne and Ciara with his presence.

"Who are you?" Elizabeth demanded.

"Our grounds manager," Rayne said.

"Why is he here?"

"You threatened us and our village,"

Rayne said. "It's a cause for concern, don't you think?"

"What do you want?" Ciara asked. "We don't have any connections in Kilkenny. The gardai can help you more than we can."

"What did you mean, that we wouldn't see a threat coming?" Rayne's mind returned to how Elizabeth might have known her grandparents. "Was Darcy a soldier? We have a picture of Dougal McGrath with Billy McGillicuddy."

"Our da was in the war. We weren't born until after." Elizabeth finished her tea. "Our mam was a nurse but just as talented as any doctor. Here in Grathton. Our parents are buried here, and now I need to bury my own brother. Or his ashes."

"And you?" Rayne asked.

"I'll be laid to rest in Dublin, with my husband and son. My daughter and grandchildren all live there now. Darcy's grandson Rian also is in Dublin with his wife. We have no need to return to Grathton. Sometimes, Rayne McGrath, things are better left to die out." Elizabeth speared her with a hard gaze.

"Our village is not one of those," Rayne assured her. "What will happen to the McGillicuddy estate?"

"Interested in buying it?"

"Maybe," Rayne said at the same time as Ciara said, "No."

"Well, you'd have to beat the McElroy's lucrative offer. The O'Briens are also interested. Darcy's homestead is between them both. They were all neighbors and friends for a long time." Elizabeth shrugged. "Darcy's children are gone. My children don't want it, though perhaps we should hold it for future generations."

Ciara was shaking her head no.

"There is no rush to decide," Rayne said. "Our housekeeper said there was something urgent you wanted to discuss? We're not responsible for anything that happened in Kilkenny. You can't sue us."

Elizabeth gripped her mug in both hands. "I find it suspicious Darcy was cremated when he'd requested to be buried in a wooden box so he would be one with the earth. He didn't even want to be in the mausoleum itself but the grounds outside the marble. It was why he had to be buried in the new cemetery rather than in this one."

The McGillicuddy burial plot was shaded with a center structure, and several headstones, surrounded by a low white fence. A bench was inside for contemplation or ease when visiting.

Rayne had been to the McGrath mausoleum, ten times as grand, and the surrounding spaces for their dead around it, when they'd interred Uncle Nevin.

Ciara would be buried there. Rayne hadn't given it much thought but when her time came it would probably be here that she'd be buried, though her father, Conor, had been cremated and his ashes buried beneath a tree in their backyard in LA. Her mother wanted to join him.

Elizabeth's eyes welled. She blinked and turned to walk into the kitchen. Father Patrick followed her, as did Rayne, Ciara, and Amos.

The church kitchen was large with a table that could seat twenty. Father Patrick set his cup down on one end as Elizabeth placed her mug in the sink.

She turned, no more sign of tears. "I want my brother's body back."

"That can't be done," Ciara said.

"I'm aware of that." Elizabeth lifted her chin.

"So?" Rayne asked.

"My brother was very secretive about his time as a solider in the Irish Free Army in 1935. He wouldn't tell me what he saw or what he was up to, but I knew it was very dangerous. Our da was the same. I lost a son in the Troubles in 1970. Our family has always been patriotic." Elizabeth added, "We shed blood for Ireland."

Rayne watched the older woman closely. Would she know about the secret society? Could Darcy, or their father, have been part of it?

The Republic of Ireland had been established for a hundred years. Nobody was alive now to punish, or reward.

"Our ancestors also died for the Republic," Ciara said.

"They are gone. We are all that's left," Rayne seconded.

"I feel like my brother is being dishonored in some way," Elizabeth said, placing her hand over her heart. "I don't understand why but I will get to the bottom of it."

"How so?" Father Patrick asked.

"I am not sure that he died of natural causes, and now we will never know, will we?" Elizabeth demanded shortly. "Any proof of wrongdoing just went up in smoke."

"And while we are very sorry for that happening, it's not our fault," Rayne said. "You had no reason to threaten to sue us."

"I knew it would get you down here for a meeting." Elizabeth's brows rose.

"We are here."

"Finally," Ciara drawled. "The point."

Amos rocked on his heels, his hands behind his back.

"No need to be rude, young lady," Elizabeth said. "You have no idea what I am going through."

"That would be incorrect," Ciara countered. "My da was murdered on our property and everyone thought it was an accident. I know."

Elizabeth straightened. "Oh?" She turned to Rayne.

"Yes," Rayne said. "Ciara was right in her speculation that something was wrong. And now you believe the same for your brother?"

"You think Darcy was murdered?" Father Patrick spluttered with indignation. "He was ninety and died in his sleep. A very peaceful way of meeting our Lord."

"Darcy and I talked on the phone that night. I tend to be a night owl. He had something he wanted to discuss that concerned our past. He sounded very worried, which isn't like him. He asked me to meet in person and wouldn't tell me over the phone what was bothering him. I had planned to visit with him over this weekend — only to find out that he'd died during the night. I just don't believe it." Elizabeth quivered with rage.

Considering the conversation they'd had,

Rayne didn't blame her for being suspicious but odd things happened all the time. It was a sad fact of life.

To be ninety and die in your sleep without illness or dragging sickness out for years was a blessing, as Father Patrick said.

"What do his friends say?" Rayne asked. "Did he have a housekeeper? Staff on the farm to help?"

"He lived alone. Murray and Olivia O'Brien live on the other side of the McElroys. Sheff and Dorothy. Shauna and Luke Dennehy, bless their souls, having to bury their grandson, Aiden. That's a shame in truth but my brother's death is no less a tragedy, even if he was old as Methuselah. Those four men were thick as thieves."

"Was Darcy part of the club?" Rayne asked. "And our ancestor too?"

"Darcy, yes, your grandfather Lorcan not so much."

Rayne wondered why Elizabeth was rather sour-faced about it.

"The Randalls used to have much larger property but sold it over the years as their crops failed," Elizabeth shared.

"Who bought it?" Rayne asked.

"The McElroys. Now, that family has a head for business that is to be admired. Darcy kept a small flock of sheep, some goats, and enough of a garden to keep himself in veg. I know he traded with the McElroys for fruit and jam. He paid one of their daughters to help with his laundry."

Rayne was very curious to see the McElroy farm. They'd made a success where others hadn't.

"The Walshes also downsized considerably. The Dennehys and O'Briens have held onto what they own, which is a feat in itself with the way times have changed." Elizabeth shrugged. "Moving the main motorway was the death of Grathton Village."

"We are not dead!!" Rayne protested. "This is the perfect time for a comeback, anyway. People can work remotely. We have Wi-Fi. We are offering the perfect quaint Irish wedding getaway."

"I heard about the tower going up in flames," Elizabeth said with a smirk.

"An exaggeration!" Though probably not much of one.

"My brother had no reason to lie." Elizabeth wouldn't look away from Rayne or Ciara. Amos walked behind them, his hand on Rayne's shoulder.

"Darcy McGillicuddy was known for his stories," Amos said. "He had the perfect storyteller beat, like a bard of old. He was famous in the pubs for it."

"Was that an actual skill?" Rayne thought it sounded cool. Just as cool as Bronagh's grandmother as the village matchmaker.

"Yes. And now that gift has been silenced," Elizabeth said. Her mouth thinned.

There was no winning in this situation. "I'm sorry," Rayne said again.

They all bowed their heads.

"Elizabeth, dear," Father Patrick said in a gentle voice. "I had the funeral service scheduled for Sunday per your request. It was in the church newsletter. What would you like to do?"

"That was before the fiasco of the cremation." Elizabeth held up three fingers. "The third red flag."

Rayne was intrigued by the phone call between Darcy and Elizabeth where he'd been concerned. Had he feared his phone being tapped and that was why he hadn't shared his worries?

"I've talked to Garda Lee and the incompetent woman will not do anything more to investigate. Her attitude is to get on with my life." Elizabeth hefted her chin.

Ouch, Rayne thought.

"Darcy told me how nosy you are, Rayne, and you Ciara, are friends with Garda Williams." Elizabeth held her arms to her sides. "This is what I want. I want you two to get to the bottom of this dilemma, and in return, I will give you my blessing with the villagers."

"We don't need your blessing," Ciara said.

"Trust me." Her nostrils flared in anger. "You don't need me for an enemy."

Chapter Fifteen

Elizabeth, after collecting her coat and purse, instructed Father Patrick to go ahead with the service on Sunday as her family had already made arrangements for time off. She stopped before Rayne and Ciara. "Do not simply accept Darcy's fate." She swept from the church.

"She's something else," Ciara complained.

"We can't be sued for what happened," Rayne reiterated. "I was worried that she had some ancient trick up her sleeve."

"No tricks — just threats." Father Patrick brought his mug to the electric kettle and poured water into it. "Between us," the priest eyed the ceiling before returning his gaze to Rayne, Amos, and Ciara, "Elizabeth terrifies me."

"Is there any chance Darcy didn't die in his sleep?" Amos asked.

Rayne tilted her head. She was curious as well.

"As I wasn't there when Darcy passed, I can't be one hundred percent sure," Father Patrick quipped. "The medical examiner had no reason to suspect foul play, as Elizabeth suggests. And now that he has been cremated, we might never have those answers."

"They could run a toxicology report on the ashes," Rayne said.

"How would you know that?" Amos asked. "Should we be worried?"

"Mom." Rayne smiled at Amos. "Lauren being on the sitcom for so many years led to somewhat outlandish plot twists, which made for interesting conversations on the set. Her best friend, Paul, is also her producer. They could brainstorm ideas all night."

"I can't wait to meet Lauren," Ciara said. "I suppose that Dominic, em, Garda Williams, would know that about the toxicology too."

"I'm sure, but it wouldn't hurt to remind both the gardai. Since it isn't being treated as a crime, I wonder if they'll be more forthcoming with us?"

"I'll text him," Ciara said. She pulled her phone from her pocket and shot off a message. She was getting pretty fast on it.

"Thank you, ladies," Father Patrick said.

"I know you will help as only you can."

Rayne patted the priest's shoulder. "Father Patrick, we have a dilemma at the manor that you might be able to assist us with. Lenni McGee and Pete O'Shea are arriving this afternoon and the person who was supposed to marry them bailed. I don't know the ins and outs here in Ireland but back home they could get married by a Notary Public or a Justice of the Peace. Or a boat's captain . . . not sure the whys of that last one, but it's true."

"Another episode of Family Forever?" Amos teased.

"You got it. I was raised on a thin line of reality." Rayne pinched her forefinger and thumb together.

"Well, bring yourself back to earth, Princess," Ciara said. "Father Patrick's frowning. Can you marry the couple even though they haven't been to your classes?"

"I'm afraid I wouldn't feel comfortable," the priest said. "Unless they happen to be Catholic?"

"They are not religious," Rayne said. "Lenni is a businesswoman, and Pete is a history professor. They are both from Ireland, so natives."

"They will need to get a solemnizer from Kilkenny," the priest said, sounding truly apologetic that he couldn't help.

"All right. I thought I'd ask," Rayne said. "On that note, though, we need to get back to the manor. Lenni wants a phone call, poor thing. She's been the least stressed bride I've ever known until now."

"Go on, then," the priest said. "But don't forget to talk to Garda Williams about further possible testing for Darcy McGillicuddy. I feel terrible that one of my flock was cremated by mistake. To be human is to err, and heaven help us we all do, but that doesn't help the McGillicuddy family."

They said goodbye and left the church as Colleen Randall, with her daughter Corrine, entered the foyer.

"Hi!" Rayne said. She wanted to get to know Colleen better and find out if there was a way to help one another.

"Hello." Colleen scanned the interior to the lost and found box then smiled with relief. "There is your hat, Cor."

Sure enough a bright pink hat with a fuzzy ball on top poked from a mesh box, laid over several coats, single mittens, and scarves.

Corrine broke from her mother with a squeal of delight and rescued her beloved hat that happened to be the same color as her glasses.

Father Patrick chuckled. "And now all is right in her world. So precious. Children are a joy."

"She can be a handful at times, but I swear I love her more every single day," Colleen said. Sadness, similar to what was in Elizabeth's eyes, glimmered below the surface. Was she grieving a loved one as well? Even if Aiden was a louse, it was obvious that she'd cared.

"She's so cute," Rayne said.

"Thanks. Come on, Corrine, or we will be late for school." Colleen read her watch. "Nine. We are already late. She refused to go without her hat. If it wasn't here, I didn't know what I was going to do."

"That's worked out then," Father Patrick said. He clasped his hand on Corrine's shoulder. "You be a good girl at school today."

"I will!" Corrine put her hat over her braided brown hair. It did have hints of red, like Sheila had suggested. Her glasses slipped down her upturned nose. She whipped them off and glared at a smudge. Her green eyes welled.

"Let me help," Colleen said in a quiet voice. The little girl gave them to her mother, who cleaned them, and put them back on her daughter. "No more smudge."

Colleen's hair was a rich brown with auburn highlights and brushed back in a ponytail. Her skin was porcelain, cheeks rosy from the cold, her eyes near-black as Beetle's were. Rayne didn't see any obvious tattoos.

As Ciara had countered to Sheila's suggestion, this was Ireland and almost everybody had a little bit of red in their locks, so it didn't mean anything. The McGraths were black Irish so an exception to that theory.

"You are always so calm, it seems," Rayne said. "Does Corrine take after her dad?"

Colleen winced. "She's more like her Uncle Beetle, right, love?" She held out her hand and flexed her fingers. "Let's go."

Corrine raced toward the altar instead, her hat jammed on her head, braids flying behind her.

"How's that going?" Rayne murmured.

Colleen turned to scowl at Rayne. "Do you mean, has the gardai arrested my brother for killing Aiden?"

Rayne's cheeks heated at being the direct object of the woman's ire.

"Or are you talking about the slanderous rumor of Aiden being Corrine's da?" Colleen crossed her arms, her scowl deepening.

Amos's jaw set. Guess he hadn't heard

that particular rumor.

Rayne swallowed, hard.

"I will tell you the same thing that I told Garda Kaitlin Lee." Colleen exhaled, far from calm now. "It is none of your business. Corrine is just fine."

As the little girl was now sliding along the floor on her back, as if swimming, that clearly was a stretch. High energy was something that lots of kids outgrew.

Now was not the time to press, obviously. Could the gardai insist that Corrine take a DNA test? Not a plot twist Rayne was familiar with — she'd have to share it with her mom.

"Please know that I am not judging you or your daughter at all." Rayne clasped her hands together and held Colleen's gaze. "I've wanted to talk with you because I like Beetle very much. Ciara and I don't think he killed Aiden."

"Well," Colleen blustered, her hands lowering to her sides. "That's all right then."

"In fact, Ciara and I were wondering if there was a business you might be interested in running?"

"You were?" Colleen's cheeks turned a darker pink, from cold to embarrassment.

"Yes. Forgive me for not making more of an effort to meet you. Moving here from

LA has been a whirlwind. I miss having friends. Ciara is amazing, and Sinead . . ."

"Sinead and Liam both speak highly of you. Me and Sinead went to primary together. She's always been a good judge of people. Better than me for sure." Colleen turned to Corrine, now putting her glasses on the Virgin Mary statue. "Corrine, let's go! I am counting to three. One. Two. Three." Corrine, without her glasses, joined them. She tugged on her mom's hand. "What businesses were you thinking of?"

"We want to fill niches that are needed, but honestly, we aren't that picky. We've got to get some younger people in the heart of the village," Ciara said.

"I hear you." Colleen sighed. "I don't know how to do anything."

"What are your hobbies?" Rayne asked.

"Being a single parent doesn't allow much time for anything. Laundry, meal prep, helping Corrine with her schoolwork. I love to escape in a book, though."

"You've always had your nose in a book," Father Patrick said. "I remember that about you, even when you were this age." He rescued Corrine's pink glasses, plopping them on the little girl's nose where they belonged.

"Ta!" she said. Her smile was so sweet,

how could anybody be mad?

"We were thinking of a lending library," Rayne said. "We wouldn't be able to pay very much but you could choose your hours."

Colleen waved her fingers. "Beetle and I have small trusts from our grandparents on Mam's side. We'll inherit our family's land, after our folks go, but we have enough to get by. I help out at the school, and then at the pub for Beetle. He owns the Sheep's Head."

"Pubs are the heart of the community," Amos said. "It was a smart investment."

"That's true. I have a little cottage on my parents' property. Da can fix anything and Mam was a nurse. She's writing a novel but can help me with Corrine. My necessities are minimal. Whatever Corrine needs. Let me think about the idea of a library." She smiled and it brightened her entire face to one of beauty. "It sounds like heaven. I could create a children's area."

"You could," Ciara said. "You'd be able to bring Corrine with you."

Those magic words chased some of the sadness from the young mom's shadowed eyes. "I'll be in touch!"

Did it really matter who the little girl's dad was? Colleen had a wonderful support system here in Grathton. Rayne didn't see her as a killer. She didn't need Aiden's money as she had her own and wasn't flashy.

Colleen and Corrine left, and the foyer of the church was very quiet without them.

"A library is a very good idea," Father Patrick said. "What did the council say about making Grathton a tourist town?"

"There is no law that says we can't," Ciara said in a cautious tone.

"But Freda Bevan was pretty rotten about it. She wants to incorporate us into Cotter Village — us and the other villages too. My mom had wondered if Freda might have a political agenda, and this could build her name."

"She showed her true colors last night though, so she might not have the support that she thought she did." Ciara shifted her gaze from Rayne to the priest.

"Power can change people," Father Patrick said.

"I know it!" Rayne agreed.

Her phone dinged.

"It's Don again. Father Patrick, Don and Paddy won't sign a lease if we do the tourist village in a historical manner, and they are the only ones willing to sign on the dotted line."

"Don McElroy and Paddy O'Brien?" The priest rubbed his chin.

"They want to run a mobile phone service," Ciara said. "Mobile phones and churning butter are at opposite ends of the spectrum."

"Churning butter?" Amos showed his very large hands. "I don't know that these are made for that."

Rayne touched a callous. "You won't even need gloves."

"You must decide what it is that you want to do and what you feel is right. That was an idea, is all," the priest said.

"I like that we are brainstorming. We offer that charming village vibe at the manor, right down to the bungalows."

"It's not modern," Ciara said. "Da wanted modern."

"He wanted us to save the village." Rayne crossed her arms.

"By modernizing," Ciara said.

Rayne sighed. She had a point. "I don't know what to do."

"What is the rush?" Amos asked.

"Well, Don and Paddy not signing for one. For two, we need a direction." Rayne loved a plan. It's how she made forward progress.

Maeve also loved a plan and together they'd gotten a lot accomplished. The staff was mixed on going backward rather than forward.

“What if we somehow straddle the line of modern and historic? Like you are doing now,” Amos said.

“What do you mean?”

“Well, a blend of historic and modern. Take what is best from each era.”

Rayne’s body began to hum with excitement.

“I like it.”

“Me too,” Ciara said. “And it would be following Da’s will while giving us a gimmick, as Haley McGavin suggested. The perfect blend of old and new.”

The four inside the church nodded at one another.

“I guess I’ll let Don know that he can move on if he doesn’t want to sign a year-long lease.” Rayne grinned. “His choice. We will be a mix.”

The four gave high-fives all around.

Even though it went against the grain to turn down opportunity for short-term, the merit in the long-term mattered most. It was all about saving their home for future generations.

“Let’s go,” Rayne said. “We have a trunk to move.”

The rain was awful and remained a torrent all day. Ciara had a migraine and took a nap. Lenni had thankfully found a substitute solemnizer, so that was off the to-do list. The zipper on the gown would need to wait, so Rayne concentrated on the torn silk in the lid of trunk, able to mend it. There were no more hidden items inside. She'd moved the stack of history books and combined the loose photos.

Her favorite was still the four men in the Polaroid. They were so sure of themselves. She wanted to know their stories. The nose on one man, had to be a McElroy. Blue eyes? A McGillicuddy. Green . . . reminded her of the O'Briens. And of course, the stormy gray belonged to a McGrath.

Cormac hadn't located a family tree, but he had brought out the family Bible. No Thomas McGrath was listed around that time period. The popular family names were Donald, Dougal, Duncan, Andrew, Lorcan, Conor, Nevin.

It seemed that great grandfather Conor, the youngest son, had inherited because the others had died.

"So sad," Rayne said aloud. She was grateful for Blarney at her side.

"Ready to move that over?" Amos asked. He and Richard were draped in rain gear and covered the trunk as well.

"Thank you!"

Ciara, headache gone, joined Rayne in the blue parlor. She showed Ciara the hidden message, including the sketch. They spent the afternoon online. No matter how much Rayne and Ciara searched, the shamrock, and the crown, didn't show up and set off any alarms for a secret society.

The thing about secrets?

They almost always came to light.

CHAPTER SIXTEEN

At seven that Friday evening, the inhabitants of McGrath Castle gathered in the foyer, with Rayne constantly checking her phone.

"They should be here any minute. Maeve, can you put in a request to the Weatherman in the Sky to stop the freaking raining for like, ten minutes, so that Lenni and Pete don't get drenched upon arrival?"

"Prayer sent, but I'm sure He has other things to do," Maeve said in a tart tone.

The affianced couple had driven from Cork to Kilkenny, where they'd hired a second solemnizer. Their best friends wouldn't arrive until tomorrow. They'd had a relaxed dinner together and now wanted to hole up in the main bungalow, yes, together, before their posse arrived the next day for the ceremony.

Rayne and Cormac, in rain gear with giant umbrellas, would meet them outside, point the way to the bungalows, and escort them there.

She and Cormac each had on wellies that reached their knees. She did her best to hang onto fashion, but it was a challenge when the torrents of water made her resemble one of their wet barn cats.

She recalled Aine sweetly explaining about Irish rain back in June when she'd first moved here — a misting, she'd called it with a wistful smile. This was a waterfall and not to be confused with romantic drizzle.

Her phone dinged. "They're here!"

"The whiskey!" Frances said, dashing into the kitchen to retrieve a small bottle of spiced liquor for the couple as a treat to warm their bones before a crackling fire. Rayne and Ciara had discovered the antique bottle in the attic and Frances had cleaned it up.

The trunk had been moved to the third bungalow, where Amos had promised it was centered appropriately. He'd even sent video until she and Aine agreed it was right.

The fact that they had achieved *most* things on the list was because they'd worked together as a team.

"Thank you," Rayne said, gently pocketing the lovely antique filled with spiced whiskey.

They'd sampled some with their dinner of roasted beef and Rayne was a fan.

Blarney took one look at the howling weather outside and decided to stay in the covered warmth of the foyer.

"Smart boyo," Ciara said with approval.

Rayne and Cormac opened their umbrellas outside on the section of covered porch. One didn't open umbrellas inside the house or risk bad luck — the same superstition in the US, like spilling salt and needing to immediately toss some grains over your left shoulder to blind the devil, but Ireland held the very real fear of aggravating the fairies and making them an enemy.

Fairy doors, cute and inviting, were actually traps to keep them away from your actual house. It seemed mean, because the fairies were so stinking cute, but Maeve was insistent. They had fairy doors on some of the trees in the apple orchard. They'd added them to two of the three bungalows for luck as well. And, of course, the one in the cemetery that the sensible Moira Morton had appeased her granddaughters with.

The large umbrellas at the castle were sturdy and meant to withstand the windy rain or at least put up a valiant effort against the blast.

They were not the stylish umbrellas one

used in the states. Well, Rayne hadn't ever owned one, living in Hollywood and sunny LA.

A sleek Mercedes in black with shiny silver chrome rolled toward them. Rayne and Cormac gestured for the couple to follow them down the dirt and gravel path.

Luckily, the animals were all in the barn or shelters around the property. Dafydd would be taking care of the sheepdogs and horses in addition to the sheep. Mama sheep was back with the herd.

Amos was at the biggest bungalow, lighting the fire in the indoor fireplace to welcome the couple. He'd meant to bring the whiskey earlier but had forgotten.

Not a big deal in the scheme of things.

They reached the bungalow with Rayne and Cormac leading the way. Golden light glimmered from the porch as well as from inside the window. The drapes were open to see the fire inside. Old-fashioned paned glass made the images blurry for privacy.

Rayne went to Pete's side of the car, and Cormac to Lenni's, covering their doors with their umbrellas.

"Thanks. What a mess!" Pete said as he exited with a grateful nod.

Amos had the front door open, and Pete dashed inside, right behind Lenni and Cormac. They kept the umbrellas in place on the porch so Amos could retrieve the luggage from the car.

In minutes the couple was inside, still dry. Even Amos, Rayne, and Cormac were only slightly damp. The umbrellas were awkward, sure, but worth their weight in gold.

"Welcome!" Rayne said with a grin.

Lenni was just under six feet. She took off her knit cap and jacket. She had caramel-colored springy curls, dark skin, and catlike green eyes. She wore an emerald pantsuit fitted to her curves. The woman was stunning.

"Hi! Howareyetheday? What a trip."

"I offered to drive, but she prefers it, so." Pete O' Shea, her beau, was her exact height, pale with freckles, red hair, and blue eyes beneath bushy red brows.

Rayne recalled a conversation with Lenni where she'd shared that they were both in their forties, had dated for a long time before deciding to tie the knot and make their union official.

"I feel more in control behind the wheel, and Petey says he doesn't mind." Lenni smiled.

"I don't!" Pete removed his coat — a canvas material that was weatherproof, and hung it on the coat tree, then he hung up

Lenni's too. "There you are."

"Thanks, love."

The pair, though opposites, seemed to be one unit with the easy affection of love cherished and shared.

This would be a happy wedding, Rayne felt it in her bones. At last, their McGrath luck was turning around.

Rayne stuffed her hand in her pocket of her raincoat, worrying the Jimmy Choo crystal. It had been a comfort to touch. "I'm so glad you found a solemnizer."

"Us too, though we'd decided to simply handfast if we didn't find a replacement," Lenni said. "Our friends will be here tomorrow, and it will be a treat to see them no matter what. We all live in Ireland, but different parts. Six hours shouldn't be a continent apart yet sometimes it feels that way. Sharon runs an all-girls school that has a waiting list years' long."

"Brandon Garrett is an artifact restorer who travels the world, and his fourteen-year-old son, Drake, runs track. They think he might be good enough for the Olympics." Pete smiled at Lenni before turning to Rayne, Amos, and Cormac. "Drake is our godson. It's been wonderful to encourage him along the way, since we never wanted kids of our own."

"We get to spoil him, guilt free." Lenni scanned the interior with a speculative gaze. "This is a lovely home."

"Thank you! This way is the kitchen — over there are the two bedrooms. The main bedroom has an ensuite and there is a shared bath off the hall, if you had other guests."

Rayne flipped on the light to the kitchen, bumping into the doorway with the bottle. She withdrew it from her other pocket, hoping it was all right, and placed it in the center of the round wooden dining table. She'd arranged fall flowers for the centerpiece that gave off a cinnamon scent because of the pale orange carnations. "We thought you might like a dram before bed. Our cook is quite talented. This is spiced whiskey she's made. You said you had dinner in Kilkenny?"

"We did," Lenni said.

Pete stood next to her in the threshold while Rayne crossed to the fridge, which she opened. "We have the basics in here — milk, jam, eggs." She pointed to the cupboard on the opposite side of the room. "The pantry has bread, crackers, and assorted snacks."

"I'm stuffed." Pete gestured to the whiskey. "But a nightcap will be just the thing."

"Coffee?" Lenni asked. "I'm an addict. I hope you have a machine."

"And I like tea," Pete said.

"We have a Keurig under the counter so you can choose what you like. A two-burner stove, and a microwave should address all your needs."

"This is far fancier than what I'd imagined when I'd booked rustic bungalows at the castle." Lenni nodded with approval. "It's just the right mix of old and new."

That made Rayne happy, and sure that they were on the right track for the village itself. "Good to know."

Pete picked up the whiskey bottle and admired the facets in the glass. "Is this an antique?"

"Yes," Rayne said. "We discovered the bottle in the attic."

"If you want an exact date, Brandon is an expert on artifacts. He's an expert because he is nosy," Pete tapped his nose, "and can't stop asking questions."

"Sounds like Rayne," Amos said.

Lenni smiled. "And you are?"

Rayne shook her head. "I'm so sorry — I'm Rayne McGrath, this is Amos Lowell, grounds manager, and Cormac Lloyd, who manages the house."

"Lenni McGee and Pete O'Shea," Lenni

said. “We’ve done everything online, so this is the first time we are meeting face to face.”

“You have a partner?” Pete asked.

“My cousin, Ciara,” Rayne said. “You will meet her tomorrow. We are all at your service to make your wedding special, though it’s gotten off to a bumpy start.”

“This is nothing,” Pete said. “Remember a few years ago when we went to the Bahamas?”

Lenni chuckled. “How could I forget? We almost drowned on a fishing tour of the island. Our boat hit a coral reef, and we had to swim to shore.” She shuddered. “I am not a fan of the water in the first place. Add sharks?” Her eyes widened. “We flew home the next day.”

“That’s awful!” Rayne said.

“The second attempt,” Lenni said in a lowered voice, “was at a romantic Scottish hotel on the loch. It was haunted. Legit haunted. I am a strong woman who manages a company of a thousand people. I was shaking in my boots. This one wanted to check out the noises. You are never supposed to go check out the noises, right?”

Pete laughed. “I had no idea my goddess was afraid of anything — the water, and ghosts. I didn’t mind holding you all night, did I?” He caressed her arm.

"No." Lenni smiled fondly.

"Did you find out what was causing the noise?" Amos asked.

"We asked the property owner the next day and she said it was haunted by Scary Mary Scott, the widow of a pirate hanged from his own ship that had been sunk in the loch outside," Pete said with a grin.

"Scary Mary Scott!" Rayne exclaimed.

Lenni sighed. "We'd planned to stay four days that time but decided instead to watch Drake compete. We try to make each of his meets but that one had come up suddenly."

"So, this is our third attempt. If it doesn't happen, it's okay." Pete clasped Lenni's hands and kissed the fingers. "I love you and you love me."

"We are very serious about handfasting this time around. Drake wants to be our witness as does Sharon and Brandon. Why not?"

"Sweet!!" Rayne loved the romance of it. They were sincere.

"What about your parents?" Cormac asked.

"Deceased." Pete put his arm around Lenni's waist. "We only have each other."

"It seems that you have found your best friend to travel through life with," Cormac observed.

"Let's go over the plan for tomorrow," Lenni said.

"When will your friends arrive?" Rayne asked.

"Sharon by noon — Brandon and Drake around the same time."

"You are welcome to have breakfast with us at the house. It would be casual, around nine. We didn't plan anything, not realizing you'd be here early."

Lenni and Pete shared a look.

"Or," Rayne said, easily able to decipher that was not of interest for the couple. "We can get together for a light lunch at noon. Up to you. The ceremony is slated for four to get the afternoon setting sun. The gazebo is weatherproof."

"We don't care about early. We work so hard during the year that being able to sleep in is a treat," Pete said.

"We have things here to tide us over for a bite to eat until later," Lenni said. She patted her duffle bag.

"The fridge and pantry are stocked with the basics," Rayne said.

"That sounds perfect," Pete said.

"If you'd like, we can go to the Coco Bean Café for food, or the Sheep's Head pub for a small bite. We've planned a full Irish dinner at five-thirty or six," Rayne said.

"I can't wait to see the castle," Pete said. "I love history. When Lenni told me about this place, I had to do a search on the McGraths."

"You did?" Rayne put her hand to her chest. It was funny to hear him be so enthusiastic. Heck, she was too.

"Pete loves history, just as much as Brandon adores artifacts. They have the old days in their blood. Me and Sharon are modern businesswomen. We met in college and have been fast friends ever since."

"Is she married?"

"To the school," Lenni said. "She's happy."

"Brandon is on divorce number three." Pete gave a shrug. "His travels don't provide security in the sense that he is rarely home."

"Drake is surprisingly well-adjusted," Lenni said.

"He knows he is loved, that's why," Pete said. "You just need one person in your corner in this crazy life and he has four — five, counting Sharon."

"She dotes on him too," Lenni agreed.

Cormac's phone dinged. "Maeve needs me at the house," he said. "Rayne?"

Her indecision to leave just then must have shown on her face. She wanted to make sure there was nothing else her guests needed.

"I can walk you back," Amos said. "I have my own giant umbrella."

"Nice to meet you both," Cormac said. "Congratulations on finding your true love through any challenge."

"Ah, thanks, Cormac," Lenni said.

"Any chance we can see the attic tomorrow?" Pete asked.

Cormac sent Rayne a panicked look.

"Cormac will be happy to show you the downstairs rooms," Rayne said. "The attic is very dangerous with all the junk piled in it."

"All right," Pete conceded. "But we'd be careful."

Cormac left, the door revealing pouring rain. Rayne accidentally dropped the crystal from the Jimmy Choo.

"What's that?" Pete picked it up and admired it before handing it back to Rayne.

"A crystal from a high heel that my dog stole and buried pieces of across the property," Rayne said with a laugh. "If you find any shiny objects, please return them to me. I have the other shoe at the house just in case."

"Are you sure that's from a shoe?" Pete asked. "It is remarkably clear."

"It was fancy," Amos said. "I saw it myself. The dog raced off with it like he knew he'd won the prize."

"We don't have pets but love them." Lenni took Pete's hand.

"Blarney is my first. Lenni, we'll need to go over the final fitting for your dress," Rayne said. "We can do that when you get up. Shoot me a text and I can come get you."

"We can walk," Lenni said. "We both love to be outside during our free time. Pete's cooped up in the college, and I'm trapped in my office."

"We've got horses, sheep, and ducks. We could offer a carriage ride if the weather co-operates," Rayne said.

"I'd love a pint at the pub," Pete said. "Having low-key time together is the best gift we can have, so don't feel like we need to be entertained."

"You might be the perfect guests," Rayne said.

"How about eleven for the fitting?" Lenni suggested. "We'll come to you."

"Great," Rayne said. "Good night."

Amos and Rayne grabbed their giant umbrellas as they stepped from the bungalow to the porch.

Rayne moved toward the manor house in

the distance, but Amos took her arm and bent to kiss her beneath the protection of the umbrella.

He peered into her eyes. “Ready for that cup of coffee?”

“Yes!” Rayne didn’t even hesitate.

“This way, milady,” Amos teased. “My place is behind these cottages.”

Rayne’s stomach fluttered with excitement.

It had been six months since Landon had broken her heart and destroyed her faith in her own common sense.

How hadn’t she realized what he’d been up to?

Amos had been patiently waiting for her. They’d become friends and shared a solid respect for one another.

He closed his umbrella to share hers, their shoulders together as they dashed across the grass to a stone bungalow. He opened his wooden front door. Inside the layout was similar to the refurbished ones but had older appliances and furniture that he’d personalized with blankets and pillows. There was an array of photos on the wall.

“These are great,” Rayne said. “Did you take these pictures?”

“A hobby of mine,” Amos shared.

“You are very talented.” She examined the

pictures closely. He'd gotten one of Blarney chasing the geese in motion, black and white, with Rayne on the edge of the lake.

"I love this one," Amos said. He tapped the image.

"I do too! Will you make me a print?"

"Of course," Amos said. "Would you like coffee? Whiskey?"

"That sounds perfect."

Amos went to the kitchen and turned on the lights. "You can take your jacket off and stay a while," he said.

Realizing she was clutching the lapels of her raincoat, though she'd left the umbrella by the front door, she released it.

The crystal again dropped from her pocket. "I've got to put this with the others before I lose it again."

"How many have you found?"

"I'm not sure. I drop them all in the vase." She draped the coat over the kitchen chair.

Amos poured them each two fingers of oaky whiskey. "Slainte," he said.

"Slainte," she replied. She sipped, her mouth dry.

Suddenly, she didn't know where to look. Amos took up the whole kitchen. He crossed to her in four strides.

"Don't be nervous," Amos whispered as he peered down into her eyes.

"I can't help it. I made an awful mistake."

Amos's brow furrowed. "Landon."

"Yes."

"He was an idiot who took advantage of you and your dreams."

"Yes." But she hadn't known that at the time. She'd been naïve.

"The Rayne McGrath I know would kick his ass if he ever tried such a thing again." Amos brushed her hair off her cheek.

She chuckled. "You're right."

"Sometimes we need to learn that we are able to stand on our own two feet, before we are ready to be part of a couple."

"You sound like you know what you're talking about," Rayne said.

"When I was at university, I thought I'd found the love of my life. I had plans for us. How we would take our place as a couple after graduation." His blue eyes clouded.

"What happened?"

"She didn't have that same vision. Loved me but not enough to commit to my dreams of staying in Ireland."

Rayne ran her knuckles across Amos's strong jaw. "I'm sorry."

"She moved to India, to be a nurse for doctors across borders. I couldn't be mad. It was my fault for not listening to her."

"How could she leave you?"

Rayne placed her hand on his strong chest.

"Her destiny was greater than Ireland." Amos gave a good-natured smirk.

"Are you still friends?"

"We send holiday cards. She married a doctor, and they live in Africa now. They really do want to save the world."

"Do you have regrets?" Rayne asked.

"No. She was right to leave, for her dreams. I love Ireland. Mine are here."

"Amos, I am going to return to America at some point," Rayne said.

"I understand." Their mouths were inches apart.

"Is this smart, to start something?"

"Smart?" Amos shook his head.

Rayne, drawn to him, stood on her tiptoes. "Then what are we doing?"

Amos gently, slowly, cupped her nape. Shivers tingled down her spine.

"Kissing, lass. Just kissing."

Chapter Seventeen

The next morning, Rayne realized that she'd overslept. She woke and patted the bed, but Blarney wasn't there.

"Blarney?"

Her pup rose from where he'd been sleeping against the door. He gave a great big shake of his furry body, one ear lopsided.

"Rough night?" Her grin remained in place, even though Blarney was disturbed over something.

Amos was an expert kisser. They'd spent an hour, just kissing. It was like learning a new skill all over again as he taught her how he liked to kiss.

He'd walked her home by ten — a perfect gentleman.

The manor had been dark as everyone had already been in their rooms. Rayne was glad as she didn't want to break the spell Amos had created for them. Two people with insane chemistry on the verge of combustion.

Now, it was already past nine and she'd missed coffee and breakfast. She showered, dressed, and raced down the stairs, poking her head into the kitchen. Frances was taking a break over a cup of tea at the table.

"Morning. Where is everyone?"

"Maeve and Aine are in the laundry room, Sorcha will be here at one to help decorate for the wedding, and Ciara is with Dafydd in the blue parlor. She asked not to be disturbed." Frances peered wisely over her mug. "It's been a half hour."

"Oh." Of course, Rayne wanted to check on her cousin despite the butt-out vibe she was getting from their chef.

"Cormac is in the office searching for a Thomas McGrath in the family records," Frances continued, "since he wasn't in the bible. I'm sure there had to be more than one as it is a popular name even now. When will the couple be here?"

Rayne snagged an apple from the fruit bowl and sat down. It would do for breakfast.

"Lenni and Pete? Lenni for sure for her final fitting will be here at eleven. She gave me her measurements online. I won't tighten the zipper until the last minute just in case."

"Smart," Frances said.

"Experience," Rayne agreed. "The fall colors will be really pretty. Her dress is an ivory, like old lace, with soft peach accents. Pete is wearing a cocoa brown suit." She recounted the couple's complicated history. "This is the third attempt to get married."

Frances exhaled. "My husband was my best friend. It sounds like they have the same kind of relationship. I would have stayed with mine through thick and thin, but his death left me alone. He went where I couldn't follow, though I was tempted."

It was the first time Frances had opened up about her husband. She'd left Cotter Village, and it had been their good fortune to get her at McGrath Castle.

"Would you ever marry again?" Rayne bit into the crisp apple, chewed, and swallowed.

Frances shook her head. "No. I couldn't stand the loss. I'll pour what's left of my heart into the meals here."

A door opened from one of the rooms, a masculine voice shouted a curse, then the front door opened and slammed closed.

Rayne stood, the chair scooting back.

Frances nodded. "Ciara will need you more than Cormac. The whiskey decanter is full already. I added some of the spiced in a blue bottle."

"Thanks," Rayne said.

She hurried to the parlor door which remained open. Ciara's back was to her, her shoulders shaking. Blarney appeared and entered the room.

Rayne closed the door behind her to give them privacy. She went to the hidden compartment. "Ciara?"

Ciara lifted her tear-stained face and held out her hand. On her palm was the simple gold Claddagh ring Dafydd had proposed with. "He wouldn't take it back," she said. "I don't want it anymore. It belonged to his Gran."

"I'm sorry, Ciara."

"I didn't love him enough to forgive him." Ciara placed the ring on the desktop. "He's really mad. Claims that I'm the one who broke the promise."

Rayne poured them each a drink, giving Ciara hers. She stayed quiet so her cousin had the room to talk.

"He hates me now."

Ciara sipped. Blarney leaned against her leg.

Rayne patted her shoulder.

"I don't blame him for hating me. I can't keep the ring." Ciara glared at the gold shining on the desktop, her mouth a thin line.

"You can give it to him later. Once he's

had time to process," Rayne said, "what he's feeling."

"I'm relieved." Ciara lifted her face, her expression one of guilt. "I am relieved to not follow through with the proposal. What kind of person does that make me, Rayne? I loved him at one point. I know I did."

Rayne placed her tumbler on the desk, and then Ciara's. She pulled her cousin into a hug.

"I'm a terrible person," Ciara sobbed.

"No, you're not," Rayne countered.

"How can you say that?"

"You are a smart woman. Feelings change all the time. What if you'd gone through with the ceremony?" Rayne tipped back, hands on her cousin's shoulders, and studied Ciara's face. "You have integrity and would have done it because it was expected of you. Right?"

Ciara sobbed more. "Damn it, Rayne."

"You would have been miserable." Rayne made circular motions on Ciara's back.

"How can you know that?"

"Because you are an incredible person. You are loyal to a fault. Marrying Dafydd out of expectation would have been the wrong move for the *right* reasons. This gave you a chance to reflect. His dishonesty regarding his past allowed a window of opportunity and reflection for you to make the right choice for you. There is no wrong in that."

Ciara slowed her sobs. The cousins grabbed their drinks and made their way to the blue love seat.

"It was a close call." Rayne sat and Blarney jumped up between them on the cushions.

"What will people think?"

"Who cares? They aren't living your life."

"Dafydd wanted to know if he should leave the manor."

"And you said?"

"No! He's a brilliant shepherd. Unless he wants to. It's not like we will run into one another all the time." Ciara sipped her drink.

"All right. I support you, whatever you want. While we are busy remarketing Grathton we might be smart to look for another shepherd, just in case."

"I can't imagine he'd be happy here," Ciara said in a sad voice.

"No. But maybe he will focus on the sheep and pour his sorrows into that."

"He says I ripped his family from him," Ciara glanced at Rayne over Blarney's head, "I guess it is true."

"Don't let him guilt you into taking him back, Ciara. You have a right to live your life for yourself and what makes you happy. If he steps over the line, we should let him go."

"In the spring," Ciara said. "We can't manage the sheep without him. Was I stupid to break it off now?"

"Being true to yourself is never stupid. Does it complicate things?" Rayne shrugged. "We are getting to be pros at handling complications."

"Come June, at the end of Da's insane deadline of a year, we will know how things turn out."

"A bright spot, cuz? You should take the McGrath name, as Uncle Nevin wanted."

Blarney barked and wagged his tail.

"You're right." Ciara patted Blarney's head. "It's time. I'll have to find the paperwork."

"It's in the office, locked in the file cabinet," Rayne said right away.

"The harder I try to hold onto what no longer serves, the bumpier life has been." Ciara fisted her hand and then opened it. "I'm ready to step into the flow."

"That sounds great to me too. If we don't connect with Fionagh Quinn, maybe we need to look for a different solicitor?" Rayne didn't finish her drink as she hadn't had breakfast yet and had a dress to finish. "Haley highly recommended her so she'd be my first choice. Treasa was no help."

"She was full of herself, wasn't she?"

"That's being kind. Snobby totally fit her." Rayne tapped her cell phone. "We can check the online directory."

"That's a grand idea. Never thought I'd miss a physical copy of a phone book," Ciara said. "Want me to do it since you have a dress fitting today? I'll keep phoning Fionagh until she answers out of annoyance."

"Yes, please." Rayne was relieved to delegate the task to her cousin. "Our situation is complicated, and it's important to have our legal stuff sorted out. My American brain might miss something."

"I'll also chat with Maeve about the antiques appraiser." Ciara drank the rest of Rayne's whiskey. "We can sell the spiced whiskey. It was delicious and unique to McGrath."

"I like that idea." Whiskey, jam, and weddings — adding on the expense of making Grathton a tourist destination, creating a village from yesteryear just wasn't the right direction.

A knock sounded on the door and Maeve entered. "Lenni and Pete are in the foyer. Should I put them in the library?"

"Oh, that's all right." Rayne walked toward Maeve. "I'll need Lenni upstairs. Is Cormac free to show Pete around? By the time we're done, they should be too."

"Sure." Maeve's astute gaze zeroed in on the empty tumblers and the gold Claddagh ring on the desk.

Ciara busied herself with scanning her cell phone.

"I'll be back," Rayne said to Ciara. "You're on lawyer duty." She and Maeve left the blue parlor, Rayne closing the door behind them.

Maeve didn't comment as she and Rayne walked down the hall. Lenni and Pete admired the bogwood statue of the Irish warrior in his kilt, sword, and shield.

"This is incredible." Excitement filled Pete's voice. "The details are complete down to tiny fingernails."

"To be honest, I've never examined it that close," Rayne said.

"Don't worry, Rayne." Lenni put her arm around Pete's waist. She'd dressed in leather flats and a calf-length denim skirt and top. "My dearest has an eye for detail. Used to make me batty, but I learned to let it go or else I'd spend my time tearing my hair out." She pulled her fabulous curls.

"We can't have that." Pete reluctantly looked away from the statue but exclaimed again when he saw the McGrath shield on the wall. "When is this from?"

"Cormac can tell you," Rayne promised. "Cormac, you remember Lenni and Pete from last night?"

"Yes, nice to see you again. Gray skies are forecasted for the rest of the day but no rain." Cormac wore his uniform of black suit jacket over slacks. Their butler occasionally wore more casual clothes, but it was a rare sight and usually due to working outside.

"Hi," Lenni said as Pete smiled.

"I'll gladly answer all of your questions." Cormac gestured to his left. "Let's start this way. The hall eventually leads to the tower which has been refurbished."

"The tower?" Pete took Lenni's hand. "Babe, why didn't we stay in the tower?"

"We had too many people for that to be comfortable. Why don't we come for our anniversary?" Lenni laughed. "This place isn't going anywhere."

Rayne bit her lip and changed the subject. "Lenni, my sewing studio is up this staircase."

Pete kissed Lenni's fingers and released her hand. "Until later."

The men went one direction, Maeve disappeared, and Lenni and Rayne climbed the stairs.

"How did it feel to inherit a castle?"

"Surreal," Rayne said. "I still can't believe it."

"I happened to be scrolling social media when I saw the advert for Modern Lace, run by a talented young American — you. I put in your name, and that awful Landon Short showed up, with him fleeing authorities in Mexico. What an arse. Is he still in jail?"

Her face flamed. "You saw that?"

"Don't be upset, Rayne. I wanted to give you a fair shake. And, I thought the story of you inheriting was quite touching. I was tickled he'd shown his true colors before you married him or the gombeen might have gotten half."

Gombeen? Rayne would ask Aine and add it to her vocab list. "Ciara is the best. I couldn't ask for a better partner."

"Ciara Smith. From the pictures on the McGrath Castle website, you bear a striking resemblance. Eyes, stature, natural hair color." Lenni grinned. "I change mine all the time."

They arrived at the sewing studio. Rayne unlocked the door, and ushered Lenni before her. "Here we are."

Lenni's face morphed from happy to radiant as she walked toward the wedding dress hanging on a rolling clothes rack. The gown was a stretch silk satin that was formfitting yet allowed some give. The delicate antique lace on the sleeves and mermaid skirt exuded luxury, as did the silk ivory buttons at the wrist and up the nape. It was a classic style.

"It's gorgeous, Rayne. I can't believe you created this from our conversation. It's like you read my mind. And you made this by hand! Each stitch is precise." Lenni smoothed her fingers over each detail.

"Ready to try it on?" Rayne had a privacy screen near the closet.

"I wore the same undergarments so it would fit," Lenni said.

"Smart. Let me know if you need help." Rayne wheeled the dress toward Lenni, who stepped behind the screen.

"Would you like champagne?"

"No. Let's wait for later." Lenni's voice was barely a whisper. "Rayne, this is magical. I had no idea that putting on this dress would make me feel this way."

This made Rayne's day. "The zipper is loose, so let me do the back."

"Oh, Rayne." Lenni caressed the front of the gown over her hips. Her green eyes shimmered with pure joy. "I feel beautiful."

Rayne blinked happy tears away. "That's what this day and this dress is all about." She carefully zipped the back. Snug as a glove with no alterations necessary.

"How does it look?"

Rayne brought her to the full-length mirror on the closet door. "Stunning. Let's do a twist for your hair to show off the neck on this gown." Rayne lifted her curls to give her the idea.

Lenni's perma grin said it all. "Pete will be blown away."

"I'm glad you like it," Rayne said.

"Love it," Lenni countered. "Pete and I will splash the news of our wedding all over social media. We're all about a good underdog story."

Rayne placed her palm over her heart. "Thank you."

"Not that inheriting a castle makes you an underdog, but you know what I mean." Lenni twirled to see her dress from all angles.

"I do. It hasn't been an easy transition for some of the villagers. You are a smart CEO. Would Grathton hold more appeal if we made it a tourist destination, by creating a village from the eighteen hundreds?"

Lenni returned to the privacy screen and stepped behind it. Slipping out of her gown, she gently returned it to Rayne. "Interesting proposition. There are historical places all over though. I suggest a cost analysis. Pros and cons. Goal?"

"To grow the populace with a younger demographic that want to establish roots. We have old-timers in their eighties and nineties that still showed up with shovels the day we cleared the cemetery."

"You have a cemetery attached to the property?" Lenni shrugged into her denim dress and pulled the phone from her pocket. Though silenced, it vibrated with notifications.

"We do."

"That will make Sharon's day. Or night. She loves all things spooky. Not me so much. I will sleep with the light on at the slightest sound."

Rayne laughed.

"Sharon will be here in thirty minutes and is starving. Drake and Brandon will be here around the same time. Should we meet them at the café?"

"Sure. But, Pete mentioned wanting a pint. We could split up, boys and girls. Or all go to the pub. Excellent fish and chips. Oh, but Drake is under eighteen."

"Pub works for us. It's a common thing to allow all ages until after nine PM and Drake loves his fish and chips."

"Beetle serves awesome food and drink. The Coco Bean is right next door, anyway — Sinead and Liam own that, and Sinead is making your wedding cake."

"All right! How wonderful." Lenni put her hand on the door. "Let's meet at the pub at noon. I'll drag Pete away from Cormac, who I am sure is overwhelmed by questions. I'll think about your challenge with the village. I love solutions."

With that, Lenni departed. Rayne tightened the zipper, just in time to grab Ciara for a walk to the pub. "Can't wait for you to meet the guests."

"I overheard Lenni and Maeve talking about lunch. Cormac wore a dazed look after the tour with Pete, so I figured I'd join you for moral support."

"Any progress with Fionagh?" Rayne asked.

"No, but we have an antiques appraiser coming out next week." Ciara buttoned her jacket. "Maeve had a list of numbers, and we got lucky on the third attempt. Nobody better talk about Aiden's death or that might sour their experience."

"I didn't even think about that." Rayne adjusted her charcoal scarf that doubled as a shawl. Would Beetle be at work, or laying low from the gardai?

"Show time," Ciara said.

Rayne and Ciara crossed the street as Lenni and Pete hugged a petite woman with Asian features. A teenager with a very lean physique who had to be Drake, jumped from the car as a tall, handsome man with dark hair like the young man's, climbed from the driver's side of a parked sportscar.

Brandon Garrett?

Her guess was answered when Sharon called out, "Brandon!"

And then, to her horror, a man on an electric bicycle whizzed past them, pausing. Bran Wilson chortled, "Another murder in Grathton Village. If I were you, I'd cheek it back to where you're from. Strangers don't belong here."

Chapter Eighteen

Mortified, Rayne sucked in a shocked breath. "Bran Wilson! I'm going to tell your mother what you're up to," she said with a wag of her finger. She'd worked with Bronagh just a few days back, and the lovely woman had expressed nothing but support for Grathton Village.

Lenni and Pete exchanged amused looks.

"You'd better not," Bran said, sounding concerned.

"Back off," Ciara said, standing at Rayne's side — a united front against a forty-year-old bully who lived with his mom.

"Afraid of the truth?" Bran balanced on the bike. "Aiden was killed in the cemetery."

The man rode off, sending the Irish equivalent of shooting the bird over his shoulder as he went.

"What a tool," Ciara said.

"He seems like a right spanner," Lenni said. "What did he mean about a murder, though?"

"Should we be worried?" Pete seconded.

"Bran is against the revitalization of the village, something that Ciara and I have been tasked with." Rayne tried to keep it light. "The councilwoman for Cotter Village would like us . . . to be combined."

"What are the benefits to combining the villages?" Lenni asked.

Pete looked at his wife in horror. "You can't think that there would be any worth giving up the quaintness of these streets and buildings."

"I have my own opinion," Lenni said. "I am gathering information."

Pete spread his hands and eyed the gray, but dry, sky.

"I'm happy to answer those questions," Rayne said. "How about we head inside, though?"

"Over a pint of the black stuff," Brandon said, referring to Guinness. This was echoed by Sharon and Lenni.

"I want a Club Orange," Drake said. "Do they sell soda?"

"Yes," Ciara said. "Club Rock Shandy is my favorite."

Rayne opened the door to the pub and the latest guests trickled in. She'd never tasted the Rock Shandy flavor before, but the Orange was good.

What could she tell them about Aiden and his death?

Garda Williams was in the pub, speaking to Beetle in a low voice. Colleen, his sister, came out from the kitchen with an apron and an order pad.

Colleen gave them a wry smile. She read the time on her watch then said, "Afternoon, folks. Let me clear off a table in the back. Follow me."

Rayne pulled her gaze from Beetle and the garda. "Don't leave town," Williams said. "I want your promise, or I will put you in a holding cell. You are our most likely suspect and every question we have comes back to you."

"I won't leave," Beetle said. "I didn't touch a hair on Aiden's head. I'd like you to go before you ruin my business."

"We have witnesses that say differently," the garda eyed the bruises on Beetle's knuckles.

"I've already explained about that night," Beetle said.

Lenni cleared her throat to get Rayne's attention. "Everything okay?"

"Yes, of course," Rayne said, following Lenni to their table for seven.

Colleen handed out menus, glancing often

toward the front door, the garda, and her brother. As soon as Garda Williams left, she excused herself. "I'll be right back to get your order."

"What is that all about?" Lenni asked. "Is the tattooed bartender a suspect in the man's murder?"

"Unfortunately," Rayne said. "I think he's innocent though. Colleen, the waitress, is his sister."

"She's beautiful," Sharon said. "Was it over Colleen?"

Rayne knew this wouldn't win her any points with the gardai or her curious guests. "Beetle and Aiden did have an argument about her, though I don't know all of the details. Now, let's focus on our order."

Colleen untied her apron and threw it at Beetle's chest. "I won't help if you continue to be so fecking stubborn!" She went into the back, and Beetle followed.

"It might be a while before we get to order, if at all," Ciara said. "We can go next door to the Coco Bean."

"I don't mind waiting," Lenni said. "You can fill us in on what happened to Aiden."

Brandon, Sharon, and Pete all agreed to wait, though Drake was restless. "I'm hungry!"

Lenni pulled a granola bar from her purse

and pushed it toward the teenager.

"Thanks," Drake said.

"He's growing. Again." Brandon studied Rayne and then Ciara. "You got kids?"

"No," Rayne said.

"Nope," Ciara seconded. "I'm Ciara Smith, by the way. Rayne's cousin."

The guests all called out a hello.

"Kids are a pain in the arse." Brandon tossed a napkin at his son, who grinned back at his father, while demolishing the granola bar in two bites.

Rayne gave the barest bones of what had happened and what they had discovered when finding Aiden over Thomas McGrath's grave.

"I'd like to see it." Brandon's statement was applauded. He continued, "Cemeteries are interesting. One where a murder was recently committed? Even more so. The mysteries are usually a hundred years in the past."

"Do we have time after our pint?" Pete asked.

"*If* we get a pint," Sharon said.

"The beauty of Grathton Village," Ciara said, "is that everything is in walking distance. The church and old cemetery are a few blocks away."

Colleen and Beetle exited the kitchen,

both with red cheeks and flashing eyes. Matching tempers?

Smoothing her hair from her forehead, ponytail in place, Colleen searched for a tablet on the counter, grabbed a pen, and returned to their table. “Sorry about that. Now, what can I get you?”

“Club Orange and fish and chips. Large.” Drake propped his elbows on the table and smiled at Colleen. “Extra-large?”

“Got it. I can add extra chips,” Colleen said with a half-smile. “Curry sauce?”

“No, thanks.”

“Next?”

Colleen quickly took their orders, dropped the drink ticket with Beetle, and ducked back out of sight to the kitchen.

Rayne watched as Beetle put together the drinks and when they were done, she went to get them and bring them back which would give her a chance to check on him as well as save Colleen a trip.

“Hey,” Rayne said. “How are you holding up?”

“It couldn’t be worse,” Beetle shared. “Did you know that Aiden might be Corrine’s da? And Colleen won’t tell me! I had to hear it from Paddy O’Brien. The McGillicuddys are in town for Darcy’s funeral tomorrow. Anyway, him and Don were in last night drinking and let it slip. On purpose, I bet."

Rayne picked up the tray of drinks. The comment didn't require an answer.

"It's why Garda Williams has me under such scrutiny. If I'd known about it, I wouldn't have acted any differently. Well, maybe insist he pay for Corrine's school or something." Beetle narrowed his eyes. "I'm not a killer."

"I know that," Rayne said.

"It's you and Ciara sticking up for me that has stayed the gardai from tossing me behind bars." Beetle held her gaze. "Thank you."

"If there is anything else we can do, just say the word." She really did believe in his innocence.

"Colleen told me you're discussing helping her run a business?" Beetle wiped up a small beer spill on the tray.

"Yes." Rayne nodded. "She explained she doesn't require a big income, thank heaven, since we are on a tight budget. We've got to get new, younger, people in those businesses."

Beetle crossed his arms. "Like, what were you thinking?"

"We threw out the idea of a lending library, since her hobby is reading." Rayne carefully slid the tray off the counter.

"Colleen always has her nose in a book," Beetle agreed. "And she's a great mam. So patient! I have no idea what she ever saw in Aiden. It's my fault. I will never forgive myself for introducing them while she was at university, and I was playing the clubs in Dublin."

"You can't blame yourself for that." Rayne adjusted the tray. "Anyway, the library could be a neighborhood place to gather readers, of all ages."

Beetle scowled. "Not much of a reader myself, I'd rather play music, but to each their own."

"Agreed. My passion is creating dresses. Ciara loves horses." Rayne lifted the round tray, careful not to spill. Three pints and one Club Orange. She and Ciara were sticking with water.

"Thanks for caring about the village. Mam and Da have the family homestead. We've had to sell land to keep it going, to the McElroys, or the O'Briens, but we're still here, which is more than other families can say. I wonder if the Dennehys will stick around with Aiden gone?" Beetle's eyes were sad.

Rayne recalled Sheila saying that Aiden's mom had remarried, and his dad had taken off. Would there be an heir? "The McGillicuddys have lost Darcy."

Beetle wiped the counter with a towel. "A whole generation will be dying off. Where does that leave us?"

Rayne sighed. "Hopefully with room to grow. What do you think of merging with Cotter Village?"

"No, thanks. You keep bringing in business and I won't complain. Cotter is too expensive. I heard a rumor that you are considering making the village historical for a tourist trap." Beetle shook his head. "That wouldn't be for me."

"All right. Thanks for that feedback. Onward then," Rayne said with a laugh as she delivered the tray of drinks to their table. Paddy and Don had been busy boys spreading tales.

Perfect timing as the food also arrived, steaming hot deep fried fish filets, French fries, and bowls of clam chowder. Colleen delivered the food and ducked back out of sight.

"Let's save the cemetery trip for tomorrow, all right?" Rayne suggested. "We have a wedding to prepare for." She read the time on her phone and widened her eyes. "In two hours!"

Lenni, Pete, Sharon, Brandon, and Drake

all cheered. Beetle sent over a bottle of champagne on the house.

The ceremony uniting Lenni McGee and Pete O'Shea in the heated gazebo went off without a hitch. The solemnizer, a woman in her fifties with merry hazel eyes and a subtle gray suit, arrived on time and read the vows written by the long-term couple.

Brandon and Drake stood on one side, and Sharon the other. Lenni's simple bouquet of peach roses was something she and Sharon had put together, with a rose in Sharon's hair, and a rose for each of the guys' suit jackets. Rayne watched from afar — on hand if needed, but not part of the group. It would be the same for dinner later.

It was a skill to be there but not there. She wanted to fuss at the way the hem of the gown flowed but remained off scene. Like most things, this new venue was a work in progress.

Blarney and Amos joined her. Rayne kept hold of Blarney's collar so that he didn't make his way to the happy people in the gazebo.

"This is so romantic," Rayne whispered to Amos.

Amos slipped his hand around hers and squeezed, keeping it there rather than release it. "You are a romantic," he said with a glint in his blue eyes.

"What gave it away?" she countered. "The sketches of wedding dresses? My business model to design that perfect gown for happily ever after?"

"The lingerie," Amos teased.

She blushed as she recalled Blarney getting into the silk slips. "I suppose I am, but I don't mind. Do you believe in romance?"

"Romance, or love?"

"Are they two different things?" She hadn't really considered that before. Romance did not necessarily equal love.

"I would like to romance you, Rayne McGrath," Amos declared. "When can you come over for coffee again?"

"I dreamed about your kisses," Rayne said, meeting his gaze.

The heat there, desire for her, banished any chill in the November air. "And I dreamed of you," Amos said. They held one another's eyes for some time.

Before Rayne knew it, the McGee-O'Shea ceremony was over.

Because this was a very intimate affair, it would be just the guests in the formal dining room. Prime rib, roasted potatoes in a medieval setting. They'd asked Rayne to join them, but she'd declined, opting instead to oversee from a distance.

Sinead had delivered the wedding cake. It looked rich and decadent with glossy chocolate ganache, white pearls, and peach trim. They had the expensive champagne for many toasts.

After a special feast, the wedding party had moved to the gazebo for music off of Drake's Spotify account and dancing under the starlight. They'd made plans to meet tomorrow after church to check out the cemetery.

Father Patrick was combining Darcy's service with the Sunday eleven o'clock mass so Rayne would attend in the morning, rather than her usual Saturday. If she'd learned anything in this journey it was to be flexible.

After the staff dinner, Frances and Maeve cleared the dishes. Dafydd, Richard, Amos, Cormac, and Aine sat at the table. Rayne handed out flutes while Ciara passed around the amazing cake that Sinead had made for them that was the same chocolate Guinness flavor but without the fancy decorations.

"I scored the good champagne for us too," Rayne said. "We deserve a toast. Ciara and I could not do this without you. So, thank you. Slainte!"

Everyone drank, and Rayne topped off their glasses.

"We can celebrate our possible new solicitor, Fionagh Quinn," Ciara said. "She won't sign us on until after we meet with her, Monday at ten."

Rayne clapped her hands. "Persistence paid off." They'd need to figure out a way to pay for the solicitor Haley had highly recommended later. She exhaled, going with the flow. "That is great, Ciara."

"So, what does everyone think of our second wedding event?" Ciara took a bite of the cake and closed her eyes in joy.

"I've heard nothing but good things from them," Maeve said. "Lenni and Pete are incredible guests who appreciate that this is a home. Why couldn't they have been our first?"

"We learned a lot from our mistakes," Rayne said.

"Our many, many mistakes," Dafydd complained.

"That is true success, right mate?" Amos said. "Taking failure and turning it around despite the odds."

"We have had so many challenges," Rayne said. "But, Lenni looked beautiful in her dress, and she was thrilled with the wedding itself. It makes everything worth the pain to have a happy bride."

Ciara raised her champagne glass. "To

you, Rayne. You talk about us being a team, but you are our fearless leader. Without your . . . *misneach* . . . I'm not sure we would have gotten as far. Da was right to choose you to be at the helm."

"*Misneach* means courage," Amos explained. "You have bravery in spades. You'd make your ancestors proud."

"That's sweet of you to say, but without you all, I am a terrified American afraid of making more mistakes that could cost us not only the village but this home." Rayne took a bite of chocolate cake.

Sinead was a genius.

Ciara winced. "It won't come to that. It can't. There has been such a high price to pay that we can't lose sight of the goal. I know we talked about what Da wanted. Not just with modernization. I'm not sure."

"Oh, no. No trying to back out of going through with the adoption." Rayne gestured at her cousin with her champagne flute and shook her head. "Uncle Nevin wanted to adopt you. He just ran out of time."

All eyes turned to Ciara, but while most gazes held congratulations, Dafydd's were filled with anger.

Chapter Nineteen

Rayne was woken in the middle of the night by sounds that very well could be ghosts. Whatever they were, Blarney didn't like them. She sat straight up on her mattress, clutched the comforter, and stared toward the door.

The pup got off the bed for the third or fourth night this week and growled at the door before sprawling before it.

Her protector.

Instead of dreaming of Amos's kisses, she tossed and turned — sleep eluding her until she finally got out of bed. Elizabeth's demand that they help her find out what happened to Darcy hadn't gone anywhere. She put a note on her phone to ask Garda Lee and Garda Williams about it. The woman had seemed as sincere in her belief of foul play that it reminded Rayne of Ciara.

She studied the two purses displayed on shelves on her wall. The bubble gum pink

Hermes she'd gotten from an estate sale that was worth far more than she'd ever realized, and a bag from her mom that she would never sell. The Hermes was a safety net in case something happened to the sheep, or the village, or the manor.

They might need to sell it to pay for Fionagh Quinn's services.

Blarney, realizing that she was awake too, left his position by the door and jumped back up on the bed to watch her pace before her shelves. She'd put the crystals from her Jimmy Choo heels that she'd found since her pup's theft in a clear vase. They were cubic zirconia in a variety of shapes and colors — even ones that resembled diamonds.

She'd toyed with the idea of making Blarney a collar with some of the gemstones as he liked bling.

There was no way the other shoe would be found. It could be eaten or lost in the lake — possibly digested by a certain dog.

"Unless you buried it in the cemetery?" Rayne patted Blarney's soft, furry head. Various crystals had been found but never the actual shoe.

Her pup stared at her with adoring eyes that admitted to nothing.

"By Thomas McGrath's grave?"

He blinked, tongue lolling.

"But if I made you a custom collar that would reward you for bad behavior." She tilted her head. "You deserve nice things though."

She got the vase down that had the gemstones in it. Where was the one she'd just found? If she didn't put it with the others, it was bound to get lost.

"My rain jacket!"

She reached into the pocket of the rain jacket she'd hung on a hook in the bathroom so it would dry. It was nice to have the en-suite.

She'd asked Ciara to take her dad's bedroom, which also had an adjoining bath, but her cousin wasn't interested.

Last night she'd called Ciara out for trying to back away from Uncle Nevin's plans to adopt her. Boy, Dafydd had been upset that she was actually considering it. Maybe, if they didn't scare off Fionagh Quinn, the solicitor could handle the paperwork for that as well.

Rayne pulled out the smooth crystal and was about to add it to the others when she gave it another look. It didn't really match in shape or size but that didn't mean anything.

Some of the gemstones still had glue on

the back of them.

This one didn't.

She held it to her eye.

It was so clear she could almost see through it.

"This isn't from the Jimmy Choo, Blarney." Rayne put her hand to her temple and dropped to her knees on the mattress to peer into her dog's eyes.

He lowered his ears.

"Where did you get this, bud?"

If she was hoping for an answer, none was forthcoming.

"I hope Maeve is right about the fairies and leprechauns bringing these to us, otherwise you might have a real problem with the law."

A soft knock sounded on her bedroom door. "Rayne?" Ciara whispered.

"I'm awake!"

Rayne opened the door and stepped back to invite her cousin in. Ciara peered around the room, taking in Rayne's silk pajamas, sleep mask on her head, and bare feet. Her cousin wore sweatpants and an oversized tee. Thick fleece socks with Santas on them covered her toes.

"Come on in." Rayne gestured to the unmade bed. Once she got up for the day, she liked to make it but for now, Blarney remained on the mattress, the covers rumpled.

Ciara patted Blarney's head, then sat cross-legged next to him to rub his belly and back, scratching under his collar.

His tongue lolled and his eyes rolled back in delight.

"You've made his morning," Rayne said. "We didn't sleep well last night."

"Neither did I. I heard noises. That's why I wanted to talk to you, actually." Ciara pointed to Rayne's palm. "What's in your hand?"

"The crystal we found by the headstone. Should we move Thomas, do you think?"

"Nah — for now, let's leave the poor bloke where he is. Besides, we have a lot of other things that take priority."

"Like, deciding on the direction of the village. Historic, or modern? Or a mash-up of both. That's my favorite."

"It would be the fastest," Ciara said. "And make the most sense. But then what? How do we get people to the village? We barely have paying guests for the weddings. The next wedding on the books isn't until April."

"It's been a slow start," Rayne agreed. "Haley had suggested ads targeting digital nomads, which works with our mash-up of old and new. So far, we haven't paid for advertising. Aine has been posting to social media for free. We could set aside some money toward it. Now that we have positive reviews to share, things should pick up."

"I hope so. I don't have any fancy bags or clothes to sell. I'm sorry you've had to shoulder the burden of income. What a fool I've been to never really think about money. I had a roof over my head." Ciara scowled.

Rayne sat next to Ciara and Blarney, clutching the crystal. "I feel like an idiot too. I never, ever should have trusted Landon the way I did. I was naïve."

Ciara's eyes welled. "We are a couple of prized eejits," she said in a thick voice. A tear slid down her cheek. "I miss Da. I miss his way of telling stories and sharing our history. Like maybe he knew we didn't have much time. He never mentioned secret societies, though he was very proud that the McGraths took part in the rebellion and fought for freedom."

"My dad was proud too," Rayne said. "The Republic of Ireland."

"It wasn't the first try for freedom from England." Ciara straightened. "Want to go rummage through the attic for more history?"

"I haven't read the books that were in the trunk we just brought down. Let's light a fire and get caffeine. We can see what's there to start. Maybe we'll find information on Thomas. Cormac said that the Thomas's in the family bible don't match the timing of his death."

"I'm in." Ciara gave Blarney a last pat and hopped to her feet. "Bobby Fitzroy thinks the limestone matches the early twentieth century, so 1900s, which coincides with the 1923 date on the grave. He just keeps repeating how that grave shouldn't be there."

"I wonder how the investigation is going for poor Aiden?"

"I sent a text last night to Dominic asking for an update on the case, but he hasn't answered. I should know better, right? Crime happens on our lands and he's absent." Her nose scrunched.

"Want me to try Garda Lee?"

Ciara waved her hand. "I tried her too."

"Maybe they have answers and are sifting through the information," Rayne suggested.

"I would love for them to share!" Ciara said. "It doesn't look good for our village to be struck by tragedy yet again and have the gardai dawdle. And, Garda Lee didn't reply to my text about Darcy McGillicuddy either."

Rayne bit her lip and opted to change the

subject. It had been less than a week since Aiden had been stabbed in the back with garden shears but so much had happened since that it seemed ages ago.

"We have Darcy's service today. I wonder when the funeral will be for Aiden?" Rayne asked.

"I have no idea. Back-to-back funerals isn't good for our community." Ciara's shoulders lowered. "Tea, and toast. I'm hungry. I bet Frances isn't even up yet."

Rayne, about to drop the crystal into the vase, thought of the intact Jimmy Choo. "Hang on." She opened the drawer of the wardrobe and retrieved the lone high heel, comparing it to the dozens of crystals on the shoe. None of the sizes were the same. "This crystal doesn't match."

Ciara took the crystal and examined the high heel. "You're right."

"Not even close. I should show it to Maeve and Aine. They might be missing a piece of costume jewelry."

"It's not mine," Ciara said.

"That I gathered," Rayne said. "You have never been the blingy type."

"I like the oval shape." Ciara held out her hand and Rayne placed it her cousin's palm. "I can't believe the design on those sandals. That is very fancy."

"I didn't buy them but there are a pair of Jimmy Choos with a crystal bow for the flower at the toe. Almost five thousand smackeroos, but some brides wouldn't flinch at that price. They know what they want. Luxury."

Ciara flipped the crystal like a coin in the air. "I'd prefer not worrying about one coming loose while walking down the aisle." She gave it back to Rayne, who dropped it in the pocket of her silk robe. It made a great stress reliever. "Could it be a match for another of your shoes?"

"Nope." She planned on showing it around though just to be sure before she added it to the vase of loose crystals. "Maeve thinks the leprechauns are leaving little crystal gifts around the property."

"Why can't it be things like diamonds worth actual money?" Ciara groused.

Since it was only six in the morning, the cousins tried to be very quiet as they heated water for tea and coffee, and toasted soda bread for their pre-breakfast snack. The jam was good, but the McElroy jam was better.

Rayne put everything on a tray, while Ciara was in charge of opening and closing doors. They let Blarney outside and went to the blue parlor.

The books and photos from the trunk had

been placed in a box by the sofa rather than the stacks and piles Rayne had created. Ciara took one side, and Rayne the other. They each had an end table to put their drinks and toast on.

Rayne picked up the letter that had been hidden inside the silk lining that Maeve had placed on top of the stack of books and removed it from the envelope.

"Long Live the Republic," Rayne said. "The slogan was a point of pride." She sipped her coffee, ideas swirling in her head. Her fingers traced the sketch of the shamrock on an inverted crown. "What if our ancestor, possibly Duncan, hid this away and then died during the war? He could have belonged to a secret group of soldiers fighting for freedom, like Bobby talked about. It wasn't the first time Ireland was fighting for independence."

Ciara sipped her tea. "Duncan died, and obviously nobody knew this was there. Duncan never knew that they'd succeeded and won against Great Britain."

"That's really sad." Rayne exchanged the letter for the photo of Billy McGillicuddy and Dougal McGrath. Missing Duncan. 1923. "Fighting for the Republic didn't need to be a secret anymore."

"And without realizing what was in here,

someone just packed up the trunk and stuffed it in the attic." Ciara narrowed her eyes. "Makes sense. There's no rhyme or reason to the contents up there. It'll be nice to have the appraiser come check it out."

Rayne put the photo next to the letter. The angle definitely reminded her of two letter Cs on the crown. "I'm glad you found one. We need to be sure that whoever inherits after us doesn't have this same uphill battle."

"There could be treasure," Ciara said with a wink.

"That would put us in a bind," Rayne said. "Would we sell it, or keep it?"

Ciara sighed. "We'd have to keep the piece for posterity, wouldn't we?"

"Unless we fail, then everything will be up for grabs, according to the will," Rayne said with a hitch in her chest.

Ciara smacked her palm to the sofa between them. "You don't know the meaning of quit, and neither do I. Failure is not an option."

"You're right, cousin, we won't fail. But it would sure be nice to find treasure. We could open a museum." Rayne's mouth gaped. "We should open a museum, in one of the buildings in the center of the village that we just cleaned. What do you think?"

"Share what we have here that makes us unique." Ciara nodded, instantly seeing the appeal. "We can charge admission. Unlike the idea of the lending library, which has no way of bringing in funds. We wouldn't have to change the whole village but showcase what is great about our history."

"What about a café inside?" Rayne suggested.

"And take away business from Sinead and Liam?"

"No, you're right." Rayne reached for the photos. "I'll go through these looking for any names. One of them has to be Thomas."

"Why do you think so?"

"The date on the grave is 1923. Thomas McGrath is buried there but shouldn't be." Rayne's eyes widened. "What if he was a coward, or an English sympathizer?"

Ciara's expression froze. "That would explain why he was hidden away, all right." She gestured toward the photos. "You start there, and I'll scan these books. The answer has got to be here."

At ten, a knock sounded on the door, and Aine brought in a tray of fruit, meats, and more coffee and tea. Blarney slipped in with a bark of greeting.

"Sorry to disturb you. Blarney was outside the door, or I wouldn't have realized you were in here."

"Oh, thanks Aine." Rayne tossed Blarney a piece of ham. She stood and stretched from her cramped position.

"Any luck?" Ciara asked Rayne.

"No. No Thomas anywhere."

"We were trying to be quiet and lost track of time." Ciara closed the book she'd been immersed in. "I didn't find any mention of him either. Our history has been a series of bloody battles, with the last ending right before the turn of the twenty-first century."

Rayne thought of her poet father and his moody phases. "Conor rarely talked about it, actually. He mentioned like second cousins or something who'd been killed by the loyalists. Our family has always staunchly believed in freedom, whether it be from religious persecution, or British rule."

"Mam lost her uncle in a bombing incident," Aine shared in a quiet voice. "They were close as he'd been her favorite."

"Where? Northern Ireland?" Ciara asked.

"Dublin. It scarred my gran." Aine crossed her arms. "I've never seen violence like that in my lifetime."

"You're a baby," Rayne teased.

"It happened fifty years ago, so you weren't born either." Aine lowered her arms to her sides. "Hard to believe that our peaceful countryside was ever torn up in that way. We are taught what happened in school. I like to think that today we might choose peace instead of war, you know?"

Maeve entered the room, having heard her daughter's statement. "It was more complicated than that, *leanbh.*"

Aine blushed. "Sorry, Mam. Didn't mean to simplify your loss!"

"I pray for peace every day," Maeve said. "But why is the subject of war on your tongue in the first place?"

Rayne lifted the small sheet of paper with the Gaelic writing. Long Live the Republic. The sketch of the shamrock, and the inverted crown. The Lloyds hadn't seen it before either. Ciara and Rayne had decided to keep their discovery close within the family. Not Bobby, until they found out more about Thomas McGrath. "Talking about this again."

"It's important that we never forget. Now, who is ready for church? It's poor Darcy's funeral so it will be packed, and we should arrive early."

"We have family seats in the front," Ciara said.

"Elizabeth McGillicuddy has already called the house wanting to make sure you both will be in attendance, in black, if you please. She had the cheek to suggest we host a meal for her brother here at the castle, with no warning! Frances turned the color of a plum."

Ciara and Rayne exchanged a look. "Er, should we have hosted something?" Rayne asked. She worried the crystal in the pocket of her silk robe.

"It would be nuts at this late notice," Ciara said.

Aine watched her mom closely. Whatever Maeve would suggest, Aine would support. How awesome that Maeve always knew she had Aine in her corner.

Rayne had her mother.

Her mother! They'd been playing phone tag.

If it was important then Lauren would have left a voice mail. Right?

"What did you say to Elizabeth?" Ciara asked Maeve.

Rayne's brain scrambled as she tried to imagine how to fit a buffet in. With the wedding guests here, it would be impossible to come up with something last minute.

No matter how hard they tried, it seemed they were letting someone down.

"It's fine," Maeve assured the cousins. "It's not like Nevin and Darcy were close.

As argumentative as your uncle was, Darcy McGillicuddy put him to shame."

Chapter Twenty

Rayne, Ciara, Maeve, Aine, Cormac, Amos, and Richard all walked together to church. Dafydd had claimed a stomach bug and opted out.

"This will be awkward," Ciara complained.

"Only for a little while, until the new normal sets in," Rayne assured her.

"How do you know?" Ciara murmured.

"I had a serious boyfriend in high school who dumped me our senior year to date a cheerleader."

Ciara's brow rose in surprise. "You were dumped?"

"It happens," Rayne said.

"It's just that I imagined your life as pretty perfect."

"I had to go to deportment classes," Rayne protested. "My life was a hot mess — similar no doubt to anybody in their teenage years. Boys didn't like that I was tall. Lauren said it was because they were intimidated. Not that it mattered when I was being snubbed."

"Sorry," Ciara said, sounding sincere.

"Thanks. Anyway, despite my intense humiliation over not having a date for the dance, I still had to suck it up and show up to school. I was sure that the next day everyone would be making fun of me." Rayne shrugged.

"Did they?"

"Yeah. It was awful — but by the following day, they'd moved onto something else. I think the basketball championship. The point is that I didn't die and while it sucked rotten eggs, the angst passed. It will between you and Dafydd too. Unless you want me to fire him right now."

"No, thank you," Ciara said. "It's not Dafydd's fault that I fell out of love. I am not sure when or how."

"That's sweet of you. I totally blame the sexy cheerleader showing more than her legs, if you know what I mean." Rayne motioned curves over her hips.

"I hate her too," Ciara promised.

The cousins bumped knuckles.

"If only we could solve the fate of the village as easily," Rayne said.

"What if we brought it to a vote?" Ciara

suggested.

"How would we reach everyone?"

"A church announcement," Ciara said. "A mailer. And a poster on the door of An Post."

The post office was the second hottest spot for news outside of the church. Thanks to Ciara's advice she still managed to avoid Gossiping Gerda Meyer.

They crossed the street, trailing behind the Lloyd family. Amos and Richard were in the lead. Everyone was dressed in black, as Elizabeth had instructed.

A part of her resented being bossed around by the older woman while another part understood, or tried to anyway, that Elizabeth was grieving. The funeral home in Kilkenny had really messed up but what could they do besides apologize?

Darcy was ashes now.

Father Patrick had promised his soul would still go to Heaven — Rayne wondered if Elizabeth was looking for a cash apology in addition to the priest's assurances.

The church parking lot was so full that parishioners had to park on the street as well. The church door was propped open and people milled around outside and in the foyer.

Organ music drifted toward them.

Richard scooted to one side of the doorway to allow others to go inside while Amos waited, smiling at her.

"Don't you look lovely, Rayne?" His gaze sparkled. "Black looks very, very good on you. Matches your hair and stormy gray eyes."

Richard snorted. "What about my eyes, Amos? You're blocking the entrance to God's house to pass out compliments, so I want one too."

Amos, unabashed, stepped backward, his thumb to his chin. "All right, then. Richard Forrest. Hmm. You have hair the color of mud and muddy eyes as well."

Richard punched his arm — playfully of course, and said, "Since when does Irish red look like mud? Eejit."

"Don't you mean sediment?" Aine batted her lashes. "I'd prefer a compliment that doesn't include dirt, Amos."

"Aine, lass, your hair is the color of flame at midnight," Amos said, his hand over his heart.

"And that will be enough jokes, boyo," Cormac said in a stern tone. Luckily his lips were twitching to stop a smile. "Aine, leanbh, on this side of me if you please. This is church and we don't need the roof falling on our heads from such malarkey."

Maeve had topped her red hair, the same shade as Aine's, with a black hat. Theirs was a lovely copper to Richard's auburn. As a designer, Rayne loved the many, many shades of red. "What if Elizabeth heard you joking around?"

"She wouldn't be as forgiving as Father Patrick," Richard said. He put his finger to his lips.

They entered the church, Amos falling into step behind Rayne, who followed Ciara. Her cousin sucked in breath.

"Dominic is here — Garda Williams, in street clothes. What on earth could he be doing at our church?"

Rayne started to turn around, but Ciara tugged her forward.

"What?" Rayne asked. It would be fine to say hello, and neighborly even. His attire had her wondering if it was business, or because he wanted to hear Father Patrick's sermon.

"Don't stare!"

"I've heard of the police coming to the funerals to observe their suspects," Rayne said. "Are you sure he's in street clothes?"

Ciara nodded. "Not a garda hat or a hint of blue uniform."

"Maybe he's under cover." Rayne chanced a glance behind her, but the church was so full she couldn't see past the row directly at her back.

People were chatting and catching up. There'd be tea and pastries afterward in the kitchen hall — the voices stopped as the pianist, a white-haired woman named Eltha, played her last note, which reverberated in the air.

Father Patrick started the service. Two altar boys about thirteen with acne and freckles assisted him.

The main service was going to be combined with Father Patrick saying a few words about Darcy McGillicuddy.

Elizabeth McGillicuddy was two rows to the right. The McGrath's section of pews was to the left. Rayne had a good view so long as everyone stayed seated.

They'd had two deaths in the community. Would Father Patrick address the issues of what had gone wrong for Darcy, or for Aiden? He kept the sermon vague, and Rayne felt Elizabeth's anger, but the older woman didn't dare interrupt the priest.

"The ways of the Lord are a mystery to us here on earth, and we only ask to remain your humble servants," Father Patrick said.

Elizabeth spluttered.

"We pray that God's love offers comfort during these troubling times." Father Patrick bowed his head.

Shauna and Luke Dennehy appeared upset that their grandson's death hadn't been addressed. "Prayers, my foot!" Shauna whispered — unfortunately, her hearing loss made her whisper a shout.

Elizabeth turned to commiserate with the woman. They were around the same age.

Olivia and Murray sat next to Dorothy and Sheff. Shauna and Luke sat behind them all. Colleen, with Beetle, and Corrine, was in the third row back.

Corrine played on a tablet with her earbuds in. The little girl's pink glasses slid down her snub nose. Adorable. She hadn't paid attention to Elizabeth's all black rule — or maybe she hadn't gotten the memo. Her bright pink sweater and jeans was a bright spot in the church full of black.

On that same pew was a woman with the near-black eyes of Beetle and Colleen. Was it Connie Randall? No Mr. Randall.

Dominic Williams had also worn black though he wasn't in a suit. Black button up shirt with a color, top button undone, and black jeans. He was very fit. His boy next door's looks had more than one woman sending glances toward the handsome newcomer.

No Garda Lee, or anyone in uniform.

What would it be like if the garda actually moved to Grathton Village?

Rayne turned to ask Ciara her thoughts, in a whisper of course, and saw that her cousin was already focused on Dominic.

When he wasn't on a case, they were welcome to use his first name.

Since Ciara and Dominic had dated, Ciara had struggled to call her ex, Garda Williams. When he hadn't originally believed that someone had murdered her da, she'd taken it to heart. He'd questioned Dafydd, and Ciara had quickly and immediately come to Dafydd's defense.

He'd told her about the reason he'd been in jail. She'd supported his stealing to feed his siblings, who were grown now. There'd been ample time in their history for Dafydd to tell her that he'd been married before.

Had Dominic known that already? Did he realize that Dafydd hadn't been entirely truthful? That would explain some of the hostile vibes she'd picked up from Dominic. She'd attributed them to jealousy.

Still could be jealous, but also protective of Ciara.

Amos nudged her arm and arched a brow, but Rayne wasn't going to get into trouble by talking in church. It would have to wait for the service to be over. When would the service be over?

At last, Father Patrick gave them all a blessing and told them to go in peace.

"There will be a light refreshment in the hall."

And like a tide had been released, people moved from the pews toward the hall to the right.

Shauna, Dorothy, and Olivia all took turns managing the coffee, tea, and sweets. This time, it was Olivia who was in charge.

When Rayne turned to ask Ciara if she wanted to skip the refreshments, her cousin was already halfway down the aisle toward Dominic.

He saw Ciara coming and his eyes widened.

Rayne hurried past Amos to her cousin in time to hear her say, "What are you doing here?"

"Trying out the church, that's what," Dominic said. "If I move here, I'd want to know if I'd be comfortable."

"You haven't answered any of my texts!" Ciara stopped at the edge of the pew. Rayne bumped into her.

"Sorry." Rayne put her arm on Ciara's shoulder to steady herself.

Amos had slowed enough so that his stop wasn't as abrupt.

Dominic smiled at Ciara with good-natured patience. "I can't talk about the investigation. You know that. Not about Darcy McGillicuddy either. If you want to suggest a time to check out a flat for rent, then I'm all in."

Hmm. Dominic moving to Grathton Village. It had many plusses to the situation. If a garda lived in the village, people might feel safer despite the recent crimes.

Ciara realized that she'd overreacted to his presence and her face turned scarlet. "Aiden . . ."

"Not the time, Ciara," Dominic said. He smiled at Rayne, then Amos. "Hey." He returned his gaze to Ciara.

Her cousin was about to burst into flame from mortification.

Rayne stepped in to take the attention from Ciara and pointed toward the line of people headed for the hall, and refreshments. "You may not know this, but Dorothy McElroy, Shauna Dennehy, and Olivia O'Brien have a rivalry over who makes the best scones in the parish."

"I did not know that." Dominic looked to the line that grew shorter as people entered the large meeting room that had a kitchen.

"Oh yes," Amos agreed. "Father Patrick is quick to say that whoever has baked scones that day is the best. He's gotten quite skilled at appeasing them."

"Whose really are the best?" Dominic asked. He rubbed his bare upper lip in contemplation. He smelled like shaving cream and cologne.

"Well, today will be Olivia — but you should try them all to see for yourself," Rayne said. "All I know for certain is that Dorothy and her family make amazing jam."

"We are thinking of asking the McElroys to be one of the new businesses," Ciara said. Her cousin nodded her thanks at Rayne.

High emotion. Passion. Rayne never saw her react that way around Dafydd.

They shuffled across the pews to the hall and the kitchen. Elizabeth saw them coming and stood from her chair at a long rectangular table where she plucked at a scone with several other people that Rayne assumed was family. Their blue eyes were brilliant.

"There you are!" Elizabeth said.

Rayne stepped back, startled by the attack.

Aine waved from a table near the window with four chairs. "Rayne and Ciara — we are over here!"

Elizabeth crumpled her napkin, moving between Rayne and Aine. "I can't believe you would turn down my request for help from the McGraths. It is not how things used to be done back in the day."

Everyone stopped talking to stare at Rayne, Ciara, and Elizabeth.

"What do you mean?" Ciara asked.

"A cry for help to the lord of the village was always answered, no matter the hardship." Elizabeth's chin trembled with legit anger as if she felt entitled.

"You just called this morning," Rayne said. "Even at such last-minute notice the only reason we didn't offer our home, despite the lack of supplies of food or whiskey, is because we have wedding guests on the property."

"Excuses!" Elizabeth said. "You have the staff to handle these things."

"We have five staff members," Ciara said, "and they are all here at this service. Should they have missed praying for Darcy's soul to put out a paltry buffet? Or is it the whiskey that you want?"

Dominic and Amos each straightened behind the ladies but what could they do?

There wasn't anything to do, Rayne realized. She swallowed her own ire.

"I'm sorry for your loss," Rayne said, for the second or third time. She meant it. Losing a loved one was hard to handle. "Perhaps we can bring," she began.

Elizabeth spoke over Rayne's offer of bringing whiskey from the castle to share here now at the church. "You *owe* us, the McGillicuddys, who have been loyal allies for centuries. My kin arrived with the original McGrath clan. To be treated so poorly is a shame."

Olivia snorted and barreled between Amos, Dominic, Ciara, and Rayne. "You are a drama queen, Libby, always after the attention. You haven't changed since you were a babe."

Aine, Maeve, Cormac, and Richard all stood, as if uncertain what to do from across the room from a troublemaker.

They stepped closer to join the McGrath ranks.

"How dare you, Olivia!" Elizabeth said.

The people at Elizabeth's table appeared shocked at Olivia's declaration. Even if it was true, it probably wasn't the right time to say so.

"You are selfish," Olivia continued, on a tear. "The McGraths don't owe you a darned thing, Libby. Not a one. You own your land, just like we all do. Why don't you take your diva self back to Dublin? We don't miss you here."

Elizabeth's hand reached out quick as a

snake to slap Olivia's cheek.

Dominic stopped the blow from landing. "Enough."

"I'll tell you when it's enough." Elizabeth's gaze filled with anger. "Who the hell are you?"

"Elizabeth McGillicuddy!" Father Patrick denounced. He pushed away from where he'd been getting tea. "Language, please. This is a house of God."

"I don't care," Elizabeth said.

Olivia nodded like she'd been right about Elizabeth's character all along.

"He's the garda," Shauna crowed, her expression one that shared she hoped right along with Olivia that Elizabeth might at last get her comeuppance.

She'd tried to assault someone in front of a police officer.

"The garda?" Elizabeth dove for Dominic's throat with her hands outstretched. "Why are you here when my brother's murderer is still at large? And Aiden Dennehy's too!"

Chapter Twenty-One

Chaos erupted.

Murray, Sheff, and Luke grabbed their wives back from collectively charging at Elizabeth.

Dominic easily evaded Elizabeth's outstretched hands. His demeanor remained calm as the ladies wiggled free from their men and continued to go for Elizabeth. He braced himself and stood before the woman who had charged him, palms up to the crowd.

Rayne and Ciara, along with Amos, joined Dominic to form a human barricade between the furious ladies and Elizabeth as the tables had turned.

Dominic gave a shrill whistle. When he had everyone's attention he said, "Please take a seat. We will get to the bottom of this situation right now. We can talk here, or the gardai station in Kilkenny." He counted the number of people wanting coffee, tea, and scones. A little drama added spice. "I can call in a small bus with handcuffs for a hundred."

Rayne estimated that there were seventy-five folks here today.

Colleen's little girl, Corrine, had put her tablet down and sat on her mother's lap, her thumb to her mouth.

Alarm filled Colleen's eyes, mixed with sorrow.

Whether or not Aiden was Corrine's baby daddy, Colleen had cared for, *loved,* Aiden Dennehy. She didn't kill him. She couldn't have. What about Beetle?

Don, Paddy, Treasa — and Sheila — were sitting here today. Out of respect for Darcy? To catch up with news about Aiden? For Sheila to add fuel to her gossip mill?

Bobby Fitzroy sat at the same table with Bronagh Wilson. No sign of Bran but that was just fine with her. She'd had it with the overgrown manchild and wasn't sure how kind Bronagh had spawned someone like Bran.

"What's it going to be?" Dominic asked again.

"We can talk," Dorothy decided. She of the three seemed embarrassed by the outburst. Olivia and Shauna remained visibly upset. To have lost two of their community so quickly had to be the reason for their unusual behavior.

Rayne, with Amos, went to sit with the Lloyds, but Ciara perched on a chair closer to Elizabeth, her gaze on the emotional older woman, her body poised to jump between Dominic and Elizabeth if she acted out of line. Everyone at least was seated.

Dominic scanned the ladies' faces. "Olivia, why don't you start?"

Murray, Sheff, and Luke all groaned. Shauna and Dorothy sat straighter, glaring between Elizabeth and Murray.

Rayne was also on the edge of her seat drawn in to the intense tableau before her. What was going on here? They brimmed with secrets begging to be spilled.

She could imagine them all, sixty years younger and in their prime. Could people hold onto resentment for that long?

Landon's manipulation of Rayne was still very fresh, and she didn't see it as something she'd ever forget, so maybe it was the same for them.

"Elizabeth McGillicuddy has always thought a touch too highly of herself," Olivia stated.

Elizabeth's skilled use of makeup suggested she'd taken care of her skin and while it was clear she was an older woman, she didn't look quite as old as the other three.

"You're just jealous," a woman, maybe fifty, from Elizabeth's table stated. "My gran is still pretty despite her age. You're a has been."

A young woman who must be that lady's daughter said, "And Gran stole your man. Right, Olivia?"

The ladies wore matching black suits that Rayne recognized as tailored. They were handsome rather than pretty, their faces lacking any hint of softness. Bright McGillicuddy eyes. They had the look of career women. Could be lawyers or doctors.

Olivia's face split into a wrinkled grin. "Hardly stole. Your gran wasn't so great after all — right, hon? Not enough to keep him." She jerked her gnarled thumb over her shoulder to a mortified Murray. "Been together all these years. And what, Elizabeth, do you have? You are all alone."

"She's got us, her family," the youngest woman said. Her voice was firm.

Two men, as tailored as the women — in their thirties, or forties, watched the scene very closely. They had the same features as the young woman. Maybe they were all three children of the fifty-year-old. There was no sign of Rian McGillicuddy, Darcy's only grandson.

Rayne bet that their social calendars would all be full — attractive, well-dressed, and successful. Were they wealthy too, beyond the day to day? She straightened. Three new McGillicuddys to the village, even parttime, could bring in social cache and desirability.

"I had a brother," Elizabeth said. "My brother was my closest relative, and friend. Something went wrong. Darcy was worried." She spun a gold bangle around her wrist. "And didn't sound like himself."

"Darcy was old," Sheff said, commiserating. "Like the rest of us." He tapped his temple. "Things aren't as sharp as they used to be. You hear things that aren't there, or sense things that just might not be true."

"I haven't changed," Elizabeth said. Her expression dared anyone to argue.

While the others of the old gang had double chins, hers didn't wobble. A face lift? If so, it had been skillfully done.

"I'd like your mirror, love." Dorothy sounded sorry for Elizabeth, fighting her age so hard. "We were something back in the day." She chuckled and raised her intelligent gaze. "I'll miss Darcy, Libby. We've all been friends and neighbors for so long. You claim to know him so well, but it's not like you've stayed to visit more than a night or two. Pretty face and a cold heart. I guess that hasn't changed, despite the wrinkles you can't erase."

Elizabeth hiked her chin. "Never knew you to be mean, Dorothy."

"I am calling the truth how I see it. I overlooked what happened back then with Olivia and Murray, and you, to keep the peace, and your friendship." Dorothy's shoulders bowed. "You haven't been back to Grathton more than a minute to see that things truly have changed. You aren't the belle of the ball."

Olivia's eyes welled and some of the fight went out of her demeanor. "It was a hard time."

"It was," Shauna agreed.

"What did Darcy think of what happened?" Ciara asked. She'd been caught up in the story of the love affair.

"He was my brother," Elizabeth said. "Darcy told me to end things, if I wasn't serious about splitting up the O'Brien marriage. I wasn't, so I did."

"And made yourself scarce," Shauna said. "I understood why. Shame is a poison."

"Let's leave judgment out of things." Elizabeth's gaze switched to Luke and Shauna. "Darcy mentioned that he might sell to you, so that you could enlarge your property, and gift it to Aiden."

Dominic straightened with interest, and Rayne and Amos exchanged a look. Could this have to do with Aiden's death?

Would the sale of the property leave out Darcy's heirs?

"Your brother never had cause to fear me or my family," Shauna said. "Before my Aiden was murdered in cold blood, I would have said that nobody in Grathton needed to fear." A controlled sob slipped before she swallowed her angst.

Luke patted her back.

"We are investigating Aiden Dennehy's death," Dominic assured the spectators of this age-old feud. "I will share what I can when I can."

"Not true for my brother." Elizabeth glared at Dominic.

"The autopsy report reads that Darcy McGillicuddy died a nocturnal death. There is no more to it that I am aware of," Dominic said. He kept his demeanor calm. "I am very sorry that there will be no burial."

"Cremated against his will — who is responsible for that, eh garda?" Darcy's grandniece asked in a loud voice.

"Your great-aunt has already filed a complaint against the funeral home," Dominic said. "It is all that can be done."

Murmurs of discontent sounded.

"It's clear you share a common history that should be honored, despite the sadness we are all feeling today. Let's have a moment to think of Darcy, and Aiden." Dominic bowed his head and after sixty seconds raised it. "I'd like to try the scones I've been hearing so much about."

Ciara got up and poured him a cup of tea while Olivia placed a scone with clotted cream and jam next to it.

"They're delicious, if I do say so myself," Olivia said in a demure tone.

"Of course you would, old bat," Elizabeth sneered.

The complaint went no further as nobody else wanted to risk the fragile peace that Dominic had created.

"That was quite impressive, Dominic's work," Amos said to Rayne and the others at their table. "Scone?"

Rayne nodded. In the end she ate two, with a strong cup of coffee. Ciara sat with Dominic, and the Randall family.

Corrine had stars in her eyes as she gazed at Dominic.

For that matter, Ciara did too.

Her phone rang. She answered, thinking it would be her mom, but it was Lenni McGee-O'Shea.

"Hi!"

"Hello — are you still interested in showing us the cemetery?" Lenni's voice was friendly.

"Sure."

"Good." Lenni laughed. "We were hoping you'd say that, since we're at the church already. Didn't realize the service would still be going on."

"This is the social hour. I'll come out in a few minutes. It might be just me for the cemetery tour," Rayne said, her smile not budging as she watched Ciara and Dominic converse.

"I'll join ye," Amos said, overhearing her comment. "Got the afternoon free."

Rayne nodded as she ended the call. It would be a fun time.

Richard and the Lloyds were headed back to the manor — Richard for a nap and the Lloyds to watch a movie together in Maeve and Cormac's suite.

"Thanks for all of your help," Rayne said as they bundled up to leave.

"We will always step in," Cormac said. "I just wasn't sure what was happening. Dominic got the crowd settled down without needing to file an assault charge against Elizabeth."

Richard snickered and snugged his hat

down to his ears. "A miracle."

Maeve and Aine linked arms. "This village may be small, but it isn't boring," Aine said.

"See you all later," Maeve said. They exited the hall.

Rayne noticed that Ciara and Dominic were helping to clean up the kitchen, with Olivia and Shauna. Father Patrick was in a conversation with the men. The McGillicuddys, all generations, had left without a goodbye.

Rayne put on her coat, waiting to catch Ciara's eye to wave before putting her arm through Amos's and exiting.

They went out the side entrance of the building to avoid tromping through the foyer. Walking around with Amos to the parking lot and the cemetery gate, Rayne grinned at her wedding guests.

"Cormac told us that the site of the murder happened on the grave of your illustrious ancestor." Brandon tucked his hand into his coat pocket.

"Elusive might be more appropriate, actually," Rayne said.

"How so?" Pete asked.

"Oh, here we go," Sharon gave a good-natured chuckle.

“What?” Pete and Brandon asked in unison.

“Anything old and we modern, living, breathing humans, are left in the dust,” Sharon said.

“I warned you already, Rayne,” Lenni echoed.

“I know. It’s fine. I like history too.” Rayne zipped up her coat against the chill and glanced at Amos. “You?”

“Love it. How could I not?” Amos wrapped a scarf around his throat. “Ireland is in my blood.”

Drake, dressed like it was sixty degrees instead of in the forties, meaning no hat or gloves. His hoody was unzipped.

“Blarney came with us,” Drake said. “I hope that’s okay?” He chucked a stick along the grass toward the cemetery fence. The gate was closed. They had talked about a lock but not followed through with it yet.

Blarney chased that stick at top speed, paws kicking up dirt when he stopped before hitting the fence. Her dog raced it back to Drake.

“Blarney has a mind of his own.” Rayne didn’t mind her dog’s fervor. “Ciara and I spent all morning looking through photos and family history searching for any mention of Thomas McGrath, but we didn’t find a thing."

"Oh, that's what you meant by elusive," Lenni said.

"I'm a fan of history as well," Sharon said. "The dorm I teach in was built in the eighteen hundreds."

"That's cool — and probably around the same time as our manor. 1770-ish?" Rayne looked at Amos.

"Sounds right to me. I studied architecture for one of my university classes," Amos said, surprising Rayne. "I enjoyed learning the lines of buildings from Roman times to modern-industrial."

"Modern. Not my favorite," Pete said.

"Or mine," Amos admitted. "I prefer curves to straight lines."

Everyone cracked up.

"What?" Drake said, wanting to know the joke.

"It's not important," Lenni said. "Silly man stuff."

"I'm a man!" Drake protested, his voice squeaking at the wrong time.

Lenni pulled him into a brief hug. "You are growing too fast for my liking, so, just — slow down, would you?"

Drake patted the top of her head which he had a few inches on, despite Lenni's height. "All right, Aunty."

Lenni tickled him in the ribs and Drake doubled over with laughter.

For once, Rayne felt the pang of not having children of her own. She'd been so focused on her career that she hadn't given kids a second thought.

She was only thirty so had time if she changed her mind from what had been a definite no. Hell no.

Amos seemed to read her thoughts as he clasped her hand in his. "We'd make cute babies, Rayne McGrath."

Rayne shoved her arm into his, but didn't release his hand. "Would we?" She shook her head. "Kids are not on my agenda."

"Neither was inheriting a castle," Amos said. "Things change."

"Things do indeed change," Rayne said, choking on the word.

Amos opened the black metal gate around the cemetery. "Father Patrick and I are going to the hardware store tomorrow to get the padlock. We just ran out of time on Friday."

"It's a shame to lock it," Pete said. "But I suppose necessary. You've had trouble with vandals?"

"Pete, hon, a bloke was killed here. Remember?" Sharon shook her head.

That quieted the mood. They ambled

around the graves, none of them surprised to see the fairy doors on the tree trunks.

"The McGillicuddys are quite grand," Pete said as he and the others admired the mausoleum behind the white picket fence. "Isn't he the fellow that just died?"

"Yes," Rayne said. "Darcy. He was ninety."

"A venerable old age," Brandon said. "Are we getting close?"

"Yes, around this path," Rayne said. At last, they arrived at the Thomas McGrath tombstone.

Blarney ran directly to it, digging in the soft dirt to bury the stick from Drake that he'd dropped next to the grave.

"Here we are," Amos said.

Blarney started to dig around the limestone.

"No, Blarney," Rayne said fearing what else he might uncover. The dog sat on his haunches with a whine.

"This is nice," Brandon said as he and Pete both went to the stone and studied the calligraphy and date. Brandon ran his hand over the curve of the stone as if it was a woman's shoulder, his thumb tracing an indent. He peered closer, then called, "Pete, check this out."

Pete eagerly walked over to his friend with a nod. His brow lifted in surprise as he traced the place where Brandon had had his thumb. "No way." Pete gestured with enthusiasm at Lenni. "This is incredible. Come here."

Rayne and Amos looked at one another. Blarney wagged his tail and bumped his head against Rayne's hand.

Lenni joined the guys. "I see old rock. Possibly granite or limestone. What am I missing?"

Sharon went too, wanting a closer peek.

"Now, who here believes in secret societies?" Pete asked with a barely suppressed grin as he stared at Rayne.

"What are you talking about?" Rayne's cheeks heated.

Lenni nudged Pete. "Will you behave? Cormac may have let it slip that you'd found a message in the liner of the trunk that's in Brandon and Drake's cottage. They were talking about history, and Thomas McGrath. Why he wasn't buried over with the others. Brandon's like a bulldog with these things."

"It's not Cormac's fault," Pete said.

Sharon shook her head.

Rayne exchanged a look with Amos. She hadn't told Cormac not to tell their guests. It was possible he'd shared to find answers about the age of the stone.

"Can we read the letter?" Brandon asked Rayne.

"Yes, sure. It's at the manor." Rayne stepped toward the grave. "But I want to know what you found just now. We spent the day gently cleaning these headstones. I didn't see anything suspicious."

"Me either," Amos said.

"Here!" Brandon said, showing them a divot in the stone toward the top.

Pete chuckled.

"You guys are crazy," Sharon said. Lenni nodded.

"Show me!" Rayne narrowed her eyes. She'd been drawn to that spot before. It couldn't be a shamrock, could it?

"Let me help you see what I see," Brandon said as he took a multitude of photos. "The curve of the stone here was popular in the nineteen hundreds."

"That matches what Bobby Fitzroy said. He's a local history buff." Rayne didn't mention that his garden shears had killed poor Aiden Dennehy right here. The fact that his prints had been on the shears didn't matter as the trailer was open for all, and his alibi was iron clad for the time of Aiden's death. "We figure that Thomas McGrath must have been a rebel or a bad guy, or maybe illegitimate, possibly Protestant, as to why he wasn't buried with the other McGraths in the mausoleum across the street."

"Interesting," Sharon said, patting the headstone with a wink. "I've always liked the bad boys."

"Aunt Sharon!" Drake said.

"It's why I've never married," Sharon clarified. "I can't be trusted with my own judgment when it comes to men."

Rayne nodded. She knew exactly what Sharon meant.

Amos shook his head at her in disagreement.

"Relationships can be very complicated, which is why we have family and amazing friends, right, Pete?" Lenni said, taking her new husband's hand.

"You're very right, my love." Pete kissed her fingers.

Sharon sighed romantically.

Brandon continued to ignore them to focus on the headstone and the pictures he'd taken. He said, "Pete, Rayne, have a gander."

They gathered around his outstretched phone. It was a blurred image that none of them could make out.

"Hang on." He chose a different picture and enlarged it to a blurred three-leaf shamrock with points at the stem. Smudged — or a crown?

Rayne briefly touched her hand to her lips and exclaimed, "Amos! This was on the letter."

"Long Live the Republic." Amos nodded.

"This, my friends," Brandon announced like a game show host. "This is the symbol of the Cavalier Clovers. Your man here was a member."

Chapter Twenty-Two

Rayne shrugged, at a loss. "I've never heard of the Cavalier Clovers before. Have you, Amos?"

"Nope."

"It was a secret, secret society," Brandon said.

"Kind of like the Order of the Knights of Saint Patrick," Pete chimed in. He rubbed his hands. "There has been zero hard evidence of this clandestine group."

Rayne thought of the Cs she'd thought she'd seen on the drawing. Were her guests onto something big?

"Until now. Show us!" Brandon said. "This could be a major discovery in Irish history. On the other hand, we might be wrong."

Rayne's eyes were wide as she sifted through the possibilities.

"You have a nose for this stuff, Brandon," Pete said.

"What did Dad do now?" Drake asked. He'd been creeping around the trees to try and scare Lenni and Sharon.

"We aren't sure yet. We need proof," Pete said. "Always the hard part but one must do due diligence."

"Let's go then. Come on, Blarney boy." Rayne clapped her hands for his attention as the pup was chasing a very fat and sassy squirrel around the headstones.

"This is a beautiful cemetery," Sharon said as they walked back toward the black metal gate that fed into the church parking lot.

"We just had a community cleanup day to clear the brush," Rayne said. "Last week at this time it could have been in a horror movie set."

"Scary movies are pure craic," Drake said. He leaped to touch an overhanging branch, constantly in motion.

Blarney raced toward them with his tail wagging — he had the same energy as Drake. Inexhaustible.

"What do you know about the secret society?" Amos asked as they left the cemetery and passed by the buildings that Bobby and his team were almost finished painting.

They already looked a million times better.

"Not much," Brandon said.

"I'm not sure if this will be important. It's a letter hidden in the lining of a trunk. That alone is cool, right?" Rayne glanced at Brandon as they walked toward the manor.

"Right," Brandon agreed. His gaze took on a faraway look.

"Back to earth," Pete said to his best friend, and steered him off the curb before he missed his step.

"What will those buildings be?" Sharon asked.

"We're hoping to attract businesses as well as families," Rayne said. "We are open to ideas of course."

"How many spaces do you have?" Lenni asked.

"In this section there are five buildings for rent — it could be a business on the bottom and an apartment on the top. Or businesses on both levels. We don't have hard plans. Then we have a row of old cottages that had legit thatch roofs — six homes, in total. We aren't sure if we want to do a thatch roof to keep the aesthetic, or a modern metal roof for long-term maintenance free solutions."

"I love the bungalows on the castle property," Lenni said. "A mix of modern and old."

"Thank you! As a team, we are putting in the hard graft of blood equity," Rayne said with a laugh.

"Do you have a beekeeper?" Sharon asked.

"No. We have a family that does jams and other vegetables, but no bees." Rayne nodded at Amos. "We should add that to the list."

"I'll remind you." Amos brought out his phone and typed something in.

"Do you have a butcher?" Brandon asked.

"Liam Walsh does sausages, so yes. He is looking to expand but has an online business. His wife, Sinead, owns the Coco Bean Café and is a baker."

"She did our wedding cake," Lenni told them.

"Chocolate on chocolate, with peach." Sharon sighed. "It might be worth getting married just for that cake. And the dress. And the venue."

"I'll buy you cake, Aunt Sharon, but you need to get your own fancy dress. Maybe Rayne can make you one?"

"Anytime," Rayne said.

"She does lingerie," Lenni suggested. "On the Modern Lace website. It might be more what you're looking for, Sharon."

Rayne raised the collar of her jacket to hide the pink in her cheeks.

"I will definitely check it out," Sharon said. "This place is a hidden gem. I'm not sure I want it to get so popular that it loses its quaintness."

"What about a restaurant?" Drake asked.

"Sinead serves light foods, and you can get other fare at the three pubs, and I believe there is a diner, but the food choices are limited," Rayne admitted. "Nothing exotic."

"I love curry," Drake said.

"Same here!" Rayne said.

"I'll add it to the list." Amos had a twinkle in his eye as he did just that.

"Thanks," Rayne said. Now that they'd kissed, she couldn't stop thinking of those full lips against hers.

"Lenni told me about your goal to revive the village. What would it take to make this place an authentic village from the eighteen hundreds?" Sharon asked. "You have the bones of it for sure. The school is always looking for examples where the old ways haven't been disturbed to show our students."

"We'd have to thatch the roofs," Amos said. "Not pave the streets. Hide the cell towers and signs of internet."

It felt backward. "When I first arrived here from LA, I thought I'd landed in the middle of nowhere BUT there was something so peaceful about being in nature and not tied to my cell phone."

"Yet," Amos reminded her, "you needed Wi-Fi to access internet and your online business, because you had to change from a brick-and-mortar store to an online one for Modern Lace."

Rayne looked at Amos, surprised that she hadn't thought of this before. "I can have one of the business storefronts for Modern Lace. A place to advertise and bring people to that also showcases our new business."

"Modern Lace — a combo of old and new," Lenni said. "I'll tell everyone about your gowns and this venue."

"Me too! Having access to the internet is a big deal for me," Sharon said. "I'm always on call even when I am not."

"I could care less about internet," Pete said. "Give me stone tablets and I'd be fine."

"Cave man," Lenni teased.

"My work requires internet for global access," Brandon said. "The modern allows me to protect the old."

"I like that, Brandon," Rayne said.

It was on par with what her uncle had wanted too. It had to be enough to blend the old and new, but it would require people living and working here. Spending money here as well as time.

She did a gut check — no churning belly, and heart check — it was light, free, allowing her to breathe. Hope. “Ciara and I discussed this already this morning, and we think it would be the best solution.”

“It’s nice to have someone to bounce ideas off of. Have you and Ciara always been close?” Sharon asked.

“I inherited my cousin along with the castle,” Rayne quipped. She glanced up at Amos. “Best day of my life — though I wouldn’t have thought so, in hindsight, it’s true.”

“What is that saying about hindsight always being twenty-twenty?” Brandon asked. He made circles around his eyes to mimic binoculars.

“What does that mean?” Drake asked. He was jogging backward to keep them in view while Blarney darted around him with excitement.

“It means,” Sharon said in a teacher’s tone, “that our past always holds the answers, but we don’t know the past or the pitfalls of the future until we move forward.”

“Bummer.” Drake turned around, waiting impatiently at the edge of the main road. Several cars passed. Blarney sat, also watching. When it was clear to cross, they both sped to the other side.

Drake and Blarney were soon out of sight, hidden by the curve and trees, as they raced toward the castle.

"I can't believe how tall he is, Brandon," Sharon said. "Drake was the same height as me at Easter. Now I'm the shortest one in our group."

"You've got to be feeding him constantly," Lenni said. "He is an energy machine. I wish I could borrow some for myself."

"I know it!" Brandon said.

When the next cars passed, the adults crossed the road.

"I remember being fourteen and ravenous all the time," Pete said. "Now that I'm over forty, it's not as easy to lose weight." He patted his small belly. "Eating and sleeping was all I wanted to do."

"It's all I want to do right now," Lenni said. "Winter is around the corner and if I could hibernate, I would."

Pete put his arm around her waist. "Can I hibernate with you?"

"We wouldn't get much sleep, if so," Lenni laughed.

"You two!" Sharon shook her head. "People ask why I choose to be single, and my answer is that I want a love like you both share. Thanks again for inviting me to celebrate this special day with you."

"My problem is that you two make it look easy, when marriage and a long-term relationship is work." Brandon shrugged. "I am honored to share your wedding with you. You get to be my example of how to do it right, for Drake's sake."

"Any words of advice?" Amos asked the blushing couple.

The November chill could be the cause, but Rayne didn't think so.

"Patience," Lenni said, bumping her shoulder to Pete.

"Understanding." Pete glanced at his wife. "I try to put myself in her shoes — usually after the argument, so, during or before might be more helpful moving forward."

Lenni smiled at Pete with warmth glowing from her eyes. "You do?"

"Yes, I really do. It's not like you to snap or be short with me, so when it happens, I literally imagine what you are doing and why. It helps."

Lenni stopped walking to throw her arms around Pete. "I am so glad that I married you. I will do that too from now on."

"Maybe we could put that advice on the Modern Lace website?" Rayne suggested.

"Fine with me," Pete said. Lenni nodded.

They continued walking.

Blarney and Drake were playing catch with Blarney's orange rubber ball. Drake had met his match as Blarney could fetch for days.

A car honked behind them, and they each chose a side of the driveway.

Freda Bevan climbed out of a black sedan, her body shaking with anger as she pointed her finger at Rayne.

"Just the person I wanted to see. I have called the garda to report the vandalism you did on my home. I have you on CCTV, Rayne McGrath."

Rayne snapped her mouth closed.

This wasn't good for her guests to think she ran around vandalizing people.

Sharon watched with interest. Pete and Lenni clasped hands. Drake caught the ball and held it while Blarney ambled over to sniff Freda's shoes. Brandon stepped next to Rayne and Amos.

"I didn't vandalize anything, Freda."

"Tell that to the gardai." Freda tapped her toe to the gravel. "They should be here any minute."

Rayne shook her head. "In that case, I'll let you wait outside for them, while I show our guests inside with a coffee and whiskey."

"Sounds good," Brandon said. He put his

hand on Drake's shoulder. "I'll take my son in with you."

Freda seemed to realize that Rayne was not alone. Honestly, the woman was batty. Mental. She hadn't been anywhere near Freda's home.

"When was this supposed to be?" Amos asked.

"This morning. Ten thirty. There is Rayne clear as day, bombing the door with glitter."

Glitter? Was someone playing a prank? She considered the other councilmen who had learned Freda's objective for them all. LuLu was the same height as she and Ciara.

"Well, she must have a doppelganger, as she was here getting ready for church, and then at church with plenty of witnesses." Amos whistled to get Blarney away from Freda's shoes.

"Ciara and I were in the blue parlor reading about the McGrath history. We have roots from mid-1750 here. How about you, Freda? How long have the Bevans been around?"

"Our hundred years is not insignificant," Freda shouted.

"Who said so?" Rayne asked. Yes, needling the woman. Which wasn't nice but she just poked at Rayne nonstop.

Cormac opened the front door, buttoning

his black uniform jacket. "Lady McGrath," he called. "Welcome home. I've prepared a light repast in the formal dining room." The butler glared at Freda.

"Freda will not be joining us," Rayne said. "This is a special day for our wedding guests."

Lenni snickered as she and Pete hurried up the stairs. "I wouldn't blame you if you had vandalized her house," she whispered.

"But we know you didn't," Pete said, patting Rayne's shoulder. "It would break the rules of engagement."

"He just means that you have integrity," Lenni said. "And wouldn't stoop to tricks. I'm glad you told us about Freda wanting to combine the villages. It would be alarming without context to have a madwoman accusing you of a glitter bomb."

Amos waited with Rayne and Cormac at the threshold as Brandon, Drake, Sharon and Blarney filed into the foyer.

"Lady McGrath. Shall I call the gardai about Ms. Bevan?"

"According to her, they are on their way already," Rayne said. "She is accusing me of vandalizing her house this morning."

"You never left the manor," Cormac said with assurance.

"True!" Rayne smiled. "Do you really

have refreshments in the dining room?"

"We do. Frances thought it would be nice to have a light luncheon to offer in the event you came back from your hike hungry."

"I can always eat," Pete said.

"Me too," Lenni agreed.

"Food!" Drake cried with enthusiasm.

"I'll stop in the parlor for the letter I found in the trunk, and we can brainstorm while we eat," Rayne said.

Amos led the group down the hall.

"Milady?" Cormac called.

Rayne turned and read the concern on the butler's face. She'd stepped toward the blue parlor and hadn't gotten as far as their guests. "Just let me know when the gardai arrive and I'll come out to avoid a scene."

"She's gone too far, to accuse you like this," Cormac said.

"I'm innocent until proven guilty," Rayne said with a chuckle. "At least that is how it works in America. Did Ciara return from church?"

"Yes — she coordinated with Frances about lunch."

"Is Dominic, Garda Williams, with her?"

"No." Cormac scowled. "I hope that they are closer to finding who killed Aiden Dennehy. I can't imagine a place where one of our own is killed for no reason."

"That we know of, yet."

"I told our guests about Thomas McGrath. Were they able to help?"

"We will see. Maybe." Rayne squeezed his arm and went into the parlor.

Blarney followed at her heels.

"Do you need a boy to play with?" Rayne asked. Maybe the exercise they did together wasn't enough.

Blarney sprawled, tongue lolling, on the carpet before the sofa as he panted heavily.

"It's fine to grab a rest." Rayne shook her head.

She peered into the box of books and the letter, the crystal she'd found on the top of the stack.

What to show them that might find answers regarding a secret, secret society?

She decided to bring the whole thing, including the crystal to show Maeve and Aine, and Frances. Frances only wore her wedding band, to Rayne's knowledge, but the chef might have a secret life as a dancer, for all she knew.

The more she thought about it, she wondered if the crystal had fallen from one of Aunt Amalie's outfits. The woman had always been about fashion. Rayne had assumed it was off the Jimmy Choo.

It didn't matter, in the long run, where

the crystal came from, but it nagged at her that Blarney had buried it in the cemetery.

Would a metal detector be of any use for finding more crystals?

She balanced the box as Ciara entered the parlor. "Need any help?"

"I've got it," Rayne said. "Thanks."

"Amos mentioned that Freda accused you of vandalizing her home." Ciara whirled her finger next to her temple. "Loco."

"Maybe Garda Williams will show up to talk to us about it?" Rayne asked.

"Dominic is off duty today." Ciara's gray eyes sparkled. "I forgot how fun he could be when he wasn't in uniform." She raised her palm. "Don't start. We are friends."

"I said nothing." Rayne and Blarney followed Ciara from the parlor to the hall, heading right toward the dining rooms.

The formal one had all the artifacts and McGrath medieval history in a large space. The next dining room in size was slightly more casual and closer to the kitchen.

"Good call on suggesting lunch," Rayne said. "Are you still thinking we can keep Grathton Village a mix of old and new?"

"Not a tourist trap?" Ciara winced. "You know what I mean. Yeah. It's the best option and fits both of us, as well as meeting the specifications of Da's will."

"I can't believe that I didn't think of this before, but I'd like to put Modern Lace in one of the refurbished buildings."

"It's not Rodeo Drive," Ciara said with a concerned tone.

"That dream is behind me," Rayne said. "I can never go back to the way it was, so I need to find something new. In six more months, I can actually be in both places if I want."

"Is that what you are thinking, long-term?" Ciara asked, her hand out to open the door as they'd reached the dining room.

"Sort of. I'm sorry I can't be more clear."

"It's all right. I like the idea of you having a storefront." Ciara widened the door. "After you."

"Thanks." Rayne entered and smiled at how easily everyone was chatting together.

She turned to talk with Ciara, but her cousin was gone.

Chapter Twenty-Three

Amos had been roped into staying for a bite, as Brandon had always wanted to know about how to manage a small farm.

Would Brandon be a good fit for the village? There had to be places for sale. Possibly Darcy McGillicuddy's farm. She'd call Haley at MPM and find out what was available.

"I've been very transient, because of my job," Brandon was saying.

"I don't suppose you know anything about bees?" Rayne asked.

Lenni and Sharon caught on before Pete, who nodded and clapped his friend on the back. "You should move to Grathton Village."

"Where would Drake go to school?" Brandon asked.

"We have a combined middle and high school here, but it is very small," Rayne said.

"Remote, Dad, anyway. You aren't here all the time. I can't leave my mates on my track team. I'll visit, like I do now, on holidays. Summer."

"That's fair. Maybe down the road then . . ." Sharon said.

"This place is gorgeous," Brandon said. "And practically untouched. You have Wi-Fi so that's all I really need."

"Mam will be glad to have your junk out of her garage," Drake said. "It's been ten years she says every time she wants to use it."

"Which isn't often," Brandon said. "Is it?"

"Talk to her about it," Drake said.

"I'm afraid to." Brandon shivered.

"You should be," Drake said.

"I always liked Carol . . ." Sharon said.

"She was too smart for you," Lenni teased.

"All the good ones are." Brandon sighed.

Rayne placed the box of items from the trunk on a side table next to the food. Pete and Brandon followed her.

"Is that the letter?" Pete asked.

"Is that plastic?" Brandon asked.

Each man reached for the item in question.

"Careful," Sharon said to Pete. "If it's old the paper might tear."

"That is not plastic," Lenni informed

Brandon. "What kind of artifact detector are you, anyway?"

Lenni held out her hand, but Brandon kept it, tapping it, rubbing the edges.

"It's crystal. Blarney is kind of a collector," Rayne said.

"Thief," Amos countered.

"Explain!" Lenni demanded with a quirk of her lips.

Rayne gave a quick recap to set the scene. Rayne, the upstart American, her and Ciara at odds, Rayne wanting nothing more than to leave but trapped by her uncle's will. "And when I first moved here, Blarney . . . took off . . . with one of my Jimmy Choo heels. A limited edition with crystals."

"Oh no!" Lenni said.

"Is that a big deal?" Sharon asked. "I prefer my shoes to be comfortable, like Birkenstocks."

"Not a heels person, either. I imagine Jimmy Choos would be worth a few thousand euro," Lenni said. "I don't spend more than two hundred on a pair."

It had been closer to five thousand dollars, but her brides had been worth it.

"Not crystal," Brandon said. He sounded smug.

"What do you mean?" Rayne asked.

"Do you have a piece of glass that you

don't care about?" Brandon asked theatrically.

Drake looked up from his sandwich he'd made with rolls and ham with interest, but he didn't say anything else. No doubt he was used to his father's dramatics.

"Will a water glass do?" Rayne asked. They'd had to buy a few dozen, nothing too fancy, to help with the influx of guests.

To her surprise, Brandon nodded. "Yep."

She got an empty one from the sideboard and gave it to Brandon. "Here you go."

"Thanks." Brandon took the crystal and made a heart on the glass.

"Cool!" Drake said. "It's a diamond."

"You're right, son. This crystal is a diamond. I've never seen one in such good condition. It's got to be a D or better in quality." Brandon held it to the light.

Rayne's knees buckled but Amos caught her elbow.

"A diamond?" It was bigger than any diamond she'd ever seen, and she was from LA. Hollywood.

"Yes, ma'am," Brandon said. "Where did you find it again?"

"In the cemetery." Rayne searched the room for Blarney, who was no longer in the room. "By Thomas McGrath's grave."

"This is also a find." Pete shook the piece

of paper that had been tucked into the liner of the trunk. "This symbol matches the shamrock on the tombstone. I wonder if they could be connected? What could it lead to? Secret societies are often hiding things."

They didn't get any farther with this very exciting discovery because Freda Bevan burst into the dining room. Cormac was with her, curled fists at his side.

Rayne held her hand out for the diamond, holy smokes, sugar cookies, snicklefritz, diamond, which Brandon returned with a curious expression, rather than one of greed.

It was about the artifact and not the money.

"What are you doing here, Freda?" Rayne asked.

Garda Kaitlin Lee was right behind Freda, anger in her gaze, her cheeks red.

"Ms. Bevan, I told you to wait for me," the officer said.

"And I told you that this woman spray-painted my front door with glitter. She used terrible words." Freda searched the room and found Drake. "Words not suited for children's ears."

Drake finished his sandwich, intrigued. At fourteen there probably wasn't much he hadn't heard. He could no doubt teach them all a few.

Blarney entered at the garda's side and joined Drake at the table.

Ciara burst after them all, her arm flung with annoyance. "What is happening here? I know for a fact that we do not have Freda on our guest list."

"I don't care!" Freda held out her phone to show Ciara. "Is this your cousin or not?"

Ciara studied the image but wiped the confusion from her face. "It might look like Rayne, but it is not. She was with me in the parlor all morning."

"Rayne, would you please come to the station in Kilkenny to answer a few questions?" Garda Lee requested. It wasn't exactly a suggestion.

"We have guests!" Rayne protested.

"I can ask nicely, or make it official," the garda said.

Rayne narrowed her eyes at Freda. "You are now interfering with my business. I know you want me to fail, but we aren't going to — this is a new low."

"Well?" Garda Lee asked.

"I'll come of course." Rayne turned to Ciara. "Will you stay with our guests? They were looking at our history books." She didn't say anything more, and especially not about the freaking diamond, because she didn't want Freda to overhear her.

"I'll drive you," Amos offered.

Rayne didn't like to drive, and she gratefully nodded. Her American license worked just fine in Ireland, but she wasn't used to driving on the wrong side of the road.

"Do I need to file a restraining order against Freda to keep her from barging into my house?" Rayne asked Garda Lee.

"We can talk about it at the station." The garda pursed her mouth. "It looks like you, Rayne. It really does — otherwise I wouldn't bother you when I know about the feud going on regarding the villages."

Rayne forced her shoulders down and exhaled. "Fine."

But it wasn't.

Rayne and Amos got their coats on. She had her purse and her phone. It was nice that Amos was driving as her mother was blowing up her phone with text messages.

"Landon's decided to crawl out from under whatever Mexican rock he'd been hiding under," Rayne shared with Amos. "He's taunting the US police for not capturing him."

The text messages stopped, and her phone rang.

She answered and put the device on speaker. "Have you seen Landon?"

"No. I haven't seen Landon." Her mother sounded legit concerned.

"You need to be on guard. What if he killed Aiden?"

"What? Landon has no motive to kill Aiden." Rayne couldn't see it.

"Have they found the killer?"

"No."

"Should I come early? I can change my flight."

They arrived at the Kilkenny Gardai Station. "No, you don't need to come early."

"Paul has an idea for a documentary about you inheriting a castle. It would bring eyes to your situation and possibly more wedding guests. Dresses. People to live there. The works."

Amos parked next to Garda Lee. There was no sign of Freda Bevan.

She couldn't fathom what her mother had just proposed. Freda Bevan had crossed the line. "Lauren, we are at the gardai station. Freda has lost her mind, and I have to put a stop to whatever she is up to. Love you!"

"Call me right back. Love you too."

Rayne ended the call. "I didn't tell her about the diamond."

"You can tell her afterward."

Rayne nodded and they got out of the Fiat to enter the station.

The lobby was tile — easy to clean — and seats of hard plastic.

A receptionist in a navy-blue uniform, in her early twenties, greeted them.

Garda Lee was right behind them. "I don't know what you did to make Freda Bevan so mad, but she has it in for you."

"Like Landon," Amos said. "You inspire passion in people."

"Not the right kind, evidently."

"Your ex still on the loose?" the garda asked.

"Yes." Rayne exhaled.

"He's been spotted in Mexico," Amos said. "But he could have easily gotten a fake ID to move around. I don't trust him. He's taunting the police in America for not capturing him."

The garda gestured to a hard plastic chair. "If you could wait here, this shouldn't take long."

"Not a problem." Amos sat.

Rayne followed the garda to a small office with four desks. All were vacant. Garda Lee crossed the room to one that had her name tag on it and turned on the computer.

"Have a seat."

Rayne perched on the edge of a wooden seat — not any more comfortable than the plastic in the lobby.

"I want to show you this," the garda said. She turned the screen.

It was footage from a door camera as well as security cams around the property.

The face was covered but the posture, and hair, of the figure was an eerie match. Could it be Landon? Her skin crawled with hives.

"This isn't you?"

"No." Her stomach clenched. "This is Landon Short." Her body tingled with alarm urging her to find the man who had stolen everything from her. "It's not the first time he's pretended to be me."

Chapter Twenty-Four

"You think Landon Short is impersonating you, to the point that he's responsible for a glitter paint bomb on Freda Bevan's door?" Garda Lee sat back and crossed her arms as she digested this information.

"Yes. Yes, I do."

"When was the last time that you saw him?"

"May 31st of this year." Rayne's face burned with embarrassment at how he'd taken advantage of her. Her high hopes and dreams — all while he'd been robbing her blind, right down to the silk lingerie in their shop on Rodeo Drive.

"What happened?" Garda Lee poised her fingers over the keyboard, not stopping once as Rayne verbally vomited the past.

He'd been found wearing one of Rayne's bridal dresses the day he'd been arrested. It had gone viral on social media, and he'd been picked up in Mexico, where she'd assumed he'd been hiding again.

She hadn't been the first mark he'd taken, but the biggest haul at a hundred fifty thousand not including the gowns.

"And then he escaped jail. He had carved my name all over his cell. I never felt afraid of him. We are the same size, as you can see. He might have a few inches on me."

Rayne pulled her gaze from the video cam.

"How could he know about your argument with Ms. Bevan?" Garda Lee asked.

Goose bumps dotted her skin, and she rubbed her arms. "Maybe he's been in Ireland rather than Mexico? Blarney has been sleeping in front of my door for the last few nights. Ciara asked if I'd heard noises too. We kinda think the place might be haunted, so we've gotten used to some of the noises, but this past week has been different. What if Landon has been in our house?"

"Don't you have it locked?" the garda asked.

"Of course we do, but there are a lot of entrances. Windows. Still, it can be locked down. It was used as a fortification." Rayne, uneasy, wished she could alert those at the house.

"I suggest locking it up and double-checking each window until we catch this guy. He's obviously not in his right mind."

The garda gave a shrug. "I never really understood all that was at stake when you showed up. Not about the will, either. That's really sad that it all happened at the same time like that."

"Funny but not funny. I get it." Rayne blinked tears from her eyes.

"What does Landon want from you?"

"I have no clue. He robbed me and I've had to scramble to get the brides their dresses. I love a happy ending. I am a sucker for a romance." Rayne shrugged. "I don't have anything left for him to steal."

"You are still running Modern Lace online?"

"Yes."

"Maybe he's targeting your reputation," the garda suggested. "He sounds dangerous."

"He's a white-collar criminal, which is why he was in a low-security facility in the first place."

"Which he broke out of — after carving your name all over. He is mentally unstable, which means you can't dismiss him," the garda said. "If he has a gun, being the same size won't matter one bit."

"You have a point."

The garda stood. "I will put out the alert

for Landon Short. I suggest you go home and lock yourself in your room until we find him."

"I can't do that," Rayne said.

"I figured you'd say that." Garda Lee passed a card with her phone number on it. "This has my personal mobile as well as the station. If you see Landon, even if you think you see him, call me and I will check it out. It's wrong what he did to you."

"Thank you."

"Welcome. Let's touch base tomorrow. I might have some ideas to draw him out, if you're willing."

"Sure. I hate the idea of being a sitting duck."

"I would too. You are stronger than that." The garda nodded and sat back down, focusing on the footage of Landon on camera. "He's sly."

"Like a weasel," Rayne agreed.

She left the office and returned toward the lobby.

Amos stood when he heard her walking down the hall. "Well?"

"It's Landon Short."

"No!"

"Yeah. I need to call Mom from the car."

"And what's the plan then?" Amos asked.

They left the lobby of the station and

climbed into the Fiat.

"Garda Lee gave me her number to call at any time. We need to double-check the locks on the doors and windows in the manor. I think he's been inside."

"What?" Amos sounded upset.

Rayne shared about Blarney, Ciara, and the noises. They climbed into the car and Amos started the engine.

"I don't want to take you back there," Amos said. "Let's find another spot for you to sleep. Not to be weird or alter the pace of our coffee dates, but you are welcome to stay with me."

Rayne's stomach tightened. "Landon glitter bombed Freda's place, okay? That is not the action of a killer."

"He's crazy, Rayne, which means that he is unpredictable."

She texted her mother.

Her phone rang.

"Lauren, it will be okay."

"I'm not Lauren. This is Freda. The garda just called to tell me that it wasn't you at the door. Liar." The doorbell rang. "What on earth are you doing here?" Freda asked in surprise. "What do you have in the box? More glitter?"

"Don't open the door, Freda!" Rayne shouted. An explosion sounded and the line went dead. "Amos, go back to the gardai station."

Amos quickly maneuvered the car around, the tires sliding on the dirt at the side of the road. "What's going on?"

"Landon is at Freda's, dressed as me. He delivered a box. There was an explosion just now." Rayne allowed her wild Celtic temper to chase tears away. "I don't think it was glitter this time."

Rayne called Garda Lee, who answered right away. She hurriedly shared what had just happened.

"Go home, Rayne," the garda said. "We have our EOD team on the way."

The garda ended the call.

Amos pulled to the side of the road to make sure that Rayne was all right and find out what was happening.

Rayne's hands shook. "What is that, EOD?"

"The bomb squad — specifically, Defence Force Explosive Ordnance Disposal," Amos said. "I hope Freda isn't hurt. Why is Landon escalating things?"

"My mother always says that motivation matters in a scene." Rayne dialed her mother next.

"Rayne?"

"Landon is impersonating me and glitter

bombed Freda Bevan's house!"

"What?"

"Why, Mom? It doesn't make sense. I keep running over possible motivations in my head, like you say, but I am coming up empty. If he'd stayed hidden in Mexico, he wouldn't have been caught."

"Rayne Claire McGrath — sometimes you can't account for crazy. Where are you now?"

"Amos is driving me back to the manor."

"I'm glad that the place is a fortress. I want you to stay out of sight until Landon is caught."

"What if he's coming after me next?" Rayne's voice was low.

"I will protect you," Amos said. "I won't leave your side."

"Lauren," Rayne said, "meet Amos, our grounds manager."

"Hi. That's right — don't leave her side."

"I won't. I look forward to meeting you under better circumstances," Amos said.

"Me too — until then, thank you. Rayne can be . . . singularly focused . . . if she wants something so . . ." her mom said.

Amos arched his brow. "Is that a nice way to say stubborn?"

"Gotta go — Ciara is calling in." Rayne

was glad she hit the end call button for that one.

"Rayne?" Ciara said. "Dominic just heard that Freda Bevan was taken to hospital! What's going on?"

"Dominic would probably know more than me at this point. Landon has been dressing up as me, so, be on guard. I don't know if the police have caught him yet."

"No," Ciara said after a muffled hand over the receiver. "Where are you now?"

"We are on our way home. How are the guests?"

"Packing up to go, with Brandon considering a place to buy here. Darcy McGillicuddy's property might be for sale, but even if it wasn't, we have plenty of land to rent or lease." Ciara sighed. "Haley McGavin can help us there. I really don't know what to do about Elizabeth. She has her hand out for compensation that I don't think we should pay. We didn't make the mistake."

"What time is our lawyer appointment tomorrow?"

"Ten in the morning with Fionagh Quinn."

"Let's add that question to the list."

"Done. How far away are you?"

"Ten minutes," Rayne said.

"All right. I'll have the staff here start

checking locks to make sure that Landon can't get in. Do you think he's behind the noises we've been hearing?"

"I do."

"Me too." Ciara gave a low chuckle. "And your dog just barked, so he agrees."

"Ciara," Rayne said, about to tell her the details of the not-crystal, but her cousin had already hung up.

"I don't like taking you back to the castle," Amos said.

"I don't like being scared out of my own home," Rayne countered. "If Landon is running around with real bombs, nobody is safe."

Rayne and Amos arrived as the wedding guests were leaving.

Amos pulled the car to the side to let them pass, but Pete stopped and climbed out of the Mercedes. Brandon and Drake exited as well from a Land Rover.

Sharon must have already left.

Lenni was last to get out of her and Pete's vehicle. She liked to drive, and Pete didn't mind.

Amos and Rayne exchanged a glance before they also got out.

She missed the warm interior of the Fiat but plastered a smile on her face. Success meant faking enthusiasm until the reviews came in.

Between Landon's escapades, Aiden's murder, and the McGillicuddy drama, she hoped that the McGee-O'Shea wedding still warranted five stars.

"Lenni, and Pete, congratulations again. I hope you come back for your anniversary!"

"I hope you save the village so that you're still here to be open next year," Lenni said. "Your ex is a real arse. Ciara told us that he's impersonating you. Please, take care of yourself."

"I will," Rayne said. Bonus if Brandon lived in Grathton would be friends like Lenni, Pete, Sharon, and Drake.

Ciara and Blarney came out of the manor and down the steps. Cormac waited at the threshold of the door, which remained partially open.

"Brandon and I were talking about the clarity of the diamond," Pete said.

"What diamond?" Ciara asked.

Rayne brought the *crystal* she'd been using as a worry stone from her pocket.

Ciara paled.

"Not a crystal after all. I wanted to tell you before I left but I didn't want Freda to hear," she said.

"It's probably five carats, and the finest quality," Brandon said. "In today's world, between 250,000 and 300,000. Did you ever find any green crystals? You know, emeralds, or rubies?"

"Two green stones, and one red," Rayne confirmed. "They are the same color as the crystals on my Jimmy Choos." She truly had thought they'd come from her shoe. "Where is Dominic?"

"Went home. He is hitting a brick wall at the gardai station about further exploring what happened to Darcy. He figured that he'd better not be here socially if there is a problem. He's on duty tonight at seven and will be back."

"Brilliant," Amos said. "I want official protection for Rayne. And you. You look alike enough to be in danger."

Ciara shook her head.

"Do you have the crystals now?" Pete asked, his voice lifting.

"Yes." Rayne added, "In a vase with the others."

"Can we see them?" Brandon asked.

"We are already late to hit the road," Lenni cautioned.

"So, what is another hour?" Pete said.

Lenni shrugged good-naturedly. "Your curiosity is one of the things I love most about you. All right."

"Sharon will be very upset that she left

already if this turns out to be what I think it might be," Brandon said. His voice was high-pitched with excitement.

"What's going on, Dad?" Drake asked.

"Your mam might be even more mad at me, but, this is so thrilling." Brandon ruffled Drake's hair. "We could get another clue toward the most infamous unsolved crime of the century."

"This is why you need to get your stuff out of her garage," Drake said.

"That is the perfect segue for the conversation — thank you, laddie." Brandon put his hand to his heart. "I don't have to be back in Germany until December first. I will clean out the garage before I go." He turned to Rayne and Ciara with a grin. "Can we see them?"

Ciara grabbed Rayne's hand. "I don't get a thing of what you're going on about, but I am coming with you. You are not to be out of my sight."

Amos remained glued to her other side. "I promised your mam the same."

Blarney nudged her leg with his head.

Three souls who had her back.

Maybe that is what Landon was upset about? That she had people who cared about her?

He'd gone to jail alone, but through his

own poor choices. She would have been true to him — if he hadn't been a lying sociopath.

Chapter Twenty-Five

"Let's go inside," Rayne suggested. "Where we can be warm. I want to lock these things up until we figure out what they are." Three hundred thousand dollars. Her palms were sweating.

"I have a printout I'd like to show you," Pete said. "In the car."

"Why not bring it in?" Rayne said.

Within moments the cars were all parked and the guests, and staff, inside.

"Let's meet in the blue parlor," Ciara suggested. "There's room for everyone and drinks. I am ready for a drink."

"I'll start a fire," Cormac said. His face was scrunched and Rayne braced herself.

"What is it, Cormac?"

"During our perusal of the locks for doors and windows, I discovered a broken latch in the sunroom, which leads directly to the secret staircase and the second-floor bedrooms."

Rayne exhaled. "All right. And now?"

"It will need to be replaced in the morning after a trip to the hardware store. I've shoved a heavy wardrobe in front of it, but it won't stop an intruder who wants to get in, milady."

Ciara, Amos, and Rayne exchanged looks.

"I am not staying locked in my room all night, okay? Let's hear what our guests have to say and send them on their way, then we can talk."

"All right," Amos said. Cormac and Ciara nodded.

"I'm going upstairs," Rayne said.

"With me," Amos said.

"And me." Ciara stuck out her chin.

"I think one keeper is sufficient," Rayne said with more than a touch of exasperation.

"Fine." Ciara and Cormac led the four guests to the blue parlor.

Amos, Rayne, and Blarney, who seemed to know he was on guard duty, climbed the steps, turning left at the landing to her room.

Once there, she unlocked the door and went inside.

The crystals were in the vase on the shelf. Her gaze went to her purses. The pink bag was gone.

"My Hermes purse is missing!"

Blarney jumped up on the bed and growled at the wardrobe, alert.

"Landon must have been in here," Amos said. He opened the wardrobe where her everyday clothes hung.

"My sunshine yellow dress is not there." Rayne shivered with nerves.

"We should ask Garda Lee what Landon was wearing, if she can tell," Amos said.

"My door was locked," Rayne said. She felt incredibly violated. Again. Still.

"We should change out the locks for all the doors and windows, tomorrow," Amos said. "I will take care of it myself."

"Thank you."

"We should also call Garda Lee to let her know about the missing purse and the clothes." Amos gestured to her room. "Anything else missing?"

Rayne looked everywhere. "Gloves, a yellow scarf with pink roses, and my picture of me and my dad." She lifted the crystals off the shelf in the vase. "The other Jimmy Choo is still there. Let's go, Amos. Thank you."

"We will catch him, Rayne," Amos said in a very sexy grumble.

"I am ready to face him." Rayne sent a text to Garda Lee with the information to update the officer on the Landon situation, and that she would be in the blue parlor with the wedding guests until they left.

The officer responded with a thumbs-up emoji. Then, a message for Rayne to call her as soon as her guests left.

Rayne thumbs-upped that message.

They reached the study.

Cormac was standing guard at the open door to the parlor with what appeared to be a walking stick at his side, but Rayne knew the club was a shillelagh and a dangerous weapon in the right hands.

Should she alert Cormac now, about the break-in inside her room?

"I'll tell him," Amos said. "You go in and show the baubles to the guests so we can get onto the next drama of the night."

Nodding, Rayne brought the vase into the room.

"There you are," Brandon said with an eager smile.

Drake was sprawled on an armchair with his earbuds in and his phone, eyes closed. Probably listening to music.

Lenni and Pete were drinking tea that Maeve had brought in on a tea cart.

Brandon had opted for water as he was also driving.

Ciara held a tumbler of whiskey.

Rayne would have a double as soon as the guests left.

Where could this brilliant diamond have come from? What Brandon had said about the unsolved theft, and then asked about emeralds, had her recalling the story from Dublin Castle and the stolen Irish Crown Jewels.

She worried that perhaps her ancestor, Thomas McGrath, had been a thief. That the purpose of the Cavalier Clovers with the shamrock and upside-down crown had been to overtake the government.

What would that mean for Grathton Village?

They were trying so hard to build it up again, but this could be the death knoll. Not that she thought she or Ciara could be put in jail, but what if they were forced to pay back the value of the jewels? That would put them in debt forever.

They barely had money to pay the bills through March, when the next batch of sheep would bring income.

"It's a good thing Dominic isn't here," Rayne whispered. "He'd want to make this official when right now we are simply gathering information."

Ciara frowned. "Are those ALL real?" She paled.

"I don't think so." Rayne faced Brandon, Pete, and Lenni. "Let's find out." She exhaled. "How should we do this, guys?"

Maeve, and Aine, were inside the room. Amos too.

"Cormac is standing guard outside, with Blarney," Amos said.

The office had a window, but the blue parlor was an interior room and did not. It was as protected as they could be.

And, Rayne eyed the couch, maybe a good place to hole up for the night. As tempting as staying with Amos sounded, his place had windows.

Like a proper cottage should. Would her life ever get back to normal? "Thanks," Rayne said.

"Smart to have a guard." Brandon nodded at the vase. "Where's the diamond?"

Rayne, after a moment of panic that she'd lost it, pulled it from her jacket pocket. "I had no idea it was valuable. I've been using it as a worry stone." She showed them how her thumb fit the smooth oval perfectly.

Lenni snickered. "That's very Lady of the Castle appropriate."

Ciara closed her eyes briefly, hugging her tumbler to her chest. "Oh, dear Lord."

"Jewels love to be worn," Lenni said.

"What's the point of having them otherwise?"

Pete pulled a piece of paper from his leather briefcase. "We can't be sure without proper testing that it is a match."

Rayne moved forward.

Placing a newspaper article of two pieces of jewelry on the table, Pete said, "These were created for the Order of Saint Patrick and stolen in June 1907. The reward was a thousand pounds."

Brandon opened his tablet — an iPad, Rayne noticed, that was banged up but functional. "Here — this would be the stones enlarged."

Rayne's stomach knotted.

She knew in her heart that it was a match.

Amos, Ciara, and Maeve studied the pictures too. Maeve brought her fingers to her lips. "Oh."

"Now what?" Rayne asked.

"Can we see the emeralds and rubies you found?" Pete asked. "Where did you find them?"

"Sure. Here's everything I've collected since losing the shoe." Rayne flipped the copy of the newspaper article over, as it was blank, and dumped the contents of the vase.

Brandon brought out a jeweler's loupe.

"You just happen to have one of those?"

Maeve asked with suspicion.

"Eh, I do. It helps read microscopic text." Brandon examined the jewels and set aside one green and two red baguettes. "Real." There were thirteen lost crystals in the vase, and at the end, nine were crystals. There was one giant diamond, five carat, one smaller diamond, three carat, the emerald, and the rubies.

"I'm shocked," Rayne said. Her stomach was in knots.

"It would be helpful if you knew where these were found," Brandon said. "All in the cemetery?"

"Just the big one," Rayne said.

"When?" Pete asked.

"I can't say. I just don't remember. I was laughing when they were on the porch or in the grass. I thought Blarney was bringing them to me to put the shoe back."

"Or that the fairies were bringing them to her," Maeve said.

"That's a little crazy," Pete said.

"This is Ireland," Aine said. "Fairies and leprechauns are real."

"Far be it from me to differ with the McGrath legends," Pete said, backtracking.

Lenni admired the jewels, comparing them to the cubic zirconia crystals. "The quality of these diamonds are above par."

She held out her wedding finger which had a lovely two carat. "I might need to upgrade."

"On that note," Pete said, "we should be getting back to Cork."

"What will you do with your finds?" Brandon asked. "I'm not sure you can keep them, if they are part of what was stolen."

"We need to have a family talk. Can we have the printouts and your written opinion on size and clarity of the jewels?" Rayne asked.

Pete said, "Of course."

Brandon shrugged. "Sure. I wonder where the rest of the jewels are, if these are indeed a match to the badge or the star?"

"You're sure they weren't all in the cemetery?" Pete asked again.

"I don't know," Rayne said. "I only found the one. The leprechauns, fairies, or Blarney, might have found them all over." She put her hand to her mouth. "I'm worried that we'll get a massive fine if Thomas McGrath turns out to be a thief. What was the point of the Cavalier Clovers?"

"To overturn the British government," Pete said with assurance. "The shamrock on the inverted crown states freedom for Ireland. The Cs stand for Cavalier Clovers. This is an important discovery."

"Pete's right," Brandon said.

"One way or another Grathton Village could be in the news, which might help with the wedding venue in a roundabout way." Lenni finished her tea and set the cup on the cart with a gentle clack. "We must get going or it will be eight by the time we reach home. I need to prepare for a meeting tomorrow. Don't you have tests to grade?"

Pete sighed. "Yes. But just wait until I . . . well, I can't say a thing, can I?"

"Not yet," Brandon agreed. He looked at Rayne.

"I have no idea what to do, honestly." She waved to Ciara. "We have an appointment with a lawyer tomorrow that might give us much needed advice."

"I will say just a word of caution," Brandon said. "When it comes to Irish artifacts, the government can be sticklers."

"What should we do?" Ciara asked.

"If I were in your shoes, I would put the crystals back in the vase, and then in a safe until tomorrow," Brandon said. "I'd leave them there and take the story, with the article, to your solicitor and let them advise you how to proceed."

"Even before the gardai?" Ciara asked.

Her cousin was no doubt thinking of Dominic.

"Yes. That's true," Pete said. "Although the *right* thing to do would be to call the gardai, I would follow Brandon's advice."

Lenni zipped her lips. "Mum's the word."

"But, please," Brandon said. "Keep us in the loop. I'm tempted to rent a building right now just so I have a reason to come back."

Rayne sighed. They'd need to lawyer up.

Pete took out his wallet and some big bills. "Here. A down payment for my friend."

"That's the money I just gave you for your wedding," Brandon protested.

"I know you're good for it," Pete said.

Laughing, their four wedding guests got up to leave.

"We can't promise anything. Take your money!" Rayne said, giving it back to Pete. "We will keep your name in mind after we discuss things with our property management company."

Pete nodded, as did Brandon. Drake took out an earbud, smiling. He hadn't heard a thing. "This was brilliant. Bye!"

Rayne, Ciara, and Amos, followed by Cormac and the shillelagh, all walked them outside.

The four drove off as the night sky darkened though it wasn't even five in the evening. Winter was just around the corner.

"Brandon will be a nice addition to the village," Amos said. "I like him. He's traveled all over the world. Like my ex. She had that same wanderlust spirit."

"He will be a nice fit." Rayne checked her mobile and sent a text to Garda Lee that the guests had gone.

No answer.

"I wonder how Freda is doing?" Rayne asked.

"I can call the hospitals." Cormac and Blarney went inside. "Coming?"

"Just a minute," Rayne said. "I need to catch Ciara up —"

"Why is your pink bubble gum bag in the driveway?" Ciara asked with concern. "It will get ruined." She stepped down the stairs to the gravel.

In that one second, the front door slammed closed. Cormac and Blarney were inside, while she and Amos and Ciara were outside in the cold with no coats or sweaters. A rope with a long board had jammed the door so Cormac couldn't get out. Blarney barked and scrabbled on the massive wooden door.

Ciara reached for Rayne's designer purse. "What's inside it?" her cousin stopped to admonish Rayne. "It looks like sticks."

"No!" Rayne shouted to Ciara. "It's

dynamite!" The expensive bag so didn't matter. Her cousin's life was at stake. She raced for Ciara and rushed her from the purse.

A shot sounded in the air and Rayne froze.

She slowly turned toward the porch, arm still around Ciara.

Landon, in her sunshine yellow dress, gloves, and hat, with her pink flowered scarf for warmth, pointed the gun at Amos. Wellies, a smart choice given the weather, adorned his feet. The wig of long dark hair was slightly askew.

"Amos, stand next to Rayne. Ciara, don't move a muscle. I will shoot the first one of you to disobey." His smile was made up in her favorite shade of raspberry lipstick.

Amos stepped toward Landon.

Landon shot the ground in front of Amos.

"Amos!" Rayne said. "Just listen to him."

This man was deranged. She recalled Garda Lee's prediction of Landon having a gun and having the advantage in any one-on-one scenario Rayne might have imagined. He wasn't playing by the rules, as Pete had pointed out earlier.

"What do you want, Landon? I don't have anything to give you. You took it already."

"Calm down, Rayne," Ciara warned. "You don't want to spur him on. How did he get your things?"

"I was going to tell you that he'd been in the house and stolen the bag and dress," Rayne whispered. "Garda Lee knows about it. Hopefully she's on the way."

"Well, hell."

"I'll tell you exactly what I want," Landon said in a menacing tone. He kept the gun steady on the three of them, his back to the front door. Blarney's barks shook the wood.

"I'm listening." Rayne raised her chin.

"A first," Landon said. "Listening is not your strong point. I dropped so many clues about my plan, but you were oblivious. You wanted the win and were focused on the finish line."

Rayne bristled.

"Don't let him bait you," Amos murmured.

There were perhaps two car lengths between Landon and the purse. Ciara, Amos, and Rayne were two feet from it.

"Bring me the Hermes, Rayne," Landon instructed.

"No!" Ciara said. "Let me do it."

Landon shot into the gravel near the bag. "The dynamite will go off as soon as I press this itty-bitty remote in my hand." He showed a black plastic control. "The explosion that took out Freda — you owe me for that one, Rayne, helping you, but that feeling was nothing compared to this euphoria. You bring that bag to the porch. I'll let Cormac and your stupid dog out the door, triggering more dynamite, while we all go up in flames."

"Why?" Rayne asked.

Blarney had quieted.

"You put me in jail, Rayne. We were supposed to be united. A team."

"Revenge," Rayne murmured. It was a doozy of a motivation. She couldn't let Cormac get hurt. Or Blarney. Not Amos, or her cousin, or Dafydd.

Rayne quickly ran scenarios through her mind. She noticed Dafydd, well camouflaged in his herding gear, coming to Ciara's right. He would keep Ciara safe.

"Screw that," Rayne said in a firm voice. "I'm tossing the Hermes toward the field. Ciara, run to Dafydd on your right. Amos, duck and charge Landon. On three. One, two, three!"

She could only hope that her team, her actual team that she trusted, understood her last minute plan.

On the count of three, Amos kept his head down and zigzagged toward Landon. Rayne grabbed the Hermes and flung it with all her might away from the people she cared about, as Ciara, and Dafydd, both tackled her. She felt the knees on her tights tear.

She heard another shot fire and struggled to her feet. Blarney and Cormac ran from the side of the sunroom with the broken latch of the window. The butler must have moved the furniture to get out in the same way Landon had broken in.

Amos kicked the gun from Landon's hand. Blarney pinned Landon and Cormac held the point of the shillelagh at Landon's throat.

"Get the remote from Landon!" Rayne cried.

Too late.

Landon somehow was able to press it, and the sticks tied beneath the sunshine yellow dress he wore detonated, sending Blarney and Cormac backward. Blarney yelped but Amos carried him to safety as her Hermes bag exploded into a million pieces of pink leather in the field.

Rayne and Ciara raced for the porch and patted Amos down while Dafydd, with superhuman strength, pulled the log free from the front door. Cormac was out cold on his back.

Amos smacked down embers on the porch as Aine and Maeve, and Frances, came out the front door, armed with cast iron skillets.

"We called 999," Aine said. "Da?" She dropped to her knees by his side. Maeve helped her husband on the other.

Cormac sat up and the Lloyds burst into happy tears.

"Is Landon . . ." Rayne asked.

Ciara felt for his pulse. "Alive, unfortunately. He tried to kill us all and himself for a suicide mission." She reached for Dafydd's hand. "Thank you."

"This is my home too," Dafydd said.

Ciara nodded. "I know."

Rayne buried her face in Blarney's fur, and Amos rubbed her back. "It's over now."

Chapter Twenty-Six

Monday morning, Rayne was up before her alarm, even though she'd only gotten a few hours of sleep.

Landon had died on the way to the hospital and in a twist of fate she never could have imagined, his death had allowed Freda to receive a corneal transplant to her eye, which had been injured from the blast. When Rayne had yelled a warning to Freda, the councilwoman had turned and saved herself from even worse injuries besides minor burns. A spark from the explosion had damaged her eye.

Rayne and Ciara would stop by the hospital today after their appointment with the lawyer, Fionagh Quinn. Both were pleased with the stellar reviews on her business page. How to pay her fee now that the thirty thousand bag was gone, was something to think about later.

She put her nose in Blarney's fur. "And

you, my hero, get a bath. You stink!" She hugged him tighter to her.

After the chaos of last night, once the gardai and paramedics went home, Rayne, Ciara, the Lloyds, and Amos, met for a drink in the blue parlor. As a group, they decided to follow Brandon and Pete's advice and keep the diamond, and possible Thomas McGrath theft of the Irish Crown Jewels, to themselves until after the appointment today. What if the Cavalier Clovers had financed overthrowing the government by stealing the crown jewels?

Something about the letter they'd found hidden away in the trunk niggled at her brain.

Rayne wanted to believe that her ancestors were good guys. She must have absorbed more of her mother's training on the set than she'd realized as her next question was, *why now?*

What had happened to stir the still waters from the past one hundred years?

Darcy had died, supposedly in his sleep. Elizabeth was upset and insistent that her brother had been worried about something. The funeral house in Kilkenny had *accidentally* cremated Darcy, making a second examination impossible without a court order.

Aiden, Don, and Paddy . . . and Beetle, had been childhood friends of the younger generation. Rian McGillicuddy had moved to Dublin. In the older generation, it had been Murray, Darcy, Luke and Sheff. Had a McGrath — maybe Thomas — been part of the circle? Or was it Duncan, who had died?

It was too late to ask her dad, or her uncle.

"Come on, Blarney," Rayne said. "Let's explore."

She put on her robe and slippers with the tread to keep her feet warm. The purse had been destroyed, as had the picture of her and her dad. Yes, it lived in her memories, but it wasn't the same.

Landon wouldn't face trial for his many crimes. He was dead, and could no longer harm her.

Did she, and Ciara, as McGraths, owe anybody for what their kin may have done in the name of the Republic? She reached the foyer and listened for anybody who might be up, but it was quiet.

She entered the blue parlor and saw her cousin looking through the history books from the trunk. Ciara had the vase of crystals out as well from the safe, but they were all inside the clear container.

"Ciara?"

Her cousin stifled a squeal.

"What are you doing up?" Ciara asked.

"Couldn't sleep. Obvi, same as you."

"I hate to think that Thomas McGrath was a thief. Maybe that's why he wasn't mentioned in the church roster, or the family bible." Ciara's brows rose, her expression sad.

"I was thinking the same thing, but it makes sense."

"Does it? I can't fathom it. We have got to get to the bottom of this." Ciara pinched the bridge of her nose.

"Do you remember seeing the Polaroid of those four guys?"

"Um, yes . . . here. I was using it as a bookmark in the book on the Irish struggles against the government." Ciara hefted the tome on *current* history, dated in 1910. "Being Irish wasn't good, and being Catholic was equally as frowned upon. Irish Catholic? Forget it. The English nobility had all the power. It was no wonder people rebelled." She found the book. "And this was before the Troubles in the 1960s when the country was torn apart from the inside, after winning the War of Independence from England."

Rayne accepted the tome and the photo. "So glad you enjoy this stuff. I wish there was a juicy confession or something. Maybe a diary or journal instead of these dry books on history."

Ciara ruffled her curls. "Not good if our man is part of a secret society, like Brandon and Pete think."

"Fair. Cavalier Clovers. Pete said that they were meant to mimic the placement in government as the Knights of the Shamrock."

Rayne leaned back on the sofa.

"It's been a long week," Ciara said.

"Yeah. I still can't believe that the divot I was gently cleaning turned out to be a shamrock on an inverted crown."

"I only saw that once Brandon showed me the image he'd taken on his phone, super enlarged."

Rayne tapped the letter and the Polaroid together. "What does that have to do with our mysterious Thomas McGrath?"

"Who knows?" Ciara sighed. "All of this has me wondering about our ancestors and the part they've played in Irish history. The original Andrew McGrath was definitely a hero. Da said so. His grandfather was named Andrew after him. It's been a family name."

Rayne took a picture of the four men. It was blurry but she was able to enlarge them one at a time.

"This looks like Sheff McElroy. The nose is distinctive. And this forehead reminds me of Billy McGillicuddy. Maybe not them but what if their dads or families were involved?"

"It's a stretch."

"I agree." She tossed the picture back with frustration.

"We should talk with Father Patrick," Ciara said.

"What if these guys," Rayne said, "were the Cavalier Clovers and were good guys, like, the Knights of the Order?"

"And our Thomas went rogue? He's not included in any of the photos or listed anywhere," Ciara said.

Rayne picked up the picture. "I hate to say this, but what if Elizabeth was right about something happening to Darcy?"

"She'd be over the moon if you told her that." Ciara straightened. "Why do you think so?"

Rayne picked up the hidden letter with the shamrock on an inverted crown. "Long Live the Republic. Down with Great Britain. Bobby kept saying that the Thomas grave shouldn't be there. Pete and Brandon found this Cavalier Clovers symbol on that grave. What if Darcy knew something, and for some reason, he wanted to tell Elizabeth?"

Excitement sped through her. This was proof that would back up what Brandon and Pete had been so excited about. If she was right, they were about to find the rest of the Irish Crown Jewels.

"Let's go dig up Thomas," Rayne said.

"Are you nuts?" Ciara shook her head.

"No — I've finally figured it out."

Ciara stood. "It's illegal, isn't it, to unbury a body?"

"He's our ancestor, and this is on our land." Rayne grinned. "You won't be sorry." She was so certain that she started to laugh.

"I'll give you over breakfast to convince me it's a good idea." Ciara put her hand to her stomach. "Because it's not. Maybe the others will be up, and they can talk you out of it so we don't end up in jail."

"You'd help me anyway?"

"Of course. We are family and if we've learned anything, it's that family sticks together."

Rayne said, "Tell you what — let's call Elizabeth to let her know we want a chat before she leaves for Dublin. Hopefully she hasn't left yet."

It was now eight, so early, but not ridiculous like six in the morning early. Rayne ended up leaving a message for Elizabeth, saying, "We think you were right about

Darcy being onto something. Please call us before you leave for Dublin."

"Now what?" Ciara asked.

"You owe me a fancy lunch in Dublin if we actually find a body in the grave. I bet there isn't one."

"You've lost your mind. Plain and simple. Landon's attempt on your life has gotten to you. It's okay to admit it — I was scared as well."

Rayne held up her hand. "It's where Blarney found the five-carat diamond." She tapped the picture of the shamrock on the inverted crown. "This symbol ties the grave to the secret society that wanted freedom above all else."

"How do you leap from that, to no dead body in the cemetery?"

"I think that the shamrock is a code to let others in the Cavalier Clovers know where the money is and has been hidden. I believe we will find jewels in the grave. There was no Thomas McGrath in the picture with the others. No Thomas McGrath on the church roster for that time."

"All right. Let's go."

"Seriously?"

"Yeah. Why not?"

"Okay!"

Ciara brushed her hands together. "I

really want some breakfast first. And we need to change clothes. Can we grab a cup and some toast to go?"

Rayne laughed. "Fine. But I want my lunch this weekend to celebrate. We should call Haley and have her meet us."

"Sure. I hope we get to keep the diamonds. Do you think we will?" Ciara asked.

"Doubtful. I'm worried that we might go to jail." They left the blue parlor, with Blarney at their sides. Rayne locked the door, then had to unlock it to go back in. "We forgot to return the *crystals* to the safe."

Rayne put them away. Her body shook at the amount of money in that vase. It could save them, but it wasn't worth it. Would they be responsible if a second or third heist occurred?

Ciara grabbed the photo of the men. "I think we should bring this too, in case Elizabeth calls us back. She might know for sure who these men are. The McGillicuddy farm is close to the church."

"We should call Don and Paddy about the business lease too. Let them know we aren't doing the historic tourist thing. Paddy said he was staying with his grandparents, Murray and Olivia."

"That's right."

"Our first clients." Rayne grinned at Ciara. "This has been some ride."

They left the parlor, again, and went to the kitchen.

"And your storefront, too."

Frances had breakfast ready. Everyone looked tired from the events of the night before. It wasn't often that one's home was under threat.

"Great skills with the skillet," Rayne said proudly to the ladies.

She reached for two stainless-steel mugs from the cupboard and handed one to Ciara, and poured her coffee, sweetened the way she liked it, into hers.

Ciara made herself a tea, then grabbed a piece of toast and a paper napkin. "Toast?"

"Yes please," Rayne said.

"Where are you two going?" Maeve asked. "Shouldn't you be staying home?"

"Landon is not a threat anymore," Rayne said.

"That may be, but last night was a long one," Maeve continued in her maternal way. "You have the solicitor's appointment at ten." She tilted her head. "Where on earth are you going?"

"We have a question about the validity of Thomas McGrath's grave," Rayne said.

"We're expecting a call from Elizabeth

McGillicuddy," Ciara said. "Give her Rayne's mobile, would you please? She left a message but didn't include it."

"Oops. See? Teamwork."

"Father Patrick will be up, so that's all right then," Maeve said.

"Mam!" Aine said. "Rayne and Ciara are grown women, not your children."

Maeve's face flushed.

Cormac sipped his tea. "So? We care, that's all."

Maeve sent her husband a grateful glance. "We do."

Frances put ham slices on the table. "Would you like it warmed for when you come back?"

"Don't go to any trouble," Rayne said. "We won't be long."

Ciara wrapped Rayne's toast.

"Pajamas are a good choice then?" Maeve asked, holding in her smile.

The ladies went upstairs, quickly changed into clothes meant for tromping around, then walked down the tree-lined road to the main street, munching toast as they went, Blarney at their side.

Rayne tossed Blarney a crumb.

Ciara glanced at Rayne. "Maeve is so sweet. My mam was bossy, but it didn't come across as caring."

"She does care — they all do. Even Frances, though she hasn't been with us as long. She was right there yesterday, brandishing her weapon of choice. Amos, and Dafydd. Cormac." Rayne exhaled as the memory unfolded with a sharp pang. Blarney.

Sinead Walsh was on her front stoop of the bakery and waved a good morning. The Sheep's Head Pub was dark as were the other little shops and offices that didn't open until nine.

"I wonder how the investigation is going?" Ciara tucked her hands in her jacket pocket. "Dominic shared that Beetle's prints can't be matched on the garden shears. He remains under scrutiny because of the connection between Colleen and Aiden."

They reached the church parking lot. It was empty. Father Patrick's house was also dark, his car in the space before it.

"Guess he got to sleep in," Rayne said. "We need to be extra quiet."

"Didn't Dorothy McElroy say that she and her daughters split up the time to take care of the Rectory?"

"Yes. Probably not until nine by the looks of it. If we are still here when they come, we need to pin them down about a jam storefront."

"This might be Dorothy's husband Sheff's

dad, or grandad," Ciara said, bringing out the photo. "We could ask her too."

"It is eerily quiet," Rayne said. "Bobby Fitzroy's team should be at the buildings today, finishing up the last coat of paint." She was excited to choose one for Modern Lace. She'd pay rent too, so it was income.

They opened the black metal gate to the cemetery and walked toward the grave. They'd only gone a few feet when the gate slammed behind them.

They whirled. Blarney sat on his haunches, tongue lolling. The imperious figure of Elizabeth McGillicuddy stepped toward them.

"Elizabeth!" Ciara said, her hand to her chest. "You scared me."

"You got our message," Rayne said.

"I did." Elizabeth inched ahead, Olivia and Murray on either side of her. The trio involved in the love affair. Olivia, Catholic, had forgiven the offense. Back then it would have been difficult to be a divorced woman.

"Morning." Ciara nodded to Murray and Olivia.

"Guess we're all up early," Rayne said. "We'd hoped to catch you before you returned to Dublin. We think you're right to be worried about what happened to Darcy."

"What do you have in your hand, lass?"

Olivia asked Ciara.

Ciara passed the photo to Olivia.

"Oh, yes! That's your dad, Murray. Milton. And Corby McGillicuddy." Olivia showed the photo to Elizabeth. "I don't think I've ever seen this." She shook it toward Rayne and Ciara. "Where on earth did you find it? It has all four of them in one shot."

"We found it in a trunk," Ciara said. "It was a trove of history from a hundred years ago."

Milton O'Brien, Murray's father. Could he have been one of the Cavaliers?

Olivia made a tsking sound.

"Too bad," Murray said.

Rayne suddenly realized they were in danger. These friendly old people had a past. Could they be killers? Her body tensed. They should have called the gardai. What had been an amusing idea was no longer funny. People killed for money all the time and age was not a factor.

Elizabeth's lips pursed in anger. "Let us go," she said.

"Shut your mouth." Olivia's wrinkled face exuded menace. Elizabeth squealed and winced. Olivia waved the bloody end of a knife toward Rayne and Ciara. "Not a peep."

"What do you want?" Rayne asked. Could she run for it? Murray had Ciara by the back of the jacket. Ciara struggled.

No.

"Keep moving," Murray said. "Back to the Thomas McGrath headstone. Isn't that why you lasses are here? To check the validity of the grave?"

"How did you know?" Rayne asked.

"Aine told Elizabeth when we forced her to return your call," Murray said with a cackle.

"What is your plan?" Rayne asked.

Murray had a gas can that he shook over the headstones, getting the tree trunks and dry branches. He even doused the wooden fairy doors. "A bright fire. Fire covers all kinds of evidence. It's why we had Darcy cremated. It will be unfortunate to lose more family in the village. We'll need to get a new priest, as well."

"Why?" Rayne realized that Murray O'Brien had kin in the photo. The Cavalier Clovers, willing to do anything for freedom. Bobby had mentioned this was an extreme faction of freedom fighters. Bobby had been searching for evidence around Dublin, when it turned out they'd all gone to the same church.

"Don't play dumb. I saw the diamond you

picked up that day, Rayne McGrath," Murray said coolly. "Do you still have it?"

"It's a crystal from a Jimmy Choo."

"That's the story you've been putting around, but I don't believe it." Murray's cheeks turned red with anger. "You couldn't leave it alone."

Olivia pushed Elizabeth forward to the grave. "Dig. You know the truth, Elizabeth. I don't know how these two moppets figured it out, but it doesn't matter. Three sets of hands to do the digging will go faster. We need the fire started before nine when Dorothy gets here."

"How did you figure it out?" Murray asked. When Rayne didn't move, he hit her on the back, and she dropped to her knees. "Dig and talk. Women are excellent multitaskers."

Ciara landed on her knees next to Rayne. Where was Blarney?

The dog would go home without them, something he often did. The Lloyds wouldn't start to worry for another hour or so when Rayne and Ciara weren't back yet.

"I don't know what you're talking about," Rayne said.

Murray twisted Ciara's arm, wrenching it with a pop of her shoulder. "How?"

Ciara stifled a cry.

"We found a message with the pictures from 1923. We already gave it to the gardai," Rayne said, wishing the lie was true. "They should be here any second."

"Duncan McGrath?" Murray shook his head. "Ah, shame. I looked up to him. No evidence was the motto of the Cavaliers. It's why we remained free men."

Olivia kept poking Elizabeth with the knife, smiling at her pain. She traced the photo with the knife tip. "Billy was handsome, as was Darcy. Our boys were brave. Until your Darcy wanted to confess what his da had done." She clucked her tongue.

"To what?" Elizabeth asked.

"Don't play stupid with me. You've known where your family got its money all along," Olivia said. "Why would Darcy upset the apple cart with the truth?"

"He wanted to right a wrong," Elizabeth said. "I didn't agree that a confession was the correct course of action. What did you two cretins do about it?"

"Nothing you can prove," Murray said. "We were content to let the jewels stay hidden for eternity. They'd served their purpose. We, the Republic of Ireland, are free."

Rayne glanced at Ciara as they dug in the dirt with their hands. Ciara favored her shoulder. They couldn't let these old thieves get away with murder. Darcy's demise she now understood.

"Why would you kill Aiden?" Rayne asked. "He couldn't have known anything about what happened so long ago."

"That's what you think," Olivia said. "Paddy, our grandson, has big ears and knew about the wealth in this old graveyard. What was left of it anyway. Most was sold to pay for weapons for the CC."

"Cavalier Clovers." Secrets don't stay secrets. They eventually come to light.

"You've been nosy," Murray said with narrowed eyes. "Like Aiden."

"It was Aiden's own fault for going after the jewels," Olivia said. "We didn't plan to kill him, but the lad was a drunken mess. Tripped over the headstone and saw us following him. We were content for the contents to stay hidden, with Darcy dead. Didn't think one of our grands would be so greedy. He fell and we made sure he didn't get back up." Olivia shrugged. "I found the shears in the unlocked trailer and gave em to Murray. Bobby shoulda taken care of his tools."

Rayne glared at the old woman.

"We could never be sure if Darcy had blabbed to Elizabeth. Murray had taken Darcy's written confession that night when we played the sleep fairy." Olivia mimed a pillow over Darcy's face. "Paddy found it in Murray's office and shared it with Don and Aiden. Don won't do anything about it, but Paddy, well. He's upset about Aiden's accidental death."

Garden shears to the back were no accident! Before Rayne could say so, Ciara shook her head in warning.

"Leave Paddy alone." Elizabeth sat on her heels, designer sneakers in light blue, and pursed her mouth. "He's your grandson. You make me sick."

"Dig," Olivia instructed.

"No." Elizabeth stood. She and Olivia wrestled for the knife. "Run, lasses!" Ciara and Rayne raced for the gate as they heard Murray cry out.

They smelled gasoline, and then the strike of an old-fashioned match.

They barreled out of the cemetery and pounded on Father Patrick's door. It cracked open. He was tied up on a dining chair.

Rayne put her arm out to stop Ciara from bursting inside. "Hang on!" Was it safe to go in? She didn't see any obvious danger.

Ciara called 999 from the priest's front porch.

Hearing him groan, the cousins gave a nod

and went in. "Should we move him? Lock the doors? What if the church goes up in flames?" Rayne knew she was babbling but couldn't stop it.

"Olivia has the picture of the four men," Ciara said. "What if it's important?"

Rayne patted Father Patrick's cheeks until he came around. She found a pair of scissors and cut the rope from the priest's wrists and ankles.

"What's going on?" Father Patrick moaned.

"We were hoping you could tell us," Rayne said.

His gaze remained dazed, and she assisted him to the bench seat outside.

Ciara called the manor, on speaker, and told Maeve about the fire. "What do we do?"

"I'll call the McElroys and get the phone chain started," Maeve instructed. "Stay there!"

Within moments a plume of smoke rose in the air.

Amos, Dafydd, and Richard arrived — all three men out of breath. "Brought the truck," Amos said. "Shovels. Pails."

Garda Williams, still on his shift, arrived at the church next. He relaxed once he saw that Ciara was on the front porch with

Father Patrick.

The paramedics put the priest on a stretcher and carted him off to the hospital. Garda Lee was bringing Elizabeth, bleeding from her side, from the cemetery.

A second ambulance arrived, and a third.

"We don't have any more available," Rayne heard one paramedic say to the other.

Amos, Dafydd, and Richard brought hoses and sprayed water over the lawn to stop the fire from spreading. "It was a good thing that we'd just cleared the brush," Amos said.

"The fairies protected their land," Richard announced.

Rayne wondered if it was a combination of both that saved the cemetery grounds.

Murray, in handcuffs by a larger officer Rayne didn't know, was brought out from the cemetery gate. He was struggling for all his worth to lunge at Elizabeth. "You killed Olivia! You are going down."

Elizabeth showed her bloody palm to Murray. "It was self-defense. Let's see who breaks first. I know how to keep a secret. Fool."

Murray was put into a police vehicle, and Elizabeth went to the hospital in the ambulance.

"Olivia O'Brien is still alive," Garda Williams said over a radio attached to Garda Lee's vest. "She won't make it, but we have to try."

The third ambulance medics disappeared beyond the gate with a stretcher, carrying a very still Olivia.

Dominic Williams had put the bloody photograph in an evidence bag.

"Is there anything you two want to tell me about this?"

Rayne looked at the time on the phone. Half past nine. "We actually have an appointment with our solicitor at ten. Can we call you afterward?"

Dominic blew out a breath but then nodded. "Don't make me regret this."

Chapter Twenty-Seven

Amos drove Ciara and Rayne back to the castle in minutes flat. "I am tempted to be your bodyguards on the way to the solicitor."

"We don't need that," Ciara declared. "It will be tight, but we can make it."

"Not even if you left from here," Dafydd said from the seat next to Ciara where he was squished against the window. Amos came to a stop before the stairs. They all piled out.

Dafydd looked at Ciara as if he wanted to say something, but in the end, simply turned on his heel and walked to the barn.

"I can drive you," Amos offered.

"We'll be fine, so long as the princess here doesn't take too long to get ready," Ciara said. "I have a lead foot, Amos, and you do not. Hurry, Rayne. We're leaving in five minutes. If you are not in the Fiat, I will leave without you. You can do your makeup in the car."

"You hit every pothole!" Rayne complained.

Amos opened the door for them, and they went inside. Maeve, Cormac, and Aine waited around the table in the foyer.

"Here is the paperwork having to do with the castle," Cormac said.

"I have clean clothes laid out for you each," Aine said. "Rayne in the office, Ciara in the parlor."

"Frances is preparing sandwiches for the trip," Maeve said like a drill sergeant. "We weren't sure what to do with the paperwork about the secret society you'd left on the couch, so we didn't touch it." She looked at her watch. "Go!"

Rayne heard Amos laughing as she darted to the office.

Maeve said, "A good solicitor is hard to come by. Our ladies need the best."

Rayne closed the door once in the office and slipped out of her casual clothes into a black suit with thin white stripes and white accents. Shoes, done, purse done. She snapped her fingers and pulled the adoption papers from the locked cabinet.

The jewels could stay in the safe in the parlor.

For now.

Within five minutes, Rayne was back at the table. Aine handed her black onyx earrings to accessorize. "The best assistant ever."

Aine smiled her thanks.

Ciara left the blue parlor with a glare at Aine. "This is Rayne's." The charcoal suit had minimal flare and was the perfect outfit to wear to the lawyer.

"It looks very nice," Maeve said, nodding at Aine. There were no accessories offered.

Cormac had put everything into a tote bag. "Here you are, milady."

"Thank you," Rayne said, dropping in the adoption paperwork.

Frances came from the kitchen with a cooler and two to-go mugs. "Drive safe. If you crash, you will only be later."

Rayne and Ciara exited with thanks. Aine held Blarney by the collar though the pup wanted to join them.

"You have to stay here this time, Blarney."

Amos had brought the Fiat to the front and hopped out. He kissed Rayne on the lips. "Be safe."

Ciara got behind the wheel and Rayne climbed in the front after putting the tote bag in the back as well as the cooler of food.

"We are *loved,*" Rayne said. She waved to the family on the steps.

"That we are." Ciara grinned. "It's grand."

Rayne dialed Fionagh Quinn's office to let them know they would be five minutes late, maybe ten.

Ciara stepped on the gas.

"Or not late at all," Rayne said.

Ending the call, she brought out the cooler and handed Ciara a section of hoagie. Turkey and Swiss. Light mayo. No onion. A thoughtful sandwich before a meeting. Rayne bit into hers and sighed. "Toast was a long time ago."

"I hope Father Patrick is all right. And Murray, and even Elizabeth." Ciara chewed and swallowed. "Olivia. Murderers."

Rayne's mom called while they were in the car and the cousins brought her up to speed on everything that had happened, up to the O'Briens killing Aiden, and Darcy McGillicuddy.

"I'm so glad that you are safe! Did you tell Ciara that Paul suggested we do a documentary? It will bring awareness to Grathton Village. It's a perfect true crime documentary."

Ciara scowled but out of respect for Lauren didn't say hell no.

"And now that Landon is no longer a threat, it could be the best segue into your new lives. You have plenty of outbuildings for the crew. Possibly in the spring, to get the sheep on film. Lambs are so cute. Well?" Lauren finally paused to take a breath.

"We will think about it, Mom. But we just got to the solicitor's, so we've got to go."

"Good luck! I feel like I am always trying to catch up with you," Lauren lamented.

"It won't be that way once you come," Rayne said. "Love you!" She ended the call.

Ciara turned off the engine. They glanced at one another, then the single-story brick building.

"We deserve a break," Ciara said. The sign outside read, Fionagh Quinn, Solicitor.

The time was 10:05.

"Are you nervous?" Rayne asked. Her heart was thudding behind her chest.

"Our last solicitor, well . . . this can only get better, right?" Ciara had hope in her gaze that Rayne felt as well.

"Right."

The cousins exited the car and entered the building.

A woman with short brown hair and blue eyes smiled at them. "Ciara Smith, and Rayne McGrath?"

"Yes," they said in unison.

"I'm Fionagh Quinn. I just got off the phone with Haley McGavin at MPM in Dublin. She assured me that you aren't lunatics, and I didn't need to be concerned about your speeding through Kilkenny." She eyed her phone. "Twenty minutes. It takes me twenty-five from Grathton."

"Ciara is an excellent driver," Rayne said.

"All right." She stood and said, "Please, call me Fionagh. I gave my receptionist the morning off because she will be working late, which is why I was answering the phone."

She opened the door to a very professional looking office. Like her, it was decked out in navy-blue. The office furniture was blond wood, the floors a darker wood, and covered with Oriental carpet in blues and grays. Bookshelves lined one wall, and another overlooked a fountain in a private courtyard. Two chairs sat opposite the desk. A larger leather chair on wheels was behind it.

Fionagh went to a side table that had an electric kettle as well as a Keurig. "What can I get for you to drink?" She made herself a black tea.

"Nothing for me," Rayne said. Thanks to Frances she wasn't either hungry or thirsty.

"Water, if you have it," Ciara said.

"Sure." Fionagh opened a small fridge next to a file cabinet and pulled a small bottle out. "Here you go."

"Thanks," Ciara said.

Rayne sat when Ciara and Fionagh did. Her palms were sweaty. They had so much at stake.

Fionagh kept her computer closed and smiled tightly. "This first consult is on the house. I want to make sure that we are a good fit, before we sign a binding contract."

Rayne understood that they would need to be careful of what they shared. She also knew that she trusted this woman.

"Haley said you are expensive but worth it," Ciara said.

Fionagh chuckled. "She's right on both counts." She tilted her head and looked at Ciara and then Rayne. "Who wants to start?"

Ciara jerked her thumb to Rayne. "Rayne actually owns the bloody castle so probably her."

"Castle?" Fionagh repeated.

"McGrath Castle in Grathton Village." Rayne watched the woman's lips thin. "You might have passed by it, but it's not on the main thoroughfare. You'd have to search for it."

"Let's start at the beginning," the solicitor suggested.

By noon, Rayne feared that Fionagh's glazed over expression didn't bode well for them. And they hadn't even gotten to the part about the jewels. Uncle Nevin's murder, the crazy will, trying to save the past by blending it with the future.

"Let's take a break," Fionagh said. "I'll have Marta order us some lunch. I have a feeling that I'll be needing whiskey by the end of today. I can move my two o'clock but not my three. Can you stay?"

"Yes," Ciara said.

Rayne nodded.

At half past two, Fionagh, rather dazed, quoted a price to take over from Owen Hughes that made the cousins blink.

"We have to make this work," Ciara said, looking at Rayne. "You are out of handbags."

"We will. Together."

They signed on the dotted line. No more Owen Hughes. The will could be changed. It was up to Rayne, and Ciara, how to handle things moving forward. Fionagh assured them they weren't going to jail regarding the *possible* Irish Crown Jewels. Right now, she reminded them, they were not sure about the jewels. Possibly crystals. It was only supposition.

"I've got just the person to handle this," Fionagh said. "A higher up in the CEA, the Corporate Enforcement Authority. Rayne, think American FBI. Keep them locked up and don't talk about it to anyone. Once we *know* for sure, the jewels will be confiscated. You might get a reward."

"It was a thousand pounds," Rayne said.

"We'll see about that," Fionagh said. "Also, leave *Thomas* where he is for now, until I make some phone calls. Marta found out that Murray O'Brien is being charged with Aiden Dennehy's murder. He isn't talking though. He had a note on his person from Darcy McGillicuddy confessing that their parents were part of a secret society called the Cavalier Clovers. You heard him say so, but while he might be tightlipped, Don McElroy and Paddy O'Brien confirmed that the grave is empty, like you thought, Rayne. It's where the Cavalier Clovers stashed the remainder of the . . . stolen goods, once the weapons to win the War of Independence were bought. The supposed jewels were too hot to try and sell and better left buried. The lads are singing like canaries to Garda Williams and Garda Lee."

"No Thomas McGrath body, Ciara." Rayne couldn't believe it. "You owe me lunch."

"I will gladly pay, after the sheep are born."

Uncle Nevin used to give out bonuses for

a bumper crop.

"I have a very trusted accountant that I can recommend to you, but I get it if you'd prefer to find your own. Look for someone who is sanctioned by law so that if there are any discrepancies, they will be accountable."

"We really appreciate your advice," Rayne said.

"It would be ideal for this time next year to have you each draw a salary." Fionagh raised her hand. "I know it's a lot to take in right now. While it feels like you are cash poor, your wealth in property alone makes that simply not true." Fionagh quoted a sum that brought tears to Rayne's eyes.

Ciara sent Rayne a panicked look.

"Olivia O'Brien died, as Garda Williams thought. Elizabeth McGillicuddy is in surgery. Freda Bevan is in ICU but expected to pull through. Ciara, I agree with Rayne that we should file the adoption papers. I can manage that for you." Fionagh sat back. Her exhale reached the rafters. "I think you ladies came to me in the nick of time."

Rayne and Ciara left the office just as dazed as Fionagh had been around the midpoint of their meeting. The cousins were in excellent hands to guide the village and their family toward the next generation to come.

Rayne smiled at Ciara. "How about this for a slogan: Welcome to Grathton Village, the perfect blend of past and future?"

"Love it." Ciara unlocked the doors to the Fiat. "We need to discuss your mam's idea, though. Not so keen on a documentary . . ."

Filled with renewed hope, Rayne opened her side. "Let's talk about it on the way *home*."

ACKNOWLEDGMENTS

It takes a team of people to transform a manuscript from the Word document stage to the final product. My agent, Evan Marshall, and my editor, Tara Gavin, have my thanks for their expertise and guidance. For the crew at Crooked Lane who put it all together, from dust jacket to copyedits, thank you as well.

Sheryl McGavin and my mother, Judi Potter, are my first readers — despite crazy circumstances, they always come through. I was very blessed to be introduced to Mom's coffee ladies, all avid book lovers. They had suggestions for unique names, and that's where I learned about the Catholic church not usually having a service on Sunday — it is the Lord's day. Thanks Marg, Liz, Dianne, Sister Barb, Jan, Judi, and Father Baraza.

ABOUT THE AUTHOR

Ellie Brannigan has lived in South Florida for the last twenty years. She loves the ocean and any food dish with shrimp. When she's not creating new fictional worlds, she reads, and travels . . . and eats.

The employees of Thorndike Press hope you have enjoyed this Large Print book. All our Thorndike Large Print titles are designed for easy reading, and all our books are made to last. Other Thorndike Press Large Print books are available at your library, through selected bookstores, or directly from us.

For information about titles, please call:
(800) 223-1244

or visit our website at:
gale.com/thorndike